Forest of Scarlet

FOREST OF SCARLET

COURT OF MIDSUMMER MAYHEM

BOOK 1

TARA GRAYCE

Forest of Scarlet
Court of Midsummer Mayhem Book 1

N
W E
S
Court of Ice
Wilderness Court
Court of Artisans
Goblin Court
Court of Stone
Court of Mists
Court of Islands
Harvest Court
Court of Sand
Court of Grass
Faeric Market
Court of Revels
Great Library
Tanglewood
King Oberon & Queen Titania Court
Queen Mab's Court
Court of Knowledge
Court of Dreams
Court of Jungles
Court of Seas
Queen Hippolyta's Court
Swamp Court
Fae Realm
Court of Swordmaidens

Chapter One

The young human girl hunched on her hands and knees, sobbing as the giggling fae around her forced her to lap like a dog at the cake ground into the moss. The girl licked at the earth, spitting and grimacing as dirt and moss covered her tongue. Her cheeks glistened wet with her tears. Still so innocent, still not hardened to the point where she would become a shell, no longer willing to give her fae captors the pleasure of seeing her tears.

At least her eyes remained clear, her mind her own even as she was forced to the degradation of eating dirt.

A few yards away, a group of human musicians played a variety of instruments. The harpist strummed her golden harp, a placid smile on her face even as her fingers bled. Nearby, a female violinist sawed her bow back and forth with a vague expression on her face, seemingly uncaring as her fingers blistered from pressing on the strings.

These captives had given up. To dull their pain, they'd eaten faerie fruit, willingly falling into the lulling, sweet nothingness that the fruit provided. The faerie fruit would make them pliable to faerie whims, but its addictive qualities made its victims crave the fruit even as it made them more a fae's plaything.

At the side of the boisterous crowd of fae, Brigid swirled the wine in her glass, not taking so much as a sip. Even the scent of the strong faerie wine threatened to lighten her head and turn her vision dizzy. If she drank, she'd become as empty-eyed as those poor souls.

As it was, she let some of the headiness of the wine's scent calm the burning in her chest at the sight of her fellow humans suffering the torments of the Fae Realm. As much as she wished she could rescue them all, she could only save one tonight. And her target had to be the child before she was taken by the lure of the faerie fruit or broken by the torture she'd already suffered.

Brigid's red silk dress swished around her, glinting in the glow of the yellow faerie lights that bobbed near the ceiling of the grand, garden palace. Massive rose arbors arched over the space while hedges outlined a variety of gardens, complete with burbling fountains and statues that might or might not have once been living people.

Beyond the gardens, ginormous flowers—nothing but massive buds and blooms plopped directly on the moss with no stem, bush, or leaves—provided rooms amid the folds of their petals for the fae when they stopped their revelry long enough to collapse into sleep.

Under the arched ivy arbors that formed the main throne room, the pixie Queen Mab of the Court of Dreams sat on her throne formed of flowers and thorns. The pixies, fauns, naiads, and dryads of her court danced attendance on her, even as the guests from the other courts paid their respects to their host for the lavish party.

Brigid sashayed up to a group of fae ladies from a variety of courts, from the autumn fae ladies dressed in shades of orange to the pixies of Queen Mab's court with their sheer, iridescent wings fluttering at their backs. Even in their full-sized forms, the pixies in the group barely reached Brigid's shoulders.

One of the fae ladies laughed and swigged more wine. "Hippolyta's Pet!"

Several of the other ladies tittered at Brigid's nickname, whispering to each other behind their hands.

The persona of being Queen Hippolyta's entertaining project was Brigid's protection—and protection for Hippolyta as well. If everyone dismissed Brigid as the strange human that Queen Hippolyta, ruler of the Court of Swordmaidens, had taken in as a pet, then they wouldn't realize that Brigid was also the Wild Fae Primrose, the mysterious person stealing away humans from their fae captors.

Brigid plastered on her doltish smile—an expression that came almost too easily to her at this point—and raised her glass. "Aren't I pretty tonight? The dressmaker is commendable."

That wasn't a lie. Layers of red embroidery in a sparkling, glinting thread weaved patterns over the red silk. Not wild fae primrose, as much as Brigid would have loved that symbolism. Still, the red was enough of a statement, even if only she and her few trusted companions knew its significance. The dress itself was, indeed, splendid, with layers of silk that floated around her.

Better yet, the dress had pockets.

Not just any pockets, but the magical fae pockets that could hold an impossible number of items without ever bulging or becoming full. Sadly, the pockets couldn't hold living things, either plants or people. It would have been rather convenient if she could have rescued humans by simply tucking them in her pocket and walking away.

"Indeed." Another of the fae ladies plucked at Brigid's

sleeve. "You are such a lovely doll to dress up. You humans are such fun. Alas, I lost the last human I stole away."

"The Wild Fae Primrose?" Another of the ladies grimaced, then swigged her wine as if to bolster her courage after so much as saying the name.

The lady dropped Brigid's sleeve and wiggled her wings, making her flower petal dress float around her. "I still can't believe one of our own would so brazenly break the laws of our realms and steal what we have rightfully stolen."

One of the other pixies fluttered her wings and her lashes. "If he wasn't such an annoyance, it would all be a little dashing, don't you think?"

That set off another round of titters, and Brigid giggled along with them, despite the little twist curling her own smile.

These ladies couldn't conceive that the person who had rescued so many stolen humans could be a human, someone they saw as far inferior to themselves. Nor that *he* was actually a *she*.

But Brigid gladly let them continue thinking that. The more wrong the gossips were, the safer she and those who helped her would be.

Brigid lifted her own glass, sloshing some on herself so that she would smell as inebriated as the rest of the revelers. "Sink me, I have it! A delightful little rhyme I have been mulling over to entertain my queen, and I finally have the final line!"

"Let's hear it, pet!" The surrounding ladies giggled and drank, then giggled some more.

Brigid screwed up her face, as if coming up with a simple rhyme took intense concentration. She slurred her words a bit as she spoke in a sing-song voice.

> *"They seek him here, they seek him there,*
> *Those faeries seek him everywhere.*

Is he in the Fae Realm or with the monsters below?
That elusive Wild Fae Primrose."

For a moment, the group of ladies blinked at her, as if they weren't sure if they should applaud that performance or decry it. She was, after all, not-so-subtly jabbing at their inability to catch the Primrose so far.

Then one of the ladies snorted, wine spewing from her mouth. That started the giggles all around the circle, and Brigid beamed as if she thought coming up with that rhyme had been a great accomplishment.

In truth, it was an atrocious poem. The last rhyme was a stretch, and the rhythm was off. But it hardly mattered as long as the fae around her found it amusing.

Boots clicked on the garden paving stones a moment before a tall figure dressed all in black joined their circle. His black hair was tied back at the nape of his neck while he clasped his hands behind his back. He was probably the fae equivalent of in his mid-thirties, but the dour frown that etched lines into his handsome fae face made him appear older.

"Lord Chauvlyn!" One of the ladies looped her arm through his, leaning on him with breath that reeked of faerie wine even from where Brigid stood. "You absolutely must hear the rhyme that Hippolyta's Pet came up with. She is *such* an entertaining darling!"

Several of the fae ladies started repeating the rhyme over each other, correcting one another as they each tried to remember the exact words.

Lord Chauvlyn eyed them, looking down his nose at each of them, before he turned his dark, forbidding sneer on Brigid. "The Wild Fae Primrose is no laughing matter."

"Oh, really?" Brigid raised her glass and kept her tone light, her eyes wide and innocent as if she were genuinely confused. "He seems to make those chasing him quite the laughingstock."

"He will be caught, human." Lord Chauvlyn studied her far too sharply, as if he wanted to see beneath her light words.

Perhaps she shouldn't tweak him so. Lord Chauvlyn, by appointment of King Oberon of the Court of Revels, had made it his personal mission to catch the Primrose. He had the support of many of the kings, queens, lords, and ladies across all the courts, except for the rare court like the Court of Knowledge or Court of Swordmaidens.

Brigid widened her eyes and her smile. "Perhaps he will; perhaps he won't. But you, dear Lord Chaubertin, should worry less about the Primrose and more about your attire."

"Lord Chauvlyn," the fae lord growled under his breath.

Brigid continued over him as if she hadn't heard the correction. "It's dreadful, honestly, for a lord of the Court of Revels to go around in basic black. And that tailoring…shameful, really. Surely the favorite of King Oberon and Queen Titania can dress far better."

This set off another round of tittering as the ladies jumped to agree, adding their own attempts at witty comments on Lord Chauvlyn's attire.

There had to be a reason why Lord Chauvlyn always wore black. Colors and clothing held meaning for the fae. Perhaps he truly saw himself as the cackling villain. Or maybe he despised the flamboyant nature of his court's normal form of dress and wearing black was a form of protest. If Brigid needled him about it enough, he might eventually give away his reasons for the color and lack of style. Or not. Either way, it provided an easy way for her to nettle him.

Lord Chauvlyn's jaw worked, his nostrils flaring as a redness crept up his neck. He flexed his fingers. "You mark my words. I will catch the Primrose."

With that, he spun on his heel and stalked off, his shoulders stiff beneath his stark black coat.

Brigid remained for a few more minutes before she swayed off to the next group, this time a mix of fae ladies and gentlemen. She trotted out her little rhyme several more times until nearly everyone at the party was repeating it with gusto.

Finally, the little human girl on the stage collapsed in a heap, and she was taken away from the party by a goblin servant belonging to Lady Belania, the girl's captor.

Brigid giggled and swayed with an apparent increasing drunkenness before she finally stumbled to the edge of the party and collapsed face-first onto the moss, half-in and half-out of the flower assigned to the Court of Knowledge for this event.

She lay there for a few minutes, feigning drunken slumber. A few fauns clopped by, then a few more passing fae whispered about how Hippolyta's Pet was unable to hold her faerie wine.

As it grew silent around her, a faint rustling came from the giant rose in front of her. "Brigid?"

"Is it all clear?" Brigid eased her head up, peeking at sixteen-year-old Rosaline, one of the apprentice librarians of the Court of Knowledge and part of Brigid's League. Since she was the daughter of nobles of the Court of Revels, she'd been included in the retinue sent to this party from the Court of Knowledge.

Dressed in a dark purple dress that complemented her swarthy skin and dark hair, Rosaline crouched next to Brigid's head just inside the rose's petal walls. Her gaze darted around before she nodded. "Yes."

Brigid quickly crawled into the rose, already fumbling with the clasp of her dress even before she was fully inside the safety of the rose.

With Rosaline's help, she quickly shucked the dress. Then she helped Rosaline change into it.

Perhaps it was an added risk, swapping dresses instead of having Rosaline snatch the child herself. But Rosaline was only sixteen, and Brigid wasn't going to ask her to put herself at that kind of risk. At least this way, Rosaline could deny any knowledge of why Brigid had asked to change dresses with her and claim complete ignorance if Brigid were caught.

Besides, Rosaline was fae while Brigid was human. That meant that Rosaline was a bit more bound to the Laws of Bindings that governed the Fae Realm than Brigid was. Snatching a human from a noble of one's host as a guest in that court was a bit tricky for a fae. Brigid, however, could just take the child with impunity. As long as she wasn't caught doing it.

With another glance around, Rosaline rolled out of the rose, then sprawled on the moss in the same position that Brigid had been in a moment ago, facedown, her head and hair, which was far darker than Brigid's, hidden by the petals of the flower. At her side, she clutched an empty goblet.

With Rosaline now in place as Brigid's decoy, Brigid dressed in the drab brown-and-orange dress she'd brought along for this part of the plan. She covered her hair with a wig, turning her into a redhead whose hair was more orange than red. She added a pair of fox ears clipped into her hair, plastered some fur over her nose and added whiskers, then tied on a bushy fox tail.

And people scorned makeup artistry as frivolous. As if it didn't come in handy to be able to transform one's face with a few swipes of a brush and skillful use of shading and highlights. Not to mention, Brigid enjoyed it. That was a good enough reason in itself.

In a few minutes, she stepped out of the rose, the picture of a goblin girl servant. After collecting the tray that Rosaline had set nearby, Brigid kept her head down and bustled through the crowd.

A few of the fae barked orders at her, and she quickly complied. The noble fae didn't give her a second glance as she took their empty glasses, filled their wine goblets, or brought them more food. Good. Her disguise was working.

She meandered her way through the party, then into the maze of flowers and gardens that formed Queen Mab's palace. Here, away from the main party, goblin servants, fauns, and lesser pixies flitted about, keeping their heads down and giving Brigid not so much as a first glance, much less a second. She was just another one of the servants.

Finally, Brigid reached the flower, a giant peony, assigned to Lady Belania of the Harvest Court and her retinue. A few servants and guards remained, and Brigid bustled by them with purpose.

The guards didn't give her a second glance. After all, she was just another goblin servant. A lesser in their eyes. While most of the lordly fae in all the courts looked down on goblins, those of the Harvest Court, as another Autumn Court, especially scorned goblins.

Something Brigid planned to use to her advantage.

Inside the flower, she found the fold of the petals where the young human girl had curled up on a blanket. Her blonde hair lay in tangled strands around her face while tear-streaks stained her cheeks, showing that she had cried herself to sleep.

Brigid crept up to the girl, then pressed her hand firmly over the girl's mouth.

The girl's eyes flew open, wild and wide.

Brigid's heart ached, knowing what fear and torments this girl must have suffered already in her time in the Fae Realm. She was a plaything for her faerie captors. Treated as less than a dog to be laughed at and tormented, driven to insanity if left to the fae for too long.

Dressed in her disguise, Brigid looked just like one of the

fae. When she started rescuing humans, she had wasted precious time having to reassure each human that she was actually a friend.

Now, she reached into one of the hidden pockets of her skirt—of course this dress, too, had magical pockets—and withdrew a small red flower. She held it out to the girl.

The girl tentatively reached out, then gripped the wild fae primrose in her fist. She stared at it for another moment before her gaze swung up to meet Brigid's with a look of supreme trust calming her features.

Brigid withdrew her hand from over the girl's mouth. "I'm here to guide you home, wanderer. Stay silent and do exactly as I say, and you'll be home soon, all right?"

The girl nodded, folding her fingers over the flower so that she had it pressed, hidden, inside her fist.

Brigid bundled the girl into the blanket, then picked her up. To anyone watching, she would look like she was just carrying soiled linens to the laundry for washing.

She strode right past the other servants and the guards, trying to pretend her burden was nothing but blankets and not a girl who was becoming increasingly heavy the longer she walked.

Thankfully, the girl remained absolutely still and silent.

Brigid only had to wander down a few mossy pathways before she reached a giant dandelion. The guards here were already well into their own cups of wine, and some of the servants were passed out between the petals. Only a few of the sprites remained awake and bouncing around, repeating rhymes and cackling to themselves.

Brigid kept her head down. Just another goblin servant bringing a new blanket for a visiting fae noble.

Deep inside the flower, she located the trunks. She set the girl down and unwrapped the blanket.

The girl peered up at her, blinking.

Brigid opened one of the largest trunks, then pulled out stacks of garments, cloaks, and sundries. "This next part is going to be a bit uncomfortable for you. I need you to curl up in this trunk. You'll need to stay still and silent for hours. You can doze, but when this trunk starts moving, you'll need to be awake and alert. When you hear someone outside of the trunk say, 'Welcome to the Court of Knowledge, my lord,' crack open the trunk. The next person to open this trunk will be a friend. Go with them and leave the primrose behind. I'll see you shortly after that to bring you home."

The girl nodded, then climbed into the trunk without hesitation. Brigid piled as many of the clothes on top of the girl as she could without smothering her. Then she stuffed the rest of the clothes into the magical pocket of her dress.

After shutting the trunk, Brigid gathered the blanket and strolled past the servants and guards once again.

She wandered the pathways until she found a secluded, empty bee balm flower where she stashed the blanket. By the laws of hospitality, Brigid couldn't steal from her hosts or the court hosting her. So while the child, bound to the Harvest Court, was fair game, the blanket wasn't since it belonged to the Court of Dreams where Brigid was currently a guest.

As a human, Brigid *might* be able to get away with breaking the laws of hospitality. And that was a big *might*. Such things got tricky, here in the Fae Realm. It was best just to leave the blanket. Some servant would find it and wonder how it had gotten there, but it would be an unremarkable find that no one would report to Queen Mab.

While Brigid wanted to hurry, she kept her pace brisk but unworried. Finally, she reached the rose.

Rosaline still lay sprawled before the flower. A few fae

wandered by, shaking their heads and giggling at Hippolyta's Pet.

Brigid slipped into the rose and quickly peeled off the fake nose and fur, unclipped the ears and wig, and untied the fake tail. She sloughed off her plain dress until she was down to her shift, then she peeked between the rose petals.

She had to wait for several minutes before the area around the rose was completely empty. "Rosaline, now."

Rosaline pushed upright and launched herself into the rose. Hurriedly, Brigid helped her out of the red dress, then pulled it on herself once again. She tucked the plain dress and all the parts of her disguise into the magical pocket of the red dress.

Rosaline wiggled into her own bright purple dress and settled her headdress of flowers onto her head once again. "I'd better get back out there before anyone realizes I've been missing."

It was a risk, having Rosaline go missing. But her absence would be less noticeable than Brigid's. Brigid had purposely made herself incredibly popular and visible. It was her cloak of safety, but it had its downsides. "Go on. I'll be here."

After sharing a smirk, Brigid glanced out of the rose, ensuring that it was still clear. She settled into her spot on the moss once again, wiggling to get as comfortable as she could.

Now she just had to wait out the night.

Chapter Two

Brigid only slightly exaggerated her yawn. The all-night fae parties sure took a toll on the next day.

She wore a rose-pink dress this morning, the hidden pockets stuffed with her goblin disguise of the night before. She trotted behind Helena and Demetrius, the heads of the delegation sent from the Court of Knowledge. Rosaline stuck close to her side while swordmaiden guards clustered around them. A few servants carried their trunks as they headed for the Anywhere Door in the Court of Dreams.

This morning, Queen Mab's guards wore hard expressions. A crowd had gathered near the Anywhere Door where it was set into a rose arbor.

Lady Belania was shouting, tears streaking her face, "My precious pet has been stolen! The Primrose must be behind it!"

Brigid plastered on a blankly benign expression rather than snorting. Such theatrics.

Helena strode toward the Anywhere Door, but she was halted by faun guards carrying spears. She placed her hands on her hips. "What is the meaning of this? My husband and I wish to return to our court."

"Your trunks must be searched. Queen Mab's orders. The Primrose struck again last night." One of the fauns spoke, clacking his hooves in an officious manner.

"What does that have to do with me? I'm clearly not the Primrose." Helena gestured at herself and her flowing, deep green gown.

Demetrius placed a hand on his wife's arm while he glared at the guards. "We are trusted members of King Theseus's court."

"We don't know who the Primrose might be. Everyone must be searched." The faun guards remained at their post, their spears blocking the Anywhere Door.

More faun guards converged on Helena, Demetrius, Brigid, their servants, and their trunks. Without so much as a by-your-leave, the first faun guard flung open a trunk and began tossing Helena's things out of the trunk onto the moss.

Brigid's heart beat harder in her chest, and she resisted the urge to touch the pocket where her disguise from the night before remained hidden. Instead, she blinked and let her mouth drop open in a shocked expression.

Helena surged toward him. "How dare you! King Theseus and Queen Hippolyta will hear about this!"

Demetrius quickly stepped forward and snagged Helena, whispering in her ear. He was the only one who could calm Helena down when she started to get all screechy and flustered.

The fauns ignored her as they turned to the next trunk and began tossing the things from that trunk as well.

Brigid waited, a placid but concerned expression schooling her features.

The crowd parted, and Lord Chauvlyn strode through, dressed as always in a black shirt, black doublet, and black trousers.

Rosaline ducked behind Brigid, as if trying to hide from the delegation from the Court of Revels. Rosaline had originally come from the Court of Revels before she'd made the decision on her recent sixteenth birthday to join the Court of Knowledge and become a librarian instead. Her parents—nobles of the court—hadn't been pleased, though they hadn't cut off all ties to her yet. They—and everyone from the Court of Revels who knew Rosaline—simply pressured her to return to the court of her birth every chance they had.

Ignoring Rosaline, Lord Chauvlyn stared down his nose at Helena. "We all know that King Theseus and Queen Hippolyta are far too sympathetic to the Primrose's cause."

"My king and queen have nothing to do with that rogue." Helena drew herself up to her full height, though she still stood far shorter than Lord Chauvlyn.

She and Demetrius weren't a part of Brigid's League, so they didn't know that the Primrose stood just behind them at that moment. But they were loyal to King Theseus and friends with Brigid's sister and brother-in-law.

Lord Chauvlyn snorted. "Perhaps. But they would gladly look away if he happened to be a member of the Court of Knowledge."

Brigid stepped forward, fluttering her fan. "What are you implying? Surely you don't think a librarian would have the daring to be the Primrose?"

Lord Chauvlyn's scowl deepened as he turned his gaze on her. "King Theseus claims he is merely a librarian king, but he married the Queen of the Swordmaidens. No mere librarian could pull off winning the hand of a swordmaiden. And we have all seen how he harbors humans within his court. Not as playthings, but as equal members."

Equal members, like Brigid's sister Meg, who worked as an assistant librarian right alongside her fae husband Basil, a master librarian. Like Meg's other siblings Sebastian, who had recently become an assistant librarian, and Viola, who would become an assistant librarian sooner rather than later. Beatrice, her youngest sibling, would become a librarian as soon as she was old enough.

Even Brigid, though she played at being a pet, was a true member of the Court of Knowledge.

Brigid shrugged and swished her dress. "Perhaps King Theseus finds humans entertaining when they play at being librarians."

Demetrius glanced at her, his brow puckered with a frown, as if he couldn't quite figure out why she would denigrate her own family. He knew, as well as she did, that her siblings did more than merely play at being librarians.

Helena drew herself even straighter, her blonde hair glinting nearly as much as her eyes, as she speared Lord Chauvlyn with a look. "Basil and Meg are our friends, and it doesn't matter that Meg is human. Nor is the Court of Knowledge the only court to welcome humans."

"Perhaps." Lord Chauvlyn swept another dark look over Brigid and Helena before he turned back to the faun guards. "I trust their trunks will be searched thoroughly."

"Of course, Lord Chauvlyn." The faun bobbed to the fae lord. "If you would like to return to the Court of Revels, you are free to go. We all know you aren't the Primrose."

Lord Chauvlyn nodded, then strode past the guards, motioning for his retinue to follow. Sprites and goblin servants trundled past, carrying his trunks. Including the large trunk where a little girl lay safely curled beneath Lord Chauvlyn's dirty laundry.

Brigid grinned and waved. "Farewell, Lord Chauvertin. Please convey my apologies to my queen for my delay in returning."

Lord Chauvlyn's shoulders stiffened, and he kept walking without acknowledging her through the Anywhere Door.

As little as he probably liked it, the Anywhere Doors didn't connect the courts directly to each other. They were all connected to the Hall of Anywhere Doors in the Court of Knowledge, and from there the Doors led to each of the Courts. Some long ago monarch of the Court of Knowledge had designed them that way on purpose since it gave the Court of Knowledge ultimate control over the Anywhere Doors.

It was only by King Theseus's gracious permission that Lord Chauvlyn and the others were allowed to use the Hall of Anywhere Doors to travel between the Courts, especially since the Anywhere Doors were supposed to be used to make it easy for all the Courts to seek knowledge, not seek parties and revelry.

How it must gall Lord Chauvlyn to accept King Theseus's hospitality, if just for a moment as he traversed the Anywhere Doors to return to the Court of Revels. He would be even more annoyed when King Theseus and Queen Hippolyta delayed him with well wishes to convey to his king and queen.

He would find it especially galling once he unpacked his trunk and discovered that half his clothes were missing, a little red flower left in their place. The clothes would turn up a few days later, left at the edge of the Tanglewood with another wild fae primrose blossom and a note thanking Lord Chauvlyn for the use of his trunk.

The faun guards set to work searching the remaining trunk, the one belonging to Brigid.

Brigid swept forward, catching the red dress from the prior evening before it could fall on the moss. "How dare you treat such elegance this crudely?" She proceeded to wax eloquent on the silk and the work of the seamstress until even the clothing-obsessed fae were rolling their eyes at her.

Finally, the fauns stepped back. "We apologize for the delay. You are free to go."

Helena huffed, scowling as the servants hustled to throw the clothing back into the trunks. Brigid joined them, both helping and hindering as she worried over the treatment of the silks.

When everything was back in the trunks, Helena and Demetrius strode toward the Anywhere Door. Brigid quickly followed, picturing the Hall of Anywhere Doors as she stepped through.

For a moment, she felt the shivering feeling of traveling a faerie path. This one was stable, linked as it was to the Anywhere Doors. Most people likely wouldn't even notice the feeling as they stepped through the Door.

But Brigid had trained to walk the faerie paths. She'd learned to pay attention to those feelings, those instincts.

Then she was through the Door and entering the Hall of Anywhere Doors. White marble surrounded her in a long, huge hall. White pillars framed each door set in a long line down each side of the room. Each of the shorter ends of the hall held double doors guarded by armored swordmaidens. One set of doors led to King Theseus's palace while the other opened to the Great Library.

King Theseus and Queen Hippolyta stood to one side of the Hall of Anywhere Doors, already talking with Helena and Demetrius. King Theseus wore a blue coat in a similar cut and style to the coats worn by the court's librarians, complete with light gray trousers. His black hair was a sharp contrast next to his wife's brilliant blonde. Queen Hippolyta wore a white, simple dress edged in gold embroidery that matched the gold etchings on the hilt of the sword buckled at her waist.

Queen Hippolyta glanced in Brigid's direction and met her gaze. The fae queen tipped her head in a slight nod, a hint of a smile gracing her face. The queen's only acknowledgement that the mission had been accomplished.

While King Theseus and Queen Hippolyta knew that Brigid was the Primrose, they didn't know the details so that they could maintain plausible deniability with the other courts. Even for this mission when they had agreed to delay Lord Chauvlyn, Brigid never told them exactly what was going down. Though Queen Hippolyta had likely noticed when several of her swordmaidens closed around a certain trunk, its lid cracked open, for a moment before slipping back into the Great Library.

Brigid strolled in the other direction, heading for the Great Library. At the doorway, she waved to the swordmaidens guarding the doors, a goblin swordmaiden who had a cow-shaped face and horns sprouting from her skull and a thin, tiny pixie girl who didn't look big enough to wield the sword she had strapped at her waist. "Hello, Minnie, Trixie."

The two swordmaidens greeted her, then stepped aside so that she could enter the Library.

Brigid pushed open one of the large double doors and drew in a deep breath of the Library's peaceful scent of green earth and old books.

Home.

She stepped into the Great Library's atrium, the click of her shoes on the marble floor changing to a quiet whisper on the spongy moss of the Library floor. Tiny white flowers peered through the thick carpet of moss while vines trailed along the shelves and draped down from the ceiling.

In the center of the atrium, a large tree grew all the way to the dome of a large glass skylight. The tree's leaves spread out, protecting the books below from direct sunlight. Branches and leaves grew out of the Library shelves, as if the Library itself was one large, living thing. Which, in many ways, it was.

Desks clustered around the base of the tree, manned by the master librarians wearing their black librarian coats. Lines of fae from various courts waited in front of the desks for their chance to ask for information.

Behind one of the desks, Brigid's brother-in-law Basil held out a book to a goblin man with donkey ears. Basil's tousled dark hair fell over his forehead, leaving the tips of his tapered ears visible. He glanced up, laughing at something the goblin man had said, and his gaze flicked to Brigid.

Brigid waved, and Basil's smile widened, some of the tension leaving his shoulders. He tipped his head in the direction of the book repair room.

She nodded, then wound her way through the Library in that direction. Once she was hidden among the shelves, she trailed her fingers along one of the branches.

The Library around her gave a little shift, and one of the leaves reached out to pat her hand, welcoming her home.

Brigid wasn't sure how much the Great Library's semi-sentience could understand of her mission to rescue humans from the fae, but she liked to think the Library approved. It never stood in her way when she used its nooks and crannies to hide humans as a waypoint before taking them home through the nearest faerie circle.

Perhaps that was the Library's approval. Or perhaps it was King Theseus's sense of right and wrong influencing the Library through its deep, mysterious tie between its sentience and its king. Either way, Brigid relaxed as the safety of the Library enfolded her.

Deep inside the Library, tucked beside the stairs to one of the towers that held forbidden books, Brigid reached the book repair room and stepped inside.

Her oldest sister Meg sat at one of the tables, meticulously sewing a new binding for a book that had been damaged. Meg's golden-blonde hair fell across her shoulders, brushing the light green of her dress and darker green of her assistant librarian coat. Her and Basil's second daughter Morgan slept in a cloth baby wrap snuggled against Meg's chest.

Inside of a network of Library branches corralling off the far right-hand corner, Meg and Basil's three-year-old daughter Addy alternated between playing with her toys and chasing a blue bookwyrm around the space, totally unafraid of the tiny, scaled creature.

In the other corner, the rescued girl huddled under a blanket, staring at Meg with wide eyes as if she wasn't sure if she trusted Meg, even though Meg was a human.

Meg's head snapped up, her shoulders tensing. But as soon as her gaze rested on Brigid, her posture relaxed. "You're back safe."

"Of course." Brigid swept into the room, unable to help a hint of her indolent mask as it crept onto her face. Even with her family, it was easier to fall into her feigned persona than to show her true self. She crossed the room and knelt in front of the young girl. She reached into a pocket, drew out another wild fae primrose flower, and held it out to the child. "I'll take you home soon, but we'll have to wait here in the Great Library for a little while, all right?"

The girl stared at Brigid with wide, trusting eyes before she tentatively reached out and wrapped her fingers around the flower. She snatched her hand back, hugging the flower to her.

Such trauma in those blue eyes. Brigid had rescued the girl from the fae, but how much damage was already done? Would the girl be able to recover once she was returned to her family?

Something ached deep inside Brigid's chest, but there was only so much she could do. She could rescue humans from the fae, but she couldn't help them heal. She had to leave that for others.

The door opened again, and her fifteen-year-old sister Beatrice swirled inside, carrying a bag while two bookwyrms perched on her shoulders. "I fetched food. The House was generous. Brigid! You're back!"

Brigid glanced over her shoulder, but she didn't push to her feet. She didn't dare move too quickly and startle the girl. "Did you bring enough for me?"

"There's enough here to feed the whole family." Beatrice hurried across the book repair room, then plopped onto the floor next to Brigid. She opened the bag, then pulled out bundles wrapped in linen.

The bookwyrms slithered down her arms, their snake-like legless bodies covered with scales the same color as the leathery ruffs around their necks. They perched on their tails, their eyes fixed on Beatrice and mouths hanging open in begging pouts.

The girl shrank back into the corner, tugging the blanket back up to her chin as she gaped at the bookwyrms.

Beatrice scratched one of the bookwyrms behind its ruff. "Don't be scared of the bookwyrms. They're friendly. They protect the Library from pests like mice or bugs. And they help defend the Library when it is attacked by monsters from the Realm of Monsters."

The girl stayed curled where she was, not looking very reassured. Mentioning the Realm of Monsters probably wasn't the best way to go about calming her.

Brigid smiled confidently, hoping the girl would find her confidence reassuring. "You're safe here, and soon you'll be home. Are you hungry? It's all right to eat."

Beatrice unwrapped a sandwich and held it out to the girl. The bread was bright pink while the butter and jelly inside were green and orange. It didn't look anything like what one would eat in the Human Realm.

The girl hesitated, glanced at Brigid, then took the sandwich. Still staring at everyone, she took a bite, chewing quickly as if she feared someone would snatch away the food just to be cruel.

The doors opened again, and Brigid's eighteen-year-old sister Viola entered, carrying a stack of damaged books. "Master Librarian Maximillian just got a stack of books returned by Lord Exus. Looks like the lord doesn't know how to care for a book properly. These look like a whole family of sprites chewed on them. Oh, hello, Brigid."

Brigid smiled and settled more comfortably on the floor. This happiness was what she wanted to restore to those taken by the fae. While her family had found a home here in the Fae Realm because of Basil, that wasn't the case for most of those who were taken by the fae. They would only find safety when they were once again reunited with their families in the Human Realm.

Brigid knew their families' pain all too well. For eight months, she hadn't known what had happened to Meg. Her sister Meg had gone into the forest, hoping to get snatched by a fae rich enough to buy off the man who planned to sell all of them into indentured servitude to pay off the debts of their failing farm. For eight months, Brigid had feared the worst.

Instead of torment, Meg had found a husband and love in the Fae Realm, and their family's rescue had been found by fleeing to the Fae Realm, rather than from it.

As Viola set the stack of damaged books on the table, Addy dropped her toy and pulled herself to her feet using the gate of Library branches. "Mum-mum-mum-mum!"

As Meg pushed to her feet, a Library branch gently wrapped around Addy, plucked her from the floor, and swept her through the air until it handed her to Meg.

Meg wrapped Addy in one arm and patted the Library's

branch. "Thank you, Library. You're always so good with Addy."

Brigid smiled and shook her head. Both the Library and their family's House looked after Addy with remarkable fondness, considering they were buildings.

For the rest of the day, Brigid coaxed the rescued girl into talking, asking her questions about her name, her parents' names, where she was from, and things like that. Information Brigid's League would need to know to return the girl to her home in the Human Realm.

Once the girl stepped foot in the Human Realm, the captive binding would be fully broken. The binding was already partially broken by freeing the girl from the sway of her fae captor. But the part of the enchantment that gave her the ability to communicate in the Fae Realm would end once she was fully free in the Human Realm. Brigid and the members of her League in the Human Realm might only be able to communicate on a limited basis once that happened.

When it grew dark, Brigid put on her cloak, hid the girl underneath, and headed out into the night. Even at night, fae bustled in and out of the Library, which never closed, and walked the streets of the town surrounding the Library.

But few gave Brigid more than a glance. She kept to the shadows, navigating the streets with confidence. The little girl clung to her skirts and trotted to keep up, hidden beneath Brigid's cloak.

At the edge of the Tanglewood, the magical forest that stretched along the border of the Court of Knowledge and the Court of Revels, a faerie circle was marked by a circle of trees and dotted with the little red flowers of the wild fae primrose.

Brigid reached behind her and took the little girl's hand. "Are you ready to go home?"

The girl nodded, huddling close to Brigid's side.

Brigid's own heart pounded harder, though not from fear. No, this pounding had to do with thoughts of what lay on the other side of this circle.

Or, more accurately, *who*.

Munch, forester of the Greenwood. The young man she'd been trying not to fall in love with for the past three years.

Even though he didn't know she was the Primrose and she didn't dare tell him the truth. As far as he knew, she was just a messenger girl.

Brigid gave herself a shake. She refused to let fluttering feelings cloud her mind right before she hazarded the dangers of the faerie paths with a little girl at her side.

Gripping the girl's hand in one of hers, Brigid reached down and plucked one of the wild fae primroses. With the flower to steady her, she stepped into the faerie circle.

The swirling dizziness of the magic closed around her. Disorientating. Squeezing. Behind her, the Fae Realm was a sickeningly sweet siren call while ahead, the Human Realm tugged at her, ready to claim her once again.

If she let it, the twin tugs could pull her in all sorts of directions. She might end up far from her desired destination. She might end up a hundred years in the past from when the girl disappeared. Or a hundred years in the future. She might end up back in the Fae Realm in a far different circle than the one she left.

She drew in a deep breath and gripped the wild fae primrose tighter. Little clusters of the flowers appeared amongst the swirl and haze. Brigid followed her honed senses, stepping along the faerie path outlined by the flowers.

Soon, she would lead another wanderer home. Another family restored. Another rescue complete. Another triumph for the Primrose.

Chapter Three

Yawning, Munch of the Greenwood took his seat at the long oak table in the dining room of the Duke of Gysborn's castle, grabbed a plate, and helped himself to the eggs and sausage. While getting up early was annoying, it was worth it to get to the table first and claim as much food as he wanted.

It wasn't as bad as it used to be. Now that the drought was over, the castle kitchens always had enough food. Especially now that Tuck, one of Munch's five older brothers, was in charge of the kitchens.

But even after five years of living at the duke's castle, Munch still couldn't get over the freedom to eat as much food as he wanted without having to fight his brothers tooth and nail for it. And even better, he didn't have to wash the dishes afterwards.

Alan, one of Munch's older brothers, strode into the room and plopped into the seat across from Munch. "You're up early."

"Just enjoying Tuck's good cooking." Munch stuffed another large bite into his mouth.

Alan was here for a visit, taking a break from his successful career as a traveling bard, where he told highly exaggerated stories of their exploits as outlaws before their family had reformed, thanks to their sister Robin's marriage to Guy, the Duke of Gysborn.

"Of course it's good." Tuck strode into the room, carrying his two-year-old son. A light layer of flour dusted his shoulders, but the rest of his clothes remained clean thanks to the apron he'd likely left in the kitchen. "I'm just that good."

His wife, following close on his heels with their baby daughter in her arms, rolled her eyes.

"No, I think it's the fancy new spices Guy imported on the last trade shipment." Alan motioned with his fork before spearing a piece of sausage.

"Spices are only as good as the person wielding them." Tuck settled his son into one of the many highchairs surrounding the table, then cut up eggs and sausage into bite-sized pieces while his son squirmed and banged on the tray with his fists. Once his son and wife had food, Tuck dug into the breakfast with the same gusto as the rest of them.

Marion, the brother closest in age to Munch, was the next one to trudge in and stumble into a chair. He had recently married the village seamstress. She must have decided to sleep in that morning rather than make the trek up to the castle for breakfast.

Munch shoved a plate in Marion's direction while Alan nudged the platter of eggs closer. They all knew there was no speaking to Marion until he had some food in his system.

And they all mocked Munch for his appetite. Hence the nickname "Munch."

Still, he preferred Munch to his real name of Mungoe. His mother named him after the hero of her favorite ballad, but some names were better in ballads than in real life.

When the door opened again, John stepped inside with his wife and son, followed by Will, Munch's oldest brother, and his family. Will, John, and their families still lived in the Greenwood, protecting it from both fae and faerie monsters.

While it was nice to spend time with his brothers, Munch wasn't sure he liked being surrounded by all this married bliss and children and all that. It reminded him that he was twenty-three years old—nearly twenty-four—and still bumming around both the castle and the Greenwood with no direction and no true purpose.

Before taking his seat, Will glanced around. "Guy and Robin aren't up yet?"

No, and Munch wasn't about to be the one to be sent to fetch them. His sister Robin and her husband Guy were disgustingly in love.

"Not yet." Alan swiped a muffin out of the basket before John could take it away to the other end of the table. "Or, at least, they haven't graced us with their presence yet."

"I see." Will's mouth quirked. All of them knew better than to disturb Robin and Guy in the morning.

A loud, boisterous laugh rang in the hall outside of the doors to the dining room.

Will shook his head and quickly speared more sausages, dumping them on his plate. "Robin's awake."

The double doors flung open hard enough to hit the walls on either side. Robin's tall form whirled into the room, her sword flashing as she parried a strike from her husband Guy. While Robin was fully dressed in trousers, a leather tunic, and her knee-high boots, Guy was barefoot and his shirt was open, the ties loose at the collar. He held their son in one arm, neither of their swords getting anywhere near the child.

A nurse hurried along behind them, carrying Guy and Robin's two-year-old daughter. While most children would be wide-eyed at the sight of their parents sword-fighting, Sylvia swung her own wooden toy sword, hitting the harried nurse in the face, and squealed happy cheers. Definitely Robin's daughter.

"Can I at least get my boots on next time?" Guy sliced his sword at Robin's side.

She squirmed out of the way of his sword and jumped back a few more steps. "Not my fault that you're too slow to get dressed in the morning."

"Because you woke me up by munching on an apple next to my ear. Again." Guy raced after Robin, stabbing forward with his sword once again. "And someone had to fetch Rowan from his crib."

"Excuses, excuses." Robin gave another hearty laugh as she danced backwards a few steps.

"They're still madly in love, I see." Alan munched on his muffin.

"Emphasis on the *mad* part." Tuck shook his head and claimed another muffin before Marion grabbed the basket.

"Mad as a spring rabbit." John stuffed another bite of eggs in his mouth.

Munch rolled his eyes and reached for the eggs to get another helping before his brothers ate all the food.

With another of her ringing laughs, Robin used a chair to hop onto the table and evade Guy's sword all in one motion. Before he could follow, Robin kicked the chair over.

"Robin!" Guy growled as he jumped the chair, then vaulted himself onto the table after her. "The table? Again?"

As Robin and Guy sword-fought along the length of the table, everyone lifted their plates—or their children's plates—out of the way of stomping boots and kept eating without missing a beat, though a few of the children grew a little distracted as they cheered on either Uncle Guy or Aunt Robin.

Despite the apparent recklessness of the sword fight, the swinging swords never came close to any of the family members.

Munch popped a bite into his mouth, then lifted his plate out of the way of Robin's foot. He reached over and picked up the eggs before Robin could squash them.

Will lifted the platter of sausage out of the way. Alan held up the basket of muffins, and Robin swiped one as she passed, taking a bite even as she parried Guy's sword.

After ducking Guy's next swing, Robin saluted Tuck's wife with the muffin. "Excellent work this morning."

Tuck's wife ducked her head in pleasure, twisting her apron in her hands. "Thank you, milady. It was nothing."

"You are to be commended." Guy leaned back as he dodged Robin's sword, his tone completely unruffled. In his arms, Rowan lay relaxed and snuggling happily, also unruffled by the clang of swords.

Guy pressed his advantage, and Robin was forced to jump backwards along the tabletop. Will and his wife grabbed their plates and those of their children to keep them from being stomped on.

With barely a pause, Guy dumped the baby into Alan's arms. Alan didn't even blink at finding himself in possession of his nephew, and instead he settled him in one arm while still munching away on the last of his muffin with the other.

Munch just sighed and set his plate back on the table to snatch a few bites. Hopefully Guy would keep Robin on the defensive and they wouldn't end up fighting back down the length of the table.

Robin smirked as she hopped back a few feet, then she stood on a chair, tipping it to the floor with a clatter as she landed lightly on her feet. She grinned up at Guy. "You're getting slow."

Guy smirked back, then jumped off the table, landing in a crouch before he launched himself at Robin.

She laughed and ducked away.

Munch just shook his head. His sister had always been like this. A bit touched in the head with a recklessness that got a thrill out of danger. Somehow, Guy, the stuffy and law-abiding Duke of Gysborn, had fallen in love with her.

As he went back to eating his breakfast, Munch avoided looking at Robin and Guy. Robin had Guy cornered against the wall, and it was only a matter of seconds before she'd disarm him, and they'd move on from sword fighting to kissing.

It had been fun throughout the years to see Robin all but fling Guy out of his reserved shell. It had been less fun to have to witness all the kissing that came with it.

Munch nudged his final sausage, rolling it across his plate with his fork. What was this, his fourth? Fifth? He couldn't remember. Either way, he was stuffed, and he wasn't sure he could eat one more bite, much less finish that last sausage.

Robin plopped into the chair to the right of the head of the table, next to the highchair where the nurse had placed Sylvia. Robin kissed Sylvia's cheek, sending the girl into a peal of giggles. Robin grinned at Guy as she added a few more pieces of egg onto the plate the nurse had set in front of Sylvia. "Well, that was invigorating. I always love a good sword fight before breakfast."

Guy righted the chair at the head of the table, then sat. "Always happy to oblige."

Alan handed the baby off down the line, the baby going hand-to-hand until Rowan ended up back in Guy's arms.

With the baby in one arm, Guy took a plate, then frowned when the platters of sausage and eggs were passed his way. Only a few eggs and a single sausage remained.

Robin stabbed the sausage before Guy could, eating it right

off the fork. She gestured around the table, speaking around her mouthful of sausage. "Nice to see such a full table this morning."

Munch sighed down at his lone sausage, then passed his plate along to Guy. If he wasn't going to enjoy eating it, then Guy might as well have it.

Guy quickly snagged the sausage before Robin could swipe it from him. "Will, John. Is all well in the Greenwood?"

"Incursions by monsters have continued to increase." Will shrugged. "But we've been keeping up, for now."

"Good work." Guy's jaw tightened, his eyes sharper. He had good reason to be especially wary of incursions by the fae. A fae had tricked him into a bargain that had held him captive, murdered his three wives before Robin, and caused over seven years of drought that spread throughout the kingdom.

"Just let me know if you ever need help for a good monster battle." Robin grinned, as if she looked forward to a good fight now and then, even though she had been neither an outlaw nor an official forester for the past five years.

Will poured water onto a napkin, then scrubbed at his son's egg-smeared face. "You know we can handle it. We're foresters."

"Sword fighting me isn't enough for you?" Guy raised a dark eyebrow at Robin.

"Fighting you is too easy." Robin waved her last bite of sausage at him.

"Really?" Guy snagged the fork from Robin's grasp and popped the bite in his mouth, smirking at Robin.

Robin tilted her head back in another loud laugh. "All right. Not so easy."

Munch sighed and sank lower in his chair. Did all of his siblings have to be so disgustingly in love? It had only gotten worse now that Marion was married. All of them had gotten hitched, leaving Munch the only one at loose ends. The only one they still considered the baby of the family, even if he was a grown man of twenty-three. Nearly twenty-four.

"Will, John, you'll need to hurry back to the Greenwood after breakfast." Robin leaned back in her chair. "I think our friend from the Fae Realm is going to stop by sometime today."

Munch bolted straighter in his chair. Brigid. She was coming for another visit, surely with another human rescued by the Primrose in tow.

She was so brave, acting as the traveler between worlds on behalf of the mysterious fae the Primrose.

If Robin said she was on her way, then she would be there soon. Robin had a better sense of fae magic and the call of the faerie circles than anyone Munch knew, with the possible exception of Brigid.

Even before he'd given it much thought, Munch shot to his feet. "I'm done eating. I can go to the Greenwood and meet her. Any idea which faerie circle she'll use this time?"

"It might be the mushroom circle, or perhaps the spruce circle. I can't tell for sure." Robin's smirk returned, a twinkle to her brown eyes as she met Munch's gaze. "Go get your lady love."

Munch clenched his fists, his face burning. "She's not my lady love."

"Sure, sure." Robin waved at him, then lunged half-onto the table, grasping the muffin basket just as Marion did. The two of them tugged the basket back and forth, making the last muffin roll across the cloth lining the inside.

Munch hurried away from the table before Robin or his brothers could think of more teasing. Sure, Brigid was pretty. And smart. And had that dash of daring without being as reck-lessly crazy as Robin.

But she wouldn't look twice at him. He'd thought they'd had

a spark when they'd first met five years ago. But after their disastrous attempt at a first kiss, she'd held him at arm's length. He could never be her hero anymore than he could be a hero to his family.

After all, how could he ever hope to match the heroics of Robin or Guy in the eyes of his family? Or how could he ever hope to compete with a dashing, fae lord like the Primrose in Brigid's eyes?

Not to mention, Munch was human. At twenty-three, his brown hair was already beginning to recede at his temples. He was fit and well-muscled, but he liked food far too much to ever have the sculpted look of a fae lord. At least the light scruff on his jaw and upper lip wasn't too patchy, even if it wasn't as thick as Guy's beard.

In other words, he was a completely average human young man. Why would Brigid ever give him a second glance when she spent her days in the Fae Realm working for someone like the Primrose?

That didn't stop Munch from hurrying down the corridor, snagging a few snacks from the kitchens, and rushing out the door into the castle's courtyard. Hopeless, that was what he was.

The guards at the castle gate waved to him and opened the gates. He strolled down the stone causeway from the gates before his boots scuffed on the gravel of the road that wound toward the village, which straddled the river.

While he could have taken a horse—he even had his own, a gift from Guy—he preferred to walk today. It felt right, taking the left fork of the road and, instead of heading toward town, he turned into the Greenwood.

As the dense forest of the Greenwood closed around him, he drew in a deep breath, then released it slowly. Home.

Yes, he had lived in the duke's castle for much of the past

five years. But the Greenwood would always be home. He had been born under these trees, the son of foresters. He'd lost his parents here when they had been killed by the same fae who had held Guy captive. Munch had fought alongside his brothers and sister as outlaws for much of his growing-up years. He knew these trees, these paths, better than he knew the corridors of the castle.

Munch hiked deeper into the Greenwood, following familiar winding trails between the trees. Well, they weren't trails so much as slightly cleared places where his family and the animals of the forest tended to walk. Someone unfamiliar with the forest wouldn't see a trail at all.

Once he was deep enough in the forest that he could no longer see the bright edge where forest met the fields of the village, he halted next to a large, old oak tree that dominated this section of the forest. He rested his hand on the bark, closed his eyes, and searched for that instinct deep inside him.

Legends had it that his forester ancestors had a bit of fae blood in them, giving them this ability to sense fae magic and an extra connection to the Greenwood. Munch wasn't sure how much of the story was true, but Robin certainly had a sense when it came to fae magic and the circles.

Was it his imagination, or did he feel a slight tugging deep in his chest drawing him toward the north and the mushroom circle there?

It was as good a direction as any to hike. If he missed Brigid, she knew the way to either Will's cottage in the Greenwood or the duke's castle on the hill.

Still, he didn't want to miss her. He wanted those few minutes with her without any of his siblings present. A few minutes where they could simply stroll and talk, as they did every time Munch managed to be the one to meet Brigid at the faerie circles.

Munch set off into the Greenwood, the oaks, beeches, and pines closing around him. He strode at a steady pace, reaching the mushroom circle an hour later.

The forest around the circle remained still. Empty.

But there was an extra something in the air. A tingly shiver. The rising sense that something was coming.

Munch unstrapped his bow from his back, braced it against his foot, then leaned on it so that he could slide the string into place. Once done, he climbed up a nearby, branching butternut tree and settled comfortably into a crook of the large branches. He selected an arrow and nocked it on the string, though he didn't draw it.

Something was coming through that circle. Whether it was Brigid and her rescued human or a fae monster set on destruction, Munch couldn't tell.

As he had been trained to do, he settled in to watch and wait, prepared for whoever or whatever would step through that circle.

Chapter Four

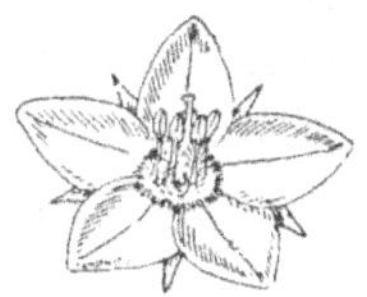

Munch kept his breathing light and steady, his muscles ready in case a monster stepped from that circle.

The pressure of fae magic increased until it clung heavy and sticky in Munch's lungs and throat. A shimmer filled the faerie circle, like a heat wave on a summer day.

Then something pink appeared in the shimmer a moment before a young woman dressed in a pink silk dress stepped from the circle, a dark green cloak wrapped around her and her brown-blonde hair flowing across her shoulders. A young girl peeked from under Brigid's cloak, her little fingers clutching the pink silk in a white-knuckled grip.

Munch waited for another few heartbeats, making sure that they were alone. But they weren't running, as if they were being chased. The fae magic receded, dulling back to a background hum.

When he was sure it was safe, he slid his arrow back into his quiver, looped his strung bow over his shoulder, and hopped down from the tree. His heart pounded harder than it had when he'd been tensed in anticipation of a fae monster, his words threatening to stick in his throat.

This was Brigid. His friend. The girl he had liked for five years. He needed to keep his cool. Act normal. Pretend he hadn't been counting down the days until she returned.

Brigid smiled, the sight sending a jolt through him that threatened to root his feet to the forest floor. She was already so pretty, but when her smile lit her face and sparkled in her eyes, the added warmth did funny things to his head.

As if immune to the effect she had on him, Brigid met his gaze, her light brown eyes as warm as her smile. "Hello, Munch."

The little girl gave a squeak and ducked behind Brigid.

Munch halted where he was, not wanting to scare the girl any more than he already had. He smiled, hoping it looked friendly and not as awkwardly infatuated as he felt. "Robin sensed you'd be coming today. I hope the trip through the circles was uneventful."

Brigid waved her hand airily. "As always." She reached behind her and rested her other hand on the girl's back, as if to give the girl comfort and reassurance. "This little one is ready to find her way home."

Based on the girl's darker coloring, she came from one of the kingdoms to the southwest. Alan and his wife should have connections there that would help get this girl home.

"Follow me, then. We'll get her some food and rest while we arrange to get her home." Munch left his bow strung as he led the way back into the forest. Now that he was responsible for Brigid and the little girl, he didn't dare let down his guard. One never knew when the fae might come after them.

Was it bad if he was almost hoping a monster would attack them? Not a big monster, just a little one. But just scary enough that he could shoot it and look the hero in front of Brigid.

Yes, it was a foolish idea, and he didn't actually want Brigid and the little girl put at risk. But he'd welcome a chance to show off to Brigid. Just a little bit.

For a few minutes, they hiked in silence, going slowly to accommodate the girl's short legs. Munch would have offered to carry her, but she seemed too scared to leave Brigid's side, much less trust a strange man.

It burned something inside him. How could the fae so cruelly treat a child, leaving her traumatized like this?

Munch wracked his brain for something to say to break the silence, since no convenient monster attack seemed forthcoming. "How are things in the Fae Realm? The monster attacks have been increasing again lately, but nothing we can't handle."

"The Court of Revels has had more monster attacks lately, though King Oberon has been cagey on that. But we've noticed more monsters on our side of the Tanglewood as well." Brigid grimaced. "That's probably why you've seen more monsters here as well."

They had, just not right now when he would have almost welcomed a monster or two. Just small ones.

But Brigid didn't have his protection when she entered the Tanglewood to travel through the circle on behalf of the Primrose. She was on her own when in the Fae Realm, vulnerable even to small monster attacks.

He swallowed, his voice rough. "I hope you've been staying safe. All those monsters probably make your job harder."

"Queen Hippolyta's swordmaidens keep our side of the Tanglewood relatively safe, even with the extra monsters." Brigid shrugged, that indolent smile still plastered on her face. "Their Majesties are keeping an eye on things, but I'm sure it's nothing to worry about. Midsummer Night is only a few days away, and that night always brings an increase in monsters. I'm sure things will quiet down after that."

From what Munch had gathered over the years, Midsummer Night was the night with the most magic in the Summer Courts, to which the Court of Knowledge and the Court of Revels belonged. It didn't come around in a predictable fashion. Sometimes it would come every three months. Sometimes it would be every three years.

Perhaps this increase in monsters was the result of the coming Midsummer Night in the Fae Realm. But the last time they had experienced so many monsters in the Greenwood had been in the months after the death of the fae who had held Guy captive. Not a comforting thought.

"The Primrose is still kept busy." Munch glanced over his shoulder at Brigid and the girl she sheltered at her side.

"Yes." For a moment, Brigid's eyes flashed, a hint of a tight anger crossing her face. Then her expression smoothed, her jaw loosening and the sharpness fading from her gaze. Just like that, the Brigid he'd met years ago was subsumed into a light-hearted mask once again. "But I trust the Primrose will have a plan to rescue those who have been snatched. He always does."

Munch itched at the admiration that colored her tone. Yes, he was infatuated with Brigid. But he didn't need that rubbed in his face whenever she spoke about that heroic fae, the Primrose. No doubt the Primrose was as handsome as he was heroic.

It was Munch's own fault for bringing up the Primrose. He really should have thought of a better topic.

"And your sister and brother-in-law? Your siblings? Are they doing well?" Could he be any more mundane with his small talk?

At least this seemed to be the right topic. Brigid launched into tales of her siblings' work as apprentice librarians, Meg and Basil's children, Meg's work as both head of book repair and Assistant Librarian of Practical Things, and how much Basil loved being a master librarian.

Her voice held such love for her family that he couldn't help but smile. But he noted that, as always, she said very little about her own life. As if she was so busy aiding the Primrose that she didn't have a life of her own. Instead, she lived vicariously through her family.

Munch could relate. He didn't have much to report about his own life either. He was still riding on Robin's cloak, marching along to her orders instead of finding his own life the way his other brothers had.

"And your family?" Brigid held the girl's hand, and the girl walked a bit faster now that she didn't seem to be clinging so tightly to Brigid's skirts.

"Robin and Guy sword-fought across the table this morning during breakfast." Munch shook his head, not bothering to hide his grin.

"So a usual morning."

"Yep." Munch shared a grin with her. The path had widened so that the three of them could comfortably walk side by side. "Alan and his wife are visiting. She will likely be able to converse with this little one."

He motioned to the girl. Her gaze was flicking between them as they talked and walked, but he couldn't tell if she understood their conversation or not. So far, she had remained silent.

"Oh, good. That will make things less scary for her." Brigid squeezed the girl's hand, giving her a smile. "She likely has a long way to go before she's home."

The girl smiled back, but the smile faded just as quickly as she flicked a glance at Munch.

He kept his smile in place, but he didn't try to interact with the girl. She would approach him if she wished. Until then, he wasn't going to push her.

"We'll see that she's safe." Munch used the excuse of a tree in his path to swerve closer to Brigid.

"I know." Brigid gave a small sigh. "I just wish there was a way to deliver them directly back to their homes. It would be so much easier on them."

Munch nodded, not sure what to say.

The Primrose—through Brigid—used Gysborn as a way station because of the difficulty of trying to return each and every person to the exact place they had come from. It was much more efficient to bring all the rescued humans to Gysborn. From there, Guy and Robin did their best to help the people return home, whether that was finding safe merchants for them to travel with, providing them with money for the journey, or in the case of those who no longer had families for various reasons, giving them a home in Gysborn.

But Munch didn't want to talk about the Primrose. In fact, he had been trying to avoid that topic, even though it wasn't working.

"Alan and Sofia surprised us with the fact that they are expecting. I'm going to have another niece or nephew in a few months." Munch lifted a branch out of the way so that Brigid and the girl could pass underneath.

"Congratulations! How many is that now?" Brigid ducked under the branch, then smiled back at him.

He let go of the branch, then hurried to fall into step with her again. "A lot. There's quite the pack of them." He'd have to start counting on his fingers to get an exact number of his nieces and nephews, and even then he'd probably forget one. That was what came of having six married siblings.

Brigid gave a laugh, shaking her head. "It must be chaotic when all of you are together. I can't wait until more of my siblings are married. I love my nieces, and it would be wonderful to have a few more running around."

Munch snapped his mouth shut. He'd nearly blurted out that she could get married herself. If he made a suggestion like that, he might find on her next visit that she had up and married that elusive Primrose.

Instead, after a moment, he said, "Do you think the Great Library would survive a few more half-fae, half-human children running around?"

"The Great Library is surprisingly good with children." Brigid shrugged, then glanced down at the girl. "Do you think we could take a rest? It's a long walk on little legs."

He should have thought of that. "Of course. There are a few rocks up ahead where we can sit. I brought muffins and scones, if you're hungry."

When Brigid smiled at him again with warmth in her eyes, he felt six inches taller. He'd do anything just to keep her looking at him like that, even if he could never have more of her than these short walks through the forest.

AFTER A BRIEF REST AND A SNACK, Brigid gripped the girl's hand as they resumed their walk and tried to pretend that she wasn't sneaking peeks at Munch beside her.

When she'd met him years ago, he had been a gangly eighteen-year-old. She, too, had been eighteen, and she'd fallen hard and fast during those three weeks she'd spent with his family, training in the ways of the foresters. Even the awful kiss they'd shared back then hadn't been enough to kill the infatuation.

Over the years he had matured into a handsome man, with brown hair receding into a dignified widow's peak, a rugged scruff along his jaw, and a back and shoulders made broad and strong by years of archery, outlined by his dark green cloak and tunic. He looked quite heroic and dashing, strutting through the forest with his bow over a shoulder and his quiver at his hip. Even more appealing was his quiet, sincere manner, shown by the care he always gave to the humans she rescued.

Five years had passed here in the Human Realm while only three had passed in the Fae Realm. He was now a young man of twenty-three to her twenty-one.

Would she continue to watch him out-age her like this? He was a might-have-been. If her life was different, if she was less passionate about her mission, if she dared tell him the truth that she was the Primrose, if…

But it couldn't be. She could allow nothing to stand in the way of her mission to rescue humans from the fae. All she had to do was look at the tear-streaked faces of children like the girl she'd rescued this time or the blank, faerie-fruit-addled gazes of the adults, and her anger would burn hot and fierce, fueling her drive to keep on this path she'd chosen for herself. It didn't matter if she sacrificed the hope of a family for herself when it meant that she could reunite hundreds of families.

She couldn't let anyone get in the way of that. Not even a handsome young man.

When they reached the castle, Munch's sister Robin sauntered out of the castle's keep. She was dressed in her customary leather tunic and practical trousers with her bow on her back and her quiver at her hip. She welcomed Brigid with a smile and a laugh. When she asked after Brigid's adventures, her gaze held a bit of envy, as if she was tempted to run off to the Fae Realm for adventure, if she didn't love her family so much here on this side of the circles.

Alan's wife Sofia took charge of the girl, trying a few languages until the girl's eyes widened and the two of them were soon chattering away. The rescued child would be in good hands until her family could be located.

After Brigid passed along the information she'd gathered about the girl's family, Robin held out a piece of paper. A new list of those who had been stolen away by the fae. It seemed no matter how many people Brigid rescued, the fae always stole more.

"I wish you could stay longer. I'm sure you have some wild stories to tell." Robin's eyes danced with the reckless sense of adventure.

"Perhaps." Brigid wasn't sure what she would dare share, not even to Robin who knew that she was the Primrose. "But I need to get back before I'm missed. Time doesn't move as quickly there, but if I hurry, I can get some sleep."

"I'll walk you back." Munch was at her side in a blink. "Just in case of fae monsters."

A part of her wanted anyone else to escort her back. It would be much safer for her heart.

But most of her—more of her than she'd ever want to admit —leapt at the thought of more precious minutes with Munch. She looked forward to their walks through the Greenwood each time she rescued a human more than she cared to acknowledge.

She probably shouldn't keep encouraging him like this. She knew how he felt about her. It was obvious, by the way he looked at her.

But she didn't have the strength to let him go either. Not when she treasured her time with him so much. If all she would ever get were these scraps of moments, then she'd take it, even if she could never have what the warmth in his eyes promised if she should ever speak up.

She had plenty of practice concealing her true feelings. She clasped her hands in front of her and beamed at Munch. "Of course, I'd love your company on the walk."

Another walk through the forest where she and Munch talked about everything and nothing. Everything, except the truth of her role as the Primrose. Another moment at the edge of the faerie circle where the tension crackled between them with the memory of that dreadfully messy first kiss they'd shared. Another farewell where they didn't repeat the kiss nor acknowledge their true feelings simmering beneath. Yet another long stretch of days in the Fae Realm where she wondered what was happening with Munch as time flew by so much faster in the Human Realm.

Another sweet torment all of her own making.

Chapter Five

Brigid woke when the House dumped her out of the cozy sleeping nook in her bedroom in Basil and Meg's House. The floor was formed of the same soft, spongy moss as her mattress, so her landing didn't hurt, even though she woke with a jolt with her nose buried in the sprigs of red wild fae primrose flowers that dotted the floor.

She groaned and murmured into the moss, "What was that for?"

The House gave another shake around her, the floor bulging upward to nudge her to her feet. As she tottered her way upright, the House tilted the floor and sent her careening across the room until she stumbled against her wardrobe.

"I'm up, I'm up." Brigid steadied herself against the wooden doors of the wardrobe. The wardrobe itself was grown into the wall in a wiggly, curving shape. Brigid rested her hand on the wardrobe's latch. "I'm going to the Library today. What do you have for me, House?"

The House gave another shiver, this one rather smug.

Brigid opened the wardrobe and discovered a dress with a light pink bodice and a skirt of both green and pink that ended at her knees. A matching set of stockings and knee-high boots completed the outfit.

The House didn't create the outfit. The wardrobe took the outfit from somewhere else in the Fae Realm, where a seamstress had created the dress and placed it in a cupboard. Each of the courts had agreements to keep this free flow of food, clothing, and materials. In the case of the Court of Knowledge, it exchanged access to its Library and Anywhere Doors for the resources of the other courts.

"Good choice, House." Brigid patted the wardrobe, then changed into the dress. She was still lacing her second boot when the House opened the Anywhere Door that led from her bedroom to the main room of the House. It was all Brigid could do to stay on her feet as the House tossed her from her room into the main room.

The Anywhere Door snapped shut behind her. Only a few seconds later, it spat out Viola, still tying a ribbon in her light blonde hair.

Brigid dodged out of the way before Viola could plow into her. "The House is in a hurry to get us all going this morning."

Viola glowered up at the ceiling. "I wonder what has its beams in a twist this morning."

Dirt showered down on Viola's head. Viola scowled and brushed the dirt from her hair.

"You should know better than to question the House." Brigid strode toward the cupboards lining the small kitchen. "What do you have for us for breakfast?"

As Brigid reached for the cupboard that usually produced their food, the Anywhere Door opened again, this time depositing Sebastian. His blond hair remained tousled, and he blinked sleepily. "What put a bee in the House's rafters this morning?"

"Don't know." Brigid opened the cupboard, finding it overflowing with green eggs, pink toast, and a variety of orange and purple fruit. For all its grumpiness this morning, at least the House was still going to feed them.

To one side of the kitchen, clopping noises came from behind the double door leading to the stables attached to the House. Moments later, the upper half of the door swung open. Buddy, their talking pony companion, stuck his head into the room. He blinked his deep brown eyes sleepily. His shaggy dark brown mane stuck up in all directions while his brown coat was as sleek as always. "What does a pony have to do to get some beauty sleep around here?"

"Not our fault." Viola joined Brigid in the kitchen, brushing the last of the dirt from her hair.

Brigid handed Viola a plate of eggs, and Viola transferred the plate to the table. "The House seems to think we all need to be up early today."

Sebastian joined Viola, and the two of them took plates and platters from Brigid and set them on the table.

The Anywhere Door opened again, and this time Beatrice stumbled into the room, cradling a yellow bookwyrm in her arms. How had she even convinced a bookwyrm to leave the Library? Yawning, Beatrice stumbled across the room and gave Buddy a hug before she dropped into a seat at the table.

A squeal announced Addy's arrival as the Anywhere Door hurriedly opened to let the three-year-old bound into the room. Meg chased after her, not yet wearing her librarian coat.

Basil followed, carrying Morgan with one arm, his black librarian coat draped over the other.

A branch reached down and snagged Addy before she could make a run for either the fireplace, which wasn't lit, or the outer door. Addy squealed happily as the House lifted her from her feet. With something almost like an exasperated sigh, the House held Addy out to Meg.

"Thank you, House." Meg took Addy, then wrestled the squirming girl into her chair at the table. "How she has so much energy first thing in the morning, I don't know. She was up an hour ago already."

Ah, that would explain why the House had hustled them all out of bed. Addy was up and ready for breakfast, so that meant the rest of them needed to be up as well.

Basil passed the baby to Meg before taking his seat at the table. "And Morgan was up not long afterwards."

Brigid grabbed the last plate from the cupboard, then joined the rest of her siblings gathering around the table. Even five years later, she tried not to take this moment for granted. They had a table with abundant food. All of them had clean, good quality clothes. They were headed off for jobs at the Great Library that all of them loved.

How things had changed from their past in the Human Realm, where they had scraped out a living on a dying farm in a drought that was starving the entire kingdom.

After everyone had nearly polished off the ample breakfast, Brigid neatly stacked her dishes, then glanced at Basil. "Are you still planning to work in the tower today?"

Basil nodded, his jaw tightening. "Queen Hippolyta gave me a few more reports that she received from her scouts. I put them in the tower, but I haven't had a chance to look at them yet."

For the past few years, Basil had been helping King Theseus and Queen Hippolyta track down three fae who had stirred up trouble in the Court of Revels years before Brigid and her siblings had come to the Fae Realm. These three fae delved into blood rites so forbidden even the other fae deemed them cruel and evil. The three of them had been banished from the Fae Realm and promptly forgotten.

Except that King Theseus believed it was a mistake to forget them. Basil and Meg had discovered what had happened to one of the fae when they visited Robin and Guy for the first time, but that left two of the fae still unaccounted for.

King Theseus had given Basil the use of one of the Library towers to store their research and reports on these fae. When Brigid had begun her work as the Primrose, she had also stored her lists and research and disguises there. It was far safer than the House, guarded as the tower was by a fully grown bookwyrm and by the Library's magic.

"I have a new list of names from Robin to sort through as well." Brigid touched the inner pocket of her dress. The House always knew to include lots of hidden pockets in her dresses.

"Is it long?" Viola set down her fork, her smile dying.

Meg's face hardened as she wiped Addy's face with a rag. "Always too many names, even on a short list."

If Brigid dwelled on it too long, she'd despair. For every one human she saved, it seemed like there were three more stolen away and awaiting rescue. Yet if she didn't do what she did, then no one would be rescued. No one would return to their families. Even if she rescued only one, then she was succeeding.

Even with her League helping her, so much rested on her shoulders. Far too much, at times. If only she had someone she could trust to lean on for support. Who could help her organize the League and carry this burden with her.

But there was no one she dared trust with this.

Munch's face flitted through her mind, but she shoved the thought away. He was a human unbound to a fae court and thus too vulnerable. Besides, he was too loyal to his family. She could never ask him to leave his family and his realm to join her here. She liked him far too much to ask such a sacrifice of him.

Locking her musings away, Brigid helped her siblings clean up. Once Meg and Basil had collected everything they would need for Addy and Morgan for the day, all of them trooped through the Anywhere Door into the Great Hall of Anywhere Doors.

From there, Meg, Addy, Morgan, and Beatrice soon disappeared in the maze of shelves of the Great Library, headed for the book repair room. Sebastian and Viola reported in at the front desk to assist the master librarians in fetching books and returning them to the shelves.

Basil gestured to the tree. "I need to check in with Head Librarian Marco, then we can head for the tower."

Brigid nodded, then trotted along at Basil's side as he strode toward the great tree in the center of the Library.

Head Librarian Marco perched behind his desk tucked between two of the folds of the large roots of the tree. His white hair was cut long over his ears and flowed into a long beard down his chest. He was muttering to himself as he flipped through the book in front of him before he reached for another book and paged through that.

"Sir?" Basil halted in front of the desk.

Head Librarian Marco glanced up at them, blinking for a moment. "Basil. Yes, was there something you needed?"

"Brigid and I are going to work in the tower today, in case you need me for anything." Basil glanced over the piles of books.

"Yes, yes, of course." Head Librarian Marco waved at Basil and Brigid, his gaze already dropping back to the books in front of him.

Brigid couldn't help but smile. Head Librarian Marco and his wife had become like the grandparents she and her siblings had never had.

Basil, too, smiled as he turned away from the desk and led the way across the Library's atrium. The winding shelves quickly closed around them, filled with books and greenery and the scuttling bookwyrms. Librarians bustled between the shelves, nodding to Basil and Brigid as they passed.

Deep inside the Library, they reached the stairs to the tower they'd been given. Basil led the way up the winding, wooden stairs. The handrail was formed of a smooth branch while moss and flowers draped down the wood and stone walls.

When they were about halfway up the steps, a deep growl vibrated down the stairs underneath their feet.

"Gus. It's me. Basil. And Brigid." Basil peeked around the corner of the stairs, then shook his head. "Some guard wyrm. He's sleeping."

Brigid grinned and followed Basil around the corner. "I'm sure the Library would wake him if there was a real threat."

"Hopefully." Basil sighed as they rounded the curve of the tower.

Before them, a huge green bookwyrm filled the stairwell with his head draped facing them and his long, ropy body disappearing out of sight above. His giant ruff behind his head nearly blocked the stairs.

As Basil and Brigid strode closer, Gus cracked his eyes open, gave a grumble, then slightly rolled so that his lighter green belly was facing them.

"Oh, I see how it is." Brigid scratched just behind the book-wyrm's ruff, eliciting a deeper rumble in the bookwyrm's throat.

Basil trailed his hand over the bookwyrm's belly as he stepped around the sprawled bookwyrm. He scratched the bookwyrm's scales, and the bookwyrm wiggled to further roll onto his back and nearly pinned Basil against the wall.

Brigid picked her way around the bookwyrm, also giving Gus a belly rub as she continued upward.

The bookwyrm was so long that his tail reached all the way

into the room at the top. It twitched as the bookwyrm drifted back to sleep.

Basil continued across the room toward the desk he'd set up at one side of the round room. Small bookshelves lined the walls while drawers held various pieces of research.

On Brigid's desk across the room, a jar with water sat on a coaster. Smiling, Brigid drew a few of the sprigs of wild fae primrose from her pocket and formed a straggling bouquet in the jar. Only here and in the safety of her room in the House did she dare decorate with wild fae primroses to her heart's content.

She sat behind her desk, then pulled out the list of names. Ten names, listing the ages of those who had been stolen away and where they had been stolen from.

So many people who had been stolen from their families. So many hurting people.

She turned to her map pinned on a board leaning against the wall and double-checked the faerie circles nearest to where the people had disappeared. Through research, she had figured out which fae courts connected to each of the circles in the Human Realm.

While those skilled in walking the faerie paths between the realms could go pretty much anywhere when traveling between the circles, most people—fae or human—stepped through them with no direction. They tended to end up in the places most closely linked in that particular thin spot in the barrier between the realms.

With that knowledge, she could make an educated guess as to which fae court to search for each stolen human.

She made notes, brainstorming ideas on how to rescue the humans from each of those courts, once she received confirmation that the humans were there and which fae noble or royal held them captive.

After making a few more notes, she glanced at Basil. "Anything interesting in the reports?"

Basil sighed, his hair even more tousled as if he had been digging his hands into it. "A few more possible sightings in the Realm of Monsters, but things have become so dangerous there even the swordmaidens have had to retreat from their scouting missions. The Wild Hunt is even more hostile lately."

It must be bad, if even the swordmaidens had to retreat.

The Realm of Monsters was a lawless, desolate realm where the monsters lived, the Wild Hunt roamed, and fae too wild to bind themselves to a court could find sanctuary away from the Laws of Bindings that ruled the Fae Realm.

"There's not much else Queen Hippolyta can do but keep a watch." Brigid leaned back in her chair. She would feel better if those two fae could be found. Just one of them had caused nearly a decade of drought in the Human Realm. What damage could two of them do?

Basil nodded, then shuffled the papers and stood to file them away in the drawers with the other reports. "I fear we won't find them until it's too late."

"You will." Brigid gestured toward the drawers filled with reports. "Fae like them are too evil to hide forever. They'll poke their heads out of whatever hole they are hiding in and give themselves away."

"Perhaps." Basil sagged against his desk, his shoulders weary. "How they choose to do that is what worries me."

It worried Brigid, too. If normal fae in the Fae Realm were willing to perpetrate atrocities, then how much worse were these fae who had been deemed evil even by fae standards?

Basil grimaced at the stack of books sitting on the corner of his desk. "I've been doing some research into blood rites."

"Not light reading, I take it?" Brigid forced herself to smile, her tone light to ease the weariness that etched into Basil's face.

"No." His frown deepened, his skin looking a hint green beneath its normal coppery hue. "Blood rites aren't like the bindings. Take the captive binding, for example. It was meant to be used for captives in time of warfare between the courts, but it has been twisted to use on humans. It makes it difficult to escape and gives the captor some powers of persuasion over the captive, though the captive can resist if they have enough will to do so. On the other hand, the binding prevents the captor from killing the captive outright and gives human captives the ability to communicate. It's not exactly balanced, but it both gives to and constrains both sides."

She resisted the urge to shake her head. Basil had fallen into his lecturing tone that he often got when he was waxing eloquent on a topic. Thanks to him, she'd learned all about bindings over the years.

"Then there's the binding to a court or the marriage binding. Even if both of those can be started by being snatched from either the Human Realm or another court, they need both parties to willingly complete the binding." Basil absently nudged papers around on his desk, likely too on a roll with his lecture to notice what he was doing.

Bindings were all rather confusing and tangled, as things often were here in the Fae Realm. But the fae lived by the Laws of Bindings. The Laws kept them in check here in their own realm.

Because she lived in the Fae Realm, Brigid lived by them too. That day Basil had snatched her and her siblings, she'd seen the way her hand glowed in evidence of a beginning of a binding, something that had gone away as soon as the binding to the court was completed.

While both the marriage binding and the binding to a Court were greater bindings that even Brigid couldn't evade as a human, she was more free to disregard lesser bindings in a way the fae were not. She could steal humans away and break the laws of hospitality when a fae couldn't.

"Blood bindings are different." Basil poked at one of the books as if nudging something foul.

That wiped the smile from her face. Blood rites and bindings were nothing to joke about, even for her.

"A captive under a blood binding is totally at the mercy of the captor. If the captor gives an order, the captive is helpless to resist." Basil leaned back in his chair, as if to place more distance between himself and the books describing the practice. "It's disgusting."

"And that's why Head Librarian Marco gave you permission to research blood rites and bindings, even though those books are normally forbidden and kept in one of the towers." Brigid nudged the cheery red primroses in their jar. "You aren't at all tempted by the power found in those pages."

"Definitely not." Basil gave an exaggerated shudder.

Of course not. There was a reason Meg had fallen in love with Basil. He was one of the good ones. Too pure-hearted for the fae.

"And that brings me back to my worries about the fae who *are* willing to use blood rites. Even if we do find them, I'm not sure what King Theseus and Queen Hippolyta will be able to do." Basil shook his head, his dark brown eyes bleaker than normal. "If they are in the Realm of Monsters, there will be little anyone can do but keep watch to make sure they aren't plotting anything."

All too true, sadly. King Theseus and Queen Hippolyta would need more allies to take on the Realm of Monsters.

"I guess the monster you can see is better than one that you can't. Especially when you know he is out there, lurking, waiting for a chance to pounce." Brigid couldn't help the shiver that traveled down her spine.

She stared down at the list of names in front of her. Not just the names of those recently stolen, but the ones she had compiled who she had yet to rescue.

She couldn't do anything about the fae Basil was trying to track down. But she could rescue these humans who were suffering the torments of the Fae Realm.

Chapter Six

Munch strolled through the Greenwood, his bow across his shoulder, his quiver and sword at his waist, and a pack filled with food on his back. His boots crunched on the forest loam as he set a quick pace. As he walked, he munched on an apple, the crisp tang on his tongue paired with the sharp snap of the apple.

So far, this morning's patrol had been quiet. No signs of fae. No signs of fae monsters. And, disappointingly, no visits by Brigid, escorting the Primrose's latest rescued human back home.

The young girl, the last human rescued, had been sent on her way back to the kingdom where she belonged after a trusted merchant and his family had been found to take the girl back home to her family.

Munch tossed the apple core into the forest for the deer or rabbits to eat, then swiped his hand on his trousers. A squirrel crashed through the undergrowth to one side of the faint trail while the sun beamed down, filtering between the thick foliage overhead. The thick, dark green leaves and twining branches kept the forest below cool enough that Munch wasn't sweating in his long-sleeved tunic, which kept the mosquitoes from eating him alive. A few mosquitoes and flies buzzed near his ears, and he swatted at them as he strolled briskly enough to prevent them from swarming him.

Should he dig out another apple from his pack? Or one of the scones his sister-in-law had baked yesterday?

He probably should wait. He needed to make the food in his pack last all day. He didn't want to go through it right away in the morning.

Another squirrel dashed up trees, then back down to the forest floor, creating a cacophony of crunching leaves and cracking sticks. Squirrels were the noisiest critters in the entire forest. Deer and bear were eerily quiet, ghosting through the underbrush. But squirrels crashed about as if they owned the place.

Except...Munch froze, held his breath, and tilted his head in the direction he'd thought he'd heard the noise.

There. A crashing sound that had the distinct rhythm of running footsteps.

Munch eased behind a tree, keeping his own footsteps light and nearly soundless, and drew his bow from his shoulder. He nocked an arrow and waited, listening as the running footsteps came closer.

Too loud to be a fae. Fae flitted through the forest.

A human. Less dangerous than a fae, but strange to find someone braving the vastness of the Greenwood rather than sticking to the roads, especially now that the roads through the Greenwood were free of outlaws.

When the footsteps neared his tree, Munch whirled from his hiding place, his stance ready though he still did not draw the arrow.

"Halt and state your business." Munch found himself facing

a stick-thin boy of maybe fourteen or fifteen wearing the rough homespun of a local farmer.

The boy's face blanched white underneath the red flush of exertion. He skidded to a halt, his hands shooting up above his head. "Don't shoot me! I don't have any money, outlaw."

"I'm not an outlaw." At least, not anymore. He hadn't been an outlaw for five years now. Munch didn't ease his grip on his bow or arrow, but he turned slightly to better show his quiver. The top of it was embossed with Duke Guy's crest along with the tree and arrows symbol of the foresters. "I'm one of the Greenwood Foresters."

The boy released a long breath, his hands falling back to his sides as his shoulders drooped in what seemed like relief. "Oh, good. I've been trying to find the foresters for two days now."

"You've been wandering the Greenwood for two days?" Munch scanned the surrounding forest, but this didn't seem to be a trap. He eased his arrow from the string and slid it back into his quiver.

"Yes. I'm from the village of Corburg on the north side of the Greenwood." The boy leaned against a tree, hunching a bit.

That would explain why neither Munch nor his brothers had stumbled across the boy on their patrols until now. A large chunk of the northern Greenwood lay outside of the dukedom of Gysborn, and the duke who oversaw that territory wasn't so welcoming to the foresters. The foresters were officially sponsored by the Duke of Gysborn so their encroachment in the other duke's territory could be seen as the Duke of Gysborn interfering in another's dukedom, regardless of the fact that they were just trying to keep the forest safe.

Munch slid his bow back onto his shoulder. "What are you doing in the Greenwood? Why are you looking for the foresters?"

The boy sagged even more against the tree. Even though

Munch had put away his bow and arrow, the boy still shook, his hands trembling.

The shaking likely wasn't all from fear, but also from hunger if the boy had been running through the Greenwood for two days.

Munch sighed and shrugged off his pack. Looked like he'd have to share his food supply. So much for the fresh bread, smoked venison, and cheese he'd been looking forward to eating for lunch. "No, don't tell me just yet. I've some food and water. Eat and drink, then you can tell me."

The boy's head shot up at the mention of food. The liquid hunger in the boy's eyes made it that much easier to dig out the cloth-wrapped food from his pack and hand it over, with only a twinge of regret for the lunch he was going to have to skip.

The boy tossed back the wrappings and gnawed the bread, meat, and cheese like a starved springtime squirrel on a hidden walnut. When Munch held out his canteen, the boy gulped large swigs of water, some of it dribbling down his chin.

Munch sank onto the forest floor with his back to a tree facing the boy. He might as well get comfortable, both while the boy ate and for the story he would tell after he was done.

In moments, all that remained of Munch's lunch was a few crumbs scattered over the boy's shirt and lap.

The boy swallowed one more swig of water, swiped his sleeve over his mouth, then held out the canteen to Munch. "Thanks, sir."

Munch capped the canteen. Only a tiny slosh of water remained at the bottom. "What's your name?"

"Silas." The boy stared mournfully at the crumbs on his shirt. He licked his finger, used the spit to pick the crumbs off his shirt, then he stuck his finger in his mouth.

Munch hesitated. Should he offer the boy one of the two scones in his pack?

No, he probably shouldn't. The boy had bolted that sandwich down. After two days without food, he should probably let that settle before adding anything else, especially something sweet.

Though Munch would likely end up sacrificing that scone in an hour or so. He gave an internal sigh, mentally waving farewell to all his plans of a pleasant afternoon munching on scones in the deep solitude of the Greenwood.

"Well, Silas. Why were you searching for the foresters?" Munch shifted to get more comfortable against the tree. He couldn't seem to find a spot where the tree wasn't either jabbing his spine or bruising one of his shoulder blades.

Silas fiddled at the fraying hem of his tunic, picking at a loose thread. He drew in a deep breath, his shoulders rising and falling, as something gutted and empty filled his eyes. "My village was attacked by fae two nights ago."

Munch stiffened, catching his breath. A whole village was attacked? The fae snatched people here and there, especially those who were foolish enough to wander into the Greenwood after dark. The northern part of the Greenwood out of the range of the foresters was especially vulnerable.

But the fae rarely attacked en masse. Here in the Human Realm, they were bound by their inability to lie in this realm and their vulnerability to iron. If attacked, humans had the means to fight back, if necessary. It was only the lone, wandering human who found themselves at a significant risk from the fae.

Besides, the fae rarely had a reason to wish to attack villages in the Human Realm. Fae didn't want gold or silver or land in the Human Realm. They had far more of all of that in the Fae Realm, not to mention power and magic. The Human Realm was seen as beneath them, a place more scorned even than the Realm of Monsters.

Yes, the Fae would take the random human as a pet to torment as cruel entertainment. But that was only because they saw humans as amusing creatures far beneath them in grandeur and intelligence.

Only the rare fae, like Reinhault who had held Guy captive, did anything more in the Human Realm. Reinhault had been cast out of the Fae Realm, so he had motive to claim a kingdom in the Human Realm as his own.

When the boy didn't continue, Munch forced himself to relax, trying to add a gentleness to his tone. "What happened?"

"We had a town dance that night. We were all up and dancing and having a good time. Then they came from the forest. All tall and dark and with swords and horses with red eyes and mouths dripping blood. And we couldn't fight back. A few men tried, but there were too many, and we didn't have enough iron near to hand." Silas tucked his knees to his chin, wrapping his arms tightly as if to curl in on himself at the memories playing across his eyes.

Munch didn't know what to say. He didn't dare interrupt the boy's story, now that he'd started it.

"Everyone was running and screaming. Maybe a few got away. I don't know. The next thing I knew, they were herding us into the forest toward the faerie circle we all know to avoid. Just before we were forced through, my pa grabbed my collar and threw me to the side into a spruce tree. I curled on the ground and held still until morning. When it was daylight, I thought about going back to the village. But I didn't know if anyone was there or if the fae would come back. And someone had to get the foresters. So I set off into the Greenwood."

A brave but foolish risk for a boy untrained in navigating the forest. He had set off without food, without water, and without any idea of what direction he was going. He'd clearly been lost when Munch had stumbled across him.

"Would you recognize any of the fae if you saw them again?" Munch wasn't sure what questions he should be asking. Robin and Guy would probably ask all these questions again, but this boy's first, unpracticed answers would be the most telling.

Silas shook his head. "They were wearing black masks."

All the better to intimidate the villagers.

"If you're feeling up to it, I'll lead you back to the castle at Gysborn. The duke and the head of the foresters will want to hear your story." Munch pushed to his feet, then held out a hand to Silas.

Silas's jaw tightened, and he nodded before he took Munch's hand and let him pull him to his feet.

Munch set out along the trail once again, this time heading back the way he'd come. He'd camped out in the forest the night before so he could get an early start today. It would be late by the time he and Silas reached the nearest stocked forester camp. They wouldn't reach the castle until tomorrow.

There wouldn't even be hot food waiting for them at the hideaway. Neither of his brothers had plans to be at that particular camp, since they had scouting routes that would take them in different directions.

Munch led the way while Silas trudged behind, his steps weary after his two days of wandering. For several minutes, they hiked in silence.

Then, Silas sucked in a breath and jogged to catch up to Munch. "Will you be able to rescue them? The fae have my parents and my sisters."

The Primrose did his best to rescue those stolen away, but he couldn't keep up even with the lone snatchings. How would he ever manage to rescue an entire village of people from the fae? The Primrose was only one, honorable fae man against whoever had perpetrated this attack.

Munch glanced at Silas. The wide-eyed, desperate hope shining in the boy's eyes tore at Munch. After all Silas had been through, Munch didn't want to give him false hope. But he didn't want to leave this boy without hope either.

He awkwardly patted Silas's shoulder. "We foresters can contact the Wild Fae Primrose, the fae hero rescuing humans stolen away to the Fae Realm. I'm not sure what the Primrose can do, but I'm sure he will do all he can."

Silas nodded, then slowed his pace so he was following in Munch's footsteps once again.

Munch settled his pack more comfortably on his shoulders and relaxed into a steady pace for hiking.

He needed to bring this information to Robin and his brothers as soon as possible. This was not a lone fae snatching a random person, bad as that already was.

No, this was an organized attack by a group of fae. It was planned. Calculated. Purposeful.

And any purpose a group of fae might have for kidnapping humans could not be good.

SILENCE FELL in Guy's study as Silas finished his story.

Munch was tucked against the wall, quietly enjoying his second blueberry muffin. Guy paced behind his desk while Robin sprawled in the large leather chair, fingering the iron rod in her quiver. Will, John, Tuck, Alan, and Marion had all packed into the room, even though Tuck, Alan, and Marion weren't even part-time foresters the way Munch was.

But old habits die hard. They had been a gang of outlaws for seven years. When something bad happened in the Greenwood, they still dropped everything to rally to Robin's orders. They probably always would.

After another moment of silence, Guy halted his pacing and gave Silas a nod made all the more somber for Guy's frown framed by his black, closely cropped beard. "Thank you, Silas. We will do what we can to help your family."

Silas nodded, curling tighter in the chair in front of the desk, looking all the more wan and small with all of them gathered in this room.

Tuck pushed away from the fireplace mantel where he had been leaning. "I'll take you to my wife. She'll get you fixed up with food."

The mention of food perked Silas up. He eagerly jumped to his feet and followed Tuck from the room.

Once the door shut behind them, Guy scrubbed a hand over the scar that ran along his jaw. "I will have to send word to Duke Elridge. If he has not heard of the attack, he will soon. He needs to know what happened from an eyewitness, if no one else from the village escaped."

Robin ran her fingers over the fletching of the arrows in her quiver, a tense anticipation in her seemingly nonchalant posture. "We should go in person."

Guy raised an eyebrow. "You just wish to inspect the site for yourself."

"Yes." Robin's smirk held a dangerous tilt. "I'd like to walk the village myself. I might sense something in the lingering fae magic."

Guy held her gaze for a long moment before he nodded. "Perhaps it would be best to meet with Duke Elridge in person. I doubt this attack will be the last. We will need to work together to protect the Greenwood and our villagers."

"We'll leave in the morning, then." Robin sounded far too cheerful at the prospect.

"While you're gone, we'll step up our patrols." Will gestured between himself and John.

John nodded, rubbing his hand along his hardwood quarterstaff.

Alan, dressed in the flamboyant red clothing he wore as a bard, grinned and gestured to himself. "I'll help. I'm at loose ends at the moment."

"So will I, when I can." Marion blurted it out, as if not to be left out.

Munch was chewing a bite of muffin and didn't bother to volunteer. They all knew he'd help. He had already been patrolling the forest. Perhaps he would finally tell Will that he wanted to be made a permanent forester and that would be that. He'd finally decide on his future and put down roots.

Robin continued to finger the fletching of her arrows, as she did when sinking into her instincts and contemplating which arrow she needed to use for a particular enemy. "Good. I'll help with patrols once Guy and I return."

Guy shot her a look, sighed, then nodded. Smart man. He knew the outlaw he married all too well at this point.

Munch popped the last bite of his muffin into his mouth, then licked his fingers. That was a good muffin. Too bad he hadn't thought to grab anything more on their quick trip through the kitchens when they'd returned.

"The Primrose will need to be told about this." Robin's fingers paused on the iron rod in her quiver. "I don't think this should be communicated through our normal methods."

When they needed to get word to Brigid and thus to the Primrose between Brigid's visits, they stuck a piece of paper in a hollow of a tree just inside one of the faerie circles. Somehow, it also ended up in a hollow of a tree in a circle in the Fae Realm as well. Brigid passed messages back to them in the same way.

But the method wasn't particularly secure. Any fae could get the note, if they happened to peek in that hollow.

Guy shot a sharper look at Robin. "You want to go in person."

Her brown eyes got that faraway, reckless look to them. "Imagine the adventure to be found in the Fae Realm."

"If you go into the Fae Realm, it might be months or years until you return." Guy's tone grew tight, a hint forbidding. But he didn't voice any kind of order for her to stay.

Robin shook herself, the look fading into something almost like disappointment. "I know. I won't go. I think I could navigate the faerie paths the way Brigid does, and I wouldn't lose much time at all. But I know I can't risk leaving you and the children if I can't."

Guy's shoulders sagged, the only sign of his relief. "Thank you."

Munch patted his pockets, but he couldn't find any more food to munch on.

Guy had a point. Whoever went into the Fae Realm risked losing years, if he or she couldn't navigate the faerie paths to erase the time difference between the realms.

But Robin had a point too. Brigid, and through her the Primrose, had to be told in person about this attack. It was too dangerous to risk just putting a note in the tree. And they couldn't wait until the next time Brigid visited. Who knew what danger this group of fae could pose to the Primrose and his league, including Brigid?

Munch straightened, scrubbing the last of the crumbs from his hands and shirt. He could go. In fact, he was the only one who *could* go.

This was his chance to be the hero. For once, *he* could lead a mission without being in the shadow of his sister or his brothers. This was his job and his alone.

"I'll go."

Robin, Guy, Will, and John continued their discussion

about how to get a message to Brigid. Not even Marion or Alan looked his way.

Munch drew in a deeper breath, becoming more sure of his decision with every moment it sank in. Standing, he raised his voice, putting as much conviction into his tone as he could. "I'll go into the Fae Realm and find Brigid."

That made this plan even more perfect. Not only would he finally get to be the hero, but he'd get to be the hero in Brigid's eyes. Perhaps she'd see that he could be just as heroic as that fae, the Primrose.

All gazes in the room swung toward him. Munch refused to shift as his sister, brother-in-law, and brothers all stared at him.

Yes, they all saw him as the baby of the family. But he was twenty-three years old. Nearly twenty-four. He was perfectly capable of handling this.

Munch ignored everyone else and met Robin's gaze. Guy might be the duke and Will was the head of the foresters, but when it came to their family, they still looked to Robin as their leader.

For a long moment, Robin's brown eyes searched his face, as if reading his determination and his capabilities through his eyes.

Then, she gave a single nod. "All right. You'll go."

Will straightened, glancing between Robin and Munch. "You can't be serious. Munch? You sure?"

Munch stiffened and crossed his arms. "I can handle it."

"But...you're..." Will gestured to him, his words trailing off as if he'd realized that he better not say what he was thinking out loud.

The unsaid words echoed in the room all the same.

"I can do this." Munch clenched his fists and his jaw. This was exactly why he needed to do this. He was older than Will had been when they'd started their outlaw careers, but that didn't seem to matter to Will or the others. They all just saw him as the gangly, bumbling little brother trailing along in their footsteps.

No more. This time, he was going to do something heroic. And he was going to do it by himself without his sister or his brothers breathing down his neck.

"Munch knows what to do. He's as well-trained as the rest of us." Robin waved her hand at Munch, though she glanced at Will. "We succeeded as outlaws because we trusted each other to do our part. It's time we trusted Munch now."

That was strangely serious, coming from Robin. Yet her words made Munch stand taller, hold his head higher.

Robin saw his potential, even if his brothers didn't yet.

This was why they had always followed Robin. She might have a reckless streak as big as the Greenwood and was more than a little feral, but as their sister, she could unite them.

Robin held Will's gaze for another moment before her somber expression was shoved aside by her usual, slightly arrogant demeanor. "I know you're just going all protective. If it makes you feel better, we can both go over training with Munch before he leaves."

Will sighed, and his shoulders relaxed somewhat. "That would make me feel better." He glanced at Munch. "I know you can handle it. Just be careful, got it? The Fae Realm isn't like dealing with the occasional fae and fae monster found in the Greenwood. You'll be on their soil. Brigid has the protection of belonging to a fae court. But you won't. If any fae realizes that, they'll be able to snatch you and hold you captive. Once you step foot there, you might never leave."

Munch swallowed as the weight settled on him. The danger was real. This wasn't a fun lark. "That's why I need to be the one to do this. The rest of you have wives and children. Or a husband and children in Robin's case. You can't risk getting yourself snatched by the fae while in their realm. But I can."

"You aren't expendable, Munch." Will crossed his arms, facing Munch without backing down. John, Alan, and Marion muttered or grunted various forms of agreement.

"I know, but it isn't the same, and you know it." Munch stared at Will, not backing down. If he bowed to his brother's objections now, as he usually did, then he would be stuck in the role of the baby of the family forever. "If one of you disappears, your children will grow up without a mother or a father. If I disappear, you'll miss me. You'll tell your children about their uncle Munch and how he heroically faced the wilds of the Fae Realm. But that's it."

The picture he was painting was almost making him hope he would disappear. Not forever, but for a few years. Just long enough for his family to realize how much they missed him and for Alan to write a ballad or two about Munch's heroics.

Munch found himself grinning and relaxing into the same joking tone his family always used when talking about difficult topics. "Just promise me that if the worst happens and I disappear for years or for forever, you won't name any children after me. I couldn't leave knowing my legacy would be inflicting the name Mungoe on some hapless nephew of mine."

Robin tossed back her head and laughed. After a moment, Will joined her, followed by John with his deep chuckle. Alan slapped his knee and grinned while Marion just rolled his eyes. Even Guy cracked an attempt at a smile. Of all of them, he had yet to fully embrace the ability to joke about the deadliness of the fae. He had valid reasons, of course, but it made him a wet blanket counterpoint to Robin's brash response to dangers.

"Promise. No children named Mungoe." Robin pushed from the leather chair and sauntered across the room. "Well, if that's settled, we'd better stop nattering and get to it. Munch, go pack, then Will and I will go over your training one last time before you leave."

Munch nodded, then spun on his heel and headed for the door before any of his brothers could stop him.

This was it. He was going to the Fae Realm.

<h1 style="text-align:center">Chapter Seven</h1>

M unch hitched the pack higher on his back and faced the faerie circle. His stomach scurried like a drunk squirrel.

This was really happening. He was about to step into the Fae Realm, and he might never come back.

He'd already said goodbye to his sisters-in-law, nieces, and nephews back at the castle. But Robin and all his brothers gathered around him now. It seemed right that they were the ones to see him off, even as he stepped into this danger all by himself for the first time in his life.

Guy had tagged along as well, looking even more dour and serious than usual. As if Munch didn't already have enough big brothers breathing down his neck.

"Remember, go straight to the Great Library. Find Basil, Meg, or Brigid as soon as you can." Will glanced from the faerie circle to Munch. "Keep your head down and pretend you belong. You might look like a fae, but you aren't bound to a court. You won't be able to understand them."

Munch resisted the urge to touch the plaster ears that Marion and his wife had helped craft for him. They looked realistic, unless Munch accidentally knocked them off. But they itched and felt strangely heavy on his ears. The tips had even been glued to his head to keep them from just tipping over and sticking out in a way that real fae ears didn't.

"Though if anyone asks, claim you have goblin or gremlin ancestry." Alan tapped his chin, his gaze sweeping over Munch.

Munch crossed his arms and fake glared at Alan. "Are you saying I'm ugly?"

"I'm just saying you make for a less than impressive fae. That's all." Alan waved his hand back and forth.

Munch would have argued, but he had a point. The fae nobles were known for being stunningly handsome or beautiful. While his fae ears and close shave gave him the general look of the fae, his receding hairline and normal, human features couldn't be fully hidden.

Will gave Munch a stern look. "Just get in and get out as quickly as possible. Your disguise won't have to hold up for long if you don't linger."

"Don't listen to him." Robin's grin glinted both reckless and envious at the same time. "Have fun. You're going to the Fae Realm, willingly rather than as a captive. You'll be living an adventure few humans get to live."

There was something choked and longing in her tone. This was an adventure they all knew Robin would take in a heartbeat, if she didn't love Guy and their children more than she loved adventure.

Guy stepped closer to her and held out his hand, though he didn't clasp his fingers with hers. Instead, he simply waited, letting her choose to hold tight to him or step forward into the adventure that tugged at her.

After a moment, Robin glanced over her shoulder at Guy, held his gaze for a moment, before she clasped his hand, their fingers squeezing tight.

This was why Munch had to be the one to go. Even Robin, the most adventure hungry of all of them, chose her family over adventure.

Guy tore his gaze from Robin and instead settled the weight of his dark eyes on Munch. His short black beard framed his glower, a look that made him appear the villainous Duke Bluebeard they'd thought him to be for years. "I have given it some thought. There are only two reasons the fae would steal humans in such numbers. Either the Primrose has been too successful, and the fae have decided to snatch so many humans that the Primrose couldn't possibly rescue them all. Or..." Guy's shoulders rose and fell, his expression darkening even further. "Or they are stealing humans to use for forbidden blood rites."

A shiver crawled along Munch's arms and down his back. The evil fae Reinhault had killed Guy's previous three wives as part of a blood rite. If the blood of three women could give Reinhault such power that he could negate the effects of the Human Realm on him and create the drought, then how much power could the fae gain by killing all those people? For what purpose?

Munch cleared his throat. "I'll let Brigid know, and I'm sure she'll pass the message on to the Primrose."

Was it wrong to hope that the fae were stealing humans for the first reason and not the second? It was terrible, thinking that they wanted human slaves to torment so badly that a group of fae would get together to raid the Human Realm and snatch a whole village.

But blood rites were so terrible even most fae found them horrific.

Munch gave another shudder. If he were caught and the fae were stealing humans for blood rites, then...

He shook himself. He wouldn't think of it.

"Well, I'm off." Munch eased a step back toward the faerie circle. The signal to his brothers, sister, and brother-in-law that it was time to say last farewells so he could finally leave.

Striding over to him, John pounded Munch on the shoulder. "Stay safe."

Tuck pounded the other shoulder. "Don't eat any faerie fruit while you're there."

Munch nodded. His pack was stuffed with food. He had enough to last several weeks, if he was careful. Though, with his tendency to munch, it would probably only last him a few days. Hopefully he'd find Brigid and her family right away, and they would make sure he didn't eat anything harmful and his stash wouldn't be necessary.

Marion shifted and lightly punched Munch's arm. "Don't get snatched."

Alan chuckled and gestured, only a hint of roughness to his voice to belie the joking tone. "Come back with a story worthy of my finest ballad."

Then Will was there, and he stared at Munch a long moment before he held out a second quiver of arrows. "Don't take any reckless chances."

"Don't be like me, in other words." Robin laughed and shoved her way past Will to punch Munch's shoulder harder than Marion had. Then, her smirk dropped away into that tense, deadly look that she rarely showed. "Munch of the Greenwood, you are a forester from a long line of foresters. The fae aren't going to know what danger just stepped into their realm."

His sister was far better at inspirational speeches than his brothers. Though, Alan's was pretty good. Munch wouldn't argue with a ballad about his exploits. Unless Alan gave him the same "Maid Marion" treatment that he had given Marion.

At least Munch dressing like a fae gave Alan much less

room to twist the story around than dressing like a maid had for Marion.

Guy gave Munch a solemn nod. "Don't forget to follow the pimpernels once you are inside the circle."

Munch nodded, not needing Guy's reminder. Brigid had mentioned that she used the pimpernels—or the wild fae primrose as it was called in the Fae Realm—to navigate the faerie paths rather than just blindly stumbling through the circles.

Well, this was getting dragged out. Munch didn't like long farewells.

The sun was setting, already hidden behind the treetops so that only a pink glow remained in the sky above. The air chilled, shadows spreading beneath the stands of spruce and pine that peppered this part of the Greenwood.

If he kept lingering, he'd find himself standing in a night-time forest. It might be easier to slip through the faerie circle at that time, but also more dangerous. The magic between the Human and Fae realms was particularly thin at that time, which was why most fae snatchings happened at night in the Human Realm.

"I'm going to be fine." Munch faced his sister and his five brothers one more time. "More than likely, I'll just walk in, find Brigid at the Library, give her the message, and be back by tomorrow morning."

With Munch's luck, this whole thing would probably turn out to be another incredibly boring, glorified message run, even if it was to the Fae Realm.

Was it bad if he was hoping he did find some trouble? Not lots of trouble. He wasn't like Robin who got her kicks from danger, the more of it the better. But just enough to get a ballad written about him. Maybe two.

If this just turned out to be a message run, then his family would continue to see him as nothing but the baby of the family, good only for running messages and walking boring patrols in the Greenwood.

Robin chuckled, then waved toward the faerie circle. "That's the spirit. Now get in there. I'm sure you'll be back when your stomach starts rumbling."

And there it was. Munch grinned to hide his gritted teeth. "Fine. I'm going now. Have fun on your trip to Elridge and on your patrols through the Greenwood. If you find out anything else about the attack…"

"We'll pass it along through the message tree." Robin trailed her fingers over her quiver once again. "We'll use our old outlaw code."

A code that Munch could still translate in his sleep.

Assuming he didn't get himself snatched before he could get to Brigid. If he were captured by a fae, he'd never be able to access the message tree. And if Brigid found the note, she didn't know their outlaw code. She'd never get the message.

"You still haven't shared that code with me," Guy mumbled under his breath.

Robin smirked at him, a hand on her quiver. "An outlaw needs some secrets."

Munch drew in a deep breath. He had to succeed in this mission. Not just for his own pride, but because lives were at stake. He had to keep that in mind. A whole village had been snatched by fae, and it would probably happen again if the Primrose didn't figure out what was happening and how to help Robin, Guy, and the Greenwood Foresters to stop it.

Munch swept a glance over his family one last time, from his smirking sister Robin and her dark, brooding husband to tall, broad-shouldered John and Tuck with his favorite ladle tucked into his belt next to his dagger. Alan, who was as flashy as ever in a cloak edged in bright yellow over his red clothing with a matching yellow plume in his hat. Marion, who even now hunched with a slight sulkiness to his expression. And Will with his crossed arms and worry deepening his brown eyes.

This could be the last time Munch saw them. He'd grown up fighting at their side. Or fighting him, in the case of Duke Guy. They'd raised him more than their parents had. The Greenwood and his family had been his whole world.

And now he was leaving it all behind.

Brigid and adventure waited for him in the Fae Realm. It was time to step out from his sister's heroic shadow and start living his own story.

Munch turned his back to his family and faced the faerie circle before him. With one last deep breath of the deeply green-scented earth and trees of the Greenwood, he stepped between the mushrooms that marked the circle.

As soon as he walked inside, a shivery pressure of magic closed around him. If he turned around, he would likely still be able to see his family's vague shapes through the haze.

But ahead of him, a different forest opened before him. A mossy, green forest so vibrant it stung his eyes. A sweetness clogged the air as if he was trying to breathe underwater, if the water was a heavy floral scent. There was a deep tugging from that forest. A lilting song ringing in his head and drawing his feet toward it.

A normal human would have heard and seen nothing. Unless it was a particularly magical time of year, a full-blooded human wouldn't be able to cross into the Fae Realm without the help of a fae or a companion animal. Even the fae often found the crossing easier with the help of a companion animal.

But Munch wasn't fully human. He had a touch of fae blood, and never did he feel it as much as he did when he stepped into a faerie circle. Here, the Fae Realm called to him, sensing the piece of him that belonged to it and trying to claim him as its own.

When he'd been an outlaw, hopping through the faerie circles to evade Duke Guy and his men, this was the point where he would grip the foot-long iron rod in his quiver to keep himself grounded in the Human Realm and resist the lure of the Fae Realm.

But this time, he didn't want to resist. Instead, he took a step. Then another.

The weight of magic pressed around him even harder, squeezing at his bones until he could barely breathe, barely think. That tugging grew stronger into a yank, trying to get him to stumble forward wherever the Fae Realm wished.

No. No, he couldn't do that. Some depth of instinct, some strength of determination in him, kept his feet planted where they were. If he allowed the Fae Realm to just yank him in, there was no telling where he would end up.

His shaking fingers fumbled, heavy and numb, at his quiver. As soon as his grip closed over his iron rod, he fell back into himself with a thump, his breath a rough scrape in his chest. It was all he could do to stop himself from stumbling backwards into the Human Realm, his mission a failure before he'd even reached the Fae Realm.

Munch gathered himself, touching the iron rod but not clutching it in a way that would fully banish the cling of the Fae Realm.

Flowers. He was supposed to be looking for flowers.

The moss at his feet was dotted with a variety of flowers. Pinks, blues, whites, oranges, and yellows blurred in his vision as he struggled to hold to this brief moment of lucidity.

There. A dot of red.

He blinked, and the red focused into a tiny, star-shaped

flower peeking up from the profusion of undergrowth at the edge of this fae forest.

The flower was so small. So plain compared to the heady florals and flashy petals of the other flowers around him.

But he took a step toward it, and some of his steadiness returned.

He searched the ground, spotting another red flower growing up from the moss a few feet ahead. Keeping his gaze focused on it, he walked forward. Once he reached the flower, he located the next one, peeking between the foliage.

And so it went. He focused on the flowers, his head down, rather than looking around and allowing the Fae Realm to distract him from his path.

Then between one breath and the next, he stepped, and something shifted around him. The floral taste still filled his mouth. The background hum of weighty magic remained. But it wasn't as tugging and chaotic as before. Not as heavy.

Munch raised his head and froze where he stood.

Behind him, a forest spread out, deeper and greener than anything he had ever seen. A vibrant moss spread out beneath the trees, dotted with blooms in colors he'd never before imagined while vines draped down like the fingers of this far-too-alive forest.

Below, the moss-covered ground flowed down a hill toward a thin path that seemed to count as a road. The road wound to a cluster of stone houses with thatched roofs that wouldn't have looked out of place in the village back home.

Beyond the village, a castle of white marble and delicate spires rose on the far hill. Beside it, connected by a large white hall, was another building in white marble. But this one had a large, glistening glass dome on the top.

It fit the stories of King Theseus's castle and the Great Library that Brigid had told them, though he had no way of knowing for sure. He could be in a completely different court for all he knew.

No way to know for sure except walk down there, pretend he could understand what was said to him, and hope it was, indeed, the Great Library that he was looking at.

Munch hurried to the path, then he strode along it as if he believed he belonged. As he entered the town, it took everything in him not to jump when a tiny, glittering ball of light whizzed by him with the buzzing sound of tiny wings. If he were fae, then the sights around him would be nothing to blink at.

Ahead of him, a girl with large, tufted ears like an owl and feathered arms carried a basket as she talked with a slightly taller fae woman who looked nearly human, except for the extra edge of beauty and her pointed ears. An actual fox sat on its haunches, talking—yes, talking—to another of those glittering balls of lights, which Munch could now see contained a tiny, human-shaped creature with crystal clear wings that beat like a hummingbird's. Tall figures—people?—with leaves for hair and skin that had a bark-like texture swayed and flowed over the ground. Not really stepping, since it seemed like their legs—trunks—never lifted from the ground even though they moved forward.

The bustle increased as he crossed a curving, picturesque stone bridge over a stream and headed up the causeway to the great gates of the castle.

Two women wearing armor and carrying spears stood on either side of the gates. They didn't prevent anyone from walking inside, but their sharp gazes swept over everyone.

Munch kept walking, not meeting their gazes but not actively avoiding them either. Just pretending he belonged, as he had when infiltrating Duke Guy's palace or the village to spy on the guards.

Once inside, he stepped into a large hall. Doors lined each side of the room, framed by ornate, white pillars. Even more fae filled this room, stepping in and out of the doors and heading for the double doors on either end of the long room.

The fae here were even more strange and wondrous. Fae with curving horns wound their way past even more fae with animalistic features. Fae with green skin and standing only as high as his knee darted around the legs of a creature with a man's torso sticking out of where a horse's head should be.

It took everything in him not to gape like a dying fish at everything and everyone. That would surely give away that he wasn't one of them.

He joined the stream of people headed for the doors to the right. That would be the Great Library, if he guessed correctly.

If he guessed wrong, well, he'd have to wander back out again and hope no one noticed that he didn't belong. He couldn't even ask any of the fae around him for directions.

At this set of doors, two more armored women stood on guard. They halted each person before they let them enter.

Munch's heart pounded harder. If they asked him anything, he wouldn't be able to understand or answer.

When it was his turn, he started forward, as if fully confident that he belonged.

In a flash, the two spears swung down and barred his way. The warrior woman on the right stated something in a demanding, aggressive manner.

Uh-oh. What was she saying? Had she realized he was a human?

The woman's scowl deepened, and she barked something at him again, this time pointing at the quiver at his side, then his sword.

His weapons. Of course. Weapons probably weren't allowed in the library.

He couldn't allow these warrior women to touch his sword. If they did, they would realize it was made from human steel, which had iron in it, rather than faerie steel. They'd know he was a human.

Munch bobbed, as if in acquiescence, and slowly lowered his hands to his belt. He unbuckled it, then gently set his pile of weapons off to the side. He drew his unstrung bow from his back and added that to the pile.

He stepped back into line and started forward.

The spears flashed down again, and the woman glared and spoke again.

Munch sighed. He'd hoped they hadn't noticed his stashed knives. But these women were clearly well-trained warriors. He should have known he couldn't get anything past them.

He drew the dagger from his boot, the knife from the sheath down his back, and the final knife from the sheath at the small of his back and added those to the pile as well.

Once that was done, he held up his hands, demonstrating that he was now weapon-free.

With a thorough once-over, the warrior women stepped aside, though they continued to glare at him. The one said something, and he didn't need to understand her language to know she would be keeping an eye on him.

The doors opened, and he caught his breath, nearly stumbling at the sight before him.

A giant tree filled the space beneath the dome, larger than even the largest tree in the Greenwood. Shelves upon shelves wound through the space. Not in neat rows, but in a wiggly sprawl, punctuated by small trees and flowers and branches.

The Great Library. He'd found it, no question. He'd never seen so many books in one place, even in Guy's ducal library.

A large group of fae gathered below the spreading branches of the massive tree in the atrium.

What was going on over there? Munch meandered in that direction. Hopefully he could blend in with the crowd while he figured out what was going on. Somehow, he still needed to find Brigid or someone from her family. He'd only met her sister Meg and brother-in-law Basil once, and he'd never met any of her younger siblings. Would he be able to instantly recognize them as humans if he saw them? How would he know if the human he was approaching was one of her siblings and not a human captured by the fae?

If he saw a human who somewhat resembled Brigid, then he'd have to risk it. The information he had was too important. He had to get it to Brigid and thus to the Primrose as soon as possible.

Chapter Eight

Brigid hunched over her desk in the Tower, finishing up the last of her notes and plans. Tomorrow, she would leave for the Court of Stone to rescue two humans who had been stolen away by fae there. Unlike the last time, she would be in disguise the entire way in and out.

As she tidied her stack of papers, the entire Library gave a lurch around her, almost as if it was gagging in disgust and desperately wanted to spit something out.

Across the room, Basil straightened and turned toward the door. As a master librarian, he would have felt that even more strongly than she had.

"What was that?" Brigid stowed her papers in a drawer, turned the lock, and pushed to her feet, nearly knocking over the jar of primroses on her desk. She lunged and steadied it before it tipped over.

"Not sure." Basil shoved away from his own desk. "But I think we should check it out."

Brigid glanced over her desk one last time, checking that the most sensitive documents were locked in the desk where the Library itself would prevent anyone but her from opening it. Not that anyone but her, Basil, Theseus, Hippolyta, and Marco would be able to get past the bookwyrm on the stairs and the Library's protections, but she remained cautious, as Queen Hippolyta had trained her to be.

Basil, too, took one last glance over his desk before he headed for the stairs. Together, they picked their way around Gus, who grumbled and shifted in his sleep as they gave him a quick belly scratch on their way down.

When they reached the bottom of the stairs, Brigid rested a hand on the nearest Library shelf. A sense of agitation curled through the Library, its shelves shifting and shuddering in the way it did during a monster attack.

Had a rift opened up between the Fae Realm and the Realm of Monsters? Such things were always a possibility, and one of the reasons Queen Hippolyta kept trained swordmaidens on hand in the Library.

Basil reached into his librarian coat and pulled out the thick wooden club that he used when fighting off monsters. Something in him shifted from the mild-mannered, quiet librarian to a cautious man tiptoeing along the shelves, poised to bring the club down on the head of any giant spiders, hydras, or chimeras that might come around the corner.

Brigid reached into a magical pocket of her dress to clasp the hilt of her rapier, though she didn't pull it out. It was her last resort. While she had trained with Queen Hippolyta's swordmaidens, she had never become as proficient at weapons as they were. If she was forced to wield a weapon on one of her missions, then she'd already failed. Her cover—her best protection—was already blown.

But if she faced a fae monster, she'd have to do her best to defend herself.

They wound their way through the shelves without meeting

any monsters. They didn't meet any other librarians either, which was even odder. There should have been someone bustling about, tracking down information or putting back books.

When they reached the last bookshelf before the atrium, the leaves of the great tree spread above them, casting a brighter green light over the shelves around them. A cacophony of voices echoed off the glass dome, far more than the normal murmur that usually surrounded the tree.

Basil peeked around the corner, then froze. His forehead furrowed as he stared at the sight before him for a moment. Finally, he turned and slid his club back into his pocket. "There's some kind of gathering."

Why would a gathering put the Library so on edge? Brigid released her grip on the hilt of her rapier, sliding her hand out of her pocket, but she remained wary as she followed Basil around the corner of the shelf.

All the librarians gathered in the broad, open space of the central atrium. A few swordmaidens loitered around the edge of the group while Head Librarian Marco stood on one of the arching roots at the base of the tree.

Basil led the way through the murmuring crowd until he reached Meg's side. He took Morgan from Meg then, propping Morgan against his shoulder, he took Meg's hand and leaned closer as Meg whispered something too low for Brigid to make out.

Viola, Sebastian, and Beatrice all gathered nearby. Viola gripped Addy's hand and the toddler whined, wanting to run free.

"What's going on?" Brigid spoke in a low voice as she eased into place next to Viola and Sebastian.

"Don't know." Sebastian shrugged, his arms crossed and his posture stiff. "The Library is acting strange."

"So we all gathered here." Viola adjusted her grip on Addy's hand. "Hopefully Head Librarian Marco is about to tell us."

Beatrice trailed her fingers over the bookwyrm perched on her shoulder. "Whatever is going on, the bookwyrms don't like it." She glanced over at someone else, then stuck her tongue out.

A few yards away, a blond-haired fae boy of sixteen rolled his eyes, as if he felt himself far too mature to make faces back at Beatrice as he once used to. Behind him, his mother, a lady of the court, nudged him and scowled, whispering something that was likely a rebuke for not acting properly noble.

Brigid stuffed back her grin. That was Benedict, Beatrice's archnemesis. Or, at least, as much of an archnemesis as a fifteen-year-old could have.

At the base of the tree, Head Librarian Marco stepped onto a chair to see over the crowd and smoothed a hand over his beard, his eyes landing briefly on Basil and Brigid. "Now that you're all here, we're just waiting on our king. He will explain what is going on soon, I should think."

The double doors at the front of the atrium swung open. Two swordmaidens stood aside, then King Theseus and Queen Hippolyta swept inside, accompanied by...

Lord Chauvlyn.

The Library gave another lurch around them, as if it wanted to spew Lord Chauvlyn back out where he'd come from.

King Theseus rested a hand on the doorpost, as if to soothe the Library. Despite the soothing gesture, his expression remained tight. Beside him, Queen Hippolyta clenched her hand on her sword, danger in every graceful stride.

The Library subsided but the floor continued to give an agitated shudder beneath Brigid's feet.

What had caused the Library to give such a visceral reaction to Lord Chauvlyn? Sure, Brigid didn't like him very much. He was personally appointed by King Oberon and Queen Titania to capture the Primrose.

But while the Library helped her, it wasn't fully sentient. It didn't necessarily have a moral compass that would make it dislike Lord Chauvlyn so completely.

No, whatever had made it react had to be on a very deep, visceral level.

Something to keep in mind to fit into the puzzle once she had a few more pieces.

Once the Library had settled somewhat, Theseus held out his arm to Hippolyta, and the two of them led the way toward Marco. As they approached, Marco hopped down from the chair.

Dressed in black as always, Lord Chauvlyn strolled languidly in their wake, as if unperturbed by the Library's dislike of him. He cast his gaze around the gathered librarians, a haughty tilt to his nose.

Brigid stepped a little farther away from her siblings and plastered on the blankly insipid smile she wore in her role as Hippolyta's Pet. Now she couldn't even be herself in the Great Library, her one sanctuary.

King Theseus joined Marco, giving the Head Librarian a nod, before he faced the crowd, his expression hard rather than welcoming. "Librarians of the Great Library, please welcome Lord Chauvlyn into our Library. King Oberon has requested that we host his emissary to our court here at the Library. King Oberon is concerned by the rumors that our court has been harboring the fae outlaw the Primrose, and Lord Chauvlyn is here to alleviate his concerns. We will, of course, do everything we can to cooperate with Lord Chauvlyn."

King Theseus spoke without inflection, saying everything he was expected to say. But Brigid could hear what he wasn't saying. From the beginning, he and Queen Hippolyta couldn't help Brigid's mission overtly. For just this reason. They needed deniability before the kings and queens of the other courts.

But that meant that they couldn't necessarily protect Brigid if Lord Chauvlyn stumbled onto her secret.

She would have to be even more careful. She had just lost the sanctuary of the Great Library, even though the House was still safe.

But she could handle it.

King Theseus continued his speech, but Brigid only half-listened. The speech was for Lord Chauvlyn's benefit anyway. King Theseus was playing a role to placate King Oberon, just like how Brigid was slipping into a role as well.

Brigid glanced away, taking in the way her fellow librarians were reacting to the announcement. Some of the librarians, especially those who were also nobles in King Theseus's court, were nodding along. None of them were a surprise. Brigid already had a list of those who didn't see anything wrong with stealing humans so she knew which fae nobles to avoid, even in the Court of Knowledge.

A few of the librarians crossed their arms and looked downright mulish. King Oberon and Queen Titania weren't well-respected among most of the librarians, especially the ones who had been working in the Library five years ago when Oberon and Titania had caused a rift and unleashed the deadliest attack of monsters the Court of Knowledge had seen in years. While no one had died, it had been a near thing for several librarians and the Great Library itself had sustained a great deal of damage.

Brigid tried to avoid the gazes of those in her league. Rosaline was sneaking glances her way, and she gave a subtle shake of her head, warning the girl off. They couldn't risk Lord Chauvlyn noticing anything amiss with the way they were acting. And he was bound to notice. He wasn't an enemy to be underestimated.

Lady Hermia and her husband Lord Lysander were doing a better job of pretending they didn't care about the announcement. Neither of them so much as looked at Brigid.

Movement beyond Lady Hermia and Lord Lysander caught Brigid's eye. Something—someone?—ducked out of sight behind one of the shelves.

Who could that be? All the librarians, assistants, and apprentices were here at the base of the tree. Was it another one of King Oberon's minions? Puck, Oberon's right-hand sprite, perhaps?

No, the figure had been too tall to be the three-foot tall sprite. Not to mention the Library usually reacted to Puck nearly as violently as it did just now to Lord Chauvlyn, thanks to Puck's tendency to chuck books off the shelves and generally cause destruction and mayhem.

There it was again. A tall, brown-haired figure dressed in green and browns peeking around the corner of a shelf.

For a moment, his dark brown eyes met hers, and she caught her breath. Munch? What was he doing here? And with pointed ears?

She quickly turned away from him and made a motion with her hand. He needed to get out of sight. If Lord Chauvlyn caught sight of him…

No, she couldn't let that happen. She had to get Munch out of sight as quickly as possible.

Not just out of sight. He needed to be hidden deep inside the book repair room or, better yet, brought back to the House.

She didn't dare leave. Normally, standing out and appearing the vibrant, empty-headed girl was part of her disguise. But now, it would mean that Lord Chauvlyn would quickly notice if she disappeared. His eyes already landed on her far more often than she liked.

Keeping her smile plastered in place, Brigid nudged Viola, trying to speak without moving her lips. "Perhaps it would be good to bring Addy back to the book repair room."

"What?" Viola picked up Addy, who squirmed in her arms. Addy's squeals built into a screaming cry.

Meg stepped closer, reaching for Addy. "What's going on?"

"I think Addy needs to go back to the book repair room." Brigid flicked her eyes in Munch's direction. The fool was peeking around the end of the shelf again.

Meg glanced in that direction, then her eyes widened. She gave a slight nod, then hitched Addy higher onto her hip. "Yes. Come along, Addy darling. You must be hungry and in need of a change." As Basil took a step toward them, Meg shook her head and took Morgan from him with her other arm. "No, stay here. It sounds like they're about to give Lord Chauvlyn a tour, and Head Librarian Marco will want you along."

Basil nodded, glancing between Brigid and Meg before his gaze slid to the shelves where Munch was hiding. He gave a second, more solemn nod, before he pushed through the crowd to join Head Librarian Marco.

Good. Basil would do his best to buy them some time while they figured out how to hide Munch.

King Theseus wrapped up his speech, and Lord Chauvlyn stepped forward. He swept his glance over the crowd, and Brigid shifted to hide Meg's movement as she retreated.

As she'd known he would, Lord Chauvlyn's eyes snapped to her. Brigid widened her smile and her eyes, giving a little wave, as if she considered Lord Chauvlyn a friend.

His glower deepened, and he clasped his hands behind his back. "Thank you for your hospitality, King Theseus. I'm glad you agree that this fae styling himself as the Primrose is a scourge who must be stopped. He disregards our traditions and our way of life."

Brigid rocked back and forth on her heels, as if she was too fascinated by the broad leaves overhead to really take in Lord Chauvlyn's speech. It was all she could do not to snort and reveal the depth of the fury kindling in her chest.

As if traditions that snatched humans and ways that enslaved others were something to be cherished.

But Lord Chauvlyn and the fae like him saw humans as lesser creatures, to be given less courtesy than what one might give a dog or a companion animal. They didn't see that humans were people with hopes and dreams just like them. They didn't see the families they broke apart, the hurts they caused, the torment they inflicted.

All fae like Lord Chauvlyn saw was the enjoyment they got out of lording their power over another. In the end, they would do the same thing to their fellow fae, if given the chance. They often did to the goblins, who were forced into the role of servants in many of the courts. Humans were just more vulnerable, and thus easier prey in their eyes.

Lord Chauvlyn paused, as if waiting for agreement. He got it from a few of the nobles, but that was it.

King Theseus stepped forward. "Thank you, Lord Chauvlyn, for that." The king glanced over the gathering. "And thank you everyone for gathering. You are dismissed to return to your duties."

Brigid joined the general shuffle as everyone began to disperse, but she kept her pace casual.

At the base of the tree, Head Librarian Marco and Basil stepped forward to join King Theseus, Queen Hippolyta, and Lord Chauvlyn. All of them spoke in low tones before they moved away as a group. No doubt to start a tour.

Everything in Brigid coiled tight, eager to hurry to find out what in the Fae Realm Munch was doing here in the Great Library. But she forced her pace to remain languid. Unhurried. She even headed off in the opposite direction from the book repair room, meandering through the shelves as if she had all the time in the world.

Even once she was out of sight, she kept up her façade, just in case one of the nobles who supported Lord Chauvlyn happened to be watching her.

Finally, she wound her way around the outer edge of the Library until she reached where the book repair book was tucked alongside one of the towers.

Inside, she found Beatrice playing with Addy and Morgan in their corner, bookwyrms slithering around them. Viola, Sebastian, and Meg made a pretense of repairing books, though they weren't getting much done since their gazes kept flicking to where Munch paced back and forth alongside the wall.

As Brigid stepped inside the room, his head snapped up. "Brigid! I need to talk to you! I have a message—"

She held up her hand. "Not here. Did you notice that fae lord getting introduced just now?" She waited until Munch nodded before she continued. "That's Lord Chauvlyn. He's been tasked with hunting down the Primrose. If he finds you here, he will capture you, and he will force you to tell him everything you know about me and about the Primrose."

At least Munch didn't actually know that she *was* the Primrose. As much as she hated keeping that secret from him, this was why. That was one thing he couldn't tell Lord Chauvlyn, if he were caught.

But he already knew enough to endanger both her family and his. It would be best if he simply wasn't caught.

Munch glanced between all of them before focusing on Brigid once again. "What do you want me to do?"

Brigid glanced around at her family. Did they have enough time that they could sneak Munch through the Anywhere Door before Lord Chauvlyn noticed him?

Even if Lord Chauvlyn didn't notice him, what if one of the nobles did? After that speech, they would report anything suspicious to Lord Chauvlyn. And while Munch was wearing fake, fae-like ears, he wasn't dressed like a librarian. His green and brown clothing looked entirely too human.

Voices sounded outside of the book repair room, coming closer.

There was no time to bring Munch anywhere.

Viola and Sebastian pushed to their feet, hesitating as if they weren't sure what to do.

Meg straightened, her spine stiffening. She gestured to them. "Delay as much as you dare."

Viola and Sebastian nodded, then raced toward the door.

"Don't rush!" Brigid called after them, though she kept her voice low so those outside wouldn't hear her. "Try to look calm. And normal."

The two of them slowed their pace just before they exited the room.

"Meg, can you…do something?" Brigid wasn't even sure what she was asking. But Meg had a strange relationship with the Library. If anyone could ask the Library for help, it would be Meg.

Meg gestured to Munch. "Curl up in that corner. Think tree-like thoughts."

Munch's eyes widened, but he did as he was told. He sat in the corner across from where Beatrice kept Addy and Morgan entertained, hugging his knees to his chest.

"I apologize for this." Meg placed her hand on the wall of the Library.

After a moment, the Library gave an answering kind of

shiver. Then it shifted around Munch. He made a muffled noise as the mossy floor rose up to cover his legs while branches wrapped around him. In moments, he was entirely hidden from view, nothing but a bump in the corner. Just another odd shape in the wibbly and wobbly construction of the Great Library.

Not a moment too soon. Basil stepped inside, glancing around, as he gestured to the room. "And this is the book repair room where my lovely wife Meg works. She's in charge of all practical matters here at the Great Library."

Lord Chauvlyn stepped into the room, his dark eyes flicking over each of them, as King Theseus, Queen Hippolyta, and Head Librarian Marco strolled inside. Viola and Sebastian slipped inside, as if hoping to remain unnoticed.

Lord Chauvlyn's lips curled as he took in Meg, then Beatrice in the corner with Addy and Morgan. "Ah, yes. The humans that you took into your court, King Theseus."

"These humans are members of my court, the same as any fae." King Theseus's tone grew even more hard. Chilly, even.

"And you wonder why my good King Oberon would have doubts." Lord Chauvlyn swung his calculating eyes toward King Theseus.

King Theseus crossed his arms. "I have given you permission to visit the Library as King Oberon's emissary, but I will risk his ire and have you cast out if you insult or badger or otherwise harm any of the members of my court. Am I understood, Lord Chauvlyn?"

"Completely, King Theseus." Lord Chauvlyn gave King Theseus a half-bow. Perfectly respectful and yet with an edge of a sneer.

Lord Chauvlyn cast one last glance around the room, his eyes lingering for an extra heartbeat on Brigid, before he spun on his heels and strode out of the room, swerving at the last moment so that he didn't run into Basil.

King Theseus met Brigid's gaze and gave a nod. Queen Hippolyta even indulged in a slight smirk before she and her husband stepped from the room to continue the tour.

Basil released a breath as he reached out and squeezed Meg's hand. None of them said anything out loud, in case Lord Chauvlyn was still listening.

"Well. It seems the book repair room was too plebeian for the likes of Lord Chauvlyn." Head Librarian Marco patted his coat pockets, as if he was looking for something but couldn't remember what it was. "Oh, Basil, I forgot that paper for King Theseus in that tower of yours. Perhaps you and Brigid could fetch it for me? I'll give your apologies to the others."

"Of course. We'll hurry back with it as soon as possible." Basil swiped his hands over the front of his black librarian coat.

"Very good." Head Librarian Marco swept out of the room, on his way to catch up to continue the tour.

After a few more heartbeats, Meg exhaled in a whoosh. "Hollering harpies, that was close!"

Brigid nodded, reaching out to the table to steady herself. Her legs were more wobbly than she liked to admit. She faced cloak-and-dagger stuff like this all the time, but never in the Library. Never in her home. The Library was supposed to be her haven.

Basil spun toward them, his jaw tight. "We have a few moments. We've already led Lord Chauvlyn past the stairs to our tower, and they're headed toward the fiction section as we speak. Head Librarian Marco sent most of the librarians off to set up a display of works that have been performed by acting troupes in the Court of Revels while King Theseus sent the nobles to prepare a welcome celebration for Lord Chauvlyn.

So the path should be clear for a few minutes, if we want to move him to the tower where Lord Chauvlyn is barred from going. By the way, who are we hiding again?"

"One of Lady Robin's brothers. The youngest one, I believe, though it has been a few years." Meg hurried across the room and rested her hand on the wall. "Thank you, Library, for your help. You can spit him out, now."

The Library gave another shudder, then the branches in the corner parted and Munch tumbled onto the mossy floor, his clothing covered with little bits of twigs and moss.

He scrambled to his feet, frantically brushing at his arms and chest and heaving in huge gulps of air. "All right. All right, that was awful. I was just eaten by a building."

Brigid grinned at him, something in her easing at the sight of him safe and sound. Even if it was so odd to see him standing here in the Library rather than in the deep forest of the Greenwood. "Most of the time when the Library eats something, that something is well and truly dead. Just be glad the Library actually spat you back out and didn't decide to digest you."

"Digest..." Munch trailed off, then shuddered. "I was warned about the dangers of the Fae Realm. The Great Library eating me was not one of them."

"It doesn't make a habit of it." Meg patted the Library, and it gave a shiver beneath her hand, almost like a purring cat. "Now you'd best hurry. Sounds like you don't have time to waste, and anyone can step into the book repair room."

Hurrying up sounded good to Brigid. The sooner she secured Munch in a safe place, the sooner they could talk.

Chapter Nine

Before any of them could move, Viola slipped past Brigid, headed for the door. "I'll keep an eye on Lord Chauvlyn. I'll run back and warn you if they start heading back your way."

"Thanks." Brigid glanced at Munch. "I assume the sword-maidens made you give up your weapons at the door?"

Munch nodded, his hand flexing at his side as if wishing to clasp his sword's hilt. "Yes. And I couldn't explain what was going on. I can understand you and your family, but no one else."

Right. He'd walked into the Fae Realm of his own accord. That meant he didn't have the binding of marriage like Meg had or the binding to the Court of Knowledge that the rest of them had. The bindings gave them the ability to communicate and a measure of protection from other fae and the realm itself.

Munch didn't have any of that. He didn't even have the captive binding a snatched human had, which allowed them to understand what their captors were saying. A small comfort in their snatching, but far better than if they found themselves snatched and unable to understand what was happening around them.

"Sebastian, could you fetch Munch's weapons and bring them to the House? I don't want anyone to spot his weapons and recognize them for what they are." Brigid could only hope that no one had touched them so far. If anyone so much as brushed a finger over the weapons and realized they contained iron…

There would be questions. Questions Brigid didn't want to have to answer.

Sebastian nodded and hurried past Brigid, disappearing into the winding shelves of the Library.

She hated that her family was getting caught up in this. Normally, she tried to keep them out of her work as the Primrose as much as possible.

But she couldn't help but endanger them. They would shelter her, no matter the danger to themselves.

When Basil waved for them to follow, Munch glanced between Basil and Brigid before he crept after Basil.

Brigid took up the rear of their little party, glancing around for anyone coming up behind them.

Ahead of her, Munch ghosted through the Library, his boots whispering over the moss floor. Gone was the uncertain young man from a few moments ago. Instead, he moved with a dangerous kind of grace, his hand dropping to where his sword normally rested at his side. Here was the man who'd grown up as an outlaw of the Greenwood. Strong. Competent. A warrior when needed.

And if her heart gave an extra lurch that sent skitters through her stomach, well, who could blame her? Munch had grown up rather nice. Better than nice, actually.

Brigid gave herself a hard mental shake. Now wasn't the time for foolish fancies. She was still the Primrose, and

Munch's presence here put all of them in more danger than ever. And she didn't even know *why* he was here.

For several minutes, they wound through the Library, seeing no one. Only a few bookwyrms slithered out of their path.

Basil peeked around the end of another bookshelf, then he backed up quickly. "Get back."

Munch hurriedly stepped back, and Brigid had to grip the bookshelf to keep herself from stumbling into him.

"Basil!" a shrill female voice called from just out of sight.

"Bother, they saw me." Basil glanced over his shoulder, then pointed to their right. "You two need to hide."

Brigid grabbed Munch's sleeve, then dragged him in the direction Basil pointed. To their right, the Library shelves twisted as they reached the wall, creating a tiny, dark nook barely big enough for two people to squish inside.

Brigid pulled Munch in with her, pressing the two of them into the nook as far as they could go. She couldn't risk the tail of his cloak or the back of her pink dress remaining visible.

Based on the sound of Basil's voice, he leaned against the bookshelf a few feet away from the nook, further blocking them from view. "Helena, Demetrius. Shouldn't you be setting up for the formal reception for Lord Chauvlyn?"

Brigid released a slow breath. Helena and Demetrius were friends of Basil's, though they weren't a part of Brigid's league. Helena was flighty enough that she couldn't keep a secret to save her life, much less save someone else's. They were useful as a cover for a mission, but less useful for sneaking through the Library unnoticed.

Still, if they should discover Munch and Brigid, they might consider keeping the secret for a few minutes, at least. They wouldn't try to snatch Munch, and they wouldn't be cruel. Just dense.

"It is something, isn't it? King Oberon sending an emissary to our court over this whole Primrose nonsense. Can you believe it?" Helena's voice was high-pitched.

Demetrius's low chuckle was a counterpoint to his wife's tone. "I doubt our king and queen will stand for it long. They don't like to be bullied by Oberon now any more than they've liked it in the past. They haven't forgotten what happened on Midsummer Night five years ago."

"I haven't forgotten either." Helena's tone turned coy, and Brigid could almost picture her walking her fingers up Demetrius's chest. "It was what brought us together."

Brigid started to shake her head, only to realize that the movement brushed the top of her head against Munch's chin.

Only then did she become aware of how close she and Munch were standing. Her hands were on his chest, her body pressed up against him. One of his arms was awkwardly resting against her back, the other braced on the wall beside him. His breaths were shallow, but they still stirred her hair.

With her hands on his chest, resting on muscles that were all too noticeable even beneath the layers of his shirt and leather tunic, she was even more aware that he wasn't the gangly eighteen-year-old who had given her that first, awkward kiss the last time they'd stood like this on that long ago evening in the Greenwood.

Now, he was twenty-three and had grown into the broad shoulders of an archer and the lean body of someone who spent hours hiking the forest.

And she was pressed into a dark corner with him, their breaths hot in the space between them.

Basil's small talk with Helena and Demetrius faded into the background, drowned out by the pounding of Brigid's heart and the shuddering of her own breath in her ears.

"Brigid, I…" Munch's words came out in a hoarse whisper, as if dragged from him.

It would be so easy to stand on her tiptoes and snatch a kiss from him.

But it wouldn't be right. This was just the same spark of attraction they'd been feeling for the past three years for her, five years for him. They'd never given it a chance to develop into something real beyond mere attraction.

And it never could. Not while she was still keeping the secret that *she* was the Primrose.

She bit her lip to keep herself from spilling that secret right then and there. This would be the worst possible moment. Munch might be here, in the Fae Realm, but she couldn't forget that he had no protections. If Lord Chauvlyn caught him, he could be forced to spill every secret he held in his head.

Munch had enough dangerous secrets that he would regret spilling. He didn't need to carry hers as well.

"All clear," Basil's voice hissed from just outside of their little nook.

"We should go." Despite her words, Brigid couldn't force herself to move. Munch's dark brown eyes focused on her, his chest warm beneath her fingers.

Munch softly cleared his throat. "We should."

For another moment, they just stood there, staring into each other's eyes.

Gathering the last of her self-control, Brigid shoved away from Munch, tearing her gaze away. She was the Primrose. And because she was the Primrose, she could never let this attraction go anywhere beyond longing.

She turned her back on Munch and joined Basil in the aisle between the bookshelves. The hair at the back of her neck prickled, all too aware of Munch only a few steps behind her.

Fanged furies, she didn't have time for the distraction of an infatuation. It had been easy enough to ignore when he stayed in the Human Realm where he belonged. She only had to see him for brief moments at the end of each mission.

It was another thing altogether to have him here in the Fae Realm. Here, he might get a glimpse of the real her. If he saw the real her, this *thing* between them might become a bit more real too.

And that was too dangerous. For all of them. Far better that this remained a treasured longing rather than a dangerous reality.

"Is everything all right?" Basil glanced between them, a furrow between his brows.

Brigid plastered on a smile. The last thing she needed was Basil going all big brother on her right now. "Everything's fine. Let's get moving. We need to get Munch hidden before someone else wanders by."

Basil shot her one last, searching look before he set off again between the shelves.

She released a breath. At least this was Basil, not their talking pony companion Buddy. Buddy would likely give some sage advice, or advice he considered to be sage.

They slipped through the Library and reached the tower without any more incidents. As they began to climb the stairs, Brigid forced herself to glance over her shoulder at Munch. "Don't be freaked out by the bookwyrm. He will let you pass, once we assure him that you're allowed here."

"Bookwyrm? Like those little slithery things I've seen scuttling about?" Munch's voice came from only a step behind her, crowding her space a bit.

"Yes, but this one is…" She was about to explain, but then they turned the corner and there was Gus, awake this time. His head was up as he stared at them with luminescent teal eyes set in his large, blunt-nosed head. His green scales shone in the lights set along the tower walls while his ruff was out, blocking the entire stairwell.

Brigid caught herself before she took a step back. She had gotten so used to seeing Gus relaxed and sleepy, she had forgotten that he was still a full-grown bookwyrm, capable of protecting this tower from intruders.

And right now, he saw Munch as an intruder.

Basil rested a hand on Gus's side. "Gus, this is Munch. He is with us."

Gus slithered forward a few inches, his scales sending up a dry, rasping sound against the stone stairs. He lowered his head and faced Munch nose-to-nose.

Munch pressed a hand to the wall, but he didn't step backwards, even as his face drained of color.

Gus's eyes took on a swirling quality that seemed to root Munch to the floor. His gaze widened, unblinking, as he stared into the bookwyrm's eyes.

Two curls of smoke wound out of the bookwyrm's nostrils and twined around Munch, shimmering with an evanescent haze.

Then the bookwyrm blinked and slid back a few steps before he lowered his head back to the stone step. With a grumble, Gus shifted until he was comfortably sprawled on his back, his sensitive belly scales turned toward Basil and Brigid.

Munch blinked, then sagged against the wall. "That was…intense."

"At least he decided he likes you." Brigid rubbed her hand over Gus's scales, earning herself a shuddering, growling purr.

"And if he decided he didn't like me?" Munch eased forward with his back pressed to the wall, keeping as much distance between himself and the bookwyrm as possible.

"He would have eaten you." Brigid patted the bookwyrm's

belly as she continued up the stairs, trying to hide her smile. "Swallowed you up in one gulp."

"That was a possibility?" Munch's voice rose on the last word.

She probably shouldn't tease him like this. Sure, getting eaten *was* a possibility, but it was a very remote possibility, since he had Basil's and Brigid's permission to be here. And Munch was an honorable sort at heart, despite his past as an outlaw.

"A small one." Brigid glanced over her shoulder, then laughed at the way Munch was all but melding into the wall as he tried to edge around Gus's ruff. Perhaps she had laid it on a touch thick. This was his first day in the Fae Realm. Sure, he'd fought fae monsters for years in the Greenwood. But the wonder and wildness of the Fae Realm was something altogether different when experienced in person. "A very small one. But that's what Lord Chauvlyn will face if he tries to come up here without permission. If he tries, there's a very high chance he'll get himself eaten."

"I guess that's good." Munch still didn't relax until they cleared the tip of the bookwyrm's tail and reached the room at the top of the tower.

Brigid glanced at her desk. Nothing on it gave away that she was the Primrose.

Except for that bouquet of primroses on the corner of the desk.

Perhaps he would assume the primroses were from the Primrose, and he'd get that jealous glint to his eyes. Or he'd start putting the pieces together. Either way, she didn't want to risk it.

She turned and casually leaned against the desk, hiding the jar and flowers from Munch's view. "Well, this is as safe as it gets. We're free to talk here."

Basil sank into his chair behind his desk, remaining quiet even though he had to be as curious as Brigid as to why Munch was here.

Munch paced across the room for a moment, taking in the small windows that overlooked the Library dome. Through the windows, the peaks of the other towers and sprawling roofline of the Great Library were in view. Inside, the desks, stacks of books and paperwork, and the board where she'd pinned her map of the Fae Realm all came under Munch's scrutiny.

As casually as she could, she nudged the jar of primroses off her desk. It made a soft thunk as it hit the moss floor, but thankfully Munch didn't so much as glance in her direction. She nudged the jar beneath the desk, scraping the fallen flowers out of sight as well. There was nothing she could do about the wet splotch, but it was quickly soaked up by the moss.

Finally, Munch halted by the wall, turning so that he could face both of them. "Two days ago in the Human Realm, I was on a patrol in the northern Greenwood when I stumbled across a boy wandering by himself, searching for the foresters. Once I got him calmed down, he told me that the night before, his entire village was attacked and taken through a faerie circle. As far as he knew, he was the only one to escape."

Brigid stilled, trying to absorb his words. An entire village? For as long as she'd been doing this, she'd never heard of fae snatching a whole village.

Why now? And for what purpose?

"Robin and Guy were going to scout the area to see if they could find other survivors and work with the local duke to secure the area to prevent more attacks." Munch leaned against the wall, his face hard. "They're going to leave messages for me in our old outlaw code in the message tree. We didn't dare send an unsecured message to you, in case another fae intercepted it."

"You did the right thing. This is too big to risk in a message." Brigid swallowed, meeting Basil's gaze across the way.

His eyes were wide, his elbows braced on his desk. He would know the ramifications of this even more than she did. She might have lived in the Fae Realm for five years, but Basil was fae. He knew their laws, customs, and bindings even better than she did.

"You'll get word to the Primrose?" Munch met her gaze. "He needs to know right away."

Brigid swallowed, her voice coming out hoarse. "Yes, I'll get word to him."

A report. That was what this was. She'd have to treat it as such. Internally, she had to be the Primrose. Outwardly, she had to be the messenger, getting information to take to her leader. In either case, she had to shove aside her shock and think strategically.

"Is there anything else you can tell me? Any description the boy had of the fae who attacked his village?" Brigid forced her voice to remain level.

"He said the group of fae wore black masks and rode black horses that foamed blood around their mouths." Munch shuddered, as if imagining how horrific that must have been.

Brigid glanced toward Basil. The description meant nothing to her, but perhaps he knew more. All that book knowledge of his often proved useful in times like this.

Basil leaned back in his chair, his voice falling into that softly lecturing tone he used when he got on a roll when it came to knowledge. "Their horses could be knuckelevee. There are a few of those remaining in the Harvest Court. Though, those don't have skin, and I think the boy would have noticed the rotting strips of flesh hanging off their bodies. There are also the kelpies, which are tied to the Court of Lakes and sometimes are also found in the Swamp Court. Then there's the flesh-eating horses. Those would match the description, but they are found only in the Realm of Monsters. Actually, all of them can be found in the Realm of Monsters."

The Realm of Monsters. That wasn't good, at all.

"My brother-in-law Guy had a few theories that he asked me to pass along." Munch paused, as if he didn't like what he was about to say.

Brigid waited, letting Munch gather his thoughts without pressing him.

Munch met her gaze, holding it. "He said there were only two reasons he could think of for why the fae would suddenly attack a whole village like this. Either, the Primrose has done too good a job and demand for humans is so great that attacking a village is worth the risk. This group of fae could want to flood the Fae Realm with so many humans that the Primrose won't be able to keep up."

Brigid's stomach sank. Was that it? Were all of her efforts going to be thwarted just like that? How was she going to rescue all these people? She couldn't keep up with the humans she already needed to rescue. She ran her tongue over her teeth, trying to find some saliva in her dry mouth. "And his other theory?"

"That these fae are stealing humans for some kind of blood rite." Munch's gaze darkened, hard lines transforming his face into something Brigid barely recognized. "Guy would know. His first three wives were killed by Reinhault as part of a blood rite."

Her fingers tingled as her blood ran as frigid as the winds of the Court of Ice. The first option was bad, but this second option? That would be worse. Much worse.

Basil cleared his throat. "Due to the bindings of the Fae Realm, it is very difficult to perform blood rites here. If they were caught, they would be banished to the Realm of Monsters."

"Who says they aren't already in the Realm of Monsters?" Brigid stared at the floor, not really seeing the moss. "They could perform blood rites there."

If the horses they rode were from the Realm of Monsters, that was some circumstantial proof of their location.

Basil's gaze dropped to the stack of books on the corner of his desk. "Based on my research on blood rites, this...this doesn't look good."

No, it didn't.

"I will send..." She cut herself off, swallowed. She'd nearly blurted out something that would give away that she was the Primrose. Munch's presence here was already distracting her, making her act more the real her instead of keeping him at arm's length. "I will send this information to the Primrose. I'm sure he will check with his contacts. If these humans were stolen for the first reason, then there will have been an influx of human captives in one of the courts. Something like that won't go unnoticed."

Basil regarded her. Perhaps he'd caught her near slip. "The rest of us will keep our ears open. It's surprising how much fae love to gossip when they visit the Great Library."

Something that Brigid was more than happy to use. She had learned the locations of more stolen humans thanks to gossip gleaned at the Library than any other one source.

She turned back to Munch. "And you're going back home. It's too dangerous for you to stay here."

Munch's jaw worked, his eyes flashing. "No, I'm staying here. I'm the only one who can translate my sister's outlaw code. Without that code, we're back to passing information through unsecured messages. Or I will have to stumble back and forth through the faerie circle, and I have a feeling that would be even more risky."

Hopping hydras, but he was right. When lone fae were occasionally snatching a human here or there, it had been safe enough to pass messages without a code. She was in the Human Realm frequently enough that anything more sensitive could be passed along in person.

Now something had changed. She didn't know what it was, but she didn't like it, whatever it was.

This attack was organized. Well-executed. Done without any fear of the risks of the Human Realm that normally held fae back from attacks like this.

And she didn't even dare ask to learn his outlaw code.

The magic of her binding to the court made things like secret codes tricky. Actually, it made them pretty much impossible. The court binding granted her the ability to communicate with the fae—both in speaking *and* writing.

While she spoke and wrote in her own language, the magic translated it so that her audience heard and read her words in their own language. Same in the reverse. To the extent that when Basil taught her to read and write, he taught her in the fae language, but she had learned it in her own. A handy thing, since she could read the notes written by Robin.

While it was unlikely that a fae could read one of Robin's notes—written in the human language—there was always a chance. But between the court binding and the fact that the communication magic had played a role when Brigid learned to read and write, her notes in return were readable to the fae. And there always was the risk that the magic would deem Robin's notes, written to Brigid, as fair game to translate for anyone to read.

When Brigid had experimented with a secret code to

communicate with her contacts, the magic either automatically translated it and made it readable to any fae—rendering a code pointless—or gave up and created gibberish that even her contacts couldn't translate. Same when they tried to write in a secret code to her.

Right now, Munch's outlaw code was safe. He could write in a code that the fae couldn't read, even if they knew something of human languages. Even if the worst happened and he was put under a captive binding, he was using his outlaw code to specifically communicate with his human family. If the notes were specifically addressed to Munch in return, it would be enough to skirt around the communication magic. Not to mention that he had learned to read and write in the Human Realm, so the magic was less proprietary over his abilities than Brigid's.

Loopholes like that were essential to navigating the Fae Realm.

"I know the risks. I wouldn't have come here in the first place if I didn't." Munch kept holding her gaze, even as he crossed his arms. "I can help."

His family's outlaw code would be useful. And he had his forester training, the same training that made his family so helpful as the way station in the Human Realm.

This was Munch's choice, the same as it had been the choice of every single person who was a part of the Primrose's League. She had accepted their devotion, the dangers they were placing themselves in, every day that she gave them orders as the Primrose. It shouldn't be any different with Munch.

"All right. You can stay." Brigid tried to make her tone breezy, not showing the weight she felt as she added another member to her League, even if Munch didn't realize that was what was happening.

With each person she added to her League, she took on the

responsibility for another life.

"Good." Munch grinned at her, though he kept his arms crossed. "Because I was just going to sneak back in if you tried to send me away."

That really would have been risky. But so very Munch. Now that he'd gotten the idea that he could help stuck in his head, he wasn't going to leave.

At his heart, Munch was a hunter. He would pursue his prey —or whatever goal he set his mind on—with single-minded focus. He needed to nock the arrow, pull the string, and take down his prey with his own two hands. He had the urge to *do*.

He didn't understand that, sometimes, the best way to accomplish a goal was by sitting back and doing nothing. Doing nothing went against the way he'd been raised as a forester and outlaw.

Unlike Brigid. She was a trapper. She set the snare, laid the bait, but then she let her prey trap itself.

Perhaps not the most heroic. It was a more manipulative, sneaky way of doing things. But she wasn't a fighter. So sneakiness was all she had.

If Munch was staying, then where would he sleep? She didn't dare leave Munch alone here in the tower. He was too much of an outlaw not to snoop once she and Basil left for home. He wouldn't even have malicious intentions. He simply wouldn't be able to help himself.

If left in here alone, Munch would figure out she was the Primrose.

Beyond that, there was too much information in this room about her league. Not to mention Basil's research about the two fae he was trying to track down for King Theseus. While she trusted Munch, she didn't trust that information in the head of someone who could be so easily compromised since he didn't have any protections here in the Fae Realm.

She glanced at Basil, meeting his gaze. "Can he stay at the House?"

She couldn't take Munch home without Basil's permission. Munch's presence would place not only Meg, Viola, Sebastian, and Beatrice in danger, but also Basil and Meg's children.

Basil froze for a moment before he gave her one, slow nod. "Yes. He will place us in no more danger than we already are in."

Because of her. She'd offered to stay somewhere else numerous times. Perhaps on the island of swordmaidens in Queen Hippolyta's Court. She knew that her presence placed her entire family at risk, if her identity as the Primrose were discovered.

But they would likely be at risk either way. Perhaps more so, if she wasn't there to protect them.

"All right." Brigid glanced at Munch. "The two of us will stay here until Basil deems it safe to move you."

They'd have to sneak him from the tower to the Anywhere Door. But if King Theseus was keeping everyone busy with that fancy reception for Lord Chauvlyn, that would be the perfect time to move Munch. They would still have to deal with the swordmaidens guarding the doors, but Minnie, a swordmaiden in the Primrose League, should be going on duty soon.

And tomorrow? Or the day after that? Munch wouldn't want to sit quietly in the House while she was off trying to rescue these snatched humans.

She'd cross that bridge when she came to it. Right now, first things first. They'd get Munch safely home to the House. She'd have to check the tree for messages and send out a few messages of her own. Then she'd figure out what their next steps were once she had more information.

Chapter Ten

Now that he'd passed along his message, Munch wasn't sure what else he could do. He had convinced Brigid to let him stay. But what besides translating the outlaw code could he do? Surely there were more ways he could help. He hadn't left the Human Realm where he was just an errand boy to become just an errand boy here in the Fae Realm.

What else could he do? In the Greenwood, he was at least a trained forester. But here, he was ignorant and nearly helpless, especially until he got his weapons back.

Brigid's brother-in-law Basil pushed away from his desk. "I will check on things below. I'll come back when it's safe to go home."

"Thanks." Brigid nodded, sharing a look with Basil before he disappeared down the stairs. Brigid stared after him a long moment before she shook herself, rounded the desk she had been leaning against, and sank into the chair. She gestured to Munch. "You might as well make yourself comfortable. We could have a long wait."

Munch wasn't sure he was allowed to take the chair Basil

had vacated, so he sank to the floor where he was. The springy moss covering the floor was far softer than the trees and loam of the Greenwood, and he'd spent hours motionless and uncomplaining—mostly—while on outlaw raids.

After taking off his pack, he squirmed until he found a comfortable spot against the wall at his back. Opening his pack, he dug out an apple. It had been hours since he'd eaten. Well, maybe not hours. But it sure felt like hours since he'd stepped foot in this crazy realm.

Brigid's eyes shot to him at the sound, then her shoulders relaxed. "Good, you brought your own food. You aren't bound to a fae or a court. You won't have the protections from the food that the rest of us have. I was just thinking that I wasn't sure what we dared let you eat while you're here. Some of it might—and that's a big might—be safe. But at best, it could make it hard for you to leave the Fae Realm. At worst, you could get woozy, delirious, or just plain lose your mind if you eat the wrong thing. It isn't worth the risk unless you're desperate."

Munch nodded and took another bite of his apple, contemplating the stash of food in his pack. He'd have to make it last. Which would mean no extraneous munching.

Oh, well. If this was the cost of staying and being the hero for once, then so be it.

Even if he was going to miss eating whenever he wanted.

"So." Munch gestured at the room. "Is this some kind of command center for the Primrose? You and Basil must be pretty high in his league to have access to it."

Although her spine stiffened, the rest of her remained almost too relaxed. He could almost see the shutters close as that empty mask took over. She flashed that too-empty grin. "Well, Basil's pretty important. He's a master librarian. He has access to most of these towers just because of his job. He's the one who got the Primrose this tower in the first place. I just organize the paperwork. A clerk, if you will."

"Clerks are pretty important. Or so I've gathered from Guy and Robin." Munch wasn't sure if his words were helping or not. Perhaps he should just keep his mouth shut.

But he was alone. With Brigid. In the Fae Realm. And he didn't want to miss this opportunity now that he had it.

Especially not after that moment they shared tucked in that corner of the bookshelves.

Had she felt it too? He thought she had, with the way she looked at him as if she wanted him to kiss her. Not that he had much experience with such things, besides that one kiss he and Brigid had shared years ago.

But he had five married older brothers and one married older sister. He had seen all of them give that look to their spouses plenty of times. In Robin's case, she usually gave Guy that look after they'd had a particularly rousing sword fight across the breakfast table. But the look was still the same, no matter how it came about.

Yet Brigid had pulled away instead of stepping closer. Sure, it could have been because Basil had been about to walk in on them. And kissing in the middle of sneaking probably wasn't the wisest choice.

Still, it might have been nice to throw caution to the wind and do the reckless thing. Robin did it all the time, and it usually worked out for her.

Brigid laughed, and this one had a high-pitched tone that grated slightly. It wasn't her real laugh. "Perhaps some clerks are important. I'm not. Not really."

Strange that she was protesting so much. And that she was giving him her fake laugh.

But he wasn't going to push her. She was a part of the Primrose League. She had secrets she couldn't reveal.

He should understand that. He'd lived the outlaw life for years. But he had done it with his family. They'd had no secrets from each other.

For a long moment, they lapsed into an uncomfortable silence filled with the awkwardness of people who should be friends but couldn't figure out what to say to each other. Munch took another bite of the apple, the crunch as deafening as a falling tree in the stillness between them. Brigid shuffled some paperwork around on her desk.

"So…" Munch let the word hang in the air between them for another long moment. "This is the Fae Realm."

"Is it everything you thought it would be?" Brigid's mouth twitched into that saucy curve, and even he couldn't tell if her tone was real or feigned.

"It's definitely as dangerous as I've always been told." So far that day, he'd been swallowed by the Great Library and nearly eaten by a ginormous bookwyrm. And those were only semi-dangerous occurrences because he'd been under the protection of Master Librarian Basil the entire time.

He hadn't even run into any of the really dangerous bits yet.

Munch swept another glance over this tower. The walls were so coated with moss and wood and trailing vines that the white stone he'd seen from the outside wasn't visible on the inside, except for the window ledges. He was inside a building and yet inside a tree all at the same time. "But it's also just as wondrous as I've always heard too. I didn't know a green like this existed. My sister is going to be so jealous when she hears about everything I've seen here."

Brigid's smile widened at that. She knew Robin well enough to know exactly how adventure-crazy she was. "And being the loving little brother you are, you won't be able to resist rubbing it in."

Munch kept his smile in place, even if something inside him

prickled. It was one thing when his siblings called him a little brother. But he didn't want Brigid to see him that way. He didn't want her feelings to be in any way sisterly because what he felt for her wasn't brotherly. Not to mention, he was older than her now.

He had enough big brothers and a big sister looking out for him. He didn't need Brigid seeing him that way too.

But he didn't let the way it nettled show on his face. "Yeah, I might rub it in a little bit. But not too much. I don't want to prod her so much that she actually drops everything and takes herself off to the Fae Realm."

He suspected that Guy lived with the constant, gnawing worry that Robin would someday run off to the Fae Realm. He never voiced the fear, never held Robin back because of it. But it was there in the sad smiles he sometimes gave her when she got that reckless gleam to her eyes.

Luckily for Guy—for all of them, really—the only thing stronger than Robin's reckless need for adventure was her loyalty.

"The Fae Realm isn't ready for her." Brigid laughed, the sound filling the room with warmth. A few flowers even sprouted from the floor, as if the Library itself approved of the sound.

As much as he wanted to keep the light tone, he waited until her laughter faded before he said, "So what happens now? With the Primrose?"

Instead of her smile fading, it merely changed, shuttering into that mask. "I'll contact him, and it will be up to him." Her light, breezy tone sounded as if she had no idea what would happen next, but he knew that couldn't be the case. Brigid was too smart, even if she sometimes pretended she didn't have a thought in her head.

"I'm guessing it will depend on what the Primrose finds

with regards to the captured humans." Munch studied her face, watching for her reaction. "If they turn up here in the Fae Realm…"

"The Primrose will rescue them." Brigid smiled, waving her hand as if stating the obvious. "And I suppose he will look for a way to take down the fae noble or ruler who was behind the attack."

Well, that much was rather obvious. Munch searched the apple core, but he'd eaten every bit of apple that he could. He glanced around, but he didn't see a place to dispose of the apple core. He set the core next to him to dispose of later.

With a ripple, the moss rose up and swallowed it.

Munch jumped, then smoothed his hands over his thighs. Hopefully Brigid hadn't noticed that. He coughed to hide his embarrassment. "And if they can't be found in the Fae Realm, then they must be in the Realm of Monsters."

"I suppose that would be the case." Brigid languidly sprawled in her chair, that insipid smile grating on his nerves. "But sink me if the Realm of Monsters isn't a big place."

She was trying to sound silly, but he could hear the intelligence she was masking.

The Fae Realm was one thing. It was mapped and divided into courts. The Primrose could move about it freely, it seemed.

But the Realm of Monsters was a lawless, bindingless place. It was ruled by monsters and bands of rogue fae. There weren't even faerie circles to travel easily between the Realm of Monsters and the Fae Realm. One could only slip through a rift, and no one could predict when one of those would open.

Wait…

Munch sat up straighter. "If the fae did take the humans they captured back to the Realm of Monsters, how did they travel back and forth? While there are thin spots between the

Fae Realm and the Realm of Monsters, there aren't any established faerie circles for travel between them, right? At least, that's always been my understanding of how it works. Thin spots open up and monsters slip through at times, but those thin spots aren't exactly predictable. But if these fae really did come from the Realm of Monsters, then they needed a guaranteed method to travel both ways."

Brigid's back went rigid again before she smoothed her posture again. "Now that is a rather bright observation, isn't it? I'm sure the Primrose will make something of it."

Why was she acting like this again? Munch found himself reaching for his pack for a snack, but he curled his fingers and resisted. Nope, no munching. He had to make his food last.

"You'll let the Primrose know that I'm willing to help? And not just translating messages. I'm a trained forester. I can be an asset." Munch patted his weaponless belt. Well, he would be an asset once he got his weapons back.

"I'll let him know, but I'm not sure if he'll call on you." Brigid gave an easy shrug, her smile twisting with a hint of pity that clawed at him. "You're a forester, but this isn't the Greenwood."

He clamped his mouth shut on his objections. Brigid was just the messenger. But it was the Primrose he really had to convince. "I'd like to meet the Primrose. Maybe if I can talk to him in person, I can convince him that I can be useful."

Brigid got that rigid set to her back again. "You can't just meet the Primrose. Most of the League doesn't even know who he is. There's a reason for that. The less you know, the less you can accidentally tell someone. You're an unbound human in the Fae Realm. You're more vulnerable than most."

All true. But he still hated it. Hated that even here, he was still being relegated to the sidelines. Underestimated. Overlooked. The baby brother.

A grumbling came from the stairwell and the bookwyrm's tail twitched.

Brigid straightened slightly, turning to face the stairs.

Munch's fingers closed on empty air. Shoot. No sword.

Basil stepped around the twitching bookwyrm tail.

Munch released a breath and unclenched his fingers. Of course, it was Basil. Munch had gotten a face-to-face look at the bookwyrm. No one was going to get past the bookwyrm if they didn't belong.

Basil glanced between them, then faced Brigid. "King Theseus wants the two of us at the reception tonight. Munch, Meg is waiting at the base of the stairs. She'll take you back to the House."

Munch nodded, gritting his teeth once again. He was just a package to be passed between babysitters. This didn't match the visions of heroics that he'd hoped for when stepping into the Fae Realm.

He pushed to his feet and hefted his pack onto his shoulder once again.

Brigid, too, shoved away from the desk and swept to her feet. Her bright pink dress swirled around her, falling in waves of silk and floral-patterned embroidery. She smoothed a hand over her skirt. "I suppose this will work for the party."

Basil gestured at himself. "I'm going just like this. It isn't like I have anything nicer than my librarian coat."

"Well, you could have something nicer if you asked the House for it." Brigid smirked as she strolled across the room. "But you're too proud of your master librarian coat to want to wear something else."

"Maybe." Basil's smile widened. "Meg likes me best in my librarian coat."

Brigid rolled her eyes. "Yes, yes. You and my sister are well and truly in love. Got it."

Munch trailed behind them down the stairs, all too used to this kind of sibling banter. It brought a lump to his throat. Would he see his family again? How much time had already passed in the Human Realm during the time he was here in the Fae Realm? Had he already missed weeks, months, of time with his siblings? Had Alan and Sofia had their baby? What other important things might he have missed?

He couldn't think about that. This was where he needed to be. He'd been certain of that a few minutes ago, and he was still just as certain now.

Once again, he edged around the bookwyrm. Sure, the beast appeared to be relaxed and sleeping. But he knew better. That thing was a killer, despite its love of sleep and belly rubs.

At the base of the stairs, Meg waited, bouncing Morgan on her hip and gripping Addy's hand. "Viola and Sebastian are already at the reception. Beatrice went home."

Basil leaned closer and kissed her cheek. "You can still come. Beatrice offered to babysit."

"And spend an evening with stuffy fae nobles and that Lord Chauvlyn sneering at my humanness all night? No thanks." Meg tightened her grip on Addy's hand as Addy tried to tear away to toddle off.

"Then I'll duck out of this—what did you call it earlier?" Basil tousled Addy's hair.

"Shindig." Meg grinned and kissed Basil's cheek.

"Yes, that." Basil turned slightly to give Meg a peck on the lips instead. "I'll duck out of this shindig as soon as possible."

Brigid stepped forward, opening her mouth as if to say something. But then she froze, her eyes widening before that insipid smile plastered across her face again. "King Theseus, Lord Chauvlyn. What a pleasure! We were just on our way to welcome you, Lord Chauvlyn, to the Court of Knowledge."

Both Basil and Meg stiffened, and Basil stepped in front of his wife and children.

Munch froze. What was he supposed to do? If he ducked away now, he'd look more suspicious. It was all he could do not to check that the fake fae ears were still plastered in place. At a glance, Lord Chauvlyn shouldn't be able to tell that he was human.

That didn't keep his palms from going clammy and his underarms from getting a bit sticky.

THERE WAS no time to lose. Brigid sashayed forward, her pink skirt rustling softly. She looped her arm through Lord Chauvlyn's and smiled up at him as if she actually liked him. "Why aren't you at the reception, Lord Chauppertin? You are the guest of honor, after all."

Lord Chauvlyn flinched, leaning away from her with a sneer curling his mouth. "We were looking for Master Librarian Basil and his humans. It seemed strange that they were not present yet."

Brigid would've found his open disgust hilarious, except for the fact that his far-too sharp gaze swept over Meg and Basil before landing on Munch.

Munch, who was dressed in clothes that were clearly not from around here with a travel pack on his back. Luckily, both of his fake fae ears were in place and his family had done a good job with them. As long as Lord Chauvlyn didn't look too closely, touch Munch, or realize that Munch couldn't understand Lord Chauvlyn's or King Theseus's part of the conversation, they would be fine.

Too bad that wasn't convincing her heart to stop pounding harder in her chest.

But her voice was steady as she gave her practiced, annoying giggle. "You know us humans. Always late."

"As I told you, Basil was just seeing to his family. He has young children who need to be put to bed." King Theseus eased back, as if trying to signal Lord Chauvlyn that it was time to return to the party.

Munch's hand flexed at his side, his expression a little blank. Because he didn't have a binding—even the binding that the captive humans had—he couldn't understand any fae besides Basil, who was bound to Meg.

"Yes." Lord Chauvlyn's tone turned even more dour, and he wasn't looking at the children. He was still far too focused on Munch. "And who is this? I don't believe I met him during my tour earlier today."

A tense silence fell on them. Meg and Basil both stiffened, and Munch glanced between them with wide eyes. All of them were acting far too suspicious. While Basil and Meg might support her work as the Primrose, they didn't go on missions. They didn't have the acting skills that Brigid or the key members of her League had.

Brigid trilled her laugh again, tugging on Lord Chauvlyn's arm to bring his attention back to her, if just subconsciously. She hated throwing Basil under the runaway carriage like this, but it was the only story she could come up with on short notice. "This is Basil's cousin."

Basil straightened, blinked, then smiled broadly. A bit too broadly, and the pat he gave Munch on his shoulder was as awkward as petting a porcupine.

Munch jumped, then he grinned and lightly punched Basil's shoulder right back, as if they had known each other for years.

Basil faced Lord Chauvlyn, but his gaze was focused past him to King Theseus, as if begging his king to go along with this. "My distant cousin. From Bog's End. He's just visiting. Bad timing, I know. But…well, here he is."

It was halting, but at least Basil was normally slightly awkward, so hopefully Lord Chauvlyn would chalk it up to that.

At least Basil could lie. All the fae could here in the Fae Realm, even if they still favored truths twisted into trickiness. But thanks to his marriage binding to a human, Basil was immune to iron and free to lie even in the Human Realm.

Bog's End was a good cover story, and Brigid would have to congratulate Basil for such quick thinking. Bog's End was a backwater of the Court of Knowledge, right at the edge of the border with the Swamp Court. Lord Chauvlyn never would have been there, and it would explain Munch's clothing, travel pack, and even his looks that, while Brigid found him handsome, weren't up to the stunning fae standards. If he looked out of place, it would be because of that.

"Yes, and I was just on my way to see that he's settled for the night." Meg bounced Morgan on her hip again, nudging Addy in the direction of the Hall of Anywhere Doors.

Brigid owed her entire family a hug for this.

"Yes, we should let Basil welcome his cousin—" King Theseus trailed off, as if realizing he didn't know Munch's name. Even their king was doing his best to play along.

"Mungoe." Perhaps it was dangerous, giving Lord Chauvlyn Munch's real name. While names had power, it wouldn't give Lord Chauvlyn any more power over Munch than he would already have if he discovered Munch was a human. And if Munch was addressed, he would at least recognize his name even if he couldn't understand anything else.

And it was rather convenient that Munch's real name sounded fae.

"Mungoe. Welcome to the Great Library." King Theseus's

nod in Munch's direction was distinct enough that Munch nodded back without more than a heartbeat's hesitation, although he didn't know what King Theseus had said. King Theseus eased another inch backwards, trying to tactfully nudge Lord Chauvlyn in that direction. "We should return to the reception. My queen will come searching if we linger too long."

There was more threat in those words than it seemed. King Theseus was fully prepared to let Queen Hippolyta, his terrifying Queen of the Swordmaidens, go off on Lord Chauvlyn if Lord Chauvlyn stepped over any lines.

Lord Chauvlyn turned, dragging his arm free of Brigid's grip, and started after King Theseus.

Basil and Meg released long exhales.

But Brigid didn't relax. And when Lord Chauvlyn turned back toward them, that sneering smirk slicking his face again, it confirmed that instinct churning her stomach. The fae lord had been toying with them, letting them think he was leaving and tricking them into relaxing.

Lord Chauvlyn's gaze rested on Munch. "Perhaps Mungoe would care to join the festivities. It would be quite the thing for a fae from a backwater village to witness a royal reception of his court."

King Theseus opened his mouth but froze. If he didn't invite Munch, he would appear rude in front of Lord Chauvlyn. But if he agreed, he would not only cave to Lord Chauvlyn, but also put Munch in danger, even if King Theseus didn't know what was going on.

What should they do? If they fought this too strongly, Lord Chauvlyn would only become more suspicious. He was already far too suspicious of King Theseus and Queen Hippolyta because of Brigid and her siblings. More scrutiny would put the entire League at risk.

But if Munch went to this party, there would be so many chances for him to be recognized as a human.

Munch glanced between them. Clearly confused, since he had no idea what was going on besides that it was bad.

Brigid's smile hadn't wobbled, even with the thoughts racing through her head. But she forced it to brighten as she reached out and looped her arm through Munch's this time. "Sink me, but isn't that just a brilliant idea, Lord Chauptin? Of course cousin Mungoe should come! He will love seeing all the sights to be found at a royal event. It will be such a difference from Bog's End, I'm sure."

Lord Chauvlyn's jaw knotted, annoyed even as he was getting exactly what he'd wanted.

Munch's eyes widened, but he nodded. At least he knew enough to keep his mouth shut. If he tried to speak, he'd just give his humanity away.

King Theseus motioned toward the Hall of Anywhere Doors and the castle that lay beyond. "Then let's return to the reception, shall we?"

Lord Chauvlyn bowed in acquiescence. Of course he was all cooperation now.

Brigid towed Munch along with her. She could handle this. She just had to play her role as Hippolyta's Pet while keeping Munch to herself as much as possible.

As soon as they plausibly could, she'd send Munch off with Basil to head back to the House. If she stayed at the party and kept the attention on herself, hopefully Lord Chauvlyn wouldn't notice if the others slipped away.

Basil followed them with Meg, though they paused in the Hall of Anywhere Doors before the door that would take Meg and the children back to the House.

Brigid kept right on going, Munch in tow.

At the double doors at the far end, two swordmaidens stood

guard. At the sight of King Theseus, they nodded and pulled the doors open.

Lord Chauvlyn swept past the swordmaidens with his head high, looking down his nose as if he felt he had every right to be there in the Court of Knowledge.

Brigid followed at their heels, her arm in Munch's. She leaned closer. "Put a smile on your face. You're at a party. Oh, and feel free to gape a bit. You're supposed to be a fae from Bog's End. That's like the most backwater of backwaters around here."

Munch nodded, plastering on a smile that was just as fake as the one she wore.

Then, together, they strolled across the white marble entry hall and through the gilded doors into the swirl of a fae court in full celebration.

Chapter Eleven

Munch couldn't help the way his mouth fell open at the sight of the great hall before him. The floor was a sea of a white marble so seamless that it appeared to be a single slab from wall to wall in the sprawling space. Veins of gold and silver wove through the marble, yet the patterns of flowers and vines showed that this was no natural quirk of the stone. White pillars the size and shape of trees held up the arching, gilt ceiling while gold vines and silver flowers draped down the pillars, sparkling with twinkling lights.

Fae of all shapes and sizes packed the space, dressed in flowing dresses and clothing that seemed to be made of gossamer spider webs or flower petals. His seamstress sister-in-law would have loved to see all the different clothing and styles, but he had no name for the strange variety before him.

A golden-haired woman in a white dress that was almost too simple compared to the other costumes around them glided gracefully to King Theseus's side. Her only adornment was the gems glittering in her hair and the golden pattern on the leather belt she wore. Even the sword hanging from the belt was simple with a worn leather grip, showing that it was her normal sword rather than a decorative ceremonial sword.

She rested a light hand on King Theseus's arm, and the two of them shared a look and a smile. So simple, yet so filled with the unspoken things between them.

She must be Queen Hippolyta, King Theseus's wife.

Munch followed Brigid's lead and bowed to her. From what he'd gathered from the side of the conversation he could hear, he was supposed to be a member of this court, making Hippolyta his queen as much as Basil's or Brigid's.

Beside Munch, Brigid's expression went even more empty and…silly. It was the only word he could think of to describe it.

Queen Hippolyta sent Lord Chauvlyn a hard look before she turned to Brigid. The fae queen said something, warmth in her voice.

Brigid stepped forward, that look still plastered on her face. "Happy to entertain! I just wish there had been time to stop at the House first. I can't believe I'm showing up to a party in this old thing." She smoothed a hand over the soft pink of her skirt.

It looked just fine to Munch, but what did he know? The only sister he'd had growing up had dressed like a man most of the time, down to wearing a fake mustache when they were pulling off raids. She wasn't exactly a connoisseur of feminine fashion. And while he'd gained a few sisters-in-law in the last few years, it wasn't like he talked to them about things like dresses or stuff like that.

Brigid kept right on talking at a breathless pitch higher than her normal tone. "I'm dreadfully appalled to be seen in public like this. It has me all out of sorts."

Hippolyta smiled with a hint of indulgence, and she said something Munch couldn't understand. Then she gestured at Munch.

Munch smiled, as if he'd understood what was said. But he couldn't respond without giving away that he was human.

Brigid giggled that high-pitched, grating sound and patted Munch's arm. "This is Mungoe, a distant cousin of Basil's. He's visiting from Bog's End. Lord Chauvlyn thought it would be good to invite him to the party. Wasn't that thoughtful of him? And here this is supposed to be a party to welcome Lord Chauvlyn, but he's willing to share his party to welcome Basil's cousin!"

Without so much as a blink to give away surprise, Queen Hippolyta faced Munch and said something. Most likely a welcome, given the context. He nodded and bowed again. Hopefully his silence would just make him look like a country bumpkin fae overwhelmed at being in the presence of his king and queen.

Queen Hippolyta made a tiny motion with her hand. So slight that Munch might not have caught it if he hadn't been trained to watch for tiny movements.

Moments later, a beautiful fae woman trilled a laugh as she swept up to them. She looped an arm through Lord Chauvlyn's, despite him being as stiff as a fallen tree limb, and dragged him off, saying something that was probably about how Lord Chauvlyn needed to participate in his own party.

In seconds, Lord Chauvlyn disappeared among the swirl of raucously dancing fae. The dancers weren't following any dance step that Munch could discern. The music, too, was wild and lilting, keening and dropping in notes he'd never heard before. It seemed to have no pattern and jangled against itself.

The blankly genial expressions disappeared from both King Theseus's and Queen Hippolyta's faces, though Brigid remained languidly insipid.

Queen Hippolyta spoke to Brigid quickly in a low tone.

Brigid replied, her tone more serious even if that smile remained on her face.

King Theseus and Hippolyta shared a look, just as Basil joined them. King Theseus said something, then he and Basil moved off, even as Brigid tugged Munch so that they were more sheltered in the corner.

Queen Hippolyta spoke again, and Brigid flicked a glance between her and Munch. Something flashed across her gaze, as if she were weighing something, even if that was the only indication on her face. Then she gave a slight nod.

Munch jumped as Queen Hippolyta gripped his arm, hard. She said something, and a wave of dizziness washed over him, even as something gold burst in front of his eyes.

"There. That should do it." Queen Hippolyta's voice washed over him as he blinked to clear his vision.

"What…I can understand you." Munch glanced between the fae queen and Brigid. "What just happened?"

Brigid shrugged, as if it was no big deal. But her eyes held a serious glint. "I wouldn't worry about it too much. This was the safest option."

Queen Hippolyta regarded him with light blue eyes that were kind, despite the hard set to her jaw. "I just officially snatched you. It places you under the captive binding, so you'll be able to communicate back. It also means you'll need to be snatched from me to return to your realm, but I won't stop the Primrose from doing that when the time comes. I'm not that kind of fae."

A wave of cold washed over Munch. Just like that, he'd been snatched. He'd just been standing here, and there had been nothing he could do.

And now he was owned by this fae queen he'd just met. All he had was her word that she wouldn't use the power that she now had over him.

He blew out a long breath. Her word, and Brigid's. Brigid trusted Queen Hippolyta. After all, Queen Hippolyta was secretly helping the Primrose when she could.

"So I can talk now, if someone asks me something?" Munch needed to make sure he knew as much as possible about this new binding so that he didn't mess something up.

Was he now speaking a new language? He didn't feel like he was. His brain and mouth were forming the familiar words.

But something was different because Queen Hippolyta's mouth tilted with a smile in response to his words.

Brigid laughed and gestured as she talked. "Oh, you can talk. It's magic, you see. You talk in your language, but the magic makes them hear it in their language. So funny, if you think about it too much. Still, it might still be wise if you kept your mouth shut. I probably should keep my mouth shut more. I never know what will pop out of it. But I guess that's why everyone finds me so entertaining."

"Yes, Brigid has a point. It may be best if you talk as little as possible. You don't know our realm well enough. You might give yourself away." Queen Hippolyta held his gaze, her hands clasped behind her back. Yet she carefully worded the admonition so that it wasn't spoken as an order. "It would be best if you still pretended to be a fae from Bog's End. While my snatching gives you the ability to communicate, you can still be snatched from me and claimed by another fae if they realize you're human. It would violate the laws of hospitality and it will be more difficult to snatch you from me, the queen of this court, but it could be done."

Not a comforting thought. He was safer now, bound to her as he was, but not exactly safe.

Queen Hippolyta gave a shrug. "The only way to prevent that would be to make you a member of King Theseus's court, but that would make it harder for you to return home to your realm. As someone who has been snatched, all that needs to happen for you to return home is to be stolen by the Primrose."

Munch nodded, releasing a long breath. As much as he wanted to stay and actually do something heroic, he still wanted to return home eventually.

"Now you are Hippolyta's Pet like me." Brigid's grin turned up yet another level of brilliance. "And even better, you'll be able to safely eat some of the food now. I wouldn't suggest eating any of the food here. And you'll definitely want to stay away from the wine. Made of faerie fruit, you know. Makes you terribly loopy if you drink it, and any fae will be able to force you to follow their orders then."

"Stay away from the wine. Got it." Munch's mouth was already watering at the sweet, tantalizing smells wafting from the food tables nearby. He could avoid munching here if he had the promise of food when they reached the House that Brigid, Basil, and Meg had been talking about earlier. "But I'll be able to eat at the House, right?"

"Probably. But that's assuming Queen Hippolyta lets you leave. You're bound to her. You can't go too far away from her without her permission or unless someone snatches you from her."

There were so many rules about the bindings of the Fae Realm that he didn't know. He'd thought himself well trained as a forester, but the Fae Realm was so much more complicated.

Queen Hippolyta reached out and laid a hand on his arm again. "You have my permission to go wherever you wish."

When she withdrew her hand, the fae queen shook her head. "And this is why I don't snatch humans. It is so much work."

With that, she swept past them, returning to the party.

Brigid gripped Munch's arm again, tugging him toward the

party. A whine grated through her voice. "Come on. We're missing all the fun!"

He had barely absorbed the whole getting snatched thing, and now he found himself stumbling into the roil of dancing fae. Jumbled conversations blasted against his ears, jangling against the strange, jarring music.

Within moments, he was passed from Brigid to some random fae woman. She didn't tell him her name and didn't ask for his. He tried to flail about, as if he were a fae. Moments later, he found himself whirled over to another fae woman.

He'd never even been to a proper formal gathering in the Human Realm. Despite the fact that his sister was a duchess, she and Guy didn't do a whole lot of entertaining. Could have something to do with Robin's propensity to sword fight on tables and state the first outrageous thing that came to mind. Not to mention that Guy himself wasn't all that sociable either. Being tormented by a fae for years would do that to a man.

But he suspected that even if Guy and Robin had been the type to host lavish parties for human nobles, it would be nothing like this. And this was a tame fae court. What must the Court of Revels and other courts of its ilk be like?

Out of the corner of his eye, Munch glimpsed Lord Chauvlyn as he all but shook a fae lady off his arm, that sneer curling his mouth, before he put his back to a pillar, crossed his arms, and glared at the world. Hard to believe Lord Chauvlyn belonged to the Court of Revels. He seemed more like he belonged to a court of assassins, if there was such a thing.

Munch wasn't sure how much time passed in a blur of dancing and heady, floral scents. Any time he got too close to a glass of the wine, his head went fuzzy and everything went hazy until he found himself blinking off to the side with no clear memories of the last few seconds. That wine sure was powerful stuff.

Finally, Basil rested a hand on his shoulder in a gesture that seemed as stiff and awkward as it felt. "Come along, Mungoe. I'd like to get you settled into the House."

Munch nodded and let Basil steer him from the marble ballroom and out into the entry hall. Viola and Sebastian quickly joined them, but Brigid didn't appear as they strode across the entry hall.

When Munch glanced over his shoulder, Basil gave a slight shrug and lengthened his stride. "Brigid will head out later. She's keeping everyone distracted."

Last Munch had seen, she had been reciting some inane rhyme over and over again, eliciting peals of laughter from her fae audience.

How did she do it, flipping from this silly person back there to the person he glimpsed during the moments he saw her in the Greenwood?

They strolled past the swordmaidens at the doors, then Basil led them to one of the Anywhere Doors. He glanced over his shoulder at Munch, keeping his voice low. "You've never been through one of these before, have you?"

Munch just shook his head. That much was obvious.

"Don't worry, they're pretty simple. Just put your hand on the door and think about where you want to go." Viola reached out and rested her hand on the knob. "But this time, you're with us so it won't matter."

"You should know the concept since you're pretending you're from Bog's End. You would've had to use an Anywhere Door to get here." Basil sighed, then gripped Munch's arm. "But for this first time, we should make sure we don't get separated."

Separated? That was a possibility? Munch barely had time to swallow before Viola swung open the door and stepped through. Basil dragged Munch through.

A heavy, swirling, dizzy feeling closed around Munch, just

like the faerie circle. But it didn't last nearly as long. He barely had a chance to even register the sensation before they stepped out the other side and into a small, cozy space made of stone walls, a mossy floor, and wood paneling.

The building gave a shudder around them, tilting beneath Munch's feet.

Meg glanced up from where she was setting out plates of food on the semi-round table surrounded by mismatched chairs. "Good, you're back. House, he's with us. He's a guest."

The floor steadied, and Munch glanced down to see moss retracting from where it had started growing up and over his boots as if this House had been preparing to swallow him.

The House gave one last shuffle, almost like a huff, before it went still.

Sebastian stepped into the room behind them, running into Munch's back.

"Sorry." Munch stumbled to the side, then halted. His instinct would be to put his back to a wall, but the walls weren't exactly safe right now. Who knew when the House might decide to enfold him into the stone wall?

Basil crossed the room to Meg's side and gave her a quick peck. "Are the children in bed?"

"Yes, though Addy was still awake last I checked. She's waiting for her papa to read her a bedtime story." Meg's smile held warmth as she gazed up at Basil before she glanced at Munch. "I've been learning to read, but I'm not nearly as good as Basil."

"If she's still awake, I'll read her one." Basil gestured to Munch. "Queen Hippolyta snatched Munch, so he has some protections now."

"Well, the House was plenty generous with food." Meg waved to the table. "There will be plenty for everyone."

Basil pressed a kiss to Meg's temple, grabbed one of the

bright purple-pink fruits from the table, and rested his hand on the Anywhere Door again. When he opened it this time, it led into another mossy room. A squeal of "Papa!" came from within as Basil smiled and strode inside, shutting the Door behind him.

Munch shook his head, then followed his stomach to the table laden with food. Viola and Sebastian were already there, stuffing their faces in a way that made saliva pool under his tongue at the thought of digging in himself. Sure, the foods were all strange colors and smelled odd. But at this point, he didn't care. It had been far too long since he'd munched on that one little apple.

Meg joined them at the table and glanced over the food. "I think everything here should be safe for you to eat. The House might be grumpier than a tomcat in a rainstorm—"

The House gave a shake around them, and dirt showered onto Meg's head. Thankfully none of it fell onto the food.

Meg rolled her eyes. "You know it's true. Don't deny it."

The House gave another kind of huffy shake.

Munch was really going to be thankful to get back to the Greenwood and Gysborn Castle, where the stones stayed exactly where they were supposed to be at all times.

"As I was saying, the House is a grumpy old coon, but it's pretty careful when it comes to the humans inside it." Meg didn't say it, but there was the implication that, perhaps, they had taken in a few of the humans that the Primrose rescued.

Could that be what Basil had meant when he said Munch's presence wouldn't put them in any more danger than they already were in? He'd assumed that comment had to do with Brigid's work as the Primrose's messenger girl, but it seemed that Basil and Meg were more involved with the Primrose than they liked to appear on the surface.

"Good. Because I'm starving." Munch plopped into the

nearest chair, grabbed the first plate his gaze landed on, and dug into what seemed to be some kind of mashed vegetable, except that it was a brilliant orange that he'd never seen back in the Human Realm.

"So are we." Sebastian grinned at him across the table with that understanding of two men who'd been deprived of munchable food for too long. "We might be a part of the Court, but even we don't dare eat at those fancy shindigs with the nobles. Never know when something might be spiked with faerie fruit."

"Keeps life interesting." Viola grinned as she spread a bright turquoise spread—jam? Butter? He couldn't tell—over bright pink bread.

Munch pointed at the spread. "Hey, can you pass some of that this way when you're done?"

If he'd been with his siblings, he would've just lunged across the table and grabbed it. But he was a guest here. He might as well use some of those manners that Guy was working so hard to instill in them.

Viola nodded and passed the spread and bread his way.

Sebastian swallowed his bite of food. "The House didn't add on another room, so you can bunk in my room tonight. Hope you don't mind the floor?"

Munch bounced his feet on the spongy moss. "Nope, not at all. I grew up sleeping on pine boughs on the ground. This moss is luxury, let me tell you."

Granted, he'd gotten spoiled during the last five years of sleeping in an actual bed. But this moss was nearly as soft as his mattress back home.

He gorged on the feast spread out on the table until his stomach was comfortably uncomfortable against his belt. Now that was more like it.

Perhaps this Fae Realm wasn't so bad after all.

Chapter Twelve

Brigid crept through the edge of the Tanglewood. The mists of dawn clung to the trees like gauzy, trailing ribbons. Strange lights twinkled among the trees, ready to lead travelers astray or exactly where they needed to be—the Tanglewood was one of *those* kinds of enchanted forests, after all. One never knew quite what would happen when one stepped within its aged trees and draping moss.

At her side, Buddy tiptoed as much as a pony could tiptoe, the clop of his hooves dulled by the moss and loam. Buddy gave a low snort, his large nostrils flaring. "Looks like your guess was correct. Few fae are out at this time of morning."

Brigid nodded and scanned the trees around them. Fae tended to be up at all hours of the night, partying. She'd found through trial and error that early mornings tended to be the safest time to wander about since the night-loving fae were on their way to bed while the fae who preferred daylight were not yet up.

With another glance around, Brigid approached the ring of white stones that marked the borders of this side of the faerie circle. Instead of stepping inside, she reached around one of the trees so that her hand was in the circle but the rest of her wasn't. Her fingers grew kind of numb and tingly, making her fumble as she reached into the nook in the tree.

Paper crinkled beneath her fingers, and she withdrew her hand. When she brought her arm out of the fae circle, she found two notes pinched between her fingers.

Two notes? How much time had passed in the Human Realm?

Brigid immediately pocketed them without so much as glancing at the words. She didn't want to risk the communication magic deciding to translate for her.

"Brigid. You might want to take a look at this." Buddy's voice held a tense note that she had rarely heard from him.

When she turned, Buddy had clopped a few yards away from her, and he had his nose to the mossy ground.

To one side of the faerie circle, the moss and flowers had been trampled so thoroughly that it had yet to spring back into place. The trampled section led deeper into the Tanglewood.

Brigid followed the trail for a few steps before an item half-obscured by the ferns and flowers caught her eye. She knelt, picking it up.

A soft, floppy fabric doll lay in her hand. Black yarn hair was carefully braided while dark brown embroidered eyes stared back at her.

Somewhere in the Fae Realm there was a human child missing her doll. She was scared and suffering who knew what at the hands of the fae, and she didn't even have a doll to hug and provide a moment's comfort.

That burn filled Brigid's chest once again, and she glared at the trail as it disappeared into the dark, mysterious depths of the Tanglewood. Everything in her wanted to march down that trail, find whoever had done this, and mete out justice then and there.

But who knew where that trail would lead? It might veer into anywhere in either the Court of Revels or the Court of Knowledge. Nor was the Tanglewood guaranteed to allow her to follow the trail to its end. The forest might shift and take her in a completely different direction.

No, she needed to remain smart and cool-headed about this. It was how she had survived for so long, and it was the only way forward now.

Buddy's hoofbeats clomped closer, then he rested his nose on her shoulder. He didn't say anything for a long moment, simply letting her soak in the warmth of his presence and the distinct clover-and-earth horse scent that clung to him.

Brigid breathed out a long breath, the heat in her chest banking to a simmer. "Thank you, Buddy."

"Of course. It's part of my job as a talking equine companion." Buddy lightly lipped at her hair before he lifted his heavy head from her shoulder.

Brigid slipped the doll into another pocket of her skirt, then pushed to her feet. "Let's get back to the cottage and see what these notes say."

Though, the notes would likely confirm what she already knew. Another village had been snatched by the fae.

Brigid tried not to fidget as she sat at the table in the House and waited for Munch to decipher the messages his sister had left for them in the tree nook.

Munch held a piece of pink toast in one hand and nibbled at it as he scanned the notes. He wore the same clothes he had the day before, though they appeared cleaner than they had been yesterday. At least the House had deigned to clean his clothes since he was their guest, even if he wasn't a member of their household and thus the House hadn't provided him with new clothes.

Munch took another bite of bread, chewing as he switched to the next note. After swallowing, he glanced at Brigid. "Two weeks have passed in the Human Realm, and two more villages have been attacked. Both of them have been along the borders of the Greenwood, though neither of them was in my brother-in-law's dukedom. It seems that whoever is doing this is wary enough of the foresters to avoid Gysborn."

"Buddy and I saw the tracks of those stolen away leading into the Tanglewood. It seems that the fae are using the circles in the Tanglewood for this." Brigid leaned her elbows on the table as she processed what that meant.

While two weeks had passed in the Human Realm, only a day had passed here. The fae had most likely struck both villages last night, herding the captured humans through the faerie circles one after the other.

Once was simply an occurrence. But three times was a pattern. If these fae were using the circles that connected the Tanglewood with the Greenwood, that meant they were likely based in one of the courts that bordered the Tanglewood: either the Court of Revels or her own court of the Court of Knowledge.

It would be very difficult for something like this to be organized without the help of the monarch of the court. She knew for a fact that King Theseus disapproved of this, even if he didn't openly show his disapproval.

But King Oberon was a different story. He had a cruel streak beneath his surface foolishness. Even if he wasn't actively behind this, he wasn't going to stop the fae who was.

Could Lord Chauvlyn be the one behind this? Sure, he hated humans and the Primrose. But he wasn't the sort to be a mastermind. He was too much the loyal attack dog.

Perhaps her assumptions were wrong. Maybe the fae were from an entirely different court and were merely using the circles in the Tanglewood because, thanks to the forest's enchantment, the circles were a bit more stationary than those in some of the other courts, such as the Court of Sand where the thin spots between the Human Realm and Fae Realm were as unstable and shifting as the sands.

"Thank you, Munch." Brigid took the notes and slipped them back into her pocket. "I should head for the Library."

She didn't mention that she needed to check with her informants to see if any news had come from the other courts about an influx of humans.

The rest of her family had already left for the Library while Buddy had retreated to his stall, grumbling something about needing his beauty sleep after early morning wanderings.

Munch pushed to his feet. "Do my fake ears look all right?"

Brigid hesitated. His ears looked good enough, but that wasn't what made her pause.

He'd be a lot safer if he stayed here in the House. He'd already caught Lord Chauvlyn's attention. It wouldn't take much for Lord Chauvlyn to corner him, though the fae lord would have to break the law of hospitality to snatch a human away from the queen of the court hosting him as an emissary. But it could be done, and she wouldn't put anything past Lord Chauvlyn.

Yet Munch wouldn't stay behind, and he'd put himself in even more danger if he tried to sneak after her. Better that she took him along and made sure she kept an eye on him.

"All right, come on." Brigid checked that she had everything she needed in the pockets of the lavender-colored dress she wore. Then she strode toward the Anywhere Door.

Munch snagged the last piece of toast from the platter, wrapped it in a handkerchief, then stuffed the bread into a pocket. As if he was worried that the lunch they'd all packed earlier wouldn't be enough. Still chewing, he joined her.

She didn't dare let him go through the Anywhere Door by himself. Who knew where he'd end up if he did. The House had a bit of a mind of its own, and the magic of an Anywhere Door could be tricky even without the House taking it into its semi-sentient head to send Munch off into the wilds of the magical faerie paths.

Brigid drew in a breath and held out a hand.

Munch swallowed his bite of toast and clasped her hand. His fingers were large against her slim hand and rough with calluses against her skin, gone soft after her years of working in a library instead of on the farm.

Why did her heart give a little lurch inside her chest at the feel of his hand engulfing hers? It was just attraction. He was a handsome man with his tousled brown hair going slightly long around his fake fae ears while the receding hairline gave him a dignified widow's peak.

His shoulders were broad from years of archery and sword practice while his posture was straight, his back well-muscled. With his quiver of arrows, bow, and sword now back in his possession—now that they could vouch for him with the swordmaidens—he strode with that air of heroic competence around him that would have made many a girl's heart patter faster.

Maybe it was just a little too good to hold his hand and imagine she could lean on him in a way she hadn't been able to lean on anyone in far too long. Yes, she knew she could count on Basil, Meg, and the rest of her siblings. But in the end, she was the Primrose, and, while she relied on her League, she stood alone when it came to her decisions and the risks she took.

This attraction to Munch could never be more than that.

She'd known it when she first met Munch years ago, and she was even more certain of that now. He had his family in the Human Realm. He belonged there with them. While she belonged here with her family and her mission.

Munch's eyebrows scrunched. "Are we going to go to the Library? If not, I'm going to grab another snack. I'm not sure that one piece of bread will hold me over all day."

She laughed and shook her head. "You have your lunch. You won't starve."

"I suppose." His shoulders slumped, his frown turning glum.

She grinned and gestured toward the kitchen cupboards. "You're welcome to try the cupboard to see if the House will have mercy on you and give you more food."

His shoulders slumped farther. "Uh, no. Tried that already this morning. The House spat out a piece of moldy cheese and a rotten fruit at me. I don't think it likes me."

"You aren't one of its people. You're just a guest, and apparently the House is touchy about that." Brigid tightened her grip on Munch's hand and rested her other hand on the latch, picturing the Hall of Anywhere Doors in the Library.

When she opened the Door, it showed the bustling, white marbled Hall.

She glanced at Munch one last time, making sure his fake fae ears were in place. Then, she tugged him through the Door.

As they fully stepped into the Hall, Brigid froze, taking in the activity that was far more than the normal bustle.

A swordmaiden dashed past her, wielding a spear. With a yell, the swordmaiden speared a cat-sized spider through its bulbous black body. Green guts spattered across the white marble.

A screech came from overhead, then a harpy dove down at them, the talons on its bird feet and semi-human-like hands descending toward Brigid's hair.

Before the harpy could get anywhere near Brigid, Munch had whipped out his bow, nocked an arrow, and released. The arrow took the harpy right through the heart, and it plummeted, dead before it hit the ground.

Brigid raced forward and yanked the arrow out, ignoring the icky sounds as the arrow pulled free.

Brigid turned back to Munch, staying focused on him rather on the gore-covered arrow, and handed the arrow back to him. She kept her voice lowered so that no one else would hear. "Your arrows are tipped with iron."

"Right." Munch had already nocked another arrow. "But I can't just sit back while monsters are attacking. I'm a forester."

"I know." Brigid grimaced as the double doors to the Library opened and swordmaidens chased three more harpies inside. The swordmaidens could probably handle it, and already one of them was taking out her own bow and nocking an arrow to the string. But Munch's iron-tipped arrows would kill fae monsters that much more efficiently. "All right. But we'll have to be quick about collecting your arrows."

Munch nodded, a grim set to his jaw. He glanced at the swordmaiden with the bow and arrow, then switched his aim. Munch released at nearly the same time as the swordmaiden, and their arrows both hit their targets. The swordmaiden's harpy screeched, flapped, and clawed at the arrow buried in its chest. The harpy that Munch shot keeled over and dropped to the floor with a thud.

Brigid raced over and yanked out the arrow before anyone else got to it.

The swordmaiden shot the harpy again, and this time it gave a gargling screech and fell to the floor. Minnie, the swordmaiden with the nose and ears of a cow, tromped over and swung her large ax, chopping off the harpy's head to make sure it was dead.

Another swordmaiden sliced a spider in half while Minnie turned and chopped a second spider with her ax.

Munch whipped another arrow from his quiver and shot the third harpy. Its wings crumpled, and it fell to the floor.

Brigid skidded on yellow-green blood as she reached the harpy's side. As she reached for the arrow, the double doors to the palace creaked open. Lord Chauvlyn strode inside, looking down his nose at the mess, dressed in immaculate black as always.

Queen Hippolyta pushed past him, a hand on her sword, her chain mail tunic clinking slightly. She swept her assessing gaze around the room, then turned to Minnie. "Report?"

Lord Chauvlyn halted across the harpy from Brigid, then stared down at her. "You seem rather unbothered by the monsters for a human."

Brigid grinned like a ninny, giggled, and slid the arrow from the harpy as if she were plucking a daisy from a spring meadow. "Just fetching arrows for Basil's cousin. I can't really fight, you know. But I had to get used to a little mess living in the Fae Realm. Even if the monsters are such a bother. Just look at my dress. It's ruined."

She gripped her skirt and flapped it, showing the green spider guts and nearly black harpy blood garishly spattered over her light purple dress.

"Ah, yes…" Lord Chauvlyn began.

"Just look at it! It's ruined!" Brigid let her voice whine in a higher octave. She was only partially exaggerating. She did love this dress, and it was rather tragic that it had been ruined. "The House is never going to get these stains out! And this was my favorite dress! Well, this and the pink dress I was wearing yesterday. And that red dress I wore at the party in the Court of Dreams. You remember that dress, don't you, Lord Challerlin? You were at that party too."

"Yes, I—"

"You were wearing black. Then again, you always wear black. Why is that? I know the Court of Revels has competent fashion designers and tailors. Why don't you make use of them?"

Lord Chauvlyn brushed at his black coat, his mouth curling with even more huffy disgust. "I make ample use of—"

"Really, I'm surprised King Oberon and Queen Titania let you out of the court wearing that. Especially as an emissary to another court. You're supposed to represent their court, and you can't properly represent the Court of Revels while you look like you're dressed for a funeral."

"My good King Oberon doesn't—"

"Then again, I don't really know. What is the proper color for funerals in the Fae Realm? It's black in the Human Realm, but maybe you wear something different for funerals here in the Fae Realm. I'm sure you do, though I've never seen a funeral here in the Fae Realm and I don't want to. Funerals are so sad, don't you think?"

"I—" Lord Chauvlyn sucked in a tight breath, his mouth going all pinched and frustrated.

Good. She'd flustered him so much that he wouldn't think twice about the arrow or Munch.

Brigid waved cheerily with the hand not clutching the arrow. "No, you're right. I've abandoned Basil's cousin."

She spun on her heels and all but skipped across the room, keeping the arrow hidden in the folds of her skirt. When she reached Munch's side, she spoke between her overly bright smile. "We should go into the Library and check on my family."

Munch nodded, then led the way toward the double doors. This time, the swordmaidens didn't stop him or confiscate his weapons. Instead, Minnie nodded to him, the acknowledgement of one warrior to another. Queen Hippolyta, too, gave him a nod.

Once they stepped into the Library and the doors were safely closed behind them, Brigid let the brilliance of the smile fade, though she kept a hint of that mask-like smile in place. "Here's your arrow back."

"Thanks." Munch grinned back at her, then his gaze flicked to something past her shoulder. He nocked the arrow she'd just given to him onto the string, drew his bow, then released in one swift movement.

Brigid gasped and spun, even as a thunk sounded from behind her.

A giant spider's eight hairy legs quivered and jerked in its death spasms. Munch's arrow transfixed it, pinning it to one of the Library shelves.

The Library shelf started to wrap around the spider to swallow it, but it gave a shudder and spit the body back out.

Brigid hurried across the space and yanked out the arrow. As soon as the arrow was gone, the floor gave another heave and swallowed the spider's body without spitting it back out.

She glanced over her shoulder at Munch. "You really are an amazing archer."

Seriously, watching him that morning wasn't helping her infatuation at all. There was just something about a man shooting down monsters to protect her that made her heart go all fluttery.

Munch shrugged as he nocked an arrow to his bowstring. "Not really. Robin's better."

Brigid raised her eyebrows at him. "She's the best archer anywhere around."

"True. But Guy is better as well. And Will. And Tuck and Alan are no slouches either, when they put their minds to it."

Munch shrugged again, but she could see the slight pain to the gesture.

It must be hard, being the youngest in such an exceptional family. Anywhere else, Munch would've been the best archer. But with his family, he felt merely average.

Brigid opened her mouth to say something—she wasn't even sure what—when Basil raced around the corner of a shelf, his gore-smeared club raised high. He glanced around, likely looking for more spiders or other monsters, then relaxed when he didn't spot any.

He joined Munch and Brigid near the door. "A rift into the Realm of Monsters must have opened during the night. I've checked the Library, but I haven't found one in here. Queen Hippolyta sent out swordmaidens to scout the village and the edge of the Tanglewood for rifts."

Brigid nodded, then glanced at Munch. "I might know what caused the rift. Two more villages of humans were snatched during the night."

Basil's jaw worked, and he gave a short nod. "That would do it. Especially if…" He trailed off, as if unable to say it out loud.

But Brigid knew what he meant. If the humans were being snatched for some kind of forbidden blood rite, that was just the kind of thing that would tear a rift between the Fae Realm and the Realm of Monsters.

Rifts were torn by especially cruel actions by the fae or when the laws of bindings that governed the Fae Realm were broken. Both of those things could be in play with these snatchings.

It was more important than ever that she meet with her contacts to figure out what was going on. She was starting to get a hazy picture, and if her guesses were correct, things were dire indeed.

Chapter Thirteen

After seeing Munch to the book repair room where he could guard Meg and the children from monsters, Brigid wound her way through the Library shelves until she reached the quiet corner in the section on humans and their affairs that was usually deserted.

Perhaps it was a little on the nose to pass messages in this part of the Library, but few fae held interest in humans. Even those who snatched humans only paid attention to the things that gave them control over humans. They didn't care about human history or laws or customs. In fact, most of this section was either horribly outdated or had been compiled by Meg, with Basil's help writing it all down.

Before entering the section, Brigid glanced around. As expected, no one was here. She strode to the various books, which were the drop points for her messengers, both within the Court of Knowledge and outside of it.

While she could have had her contacts in the other courts simply hand their notes to Basil, it would give away that Basil knew her. It would put Basil and Meg even more at risk.

This way, her contacts didn't know Basil was a part of her

network. Many of them didn't even know she was the Primrose. All they knew was that the Primrose was based out of the Court of Knowledge, and that it was better for everyone if his—well, her—identity remained a secret.

With each note she found, her heart sank. No one had seen any additional humans in their court. Three whole villages of humans had been taken, and not one of those humans had turned up in any of the courts.

It pointed solidly toward the theory that the humans were being stolen by rogue, courtless fae and taken to the Realm of Monsters. Likely for some kind of terrible, bloody purpose.

How could she possibly rescue so many people from the Realm of Monsters? Even if she entered the Realm of Monsters, it was a huge place. She would be friendless and lacking the protections that she enjoyed here as a member of the Court of Knowledge. Nor did she possess the fighting skills that would be needed to take on the Realm of Monsters.

But she couldn't leave those people to their gruesome fate either. If she did nothing, they would die in horrible ways. Assuming they hadn't been killed already.

Brigid opened the last book, the one used by Rosaline to pass notes. While Rosaline knew Brigid's true identity, even she passed notes this way to keep their contact to a minimum and avoid discussing Primrose business in the main part of the Library.

Brigid opened Rosaline's note, then caught her breath. Rosaline had visited her family in the Court of Revels last night and all her note said was that she had important information to impart. Too important to trust to a note. She would be coming into the Library for her regular shift in a few hours. She didn't dare change up her schedule and tip off anyone who might be lurking.

Namely, Lord Chauvlyn, who might recognize Rosaline as a daughter of a fellow noble of his court.

Brigid and Rosaline would have to be very careful about how they met. Otherwise, Lord Chauvlyn might realize that Rosaline was a part of the League, even if he didn't put together that Brigid was the Primrose.

Brigid whistled softly.

Seconds later, a blue bookwyrm slithered out of the shelves and raised itself on its tail, peering at her expectantly.

She knelt and set the wad of notes on the mossy floor. "Please burn these for me."

The bookwyrm burped out a breath of fire that engulfed the bits of paper. The papers curled, blackened, then turned to ash.

When nothing remained, Brigid scratched behind the bookwyrm's ruff. "Thank you. Library, could you please dispose of the ashes?"

The Library's moss lifted and swallowed the ashes. After a single moment, the notes from her League were completely gone.

Brigid stood, pulled a piece of paper and pen from her pocket, then wrote a note for Rosaline in return. *Meet me at midnight in the waterfall reading nook.*

She tucked her pen back in her dress's pocket—seriously, pockets in dresses were the best thing ever—then she carefully placed the note into the pages of the book on human farming techniques. As she placed it back on the shelf, her back prickled and the bookwyrm made a chittering noise in warning.

She whirled, but no one was in the nook with her.

Still, she quickly withdrew her hand and stepped away from the book. She didn't dare check any of the other books, not until she was sure she wasn't being watched.

She bustled about the nook for a few minutes, as if she was

on Library business. Then she grabbed a random book off the shelf—one that wasn't a message drop for her people—and strode toward the rest of the Library.

As she turned the corner, she nearly ran into Munch. He was standing just out of sight around the curve of the shelves, his bow once again on his back and his quiver of arrows tucked against his side.

Her heart gave a lurch, both in fear and the memory of how heroic he'd looked that morning when he'd whipped out his bow and shot the fae monsters.

How she wished she could trust him with her secret. Something in her yearned to lean into him. It would feel so good to have someone to carry her burdens with her, the way Meg had Basil and Basil had Meg.

But she didn't dare trust him. While he was unbound to a court, he would always be a danger. And she couldn't ask him to give up his family and his home in the Human Realm for her. She'd seen his family and how close they were.

How much had he seen? Had he seen her put that note in the book?

She couldn't go back and move it, not while he was there and watching her. Nor would Rosaline know where to look if it was moved. Brigid would have to track down Rosaline herself once she arrived, and that would bring its own set of unknown dangers.

No, this was fine. Even if Munch had seen, it would likely be fine. He wouldn't purposely betray her, and it was a risk she knew about. If she tried to move the note or contact Rosaline by a different method, she would be incurring risks that she might not be able to predict or control.

"What are you doing here?" Brigid plastered on a warm smile and set out through the Library once again. "I thought you were protecting Meg and the children?"

"The monster attacks seem to have died down. Beatrice took the children back to the House to be on the safe side, and Meg was called away to help haul the damaged books to the book repair room. So I went to see if you needed my help." Munch's gaze searched her face, as if he wanted to ask to help but didn't dare.

If only she could let him help. But it wasn't safe, for either of them.

"Thanks." She brightened her smile and strode at a pace that made her skirts swish. "I appreciate the escort through the Library when there might be monsters still lurking. I know you'll shoot them faster than I can blink."

Munch grinned and his back went a little straighter. A little prouder.

And it made her heart beat a little harder.

MUNCH STRODE NEXT TO BRIGID, wishing he dared ask what secrets she was hiding. What was in that note she'd placed in that book?

It was likely a message for the Primrose. Brigid was his messenger girl, after all. If Munch could get his hands on that note, he could meet the Primrose.

He probably should leave well enough alone. The Primrose kept his secrets for a reason.

But the Primrose was a *hero*. And more than anything, Munch wanted to meet him. He wanted to ask him personally to allow Munch to be a part of his League and help in his heroics.

Sure, Munch already worked to help the Primrose in the Human Realm. But surely there was *more* Munch could do. If only he could talk to the Primrose and ask.

But Munch couldn't tell any of this to Brigid. She would keep her secrets, hiding them behind that empty-headed mask as she always did.

"Come on. Let's help Meg and the others locate the damaged books." Brigid headed toward the main atrium of the Library.

Munch mentally congratulated himself that he knew which direction they were going. After only a day here in the Fae Realm, he was already learning his way around the Library. It was much like the Greenwood. Winding and twisting, with seemingly mysterious paths.

Yet if he leaned into that indefinable part of himself—the part Robin seemed to think was the drop of fae blood that ran in their veins—he could almost sense the direction he needed to go, both here in the Library and when he was back in the Greenwood.

That part of him felt stronger, more tangible, the longer he was here.

Voices came from ahead, and soon they reached a section of the Library just outside of the main atrium. There, a pile of books appeared to have been knocked from the shelf, the covers stained with a sticky, black substance and a few of the pages scattered and torn.

Meg knelt on the ground, piling books into her arms. She glanced up as they approached and smiled at them. "Biting bats, the monsters left a mess. Do you think we can carry all this back to the book repair room between the three of us?"

Meg didn't ask where Brigid had been or what she had been doing. How much of Brigid's secrets did her family know? Another thing Munch didn't dare ask.

It was strange, all these secrets. He had lived with secrets before, as an outlaw. But it hadn't been like this. He and his siblings could talk openly with each other, at least.

"Probably." Brigid knelt across from Meg and started piling books into her arms as if uncaring about the ick getting on her pretty, light purple dress. She flashed a grin up at Munch. "Mungoe is a big strong fae. I'm sure he can manage to carry a whole stack of books."

Something in her grin made him want to stack that entire pile of books in his arms just to prove that he could.

He knelt and held out both of his arms. "Load me up."

Brigid's grin widened, and she transferred her entire stack into his arms. Their hands brushed, and for a moment, he was tempted to clasp her hand.

He didn't, and she kept on piling books onto his arms as if she hadn't felt anything when their fingers brushed.

"How's that?" Brigid paused, holding his gaze.

How was what? The shining color of her brown-blonde hair? The rich brown of her eyes? The way her voice settled inside his chest and made him want to stand taller, fight better, and be more a hero just to impress her? He blinked at her. "Um, what?"

She pointed, her eyebrows raising. "The books? Is that too heavy?"

Now that he thought about it, the load in his arms was rather heavy. He wasn't entirely sure he could push to his feet without staggering.

But he wasn't going to say that out loud to Brigid. "It's fine. I've got it. I can carry a few more, if you'd like."

As soon as the words left his mouth, he could have kicked himself. Any more, and he might topple over. His muscles were already beginning to ache with the weight he held now.

Her mouth twisted, as if she could read his true thoughts and doubted the veracity of his words. "Of course you can. But if you carry any more, there won't be any left for me. And I might as well not make the trip empty-handed."

Meg shook her head at the two of them and stood with her load of books. Brigid grabbed the last few books and gracefully stood.

Munch gathered his legs beneath him, gritted his teeth, and shoved to his feet, the muscles in his thighs burning. But he did it.

They set out for the book repair room. With every step, the books in Munch's arms grew heavier until it felt more like he was lugging around boulders than books.

But he was not going to complain. Or beg to rest. Or ask either Meg or Brigid to take a few of the books off his hands.

Finally, they turned the corner and reached the book repair room. Munch hurried ahead, his arms burning, and all but raced for the nearest table. He settled his load onto the tabletop with a sigh, and it took a long moment to convince his arms to unclench from their locked position around the books.

Brigid set her books next to his and, while she was grinning, she didn't comment on his relief at reaching the room.

Meg surveyed the piles of monster blood stained and shredded books that littered the tabletops. "Monsters always make such a mess. Brigid, are you able to help me here today?"

Brigid nodded and sat down at the nearest table. "Of course. I was planning to stay late tonight anyway. I might as well help."

Viola and Sebastian strode into the room, their arms laden with books. Viola set her books down on the end of one of the tables. "This should be the last of them."

"Unless more monsters get in and destroy books." Sebastian grimaced and shook his head. "The swordmaidens have the Library well-guarded, but a few always seem to slip through. I'm joining the librarians patrolling the Library. It's bad now, but with Midsummer Night coming up…"

"It's going to get worse. Much worse." Meg's jaw worked,

and she glanced at Munch. "It's been nearly a year and a half since the last Midsummer Night, and five years since the last truly bad Midsummer Night."

"That was the night we all came to the Fae Realm, once all the craziness was over." Viola shrugged and reached for another book. She scrubbed it with a rag. "The craziness of that Midsummer Night was caused by King Oberon and Queen Titania's antics."

"If all these stolen humans are the reason for the rift into the Realm of Monsters and if the fae steal more humans on Midsummer Night…" Meg shook her head and took the cleaned book from Viola. "It could be bad. Really bad. Actually, Munch, you might want to leave a note for your family, warning them. It could be in a few months for them, but they should be prepared for an influx of monsters."

This could be Munch's chance to slip away by himself for a few minutes. "I'll write them a note now and leave it in the tree."

Brigid straightened and started to push away from the table. "I'll go with you."

Munch motioned for her to stay where she was. For once, he didn't want her along. "I'll be fine on my own. I know my way to the faerie circle, and thanks to Hippolyta snatching me, I can communicate. I'll avoid talking to people if I can help it and be back before you know it."

Meg, too, halted what she was doing, looking between Munch and Brigid. "Perhaps it can wait until tonight after we are done at the Library? Or tomorrow morning?"

No, it couldn't wait. Munch needed to get a glimpse of that note as soon as possible. "The monsters are under control right now, but who knows how long that will last? If more come through a rift, we might not have much of a chance to go near the Tanglewood and the circle. Besides, if the monsters are already starting to attack, some might start finding their way into the Human Realm starting now. The sooner my siblings are warned, the better. Besides, it isn't like I have to worry about fae monsters."

He patted his quiver at his side to remind her of his skills. He wasn't helpless, and he didn't like to be treated that way, even if he was at a disadvantage here in the Fae Realm.

Brigid hesitated, then that bright smile crossed her face again, masking her true thoughts. "All right, go ahead. You proved you could take care of yourself this morning."

Munch nodded, then waved to her. "Could I borrow a pen and a piece of paper?"

She reached into a pocket of her dress and pulled out a slip of paper and a pen, which seemed to contain ink already without the need of an inkwell.

Munch didn't have time to inspect it. Instead, he mulled through what he wanted to say, translated it into their outlaw code in his head, then wrote out his note. Folding it, he handed the pen back to Brigid. "Thanks. I won't be gone too long."

Meg gestured to the shepherd's staff she'd leaned against the table next to her. "We'll keep our weapons handy until you get back."

Sebastian grinned and gestured toward the door. "I'll walk with you as far as the atrium. My club is all right for dealing with monsters, but your bow is better."

Munch matched Sebastian's grin and fell into step with him. Together, they strolled through the maze of shelves, walking in comfortable silence for a few moments as if they had known each other for years instead of only a day.

"Maybe you can join our patrols, once you are back from your errand." Sebastian gestured at his bow and sword. "Your weapons look a little bit more lethal than our librarian clubs."

"Sure, I can help." It would be something useful he could do, and it would give him an excuse to wander the Library. "I will just need to be by myself or paired with you or Basil. We can't let the other fae realize that..." He trailed off and tapped his sheathed sword, hoping Sebastian would get the message. He didn't want to mention iron out loud where anyone could overhear.

Sebastian glanced down to the sword and nodded. "Right. Yeah, we can work around that."

They reached the atrium, and Sebastian gave him one last grin before he headed off to join a group of fae, which included Basil and Head Librarian Marco. They seemed to be dividing up the patrols.

Munch slipped out the double doors before Basil could catch sight of him. He didn't think Brigid's brother-in-law would stop him, but he might offer to go along. And that would ruin Munch's plan.

The two swordmaidens at the door nodded to him. Had Queen Hippolyta told her people that he was actually a human, and she'd technically snatched him as her captive? Or did they believe the cover story that he was Basil's cousin from Bog's End?

Either way, they no longer stopped him or took a closer look at his weapons, and that was all that mattered.

He strolled out of the Library and through the village without incident. The streets seemed to hold less bustle, as if the fae were staying indoors after the chaos of the monster attacks that morning.

All the better for Munch. The fewer fae who were out and about, the fewer people who could spot him and question him. And no one was going to wonder why he was wandering about with weapons, even if he was more heavily armed than most people in the Court of Knowledge and he clearly wasn't a swordmaiden.

He drew in a deep breath of the strangely warm and thick air here in the Court of Knowledge.

A pang shot through him. He missed the crisp, clear air of the Greenwood and the way the firm ground crunched beneath his feet as he hiked beneath its canopy. He missed the way he felt capable there. In the Human Realm, he knew the rules. He had his training as a forester.

And more than that, he missed his family. He missed Will's mother hen leadership. Tuck's cooking. Alan's exaggerated stories. John's quiet strength. Marion's begrudging helpfulness. The nieces' and nephews' giggles and rambunctious energy.

He even missed Robin's boisterous laugh and habit of interrupting breakfast by sword fighting across the table.

He'd return to them soon. Hopefully before too much time passed in the Human Realm.

But for now, he had a job to do here. He had to help Brigid and the Primrose find the captured humans, figure out who was doing this, and stop it before more humans were hurt. Both the ones who were captured and those who would be hurt by the monsters unleashed by rifts.

And maybe by the end of this, Munch could prove to Brigid and to his family that he could be just as much of a hero as Robin or his brothers or the Primrose himself.

Munch strolled along the path as it led out of the village, then he ducked off the trail into the edge of the Tanglewood.

The deep, dark magic of the enchanted forest wrapped around him, a subtle pressure luring him to step farther into its murky depths. What would it be like to wander this ancient forest? Would it feel and smell like his beloved Greenwood to which this enchanted forest was so tied with its faerie circles? What thrills would he find, if he answered this call and stepped onto this path between the looming trees and tangled vines that opened before him, beckoning him inward, onward.

He found himself turning, taking a step toward the heart of the Tanglewood, before he shook himself and let his hand drop to the hilt of his sword.

The touch of iron, even iron diluted in the hilt, helped clear his mind and steady his feet. He couldn't let himself be lured away by the magic of the forest.

With another shake, he forced his feet back to the thin trail to the faerie circle. He kept his hand on his sword as he strode the last few yards and reached the outer edge of the circle of trees, which marked this particular faerie circle.

Were they considered faerie circles here in the Fae Realm? Perhaps, since he didn't think they'd call them human circles, even if they linked to the Human Realm.

With his right hand still on his sword, he reached into the circle with the note clutched in his left hand.

His left hand tingled, and he fumbled to shove the note into the hollow of the tree. He felt around, but no more notes waited for him. At least that meant no more humans had been snatched since that morning.

It seemed these fae snatching humans were only acting during the Fae Realm night. That was a good thing, at least. It meant the Primrose would have a few hours to figure out a plan before another group of humans was snatched that night.

His mission complete, Munch headed back for the Library. The return trip was even quicker, and he soon found himself stepping through the double doors into the Library.

A quick glance around assured him that the master librarians, like Basil, were busy at their desks and no one seemed to be looking in his direction.

He darted into the safety of the winding shelves as quickly as possible before Basil or Sebastian or anyone else could spot him.

It took nearly as long to navigate through the Library to the nook where he'd seen Brigid that morning as it had to walk back from the faerie circle.

He halted just outside of the nook and glanced around. No one lurked nearby. He might be willing to cross a few unspoken lines by reading that note, but he wasn't going to betray Brigid by letting anyone catch him looking at it.

After he was sure no one else was around, he stepped into the nook and peered at the shelves. Brigid had been standing right about…here when she placed that book back on the shelf. He ran his fingers over the titles, searching his memory for the match to what he was seeing now.

His fingers halted. This one.

He pulled out a book on human farming methods and flipped through it quickly.

Near the back of the book, a note fluttered among the pages. He glanced around once again, then read the note. It contained only a single line.

Meet me at midnight in the waterfall reading nook.

His heart pounded harder. This must be a message that Brigid left for the Primrose. Perhaps she intended to meet with the Primrose that night to discuss what they'd learned about the two villages who had been snatched the previous night.

Munch quickly placed the note back in the book and put the book back on the shelf. He had to leave this note here for the Primrose to find.

This was his chance to meet the Primrose. He just needed to find the waterfall reading nook—wherever that was—and hide there just before midnight. He'd wait for Brigid to make her report before he revealed himself. Perhaps he wouldn't reveal himself at all and would approach the Primrose later, once he knew his identity.

Was it Basil, perhaps? No, that didn't make sense. Basil already knew about the two villages who were snatched. King

Theseus, perhaps? Or one of his nobles who didn't work in the Library itself? It had to be someone Brigid didn't see every day in the Library, if she needed to leave notes.

Munch glanced around again, then left the nook. He didn't want to linger there, in case someone happened to walk by. Or, worse, the Primrose was on his way at that moment to check for notes. The last thing Munch wanted to do was interrupt and stop the Primrose from getting that note.

Only two turns away from the nook, he nearly ran into a young apprentice librarian. She gave a slight squeal and jumped back. Her gaze flashed to his face, then she released a long, gusting breath. "Oh, it's you. I was afraid you were Lord Chauvlyn." She glanced around, then lowered her voice. "He's been lurking in the shelves today. Never know when you might run into him. I know you're Basil's cousin, but you still might want to steer clear of him."

"Don't worry. I plan to." Munch nodded to the girl, then continued on his way.

He'd join Sebastian patrolling the Library for monsters for the rest of today. But tonight, he would make sure he found a way to come back here to the Library.

Tonight, he was going to meet the Primrose, the mysterious fae who held such love for humans that he would risk angering his own people and his own life to save them.

Chapter Fourteen

That evening, Munch told Brigid that he was going back to the House with her family. But he told Meg and Basil that he was staying in the Library to protect Brigid.

It probably wasn't very heroic to lie to them, especially after they had done so much to keep him safe.

But it was the only way that he could sneak away to wait for the Primrose. And he would protect Brigid once she finished her meeting with the Primrose. After all, a few monsters might attack her on her way to the Anywhere Door back to the House.

Munch stuck to the darkened section of the Library along the wall as he waited for midnight. He'd found what he thought was the waterfall reading nook earlier that day while on patrol with Sebastian. Thanks to his pathfinding abilities, he was pretty sure he could find it again.

How much longer until midnight? It was hard to judge time here in the Fae Realm, but the sky was dark and star-strewn through the dome over the atrium. Shafts of moonlight filtered down from the nearly full moon.

Around him, the Library gave a sharp shudder. Munch froze. What was that? What was wrong?

Before he could glance around, he was grabbed from behind, strong hands pinning him against the wall before he had so much as a chance to fight back. A knife pressed to his neck, drawing a rivulet of blood.

Munch fumbled for his knife, but he was pinned too tightly. Even with his strength, he was no match for the fae who held him.

"It is as I thought, *human*." Lord Chauvlyn's voice hissed near Munch's ear. Still pinning Munch with one hand, the fae lord sheathed the knife, revealing that his own palm was already bloody as if he'd sliced himself before attacking Munch. Lord Chauvlyn pressed his bloody palm against the wound on Munch's neck. "Mungoe, I claim you as mine."

The suffocating weight of those words wrapped around Munch, as tight as shackles and binding as a noose around his neck. This claiming was much harsher, much more binding than Queen Hippolyta's snatching, for it had been done in blood.

Lord Chauvlyn released him, and Munch whirled, reaching for his weapons. But as his hand fell to his sword, his fingers went numb. He couldn't seem to find the strength to grip his sword and draw it.

No. No, this couldn't be happening.

Lord Chauvlyn smirked. "You are mine now. You can't harm me."

Just like how Munch's brother-in-law Guy had been unable to harm the fae who'd bound him for years.

And now Munch was blood-bound to Lord Chauvlyn, a fae who hated the Primrose.

Lord Chauvlyn tapped his chin, eyeing Munch. "You're here because of the Primrose, aren't you? You are staying with that nest of human librarians, and I suspect that they have something to do with the Primrose."

Munch caught his breath. He knew far too much about Brigid's work with the Primrose. All Lord Chauvlyn would have to do was ask, and Munch would be forced to tell him exactly what he knew.

He flexed his fingers. His sword, bow, and arrows were *right there*. Yet no matter how much he willed his hand to move in their direction, he couldn't seem to touch his weapons. They might as well not even exist.

Lord Chauvlyn's slick smile widened, as if he could read all of Munch's fears in his eyes. "That librarian Basil and his human wife are up to something, but I don't think they are key players in what the Primrose calls his League. They are too dedicated to the Library. But that human Brigid…"

Munch tried to stuff back his flinch at Brigid's name.

But not fast enough.

Lord Chauvlyn's hand lashed out and he grabbed Munch's shoulder, his fingers gripping so tightly that they dug into muscle and bone in a way that forced Munch onto his knees. "What is Brigid's role in the League? Tell me everything you know."

Munch clenched his teeth. He couldn't betray Brigid. Especially when he was in this situation by his own foolishness.

But the words built in his chest, working up his throat, burning on his tongue. He couldn't breathe, couldn't think, past the roaring in his head.

"She's his messenger." The words burst from him on a gasp. He shook, trying to stop anything else from pouring from him.

But Lord Chauvlyn had worded his command carefully. He'd left no wiggle room for Munch to tell only a partial truth.

"She delivers the humans he rescues to the Human Realm

and takes messages back to the Primrose." At least Lord Chauvlyn had commanded that Munch tell him everything he knew about Brigid's role in the League. He could avoid telling the fae about his family's role, at least for now. "She has a tower here in the Library where she compiles the information for the Primrose as his clerk."

Munch clamped his mouth shut. He had to hold back this last bit of information if it was the last thing he did.

But the burn spread from his tongue into his nose until his eyes watered. Tears spilled down his cheeks as his head grew light and dizzy.

"She's meeting with the Primrose tonight. At midnight. In the waterfall reading nook."

Lord Chauvlyn released his grip, and Munch tipped forward, catching himself so that he hunched on hands and knees, gasping for breath.

What had he done? Thanks to his foolishness in peeking at that note, staying here in the Library, lying to Brigid and her family, he'd just betrayed not only Brigid, her family, but also the Primrose himself.

If Lord Chauvlyn caught the Primrose, then all those humans who had been captured by the fae had no hope. No chance of rescue. They would be bound to the fae like Guy had been. Perhaps brutally killed the way Guy's first three wives had been before Robin had dispatched the fae.

When Munch gathered himself, he glared up at Lord Chauvlyn, hating that a glare was the worst he could do. This sneering fae owned him now, and there was nothing Munch could do about it.

Lord Chauvlyn's sneer curled his mouth and slicked his eyes even darker. "Humans are so pathetic. So weak. I will never understand why the Primrose insists on lowering himself to be your defender."

"Because it is the right thing to do. Because he's honorable. A hero." Munch clenched his fists, trying to put as much strength as he could into his glare.

Lord Chauvlyn shook his head, as if utterly mystified about why doing the right thing would hold any appeal. "Honorable. Is it truly honorable to work against your own people? Steal from your own people? He has turned his back on his people for the sake of a people not his own."

Munch shook his head. It didn't work like that. Sure, humans and fae were from different realms. But they were both still people, in the end. People with hopes and dreams and souls. The Primrose saw that. That was why he fought so hard. Brigid saw that. It was why she did not hate the fae even as she worked with the Primrose to save humans from fae.

With a deep breath, Munch met Lord Chauvlyn's dark eyes. "You're one of the fae stealing humans, aren't you?"

Lord Chauvlyn didn't respond out loud, but the satisfied twitch to the corners of his mouth was answer enough.

"Why are you doing this? Why steal so many humans?" If Munch was going to be a captive of this fae, then he might as well gather as much information as possible. Maybe he could warn Brigid and, through her, warn the Primrose. "What do you have to gain?"

"Power." Lord Chauvlyn stated it as if it should have been obvious. "There is great power in the blood of humans, strange as it is to have such power locked in the blood of something so pathetically weak. You have been here a day, human. You are familiar with the bindings that hold us in check. But my master and I intend to free our people from the bindings that hold us captive."

Munch's stomach churned while chills prickled along his arms.

The fae were bound for a reason. Who knew the cruelties

that the fae were capable of if left unchecked. Even the Realm of Monsters, with all its evils, was held in check thanks to its separation from the Fae Realm and even further separation from the Human Realm.

Would the checks that held the fae back in the Human Realm—such as their weakness to iron and their inability to lie —still work if the Laws of Bindings were broken?

Lord Chauvlyn and his master—whoever his master was— had to be stopped. Whatever it took.

If only Munch wasn't helpless, bound to this fae before him.

Lord Chauvlyn glanced toward the atrium and gave a slight nod. "Midnight draws near. Mungoe, my pet, I order you to stay here in the Library. In three hours' time, you are to meet me at one of the faerie circles in the Tanglewood. Don't worry, you'll know the one. You'll be drawn to it by your captivity to me. You are to tell no one about our conversation or that you are now my captive. You must not attempt to warn the Primrose or Brigid or any of her family about me or my plans. Also, you must avoid Queen Hippolyta. It wouldn't do to have her realize you've been snatched from her."

Munch flinched as the orders hit him like bolts fired from a crossbow. So much for his plan to gather information to pass along to the Primrose. Now he couldn't even warn Brigid that she had been betrayed.

As Lord Chauvlyn strolled away, Munch dug his fingers into the moss of the Library.

He'd messed everything up. All he'd wanted to do was help, and instead he'd just made everything more dangerous for everyone.

So much for wanting to be a hero. Instead, he was the betrayer. The fool who'd stumbled into a trap.

What was he going to do? He couldn't warn Brigid. He

couldn't warn the Primrose. He couldn't kill Lord Chauvlyn and eliminate the threat.

Around him, the Library gave a soothing little tremble, its moss warm against his fingers. A cerulean bookwyrm slithered out of the shelves and twined around Munch's wrists, as if trying to offer comfort.

Munch stilled, then lifted one hand from the moss to reach tentatively toward the bookwyrm.

The bookwyrm gave a growling purr and lifted on its tail to rub its head against his palm, almost like a scaly, legless cat.

"I can't warn Brigid, but you can." Munch wasn't sure how much the Library or its bookwyrms had understood. But they didn't like Lord Chauvlyn. They sensed he was trouble.

Perhaps they would sense his urgency. His need to warn Brigid. Munch might not be connected to the Library, but Brigid was. Surely the Library would do everything in its power to keep her safe.

"Please." Munch cupped the bookwyrm's face and looked deep into its slitted eyes. "Warn Brigid. She must not go to her meeting with the Primrose. The Primrose must get out of here before Lord Chauvlyn sees him and realizes who he is. Please, Library. I know I'm not one of your librarians. I'm just a human. A captive of your enemy. But Brigid is bound to your court. I'm assuming the Primrose has some connection to you as well, since he seems to use the Library as his headquarters. Please. Warn them. Don't let Lord Chauvlyn catch them."

The bookwyrm almost seemed to nod against his hand. Then it slithered away, disappearing among the shelves even as the Library gave another, slighter shiver around him.

Munch slumped against the bookshelf at his back. Hopefully the Library's warning would be enough.

Chapter Fifteen

Brigid sprawled on one of the comfy couches that occupied this particular reading nook, tucked away on a far side of the fiction wing. Her couch angled toward the doorway so that she could see the entrance without raising her head from the pillow.

A stream came out of the wall from who knew where, trickled in a rocky ledge above moss and fern walls, before pouring down over the doorway in a shimmering waterfall that left just enough space behind and to one side to walk around it without getting wet. It splashed down into a pool that filled the center of the room. Lily pads with blooming white flowers floated in the pool above lazily swimming fish. The occasional frog chirruped or hopped about while dragonflies zipped above the flowers. Several turtles rested on the rocky edge of the pond.

The couches and comfy chairs ringed the little pond with just enough space that a reader wouldn't accidentally drop a book into the water if the book should slip from their fingers.

Instead of sunlight, a beam of moonlight glittered down

from the high window, reflecting on the pond and dancing in shimmering sparks at the base of the waterfall.

Brigid settled more comfortably in the couch. This could be a long night. Rosaline would arrive in a few minutes to report. Hopefully she had information that would point Brigid in the right direction. If the fae continued their pattern, more humans would be snatched from their villages tonight. Brigid didn't want to miss this chance to stop them.

The Library gave a sharp shudder around her, nearly dumping her from the couch. Brigid pushed to her elbow, glancing around. What was wrong? What had set the Library off? Had more monsters gotten inside?

Chittering came from a whole squirm of bookwyrms near the entrance to the reading nook.

"Get out of my way, you useless worms," a deep voice hissed, inciting another round of growling from the bookwyrms.

Lord Chauvlyn. Well, this was a complication. What was he doing here?

It didn't matter what he was doing here. She had to go with it.

Sinking back onto the couch, she draped one hand over the edge and let the other rest over her face. She worked to slow her breathing into a deep, slow rhythm, as if she was sleeping.

Relax. She released a long breath as her body sank against the couch, her muscles going lax. It wasn't like Lord Chauvlyn could do anything to her here. She was a member of the Court of Knowledge, a court where he was currently a guest. The Great Library itself would rise against him if he attacked her here and now.

What he might suspect when he found her here, that was a different matter entirely.

From beneath the shadow of her draped arm, she watched Lord Chauvlyn through slitted eyes.

He dodged around the bookwyrms, and he had the sense not to kick or otherwise harm them.

The bookwyrms and Library didn't directly harm him either. They clearly weren't happy with him—even more than before—but he was still officially a guest here until King Theseus gave the order or kicked Lord Chauvlyn out.

Still, they were acting even more antagonistic than before. Had Lord Chauvlyn already done something that would break the laws of hospitality? While the laws of hospitality weren't as binding as the greater bindings, there were still consequences for breaking them.

Lord Chauvlyn extricated himself from the wriggling mass of bookwyrms and strolled around the waterfall. He paused just inside the room, sweeping his gaze around the space.

It took all her discipline not to tense or let her breath hitch as the weight of Lord Chauvlyn's gaze landed on her.

He stood there for a long moment, his scowl deepening. After several, frozen seconds, he tore his gaze away and sank onto one of the couches across the pond from Brigid and out of sight of the doorway. He languidly sprawled, resting his elbow on the armrest and stroking his chin with long, deft fingers as if contemplating the sight before him.

His other hand draped over the back of the couch, a white bandage just visible.

What was he thinking? Was he putting the pieces together? *How* had he known to come here? What did the white bandage mean?

A chittering came from the bookwyrms again, and Lord Chauvlyn straightened, tensing as if prepared to leap at the first person who strode through the doorway. He'd chosen his seat so that he was out of sight of the doorway, to lure his prey inside, no doubt, but it also meant that he couldn't see anyone until they passed by the waterfall.

Brigid peeked at the waterfall shielding the entrance without turning her head. Rosaline had halted just on the other side of the waterfall in the shadows, frowning at the line of bookwyrms blocking her way. She glanced up at Brigid, as if seeking an explanation.

Brigid gave a snuffling noise and shifted, as if she was still asleep. The movement disguised the brief flick of the hand she had draped over her face. A signal to Rosaline to get out of there.

Rosaline tipped her head in a nod, then disappeared.

Lord Chauvlyn remained tense, his gaze swinging from the waterfall to Brigid and back.

Brigid waited a few heartbeats, then she made a grinding noise with her teeth, smacked her lips, and partially rolled again. She'd have to periodically make noise or movement so that Lord Chauvlyn didn't realize that the first shift had been a warning to someone.

As she'd hoped, Lord Chauvlyn's mouth twisted in unmitigated disgust, as if he found the noises a human made while sleeping crude and uncultured.

Brigid lapsed into silent, deep breaths once again. A hum of noise still filled the room between the constant background rumble of the waterfall and the chirruping of the frogs around the pond.

But a tense kind of silence stretched beneath the lulling noise. If only there was a clock in this room to tick out the seconds.

After long moments, Lord Chauvlyn relaxed back into his pensively brooding sprawl. He didn't look like he was going anywhere anytime soon.

Brigid let her eyes close, the better to concentrate on the puzzle pieces that were coming together in her head. She needed to think through the ramifications of Lord Chauvlyn's presence here, and what it would mean for her plans for that night.

Actually, she could work with this. This might be the break she had needed. She'd need to talk to Rosaline, but she already suspected some of what Rosaline had to tell her.

Her plan was still a little hazy. It was hard to put together a solid plan when she wasn't sure where they'd end up before the night was out.

She'd need a disguise, of course. She should grab a second rapier. More weapons never hurt when going into danger. And a rope. With a grappling hook. Rope always came in handy on adventures. Hippolyta should have weapons and rope in her stash here at the palace. Oh, and medical supplies. Just in case.

It would be a busy night. There were messages to be sent, people to contact. It was going to be tricky, making sure all the bindings fell into place as they should. But this might actually work.

The more Brigid plotted, the easier it was to relax despite the itchy weight of Lord Chauvlyn's gaze on her. She might have even dozed a bit. It was going to be the last few winks of sleep she'd get for quite some time.

Time passed, marked by the creep of the shaft of moonlight across the surface of the pond. Lord Chauvlyn shifted in his seat a few times. Brigid made a few more annoying noises for good measure.

After an hour, Lord Chauvlyn pushed to his feet and strode toward the entrance. At the waterfall, he turned and glanced over his shoulder at Brigid one last time with sharp, assessing eyes.

How much did he suspect? What plans had he been formulating during their silent standoff these past minutes?

Then with a determined straightening of his shoulders, Lord Chauvlyn strode from the room, stepping around the line of bookwyrms that still guarded the entrance.

Brigid waited for long minutes, just in case his leaving was a feint and he'd come back to surprise her.

But after ten interminable minutes passed, she finally let the arm fall from her eyes. Time to get to work.

A figure appeared just behind the waterfall, and the bookwyrms slithered out of the way for her this time. Rosaline peeked around the waterfall, then hurried into the room. She glanced over her shoulder, keeping her voice low. "I saw Lord Chauvlyn leave. What was he doing here?"

"He must have found out about our meeting somehow." Brigid swung upright, her head a little muzzy after lying down and pretending to be asleep for so long. She also kept her voice low, though she didn't think Lord Chauvlyn had lingered. If her guess was correct, then he had matters to attend to tonight, as did she once she talked to Rosaline and confirmed her hunches. "What information did you have for me?"

Rosaline hurried across the room and plopped onto the couch next to Brigid. "My family's estate lies at the border with the Tanglewood. The servants reported seeing lights in the Tanglewood. So I agreed to attend a court function with my parents."

Brigid placed an arm around Rosaline's shoulders and gave her a comforting squeeze. Rosaline had left her court to avoid the wild court functions. Whenever she returned for a visit, her parents pressured her to return to the Court of Revels. Some of her relatives had even attempted to trick Rosaline into returning to the court. "Thank you for that sacrifice."

Rosaline gave a little shudder, then she straightened her shoulders. "It was my honor to take the risk. And it was worth it. I talked to Puck."

Brigid wasn't sure if she should grin or grimace at the mention of Puck. He was both highly entertaining and highly destructive, depending on his mood and the mood of King Oberon. Puck was a small green-skinned sprite who acted as the right-hand minion of King Oberon. He was King Oberon's errand boy when enacting tricks on Queen Titania or spying on members of his own court.

"It took some doing to weasel information out of him. For all his trickery, Puck is loyal to King Oberon and not inclined to run off his mouth." Rosaline gave a shudder. "I had to flirt with Romeo to convince Puck that my true loyalties lie with the Court of Revels."

"My condolences. I wish I could give you a medal for the sacrifices you've made on my behalf." Brigid gave Rosaline another comforting half-hug. "He didn't cross any lines, did he?"

Romeo was King Oberon and Queen Titania's nephew and heir. He was only thirteen years old, three years younger than Rosaline, but he thought himself madly in love with her.

"No. He was just obnoxious." Rosaline grimaced. "I feel sorry for him. Mostly. When I'm not frustrated with him. He doesn't have a good example of a healthy relationship. His parents are pretty apathetic, and he has mostly been raised by King Oberon and Queen Titania."

Brigid could only shake her head at that. King Oberon and Queen Titania were either madly in lust with each other or hated each other's guts. Since they were part of the same court, not to mention bound together in marriage, they couldn't outright kill each other. So they tormented each other with malicious tricks whenever possible. Not exactly an example of a healthy marriage.

"Anyway, once I convinced Puck that I was loyal to the Court of Revels at heart, he revealed that he and Oberon have aligned themselves with a new ally who has promised to give them power and elevate their court above all the other courts of the Fae Realm." Rosaline leaned closer, as if burdened by her information. "Even Puck didn't know exactly what was going on, though I gathered that he had been aiding whoever has been stealing humans and they have been taking the humans to the Realm of Monsters. Somehow there is a way to get to the Realm of Monsters from the Court of Revels, though Puck wouldn't reveal what it was and started to get suspicious when I pushed. I'm sorry I couldn't find out more."

"You've done more than enough." Brigid patted Rosaline's arm. She had already suspected most of this, but Rosaline confirmed it. King Oberon and the Court of Revels were involved in this. They might not be the fae behind this, but they were harboring those who were.

Lord Chauvlyn would know who was behind this. Probably even more than King Oberon. Lord Chauvlyn didn't strike her as the type of person to blindly follow someone as foolish as King Oberon if he had the chance to switch his loyalties to a more powerful, far smarter master.

Brigid pushed to her feet. "Thank you, Rosaline. Your information was what I needed to come up with a plan to stop this."

"What can I do to help?" Rosaline hopped to her feet, clasping her hands before her. Even after everything she'd risked to gain this information, she was still willing to do more.

"I'm glad you asked. This is what I'd like you to do." Brigid leaned closer and whispered her instructions to Rosaline.

Rosaline's forehead scrunched, but she nodded.

Brave girl. What Brigid had asked of her was a big risk, and she normally wouldn't ask it of someone as young as Rosaline. But Rosaline had a good head on her shoulders. She could handle this task.

Brigid turned and strode toward the exit. It was time to put her plan into action and end this once and for all.

Chapter Sixteen

Munch waited a few shelves away from the reading nook, sticking to the shadows. He watched as Lord Chauvlyn entered, then saw the apprentice librarian—what was her name?—nearly enter, then quickly back away. She, too, waited in the shadows, though she didn't notice Munch.

Surely she wasn't the Primrose. She looked maybe fifteen or sixteen.

Yes, Munch had been an outlaw at that age, and he'd thought himself plenty grown up. But he hadn't been the leader. That had been Robin.

After an hour, Lord Chauvlyn strode from the room, a hint of a smirk slicking his face. As he passed Munch's hiding place, he glanced in Munch's direction, even though he couldn't possibly see him.

But Munch was the fae lord's captive. He likely knew exactly where Munch was at all times.

Giving an even wider, self-satisfied smirk, Lord Chauvlyn tilted his head in Munch's direction, as if thanking him, before the fae lord strode onward, heading off to steal more humans that night to use in his blood rite and undo the bindings on the realms.

Munch's heart pounded harder. That smirk seemed to indicate that Lord Chauvlyn had learned something. But what? No one else but Brigid had entered that room. Unless there was a hidden entrance that the Primrose had used? Did Lord Chauvlyn know the identity of the Primrose?

After a few more minutes, the young apprentice librarian entered the reading nook.

Munch couldn't hear what was said inside. He was too far away, and he doubted he'd hear anything even if he tiptoed right up to the door of the room, thanks to the steady roar of the small waterfall over the doorway.

Only a few more minutes passed before the apprentice librarian hurried out of the room. She didn't even glance around as she bustled past Munch's hiding spot.

Finally, Brigid strode from the reading nook, still wearing her light purple dress and moving at an unhurried, unworried pace.

Didn't she know the Primrose was compromised? Surely she'd seen Lord Chauvlyn enter the room. Why didn't she seem worried?

Munch stepped out of his hiding place and blocked her path.

Brigid jumped, a hand fluttering to her mouth. "Oh, Munch. You scared me. What are you still doing here? I thought you returned to the House hours ago?"

As he should have done.

But he'd been foolish, and now he'd put Brigid, the Primrose, and all those snatched humans in danger. He had to warn her. Somehow.

He opened his mouth, but the words wouldn't come. Instead, a burning pain lanced over his tongue, and he gagged.

"Is everything all right?" Brigid stepped closer, reaching out as if to rest a hand on his arm. But she halted a few inches short.

It wouldn't matter even if she had touched him. She was human. She wouldn't be able to tell that he had been snatched from Queen Hippolyta by Lord Chauvlyn.

Munch tried to shake his head, but instead he found himself bobbing his head in a nod.

No, he hadn't meant to nod. But his orders from Lord Chauvlyn prevented him from so much as indicating that he was in trouble.

The movement tugged on the cut on his neck. The cut had already scabbed over, but the dried blood was still visible. Could Brigid see it in the darkness of the nighttime Library?

Even as he had the thought, his orders from Lord Chauvlyn forced him to shift to hide that side of his neck from her.

Brigid dropped her hand and met his gaze. For once, her eyes were clear and solemn. "Don't worry, Munch. Everything is going to be all right."

No, it wasn't. But Brigid didn't seem to know that. She didn't know what Munch knew. She didn't know that Munch had betrayed her and the Primrose to Lord Chauvlyn, or that he was now blood bound.

With one last smile, Brigid strolled past him. When she reached the end of the row, she half-turned back to him and waved. "I'll see you later."

Munch found himself smiling and waving back, like he was a puppet controlled by the burning of Lord Chauvlyn's demands.

As soon as Brigid was out of sight, Munch sagged against the bookshelves, then slid to the ground. What was he going to do? He couldn't warn Brigid or Queen Hippolyta or King Theseus. He still didn't know who the Primrose was to warn him. And in two hours, Lord Chauvlyn's order would force him to a circle in the Tanglewood where, presumably, he would meet Lord Chauvlyn returning with the humans he'd captured. Munch, too, would be taken back to the Realm of Monsters to be a part of the blood rite.

A blood rite that would likely occur on Midsummer Night. That would be when the magic would be strongest.

If Munch didn't find a way to warn someone, then he would die in a few days.

He'd never see his family again. Robin. His brothers. All the nieces and nephews he'd never see grow up, much less all the ones who had yet to be born. They might never know what had happened to him.

Which was probably just as well. He wouldn't want them to know that he'd died a horrific death as part of some forbidden rite. He'd rather Alan make up a heroic death for him.

Instead of this. He wasn't going to die a hero. No, he was going to die because of his own foolish mistakes.

He never should have come here. All he'd done was mess everything up.

The wriggling mass of bookwyrms slithered away from the entrance to the reading nook. Most of them disappeared among the shelves, but the same blue bookwyrm—at least, he thought it was the same one— slithered up to him and slid onto his lap, peering up at him with slitted eyes.

A few days ago, he would have found the snake-like dragon creepy and would have shoved it away.

Now, he scratched behind its ruff. "Thank you for trying. Do you have any more ideas for me?"

The bookwyrm gave a soft, purring growl, its whole body rumbling against him in a strangely soothing sensation. Not exactly helpful, but it quelled some of the tightness rising in his chest.

"You bookwyrms sure do love your scratches." Munch found himself chuckling as the bookwyrm rolled, presenting him with its stomach.

It reminded him of the huge bookwyrm that guarded Brigid's tower. That bookwyrm, too, loved its belly rubs.

Wait. Brigid's tower. Where she worked as a clerk for the Primrose.

Munch stilled. He hadn't seen the Primrose meet with Brigid, but perhaps there was another way to figure out who the Primrose was.

He wasn't sure what good it would do. Lord Chauvlyn had forbidden him to warn the Primrose.

Though, perhaps, if he could figure out the Primrose's true identity, he could skirt around the order somehow. Maybe if he focused on warning the person behind the mask of the Primrose, that would work as a loophole.

It was worth a try. It wasn't like he could make things any worse.

Munch cradled the bookwyrm in his arms and stood. "Can you convince your big brother to let me into Brigid's tower?"

The bookwyrm just grumbled, then settled more comfortably into his arms.

Would the full-grown bookwyrm let him pass? Munch had permission to enter that one day from Brigid, but would that permission still stand? Especially if Munch didn't have Basil or Brigid with him?

There was only one way to find out. Hopefully he wouldn't get himself burnt to a crisp.

If he did, well, being eaten by a bookwyrm was probably faster than whatever terrible fate Lord Chauvlyn and his master had planned for the humans they'd snatched.

Munch wound his way through the Library, following his memories to the base of Brigid's tower. Or what he hoped was

Brigid's tower. If he picked the wrong tower and ended up face-to-face with a strange bookwyrm, then he'd be in trouble. Probably dead.

He drew in a deep breath, clutched the blue bookwyrm tighter, and forced himself to step on the first tread. Here went nothing.

His footsteps scuffed softly in the utter silence as he climbed the winding stairs. Any moment now, he'd find the bookwyrm.

A smokiness clogged the air. He forced himself up a few more stairs.

A large, scaled, green snout came into view. Then the bookwyrm's head, its eyes shut as it grumbled in sleep.

Munch released a breath. He was pretty sure it was the same bookwyrm he'd met before. What was its name? "Uh, hello. Gus, wasn't it? May I pass?"

The bookwyrm's eyes flickered open. It blinked at Munch, then yawned, its jaws gaping open wide enough to swallow Munch whole and showing off rows and rows of sharp teeth.

Munch hugged the warm, smaller bookwyrm to his chest and tried to pretend he wasn't shaking in his boots.

The bookwyrm raised its head until it was eye-level with Munch. Those teal, burning eyes grew in his vision until they were consuming him. His breath caught in his throat, his mind freezing, as a power wrapped around him, worming inside his head and seeming to scour everything inside him with a scorching claw.

Was he dying? Burned from the inside out by this bookwyrm?

He couldn't die. He needed to warn the Primrose. Brigid. His family. He had to make up for his foolishness that had betrayed them.

The bookwyrm snorted, then lowered its head, looking away from him.

The heat ceased, and Munch gasped in a breath. He blindly sagged against the wall as his legs wobbled beneath him. In his arms, the bookwyrm nuzzled against his hand, setting up an even louder purr.

That was intense. Far more intense than the scrutiny he'd experienced from Gus the first time he'd gone up this tower.

But the full-grown bookwyrm settled back to the floor, leaving space for Munch to pass on the stairs. He'd been allowed entry.

As Brigid had done that first time, Munch trailed his fingers over the bookwyrm's scaled stomach, giving it a belly rub as he ascended the stairs. It was the least he could do, since the bookwyrm had deemed him worthy to enter.

Once he reached the top, he set down the smaller book-wyrm and hurried across the tower to Brigid's desk.

It was clear of paperwork. Only a pen remained, waiting to be used.

The pinboard behind it seemed to mark the various courts, the faerie circles, and stolen humans waiting for rescue. Fascinating, but not the information he was looking for.

He strode around the desk and tried the drawers. All of them were locked.

Not a problem. He was an outlaw.

He knelt behind the desk and reached for the pouch at his waist that held his lockpicks. Yet even as he glanced down, something caught his eye.

A glass jar rested partially beneath the desk, as if it had fallen from the desk and been kicked underneath. Next to it, a cluster of small red flowers grew from the moss.

Pimpernel, as he'd call them in the Human Realm.

But here in the Fae Realm, the flower was known as the wild fae primrose.

The Primrose must have gifted Brigid with a bouquet of the flowers he used as a symbol.

Yet that was a strangely romantic gesture and, for all of Munch's envy of the fae man's heroics, Brigid never talked about the Primrose in a romantic way.

Why would she have a bouquet of his flowers displayed in such a prominent way on her desk? And why would she try to hide the bouquet, likely from Munch when he'd arrived? Had she thought it would give away something about the Primrose? But what?

The Primrose. Who hadn't shown up for his meeting with Brigid.

The Primrose. Who had such love for humans.

The Primrose. Who was based out of the Great Library.

Oh. *Oh.* Munch was such a *dunce.*

Brigid didn't just work for the Primrose. She *was* the Primrose.

And right now, she was headed for a trap of Munch's making.

Chapter Seventeen

Munch sat back on his heels and stared at the innocent red flowers peeking up at him from the moss floor. Tentatively, he reached out and plucked one of the flowers, twirling its stem slowly between his fingers.

How hadn't he seen it before? Out of everyone, he should have realized that Brigid was capable of being the Primrose.

After all, Munch had been raised by Robin, who had pretended to be the male outlaw the Hood. She'd used the fact that everyone expected the Hood to be a man to her advantage.

Brigid had done the exact same thing with the Primrose. And yet Munch hadn't seen it. Hadn't expected it. While Robin was brash and bold even without her disguise, Brigid was a lover of pretty things. She wore pretty dresses and didn't love fighting. She didn't seem to fit the stereotype of someone who would be the leader of a league of heroes.

Why hadn't she told him? Weren't they friends?

He shook his head. Of course she hadn't told him. He was a danger. Just look at how he'd betrayed her. It might not have been on purpose, but he'd still been foolish.

More than that, he'd been foolish five years ago when he'd first met Brigid. He'd simply assumed she couldn't be the Primrose. Right from the start, he'd dismissed her rather than seeing the true depth of courage, strength, and intelligence that lay beneath her beautiful face.

No wonder she'd never told him. She didn't dare trust him.

She'd been right not to trust him. Clearly.

Right now, Brigid must be on her way to try to save the humans who would be snatched that night. She must have put together that Lord Chauvlyn was the one in charge of snatching the humans.

But had she realized that Lord Chauvlyn had figured out who she was? At least, that was what he assumed Lord Chauvlyn's smirk and nod had been all about. She didn't know that Munch had betrayed her nor what Munch knew about Lord Chauvlyn's plans.

Munch had to warn her. Somehow.

He still had a little under two hours until he was called to the faerie circle.

What if he got there first? Could he warn Brigid about Lord Chauvlyn?

There was only one way to find out.

After stuffing the primrose into a pocket, Munch scooped up the tiny blue bookwyrm, which let out a little squawk, and hurried down the stairs. The full-grown bookwyrm grumbled, as if irked that Munch hadn't taken the time to give him a belly scratch on the way down, but didn't block his way.

At the bottom, Munch set down the small bookwyrm. "Thanks for all your help tonight."

The bookwyrm bobbed its head, then slithered off.

Munch hurried through the darkened Library shelves. A few librarians were still bustling about, and the atrium still had a few master librarians and patrons. The Great Library, after all, never closed and never truly slept.

Thankfully, no one gave him more than a glance or two.

He lengthened his stride and reached for the double doors to exit the Library. But his fingers grew numb, halting just short as if he'd hit a barrier.

No. He gritted his teeth, flexed his fingers, and tried again. No, he refused to be stuck here until Lord Chauvlyn's ordered time. He had to warn Brigid.

Wait a minute. He was a forester. He knew how to evade—or partially evade, anyway—a fae's bindings. Robin had done just that years ago to save Guy.

Munch reached for his quiver. This time, he wasn't trying to reach for any of his weapons. Instead, he fumbled for the iron rod all of his family kept in their quivers for just such occasions.

Gripping the iron rod tightly with one hand, he reached for the doors once again. His fingers still tingled, but he was able to grasp the door handle and slowly pull one of the doors open. It took far more effort than it should have, but he managed to crack it open enough to slip through.

The swordmaidens on either side of the door glanced at him oddly, but he didn't stop to try to explain. He wasn't sure he could, even while gripping the iron rod.

Besides, he might get only one chance to evade the magic of the blood binding. He would save it for warning Brigid.

Such a *dunce*. He should have thought of this earlier when he'd attempted to warn Brigid. He was a forester. Robin would have his head if she realized that he'd grown so lax that iron hadn't been his first thought when dealing with the fae.

But nothing here in the Fae Realm was like it was in the Human Realm. He'd been so off-kilter that he'd forgotten to rely on his training.

That ended now. He needed to be smarter. Wiser. A forester. Robin Hood's brother.

Forget about being a hero. Right now, all he wanted to do was undo his foolish actions. If he managed to warn Brigid, he'd return to the Human Realm and forget all about his dreams of heroics. He'd go back to patrolling the Greenwood and try to put the Fae Realm and Brigid behind him.

He wasn't good enough for Brigid. She deserved so much better than someone who would betray her to the likes of Lord Chauvlyn.

Munch forced himself to take a step. Then another. Step by step, he crossed the Hall of Anywhere Doors, heading for the exit.

Would Brigid be at the faerie circle? Or had she gone back to the House to consult with his family first? Should he take the time to warn Basil and Meg?

He tried to turn toward the nearest Anywhere Door, but he rammed into a barrier, the ache flaring back into agony even with his grip on the iron.

Apparently the Anywhere Doors were too much even for the iron to counteract. He could break Lord Chauvlyn's orders only so much. Going to the faerie circle early was doable, but anything else wasn't.

Fine. He'd wait there and warn her as soon as she arrived.

Gritting his teeth, he latched his gaze on the outside doors and forced his feet in that direction. His fingers were so numb he struggled to grasp the door handle to tug it open. The door cracked open only a few inches, and he wedged his foot into the gap, all but forcing the rest of him to follow, wiggling through.

As soon as he stepped outside onto the gravel path, a tingling spread over his whole body while a burning lanced down his back.

He couldn't stop now. No matter how much it hurt, he had to keep going.

He shuffled down the gravel path, keeping his head down as he passed the few fae who were out and about at this time of night. The nearly full moon beamed silvery bright overhead, casting grotesque shadows from the castle and the houses of the village. The Tanglewood beyond remained a deep, dense black, as if ready to swallow Munch and all he loved in one, great gulp.

Another step. Another. The pain spread from his back and down into his legs. His knees ached as if gravel ground in his joints. Nails stabbed through the soles of his feet with every step.

But at least he still *could* take another step. As long as he gripped the iron rod, he could push past the clawing bounds of his captivity to continue onward.

Somehow, he reached the edge of the Tanglewood. He hardly even looked where he was going, letting his feet direct him. Perhaps it was that innate pathfinding sense. Or maybe he was only allowed to walk in the direction of the right faerie circle. But he just knew that he had to go in that direction, whatever direction it was.

The black trees of the Tanglewood drew him into their depths. Within moments, he couldn't see the edge where he'd been. Nor did he have any clue which way was what.

Didn't matter. He simply had to keep going. One step. Another.

The pain spread up his torso until each breath ached hot and scratchy inside his chest.

Only a few more steps. Then he could warn Brigid and save her from Lord Chauvlyn.

Munch didn't know what would happen then. Would Brigid know how to save him from Lord Chauvlyn? What about all the villagers who were being snatched even as he stumbled through the Tanglewood? Or the poor humans who had already been taken to the Realm of Monsters and even now awaited gruesome deaths on Midsummer Night?

Surely Brigid would know what to do. He just had to get to her.

His head pounded, a throb beginning behind his eyes and stabbing at his temples. Something wet drooled down his upper lip, and when he touched his face with his free hand, his fingers came away slick with red. Blood.

His toe caught on a root, and he tripped, falling to his knees.

A part of him just wanted to flop to the forest floor right there and not get up. It hurt too much.

But if he gave up, Brigid would be captured by Lord Chauvlyn. She would die thanks to Munch's foolishness.

Blindly, Munch rested a hand against the nearest tree and shoved to his feet. He staggered onward. Surely he had only a few more feet to go. It couldn't be that much farther.

His head was going to split in two like a melon chopped by an ax. He coughed, and it rattled wet and raw inside his chest.

He was going to die if he kept this up.

He chuckled a wet, harsh attempt at a laugh. What did it matter? Lord Chauvlyn planned to kill him anyway.

When he stumbled again, he fell against a tree, then slid to his knees. He didn't have the strength to immediately push to his feet.

He blinked at the forest ahead of him. There was something about the forest. Were the trees arranged in a circle? And were those marking stones?

A faerie circle. He knelt at the edge of a faerie circle.

He sagged more fully against the tree. This had to be the right one. Surely his instincts hadn't steered him wrong.

Gathering all the breath he had left, he called into the gloomy forest, "Brigid! Are you here? Brigid!"

His voice echoed off the trees. The brief cessation of the crickets was his only answer.

Munch settled against the tree and let his eyes close. She wasn't here yet. He'd wait right here and warn her as soon as she arrived.

Once he did that, it didn't matter what happened to him. He would have at least saved Brigid. It was far from the heroic ballad he'd hoped for himself, but it would have to be enough.

MUNCH JOLTED as the agony he'd been in for hours simply vanished. One moment he had been curled into a ball at the pain wracking his joints, and the next it was gone.

His time was up. Lord Chauvlyn would be here any moment.

Where was Brigid?

Munch pushed to his feet, using the tree at the edge of the faerie circle to steady himself. He peered into the surrounding darkness of the Tanglewood, but he didn't see anyone else.

Where was she? She was the Primrose. Surely she'd be here, attempting to rescue the humans Lord Chauvlyn was snatching from the Human Realm even now.

Yet if she came, it would be a trap. Lord Chauvlyn knew she was the Primrose and would be ready for her.

The heaviness of the magic around him pressed harder, growing so thick he could barely breathe.

A shimmer filled the faerie circle a moment before Lord Chauvlyn rode through on what wasn't exactly a horse but that was the closest word Munch had for it. The creature was narrow and bony, but its head was large and blocky to accommodate the sharp, pointed teeth that filled its slavering jaws. Its coat was a dull black that seemed to soak up any hint of light that touched it.

Lord Chauvlyn's gaze landed on Munch, and his mouth twitched with a smirk.

Hard on Lord Chauvlyn's heels, two more fae mounted on the sharp-toothed, meat-eating horses herded a group of humans into the Fae Realm. Husbands held their wives close, even as blood streamed from cuts on their heads or other wounds they had received while trying to fight back. Mothers clutched their children to them, as if to protect their little ones just a few moments longer. Siblings fisted their hands and appeared ready to fight to protect each other. Old men and women staggered forward, leaning on each other for support. Younger men and women helped the elderly as best they could, even as they glared at their fae captors.

The fae deftly directed their horses as if the humans were cattle they were driving toward the slaughter. When a human stumbled, the fae cracked whips or let their horses snap at the poor human, adding another bloody wound to the growing collection.

Lord Chauvlyn scanned the surrounding forest, a wrinkle of a frown puckering his mouth and forehead. Perhaps he, too, was puzzled by Brigid's absence.

Munch tried to reach for his weapons, but even with his hand on his iron rod, he couldn't seem to get a grip on his sword or his arrows. He gritted his teeth, a growl building in his throat. He was so frustratingly *helpless*. And there was nothing he could do about it. No way to fight his way out of it. His only hope was for Brigid to rescue him.

And yet he hoped against all hope that she wouldn't even attempt it. This was a trap. *He* was the trap.

Lord Chauvlyn swung his gaze to Munch, and the smirk

returned to his face. "I see the Primrose is late. No matter. She will come. Not only do I have them—" Lord Chauvlyn gestured to the crowd of frightened humans, "—but I have you. And I believe the Primrose will come for you even if you were the only captive I had."

Munch crossed his arms and glared back at Lord Chauvlyn. A defiant glare was the only thing he had left to him, so he'd glare death at the fae lord with every scrap of courage he had in him. "You can't just steal her the way you stole me or these humans. She's a member of the Court of Knowledge."

Lord Chauvlyn laughed, a dark sound that shivered through the night. "I couldn't capture her back at the Great Library—pesky laws of hospitality and courts and all that. But if she attacks me while I am escorting humans I have rightfully stolen, then no laws prevent me from placing a captive binding on her and taking her wherever I wish. If she attempts to rescue you—and she will, I'm sure—then she forfeits all the protections of her court."

Was Lord Chauvlyn right? Did Brigid value Munch enough to risk everything for him?

Not likely. Munch might have been infatuated with her for years—falling for her, even—but he hadn't been in love with her. He couldn't, since he hadn't known the whole truth about her until a few hours ago.

Nor could she be in love with him. Love couldn't flourish with such truths withheld.

But this was Brigid. Perhaps she didn't need to love someone to risk herself for them. She put herself in this exact same danger every time she rescued a human from the fae. Of course she'd do it for him as well.

Don't do it this time. For once, save yourself.

Munch tried to will the words to wherever Brigid was, but he knew it was just futile wishing, even here in the Fae Realm.

Lord Chauvlyn lifted a hand and languidly waved to Munch. "Take off your weapons. You won't need them where you are going."

Munch gripped the iron rod in his quiver, but his body shook with the compulsion to obey Lord Chauvlyn's order. The agony flared through his bones again, and a hot trickle of blood dripped from his nose once more.

He wouldn't be able to fight this for long.

There was no point. Lord Chauvlyn wouldn't let him keep his weapons, and he owned Munch at this point.

Munch breathed out a choked breath and reached for the buckle of his sword belt with his free hand. He fumbled at the belt latch, turning slightly to hide his other hand as he slipped the iron rod from his quiver and tucked it into the waistband of his trousers at the small of his back. It was uncomfortable, since the iron rod was about a foot long and an inch in diameter.

But it wasn't a weapon, exactly. Hopefully that would evade the magic enough that he could keep it without intense pain.

He eased his weapons' belt to the ground so that his arrows in his quiver wouldn't be damaged. Not that it was such a worry with the spongy moss-covered ground, but he wouldn't want his sword to fall on top of the quiver and snap any of the arrows.

He slid his unstrung bow from its sheath on his back and gently set it on top of his sword and quiver.

For a moment, he halted, hoping that would be enough to appease the magic.

Pain lanced through his bones, and his hand shot toward the knife in his boot of its own accord.

Nope. He'd have to divest himself of all his weapons whether he liked it or not.

He drew the knife from his boot, the dagger from its sheath

down his back, then the last one from the sheath at the small of his back.

Once he set the last weapon on the pile, the crushing compulsion vanished. He let out a breath. Good. The magic hadn't counted the iron rod as a weapon. Nor had it demanded that he divest himself of the lockpicks that remained safely tucked in an inner pocket.

Lord Chauvlyn twitched his fingers. "Join the others."

Munch stumbled forward under the force of the magic, but he didn't try to fight it. There would be no point. At this point, his fate was tied to that of these captured humans. He'd rather stand with them.

He joined the crowd of frightened humans, standing near a woman with several young children clustered around her and an elderly couple. The old woman hunched, her back stooped with age, her shawl tight over her head and hair in the same way as all the village grandmothers wore their shawls back home in Gysborn. He might have smiled at the familiarity, if this old woman hadn't been clutching the shawl like it was a shield to hide from the fae. Her husband gripped her arm to steady her, sending worried looks down at her.

Lord Chauvlyn cast one last glance over the forest before he turned his horse to face deeper into the Tanglewood. "Let's move them out."

The fae rode their horses closer, and the horses gnashed their fangs, drawing blood from those standing too close. A few of the humans screamed. Children cried.

A fae on his horse lunged toward them, and Munch quickly stepped between the horse and the young family, raising his arm to protect himself.

The horse's ears flattened against its skull, and its teeth flashed. Pain lanced up Munch's arm as the fae horse sank its teeth into his forearm.

Munch stumbled back as the horse released him. Blood welled from the wound, and he pressed his other hand over it.

The woman and her children gaped at him with wide eyes. He shook his head and motioned for them to start moving. He would be fine. He'd been wounded worse than this fighting fae monsters.

As the fae herded them deeper into the Tanglewood, Munch positioned himself between a young family and an elderly couple. He helped one of the children over a large log, then he dropped back just as the old man helped his hunched and shaky wife climb over the log. She all but fell into Munch's arms on the other side, and he steadied her with a grip on her upper arms. When she was steady, he reached out and steadied the old man as he clambered over.

Once both were over the log, Munch passed the old woman back to her husband.

Her husband gave him a nod. The woman patted Munch's arm and spoke in a creaky voice. "Thank you, young man."

The thunk of hooves on the moss was his only warning before sharp teeth nipped at his back, piercing skin even through the layers of his tunic and shirt.

Munch hissed, arching his back at the pain. But he resisted the instinct to jump away and instead stood his ground between the horse and the elderly couple.

"Keep moving, human." His voice ringing deep and resonant against his black mask, the fae cracked his whip over Munch's head. He said the word *human* in the same tone one might say *cockroach* or *rat*.

Munch waited until the couple trundled forward before he set off once again.

The forest closed around them, far darker and more tangled than even moments ago. Vines draped down from the branches, blocking their way, while lights flickered in the distance among the trees.

Was the enchanted forest helping them or trying to stop them? He couldn't tell. Perhaps it was neither. The forest could be neutral, a power beyond caring about such things.

Munch tried to discreetly glance around the forest as they passed. Where was Brigid? Her League? Surely they weren't going to allow Lord Chauvlyn to snatch another village of frightened humans and take them back to the Realm of Monsters?

She shouldn't come. She wouldn't be able to rescue them, and instead would find herself captured along with them.

If he spotted her, he'd have to warn her away. She needed to stay away.

With each step, his breath wound tighter and more painful in his chest. Hope for rescue. Fear for Brigid. Fear for himself and these people once they reached the Realm of Monsters. Ache for his family.

The forest opened somewhat, the trees farther apart. More lights danced between the trees and amongst the ferns carpeting the forest floor.

No places to hide here. No chance that Brigid was planning an ambush here.

Or perhaps this was the perfect place for an ambush because it was so unexpected. That was something his sister Robin would have done as an outlaw, and surely that meant it was something Brigid might do as the Primrose.

Lord Chauvlyn rode straight and tall on his monster horse, leading them onward without so much as a hint of worry.

The little boy tripped over a root and howled, tears streaming down his face. His mother hurried to his side, but she already held a baby in her arms and clutched the hand of a child barely big enough to walk on her own.

The nearest mounted fae was turning in their direction, the hand with the whip raising.

Munch darted forward and knelt. But he glanced up at the mother before he touched the boy. "May I help?"

The mother hesitated, then glanced at the fae. Her eyes widened, and she nodded.

Munch picked the boy up, turning to shield the boy as the whip cracked, its end slapping against Munch's cheek.

The boy wailed louder and buried his face against Munch's shirt.

Munch shot a glare at the fae and marched forward, carrying the boy and sheltering him even as the whip cracked again.

How could anyone—fae or human—be so cruel to turn a blind eye to the fear and pain they were causing? These fae were marching these humans to their deaths, and yet they took pleasure in it.

It was the rawest, deepest evil bubbling to the surface, unbound by laws and encouraged by this mysterious master. All in the name of freedom from the laws binding the Fae Realm and Realm of Monsters.

As the boy quieted into sniffs, Munch glanced down at the top of his head. "My name is Munch."

The boy gave another sniff and peeked up at him. "That's a funny name."

The boy's mother glanced over at the two of them. "It isn't nice to say things like that."

Munch let himself laugh quietly, hoping to calm all the children with light conversation. "You're right. It is a funny name. It's a nickname for my full name. Mungoe."

This time, the little boy giggled. "That's an even funnier name."

The boy's mother sighed, as if giving up on trying to teach her boy good manners.

"It is," Munch agreed as he hefted the child into a more comfortable position in his arms. The boy was heavier than he looked, but Munch didn't want to set him down and risk him tripping again. "But my mother liked it. It was the name of a hero in an old ballad."

A glance over his shoulder reassured him that the elderly couple was still stumping along as best they could.

The young mother held her baby closer, her grip tight on her child's hand. "Don't worry. The Primrose will rescue us. As will your father."

The boy in Munch's arms nodded, as if with perfect confidence in both of those statements.

Munch pressed his mouth shut. He didn't want to disagree and dash their hopes. But the children's missing father had little hope of tracking them into the Fae Realm, no matter how determined he was. And Brigid still hadn't made an appearance. A good thing for her safety, but a bad thing for theirs.

The fae herded them through the open forest, and nothing happened. No Primrose dropped out of the trees to rescue them. No trap sprung around Lord Chauvlyn.

Instead, something gnawed at the edges of Munch's instincts, growing more persistent by the moment until the gnawing turned into a sharp clawing.

Through the darkness and the thick trees, a ring of stones formed of black obsidian came into view, the very sight of it setting Munch's teeth on edge and the hair at the back of his neck prickling.

Unlike every faerie circle Munch had ever seen, this circle didn't contain the heat-haze-like shimmer of magic. Instead, something dark and murky twisted and churned inside the ring of stones.

That tight knot in his chest drew taut until he could barely breathe past it. This was how the fae were capturing humans and bringing them into the Realm of Monsters. Somehow, the fae had anchored a rift into the Realm of Monsters and turned it into an established circle.

Brigid hadn't come. A good thing, and yet it meant he was going to die. Everyone here was going to die.

Chapter Eighteen

Munch swallowed and tucked the boy's head against his shoulder. "Squeeze your eyes shut and don't look until I tell you, all right?"

He wasn't sure what it would be like going through a rift into the Realm of Monsters, but if the circles from the Human Realm and Fae Realm were any indication, it was probably going to be disorienting and more than a little scary.

The young mother's face paled, and she glanced down at the tiny girl next to her. Probably worried that her grip on the girl's hand would slip and she'd get lost in the magical paths connecting the realms.

Munch adjusted his grip on the boy, knelt, then picked up the girl in his other arm. As he straightened, he met the mother's gaze. "I'll carry them through so they won't get lost."

"Thank you." The mother wrapped both arms around her baby, straightened her shoulders, then faced the blackness as the fae drove them toward it.

The first few humans halted at the edge, gripping the stones to avoid stepping inside.

Lord Chauvlyn nudged his horse forward. It bit a man in the shoulder, and the man cried out, letting go of the obsidian standing stones and stumbling forward. He was instantly swallowed by the black rift. Yet his scream echoed back to them from somewhere beyond.

The two children flinched and huddled in Munch's arms. He stuck close to their mother, though he glanced at the elderly couple behind them. He didn't have enough hands to help them all, and the children would have to be his priority. Even as he watched, a young woman stepped forward to help the couple.

The screaming grew as human after human was shoved into the rift.

As he and the young family reached the edge of the dark circle, Munch sent one last glance over his shoulder. Just dark forest, the masked fae on their vicious horses, and the rest of the scared humans, including the elderly man with his wife pressing her face into his shoulder.

No Brigid. No rescue. No way to escape.

When it was their turn, Munch sent one last glare up at Lord Chauvlyn, faced the rift, and stepped through before the fae lord set his horse on them.

As soon as he stepped into the rift, pain tore over his skin as if he'd been sliced by hundreds of tiny knives, then had salt rubbed in the thousands of wounds. With each heartbeat, the pain intensified, going from hundreds of papercuts to the claws of a thousand cats scratching every inch of his skin.

In his arms, the two children cried and squirmed, fighting him as they tried to escape the pain.

He gritted his teeth and held on tight. If he let them go, they could find themselves lost in the vast, empty darkness between the realms, too young to find the faerie paths that would lead them home.

He forced himself to move, taking another shaking step forward.

Then, he stumbled into a fetid heat and hazy twilight, surrounded by another ring of obsidian stones. In his arms, the two children sobbed, their faces buried against his shirt.

The young mother stumbled out of the darkness, her baby wailing in her arms. Tears streaked down her own face, and she reached a trembling hand toward each of her children, touching their hair and soothing with her touch.

But she didn't tell the children that it would be all right. Neither did Munch. Right now, he couldn't bring himself to lie to them.

They stood in a dead, rotting forest. The spindly, black skeletons of trees jutted from mushy, black detritus beneath their feet. Strips of bark and desiccated vines hung from the trees like strips of rotting flesh. A stench like that of a three-day dead animal clogged the air.

Even more fae mounted on those meat-eating horses awaited in this forest, though these fae didn't wear masks and they carried long spears along with their whips and the swords at their hips. Some of them faced the cluster of humans who had stumbled through the circle, but the rest pointed outward. As if their greater duty wasn't keeping the humans in line but keeping the monsters that roamed this realm from attacking.

The elderly couple stumbled out of the black rift, both of them falling to their knees in the muck. The old man shook like a leaf in a storm, and his wife patted his hand, though Munch couldn't see her face thanks to the shawl she wore over her head and the way her back was hunched with age. The young woman who had been helping them collapsed to her knees next to them, tears streaking her own face.

Munch passed the young girl back to her mother, then set

the young boy on his feet next to them. When the little family was steady and headed toward the others, Munch turned and reached for the couple. He gripped the old man's hand and pulled him to his feet.

The old man gripped Munch's arm, still wobbling on his legs. His eyes were red-rimmed, sunken in the wrinkles on his face, the toll of crossing the rift.

Still steadying the old man, Munch held out a hand to the old woman.

She took his hand, and he pulled her to her feet. She wobbled for a moment, then reached for the old man once again.

Her husband obligingly held out his arm, and she clasped his elbow.

The rest of the humans stumbled through the rift, and Munch helped each of them before sending them on to join the rest of the group.

A screech came from high above, and a harpy swooped down toward them.

One of their captors produced a crossbow, aimed at the harpy, and shot. The arrow struck the harpy in its wing, and it shrieked as it plummeted to the ground. Even as it thumped onto the rotting muck of the dead forest's floor, another fae guard spurred his horse forward and plunged his spear into the harpy.

Munch shook his head and helped another family as they recovered after the ordeal of the rift. Right now, they were safer with their captors than they would be if they tried to run, weaponless as they were.

As another human—a young man—stumbled through the rift and fell to his knees, he was nearly trampled as Lord Chauvlyn rode through, his fae horse snorting and prancing.

The rest of Lord Chauvlyn's fae riders burst through the rift, their horses rolling their eyes and snorting. Once they were all through, they pulled off their masks and stuffed them in their saddlebags.

Munch's fingers grew even colder. The fae had been wearing masks to hide themselves from their fellow fae. They didn't care if the humans saw their faces because all these humans—including Munch—were going to die.

The fae herded them forward once again, and Munch helped the elderly and the children wade through the muck coating the forest floor. Ahead, a black castle rose above the dead trees, its towers blocky and brutal.

By the time they broke out of the forest and stepped onto the castle's drawbridge over a sludgy moat, their trousers or skirts were black and damp up to their knees.

In the castle's courtyard, the fae dismounted, then used their spears to herd the people into a tower and down a curving stairway.

Munch picked up both the little boy and little girl again, carrying them while he followed their mother. The elderly couple seemed to be managing the stairs all right, though they were slow enough that the fae jabbed them with the butts of their spears several times.

The stairs continued deeper and deeper into the earth. A stale, musty scent wrapped around them, and the children Munch carried whimpered at the darkness, which was broken only by the occasional torch, flickering with a strange, deathly green light.

As the stairs finally reached a landing, passageways stretched out before them. Voices, cries, and whimpers echoed from the darkness while the stench of unwashed bodies and excrement wafted on the already badly musty air.

This was where all these people would wait to die, even the children he currently held as safe as he could in his arms.

Munch still had his lockpicks. Would he be able to pick the locks and rescue these people once they were locked in the dungeons? But how would he sneak all these people out of this castle and through the rift once he unlocked the cells?

The fae herded them into a passageway. As they passed the cells, the gaunt, hollow-eyed humans within stared at them with something akin to pity. Yet it was the pity of a shared circumstance, knowing they were all bound for the same horrible end.

At the first empty cell, the fae shoved a bunch of them inside, then swung the barred door shut with a clang.

As the fae shoved more people into the next cell, Lord Chauvlyn sauntered through the crowd and halted in front of Munch. "It seems the Primrose doesn't care about you as much as I thought. No matter. You'll make a good addition to my collection. Perhaps I'll send my riders to capture your forester brothers next. They need to be taught a lesson about the power and superiority of the fae."

Munch swallowed, gripped the children tighter, and glared back at Lord Chauvlyn. He wasn't going to dignify the threat with a reply. Will and John could handle Lord Chauvlyn. And if Robin and Guy got involved, well, Lord Chauvlyn would quickly learn he'd tangled with the wrong humans.

Lord Chauvlyn smirked, as if he found Munch's attempt at defiance highly amusing. He drew a key from a pocket. "Don't even think about trying to escape. The locks on these doors are enchanted. They can only be opened with this key. A key I keep on my person at all times."

Munch gritted his teeth, his heart sinking in his chest. So much for his idea of picking the locks. It seemed even that escape was denied him.

Lord Chauvlyn tucked the key back into his pocket. "Now, step inside. I have matters to attend to."

Heat built inside Munch's chest, but he stepped into the cell without resisting. He didn't want to give the fae any reason to whip him or beat him with their spears, thus putting the two young children in danger.

The young mother hurried to follow him inside the cell so that she wasn't separated from her children.

The elderly couple were shoved inside next. The old woman stumbled, falling against Lord Chauvlyn.

Lord Chauvlyn's smirk twisted into a grimace, and he shoved the old woman away from him hard enough that she fell to the floor of the dungeon cell.

Her husband stumbled inside and knelt next to her, his knees creaking.

Lord Chauvlyn glowered and slammed the cell door, the lock clicking shut automatically. After drawing in a deep breath as if to gather himself, that slick smirk returned to his face as he met Munch's gaze one last time. "I dare the Primrose to rescue you now. If she tries, she will be captured, and she will die right along with all the pathetic humans she tried to save."

With that, the fae lord spun on his heels and marched down the passageway, his fae cronies falling in behind him.

Munch waited, silent and still, as the sound of the fae's bootsteps faded.

This was it. He'd utterly failed at anything resembling hero-ism. Instead, he'd just gotten himself killed. Would his family ever learn what had happened to him? Would he want them to?

Once Lord Chauvlyn and his minions were gone, the murmur of voices started up again from all the cells around them. The captives in the other cells called to their group, asking where they were from and what had happened.

Munch set the two children down by their mother. They toddled to her and wrapped their arms around her legs, holding tight. She patted their heads and whispered soothing words.

With his hands free, Munch turned to the old woman, who had managed to push herself into a sitting position.

Munch knelt next to the elderly couple and held out a hand. "Here. Let me help you up."

The old woman tossed back the shawl from her head, revealing golden-brown hair tucked into a bun with only a few wisps framing her face powdered gray. The face that turned toward him was far from old as she gave him a grin and waved to the old man. "Help Percy. His knees aren't what they used to be."

Munch's hand remained frozen, stretched out to her, as he gaped at her. "Brigid?"

"Yes, yes, it's me." Brigid used Munch's shoulder to push to her feet. She extended her hand to the old man. "Thank you, Percy, for playing along with my disguise."

The old man took her hand, then tottered to his feet with her help. He shook her hand and gave her something almost like a bow. "It was my pleasure, Primrose."

Munch's brain remained frozen inside his skull. He still couldn't reconcile the sight of her here, in this dungeon. "Brigid? What? How?"

"Oh, that was easy. I let the Tanglewood lead me to the faerie circle, then I hid outside of it." Brigid shrugged, then gave a wince. "Sorry I couldn't reveal myself when you arrived. It would have ruined my plan. Once Lord Chauvlyn and his riders came through, I simply joined the bustle. It wasn't like they had even bothered to count the humans they'd captured. A human is just a creature to them. Like a herd of pigs. Percy here graciously agreed to pretend to be my husband."

"And no one else noticed? Or said anything?" Munch glanced around at the other captives.

The young mother gave a small shrug, then revealed the flower she'd tucked into the baby's blanket. "She is the Primrose."

The old man grinned and also held out his hand, revealing a small red flower.

Murmurs traveled down the passageway, this time filled with hope, as tiny red flowers were passed from hand to hand through the bars from the recent captives to those who had been enduring this darkness and misery for days.

Brigid sat up a little straighter, running her fingers through the strands of her hair to shake loose the powder. "And thank you, Munch, for providing the distraction I needed to integrate into the group. All that banter with Lord Chauvlyn and disarming your weapons, it was perfect. Just what I needed. Even the other fae were distracted, watching you and Lord Chauvlyn."

"But…how?" Munch gripped the barred door and stumbled to his feet. He couldn't quite meet Brigid's gaze. How did she even know he'd be there? "I…"

His windpipe squeezed shut under the force of Lord Chauvlyn's orders. Even now, Munch was still blood bound to the fae lord. He couldn't speak of what had happened or what he had learned.

The weight of Brigid's hand rested on his arm, and she didn't speak until he gathered the courage to peek at her. When he did, he found her eyes filled with a mix of sparkling humor and deep compassion.

"I know everything. You looked at the note I left for Rosaline, and Lord Chauvlyn forced you to tell him. I figured out as much while Lord Chauvlyn was in the reading nook." Brigid's voice remained soft and compassionate instead of angry as he would have expected. "I saw the wound on your neck and the cut on his palm. You've been blood bound to him. It wasn't too great a leap of logic to know he'd order you to join him at the circle. He couldn't leave you lollygagging around the Library forever. Your showing up early was a surprise. Well done."

His breath whooshed out as he sagged against his grip on the barred door. She had figured out everything.

Of course she had. She hadn't become the Primrose by being as foolish as he had been. No, she was fiendishly clever beneath her empty-headed mask. He should not mistake her love of pretty things—exaggerated for the benefit of her disguise—and her beautiful face as a lack of intelligence. A woman could be both beautiful and intelligent. She could love pretty dresses and still be clever.

This was what he'd gotten wrong about Brigid all those years ago. He'd only had his sister's example of strength—that of wearing trousers and boldly fighting like a man. That was who Robin was.

Brigid wore dresses and fought with wit instead of weapons but that didn't make her less strong. That was who she was.

He gathered himself, trying to say what was on his heart without triggering the binding.

"I was so foolish. I so badly wanted to be a hero that I did things I shouldn't have." Munch shook his head, staring down at Brigid's hand on his arm. "All of my siblings are so heroic. I just wanted to be like them."

"You are." This time, Brigid reached out and touched his cheek.

The soft touch sent thoughts of kissing her swirling through his head, but he pushed them aside as he met her gaze. He'd betrayed her. He'd never be worthy of loving her. "I'm not."

"Being a hero isn't about earning glory for yourself." Brigid held his gaze. "It's about self-sacrifice for the sake of others. I watched you, Munch. I saw the way you helped everyone else on the journey here, taking the blows meant for them. That is what makes you a hero."

Her hand dropped from his cheek, gently trailing over the bloody tear in his sleeve where the bite from the monster horse still throbbed and drooled blood.

He wasn't sure he believed her. But he forced himself to nod.

Brigid dropped her hand, and her grin widened. "It actually turned out for the best. He might have figured out that I was the Primrose, but I confirmed that he was involved. After that, the plan came together rather quickly, truth be told. How better to figure out where he was taking the captured humans than let him take me there himself?"

It was a rather brilliant idea, now that he thought of it. But there was one, glaring problem.

Munch rattled the door. "We're still locked in. And I can't pick the locks."

"Oh, that." Brigid's grin took on a smug edge as she reached into her pocket and drew out the key that Lord Chauvlyn had flashed about a moment ago. "That's why I took this."

A chuckle burst from him before he could stop it. "I see my sister taught you well."

"That she did." Brigid reached through the bars, stuck the key in the lock, then twisted it.

With a satisfying click, the lock opened, and the door swung loose in Munch's grip.

Brigid stepped out of the cell, turned, and grabbed Munch. She drew him out of the cell, her grip tight on his hand. As soon as he was outside of the cell, she met his gaze, the look in her eyes more somber than it had been a moment ago. "I claim you for mine."

Something sparked deep in his chest, but it was gone as if snuffed out before he could pinpoint the sensation. The weight of Lord Chauvlyn's binding still pressed on him, squeezing his chest.

"I'm still—" His teeth snapped shut so fast they clacked painfully as the words choked in his throat.

Her soft, brown eyes met his, filled with that aching compassion. "You're still blood bound. I know. It will be broken. But until then, you won't be able to leave this castle with the others. The lesser claim I've placed on you should allow you to at least leave the dungeon. You were never given specific orders to stay here. But the blood binding won't let you attempt more of an escape than that."

Munch nodded and reached for the iron rod he'd stuffed into his waistband. "I have this. It helped me push through a direct order before."

The warm smile that lit her face bolstered him, as if she saw him as more than his foolishness. It had him standing taller, straighter, rather than bowed with the burden of his betrayal as he had been a moment ago.

"That will prove helpful. Now, listen carefully." Brigid took his hand, pressed the key into his palm, then curled his fingers over it. "I'm entrusting the task of releasing these people to you. As you lead each person from the cells, please touch each one and say, 'The Primrose claims you.' My lesser claim on you as my agent should undo their captive bindings and allow them to escape."

Munch nodded, the key warm against his palm. "I will. But where will you be?"

Brigid flashed a grin at him, yet the sparkle in her eyes was somehow sad. "Distracting Chauvlyn, buying you time, and breaking your blood binding."

"Brigid…" He wanted to protest that he wasn't leaving without her. To tell her that it was too dangerous.

But she was the Primrose. She took on dangers like this all the time. As she'd clearly demonstrated, she knew what she was doing. Far more than he did when it came to the Fae Realm. He would have to trust that she could take care of herself.

She tensed, something in her expression falling.

This was what he'd done before. The reason she hadn't trusted him with her secret, even more than just the danger he posed by being a human who could be forced to spill her secrets. He hadn't seen her strength years ago. He'd just assumed that she had a background role, that she couldn't possibly be the Primrose.

But her heroics weren't those of sword and battle. She fought with her wit and disguises and sleight of hand. It didn't make her any less brave or bold if she didn't pick up a sword or bash enemies over the head.

"I was just going to say, be careful." Munch reached for her, then let his hand drop without touching her, all too aware of all the eyes pinned on the two of them. Now wasn't the time to air their feelings. They had hundreds of captives to save, a fae lord to defeat, and realms to return to.

When Brigid's grin returned to her face, it held a warmth he'd never seen before. "I will. Stay safe yourself. It's going to be no easy feat to sneak all these people out of the castle and to the rift even with my distraction."

No, it wouldn't be. Even if they weren't caught by Lord Chauvlyn and his riders, there would be the dangers of the realm itself. It was called the Realm of Monsters for a reason.

And if his blood binding wasn't broken, he could go no

farther than the gates of the castle. He wouldn't be able to protect these people from the monsters that lay between them and safety.

"If all goes to plan, you should receive help shortly." Brigid set off down the hallway, waving over her shoulder airily at him as she went, much as she'd done when they'd parted in the Great Library. "Now I'm off to have a lovely chat with our host. I'm sure Lord Chauvlyn is going to be greatly pleased to see me."

That he would. Munch's stomach clenched, but he couldn't help the slight grin that crossed his face. He'd have to trust that Brigid could handle Lord Chauvlyn. She'd been outsmarting him for years. Surely this time would be no different, even if she was walking right into his trap.

Munch turned back to the cell, where the old man and the young mother and her children still waited, staring at him.

He reached for the old man and tugged him from the cell. "The Primrose claims you."

Once the old man stood in the passageway, Munch repeated the process for the young mother and her children.

"Please, spread the word that the Primrose is here, and to stay quiet. I'll get to everyone shortly," Munch told the old man. "Ask everyone to wait for me at the bottom of the stairs."

The young mother hustled her children in that direction. "I'll wait there and make sure no one tries to leave before you arrive."

Munch nodded to her, then moved on to the next cell. This was going to take a while to release each person one at a time. He'd have to hurry, both so that he could rescue everyone before their desperation to escape overwhelmed their good sense and before the guards noticed anything was amiss.

Hopefully Brigid had a doozy of a distraction planned.

Hundreds of people didn't sneak quietly, even with the best of intentions.

But more than that, he hoped against hope that this plan of hers didn't involve her sacrificing herself for everyone else. Surely she had a plan to get out of Lord Chauvlyn's clutches once she fell into them.

Chapter Nineteen

Brigid hurried down the dungeon passageway. A few people reached for her, but most remained silent except for a few whispers of *Primrose.* Word had traveled fast, and she was counting on the force of the legends to help Munch keep the people in line. If they panicked and made a run for it on their own, they'd be caught, and Munch right along with them.

At the base of the stairs, she quickly shucked out of her old woman disguise, stuffing the old ratty dress and shawl into her pocket. Beneath, she wore a red bodice with a red, pleated skirt that fell to her knees. Pink leggings and soft leather boots completed the outfit. The bodice and the edge of the skirt were embroidered with wild fae primroses in a slightly darker, shining red thread.

The House had outdone itself when providing her with this outfit. Especially since she'd had only a few moments to let it work before she'd had to leave again to get to the circle before anyone else arrived.

She took her hair out of its bun, tucked the pins in her

pocket, then pulled out a brush. After a quick brush, her hair lay gleaming across her shoulders.

Once ready, she tiptoed up the stairs, then peeked out into the base of the tower. Thankfully, no door barred her way, so there was nothing to creak and give her away. Inside the room, two fae guards played a board game at a table.

Time to lure them away.

With a sunny smile gracing her face, she glided into the room, then took a few steps to the side so that it didn't appear quite so much like she'd just come from the dungeon.

By the time the guards jumped to their feet, knocking over the table with their game, and turned to her, she was leaning against the wall nonchalantly.

She gestured languidly at them. "Good evening, gentlemen. Could you please take me to your lord? I'm sure he's around here somewhere, brooding over his victory."

The guards gaped at her for a long moment, glanced at each other, then back at her as if still too stunned to move.

"No matter. I'll just find him myself. No need to escort me." She sashayed toward the door, and she had it open before either of the guards moved.

By the time she stepped into the courtyard, both of them were hurrying to catch up with her. Good. She'd gotten them so discombobulated that it hadn't even occurred to them that one of them should stay to guard the dungeon.

One of them grabbed her arm. "Where do you think you're going?"

"I'm going to see Lord Chauvlyn." Brigid flashed her grin up at the guard. "He will want to see me. I'm the Primrose. I'm sure he told you to watch for me."

"Um, yes." The guard blinked at her, not letting go of her arm, even though his grip wasn't that tight.

Brigid glanced around the courtyard. A light shone in the

window of the main tower rising from the keep. "Ah, I see where he is. Thank you for your help, gentlemen."

She pulled free of the guard's grip and swept off across the courtyard, keeping her pace deceptively quick.

The guards had to trot to keep up with her, and they didn't try to stop her again.

At the doors to the keep, they met with two more guards. All she had to do was announce that she was the Primrose, and the guards stepped aside before joining her little procession into the keep and up the tower.

By the time they reached the landing and stood before the door, several more guards had joined her, as if they feared she would somehow slip away if she wasn't fastidiously guarded.

One of the guards reached to knock on Lord Chauvlyn's door, but she brushed past him, lifted the latch, and flung the door open.

"What is the meaning of—" Lord Chauvlyn whirled from his spot behind his desk, but he halted as his gaze landed on Brigid. A slow, slick smirk spread across his face. "Brigid. Or should I say, Primrose."

Brigid smiled brightly right back. "You can call me whatever you want, Lord Chaublin."

"Lord Chauvlyn," the fae lord growled under his breath before he turned to his guards. "Where did you find her?"

"She was on her way to the dungeon." One of the dungeon guards gestured to her. "We caught her before she got inside."

She hid her smirk behind an empty smile. At least, that was what they thought. It didn't occur to them that she had been coming up from the dungeon.

"Good. You are dismissed." Lord Chauvlyn waved to them, and the guards bowed before shutting the door behind them.

Hopefully most of them would linger outside of the door out of curiosity, assuming that the biggest threat had already been apprehended. Those that returned to their posts would remain distracted, wondering about her presence.

Brigid swayed across the room before she perched daintily on a corner of his desk, crossing her ankles primly. "Well, Lord Chaullin…"

"Lord Chauvlyn."

"You have me now." From where she was sitting, she couldn't see much out the window through the reflected glare of the lamp in the room. But Lord Chauvlyn put his back to the window to better glare at her, meaning that he definitely wouldn't see anything. She exaggerated a frown and gestured at him. "I see your clothing choices haven't improved. I take it the Realm of Monsters doesn't have any more competent tailors than the Court of Revels."

"My clothing is fine." Lord Chauvlyn stalked toward her and stopped only a foot away, looming over her. "Now tell me, what are you planning? I have hundreds of people in my dungeon. I have your young man blood bound to me. I will torture him unless you tell me what I want to know."

Brigid's fists clenched of their own accord as she tried to quell the panic at the thought of Munch being tortured.

She let her frown deepen as she regarded Lord Chauvlyn for several more moments as if she were deep in thought. She had thrown him for a loop by showing up here rather than attacking while he was in the Fae Realm. Since she'd come here willingly, he couldn't put a captive binding on her, and he was just off-kilter enough that he didn't dare make his move until he figured out her plan.

Finally, she spoke, as if she'd found the answer to a very difficult problem. "It's the cut of the shirt. It isn't doing you any favors. If your tailor took it in a bit more at the waist, it wouldn't bag around your belt so much."

Lord Chauvlyn growled and grabbed her chin. "Don't you

understand? I have all the power! I have those blasted humans you care for so much. I have your friend. You are trapped. You won't get away this time."

Brigid's heart thumped harder in her chest, but she stuffed the reaction down as deep as she could. Hiding her hands in the folds of her skirt, she forced out a light laugh and leaned back to tug her face free from his grip. "Temper, Lord Chaubbin, temper. My mother would have scolded me nine days to summer if I'd let my temper get the best of me like that. Perhaps you ought to try some tea? I've heard it's very soothing. Maybe a chamomile tea. Or if that isn't sweet enough for you, a honey vanilla chamomile. Perhaps with some lavender undertones? I've heard lavender is very good for stress."

"Are you truly prattling on about tea at a time like this?" Lord Chauvlyn's face mottled a hint red as he gestured over his shoulder at the window and presumably the dungeon that lay beyond. "I don't have to have a civil conversation with you. I could have you thrown in the dungeon with the rest to await the blood rites my master will perform on Midsummer Night."

Perhaps he could torture her directly. But that wasn't the fae way of doing things. Fae, like her, were more trappers than hunters. They preferred to manipulate their victims into harming themselves, rather than wielding the pain directly.

So, no, Lord Chauvlyn didn't have to have a civil conversation with her. But he would, because he just couldn't help himself once the game of wits began.

"Dungeons sound like terribly uncomfortable places. And dirty. Just look at my boots." Brigid stuck her foot out, wiggling it as if to better show off the dried layer of goopy muck that covered the knee-high boots nearly to their tops. "Look at how filthy my boots already are. This realm is disgustingly dirty. I don't understand why you wish to spend so much time here while you have a perfectly clean court waiting for you in the Court of Revels."

Lord Chauvlyn pinched the bridge of his nose and blew out a long breath. "Won't you just listen for five minutes?"

"I am listening, Lord Chaubertin, truly I am." Brigid swung her legs, leaning back on her hands planted on the paperwork on his desk. Paperwork that she was subtly shifting closer until she found a moment to stuff as much of it as she could into her pocket. "But I have such a short attention span, you see, and you haven't said anything particularly worth listening to just yet."

The muscle at the corner of Lord Chauvlyn's jaw twitched, and he stalked toward the door, reaching for the handle. "I'll have that boy Mungoe brought here right this minute, see if I don't. We'll see how blasé you'll be about my threats when he's screaming in agony."

She'd pushed him too far. She couldn't let him send guards to fetch Munch, even beyond the fact that she didn't want to see him tortured. The guards were bound to notice the prisoners were getting loose if they went anywhere near the dungeons.

Brigid pushed slightly more upright, sliding a handful of papers into her pocket as she did so. "Really, Lord Chauvlyn, are such drastic measures necessary?"

The fact that she'd said his name right caught his attention enough that he turned to her, his hand falling from the latch. "They won't be, if you cooperate and tell me what I want to know."

"What do you want to know?" Brigid frowned, adding a hint of a pout to the expression. "Please remind me. The awful cut of your shirt is terribly distracting. Have you considered a change in tailors?"

Lord Chauvlyn stalked back to her, halted only inches away,

and glowered down at her. "What's your plan, Primrose? You wouldn't have come here if you didn't have a plan. But right now, I hold all the cards. I have all the power. Your hands are tied."

"Are they? They don't seem to be." Brigid lazily held out her hands, turning them over as if searching for the bindings. "And who says I have a plan? Plans are dull. I prefer the exhilaration of the moment. Just jump through the rift and see where it leads. Don't you agree, Lord Chaulloon?"

"No, I do not." Lord Chauvlyn glared down at her, his brows heavy and menacing over dark brown eyes, which studied her with a calculating intensity. "How you could possibly be the Primrose is beyond me. Are you really the Primrose? Or have you been an elaborate decoy this whole evening?"

That was the magic of the Primrose. The Primrose had gained legendary status with skills that bordered on mythical even by fae standards. And her inane chatter had gotten Lord Chauvlyn so discombobulated that he was doubting his own conclusions.

Yet she couldn't let him lose focus on her. If he started searching for a different Primrose, he might take a closer look at what Munch and the captives were up to.

Brigid smoothed a hand over her dress, her fingers lingering on the wild fae primroses in the embroidery. "Of course I'm the Primrose. See? My identity is embroidered right into the dress."

Lord Chauvlyn blinked down at her, as if he couldn't quite comprehend her answer. "You have the brain capacity of a chicken."

Brigid giggled—a real giggle. That comment had been rather funny. "Oh, you're too kind, Lord Chaubinton. I've always considered chickens to be rare creatures. I have a friend who has a talking chicken companion. They—"

"That was not a compliment," Lord Chauvlyn growled and gripped her chin again, cutting off whatever she had been about to say.

Probably just as well. Even Brigid hadn't been entirely sure what would pop out of her mouth next. That was part of the fun of playing this role.

She tucked her hands beneath her skirt as she batted her eyelashes at him and spoke through his grip. "Really, Lord Chauverton. Is that any way to speak to a lady? Don't you know that you're always supposed to speak in flattery and compliments?"

Lord Chauvlyn's fingers tightened against her jaw. "Stop with these games, Primrose. You're here for a reason. You must have some plan in that empty head of yours, though I'm beginning to doubt it."

She smiled past his fingers, tilting her head to better meet his gaze. "Oh, that's just it. I have a very empty head, but a very full heart. You, though, Lord Chauvtin, have a very full head but a very empty heart. It's sad, really."

"Does your entire plan boil down to some nonsense about love?" Lord Chauvlyn glared at her, his grip loosening on her chin. He might order her to stop with the games, but he couldn't help but continue to play them. He was fae, after all.

"Love conquers all, don't you know?" Brigid tugged from his grip before she leaned back onto her hands again. "Perhaps you should try it sometime."

"Love is foolish nonsense. It doesn't exist. Everyone is out for themselves. Even couples who profess love for each other do so for what they can get out of the relationship." Lord Chauvlyn's gaze turned a bit distant. "It's all about power and fulfilling your own needs. Anyone who claims otherwise is a fool."

It was such a sad view of love. But knowing the Court of Revels—and the example of "love" provided by King Oberon and Queen Titania who waffled between adoring passion and passionately trying to kill each other—it was no wonder that Lord Chauvlyn had never had a good example of love.

That didn't excuse his actions. Even someone as loveless as he should know, deep in his soul, that killing hundreds of people as part of a forbidden rite was awful and wrong.

But it sparked a seed of genuine pity for him inside her chest. She wasn't even acting when she gazed up at him and put all that empathy for him into her voice. "Genuine love can be so much more than that. It's about self-sacrifice and giving of yourself for the good of someone else."

Lord Chauvlyn snorted and turned away from her, clasping his hands behind his back. "Oh, so you think you are an example of genuine love. Tell me, are you truly sacrificing yourself for others? Or do you do this whole Primrose thing out of a need to feel better about yourself? Perhaps you simply enjoy the good feeling you get as you bask in the adoration of those you save. Sure, you look better than me on the surface, but in the end, your heroics are just as selfish as my actions."

His words stung a bit, and she couldn't help the little squirmy feeling it caused in her chest. Was she doing this because it made her feel good? Did she truly want to help people?

If things went wrong, would she willingly give her life to save others? She always had an exit strategy. A way to wiggle out of making the ultimate sacrifice. In the end, she placed her trust in herself and her own intelligence to think her way out of sticky situations.

Did that make her rescues selfish? She'd told Munch that

heroics weren't about glory for oneself, but had she been seeking something selfishly for herself out of this? It might not have been glory, like he had been, but she had been motivated by the feelings she'd harbored since Meg had been snatched all those years ago. She took great satisfaction in the knowledge that she was returning people to their homes.

She regarded Lord Chauvlyn, her tone coming out more her real voice than she usually used around the fae lord. "Perhaps I am just as selfish as you are. Thank you for pointing out that flaw of mine. I never claimed to be the best example of genuine love. But I can claim that I am trying. I know what love is, and I will strive each day to live more in that love than I did the day before. That's the difference between you and me."

For a long moment, Lord Chauvlyn held her gaze, his expression more open and vulnerable than she'd ever seen, as if he was truly considering her words.

Then the sneering tilt returned to his mouth as his expression shuttered closed. He crossed his arms and glared at her. "Enough of this foolishness."

"It's hardly foolish, Lord Chauvertin." Brigid brushed at the dirt encrusting her boots, sending a shower of dirt onto the red rug.

Lord Chauvlyn's eyes flashed, and he leaned so close that their noses were almost touching. "You will tell me your plan, or I will send for Mungoe from the dungeon, and I will order him to start cutting off his own fingers until you tell me what I want to know."

"That sounds terribly messy. Blood is so difficult to get out of fabric. You'll never be able to get it out of your clothes or the rug." Brigid didn't let herself dwell on the image of Munch hunched on the floor, his hand splayed before him as he raised a knife, preparing to chop off his own fingers under the force of the blood binding.

Instead, she cocked her head and gestured at the fae lord. "Is that why you always wear black? Because it hides the bloodstains better? You should have told me that years ago. I wouldn't have judged your fashion sense so harshly if I'd known there was a reason for it."

"Don't you get it, you foolish girl! I'm trying to threaten you!" Lord Chauvlyn all but yelled in her face, a fleck of spit landing on her cheek.

"You didn't have to shout. I heard you perfectly well the first time." Brigid leaned back and flicked the spit off her skin. "If you don't mind me saying so, you really ought to attend to your personal hygiene. Your breath could do with a little mint-chewing. Though it isn't too noticeable unless you get up in someone's face like that. I suppose it isn't too much of a problem, unless you wish to make a habit of yelling in people's faces."

How much time had passed? She wasn't sure how long she could keep up this act, pushing Lord Chauvlyn to the breaking point, then reeling him back in before he carried through on his threat.

But it was going to take Munch a while to individually rescue the hundreds of people in that dungeon. Brigid would just have to keep this up for as long as it took.

Lord Chauvlyn's face mottled again, this time an even deeper shade than before. He grabbed her by the shoulder, dragged her from her sitting position on the desk, and shook her roughly. "Listen, you fool girl. You have one minute to tell me everything or I will take a knife to every child in that dungeon. If the thought of that young man's torture won't break you, then their cries surely will."

The children. Surely even Lord Chauvlyn wasn't cruel enough to torture the children.

She couldn't count on that. He had stolen them away,

knowing that his master—whoever this master was—would kill them in some horrible blood rite. Perhaps Lord Chauvlyn intended to help in the rite. He seemed enough of a lackey to do whatever he was ordered to do.

"Fine, fine. I'll talk." Brigid kept her hands behind her back, not daring to reach out to steady herself against his shaking.

Lord Chauvlyn tossed her away, and she fell against the desk hard, catching herself on her forearms hard enough to bruise.

She couldn't stop her squeak of pain. But it was just as well. She wasn't trying to pretend that she was some tough, battle-hardened girl.

Blinking rapidly, she righted herself on the desk, hunching as if defeated. She folded her hands in her lap, staring down at them. "Should…should we wait for your master? Surely he will want to hear what I have to say. I would hate to have to tell this all over again once he arrives."

"My master won't be here until Midsummer Night, and he's put me in charge until he returns." Lord Chauvlyn crossed his arms and glowered at her. "You can tell me, and I'll tell him."

"Are you sure?" She tilted her head, scrunching her forehead. "I'd hate for the information to get garbled as it is passed from person to person. This is something that I really ought to tell him directly."

Lord Chauvlyn pinched the bridge of his nose again. "Enough stalling and start talking."

She drew in a shuddering breath. "All right. All right. Where should I begin?"

"Just start at the beginning." Lord Chauvlyn sounded like he was about ready to strangle her.

As long as he kept his focus on strangling her rather than any of the captives in the dungeon, she was fine with it.

Brigid smiled and shifted, as if to get more comfortable on

the desk. "The beginning. I can do that. All right, then, I was born in the Human Realm. Did you know that?"

"Obviously. You're human." Lord Chauvlyn eyed her over his fingers, which still remained frozen over the bridge of his nose.

"Oh, right. That does make it rather obvious, doesn't it?" Brigid relaxed her posture on the desk, resting her hand on another stack of paperwork that she wanted to stuff into her pocket the first chance she got. "My parents were so happy to have another daughter, even though a son would have been more helpful for the farm. Though, Meg and I proved to be plenty sturdy and strong enough to work on our family farm. Meg is my older sister. Did you know that? Oh, of course you know that. You've met Meg."

"Yes, I have. Now get on with it," Lord Chauvlyn snarled through gritted teeth. "I don't need your life's story."

"But you said to start at the beginning, and this is the beginning."

"I didn't mean *that* beginning, and you know it."

"How should I know? You didn't specify which beginning."

Lord Chauvlyn curled and uncurled his fingers, venting a wordless snarl before he paced away from her, as if he needed to put some space between them before he gave in to the urge to strangle her.

She had definitely succeeded in getting under his skin.

While his back was turned, Brigid shoved more of the papers into her pocket. The magic of the pocket meant she could stuff quite a bit inside without ever bulging out her skirt in a suspicious manner. Quite handy, that. Especially considering how much stuff she had already jammed in there tonight.

Lord Chauvlyn braced himself against the windowsill, head bowed as he gulped in tight, angry gasps.

Brigid stuffed down her tension, forcing herself to remain

nonchalantly perched on the corner of the desk. Had she given Munch enough time? Had he gotten everyone out of the dungeon?

Lord Chauvlyn lifted his head, staring out the window with an unseeing expression. Perhaps he would be too off-kilter to peer past his reflection to see what was happening in the rest of the castle.

Then he stiffened, and his eyes narrowed. He leaned closer to the glass, his nose nearly touching it.

Clopping kelpies. He'd seen what was happening.

Chapter Twenty

Munch pulled the last captive from a dungeon cell, repeating the phrase for the final time. The passageway was crowded with people since there was no more room for them to wait in the tiny space at the base of the stairs.

Pushing past the people, Munch worked his way to the front and climbed onto the first step to survey the crowd.

People packed the space at the base of the stairs and filled each of the passageways branching into the darkness. Grumbling had broken out, and there seemed to be more than a few men who were arguing against those who were blocking the stairwell, preventing them from escaping on their own.

Munch held up his hands, waiting until he had the attention of those nearest him. He didn't dare raise his voice, so he kept his voice low. "Please stay as quiet as you can and follow me."

"Why should we follow you?" One of the men crossed his arms and glared at Munch.

Why should they follow him? He was just…Munch. Robin's baby brother. The least competent of his siblings.

Munch drew his shoulders straight and glared right back. "I

am Mungoe, one of the Greenwood Foresters and a member of the Primrose's League. I spent seven years as part of the Hood's band of outlaws, and I've been fighting fae since one of them killed my parents when I was eight years old. Anyone who doesn't want to take my orders can stay here, or I will make you stay here."

The man still glared back, but he and the others who had been grumbling fell silent. All of these people came from villages around the Greenwood. Even if the legends of the Primrose hadn't been enough, the tales of the Hood and the Greenwood Foresters were. At least, for now.

"Good. All of you able-bodied men—" He thought of Brigid and his sister Robin, and quickly added, "—or women, form up as an escort around the most vulnerable. I'll need three or four of you up front with me."

The crowd stirred, then three young men and a young woman pushed through the crowd to join him. The men clenched their fists, and the woman had somehow gotten her hands on a piece of stout wood. By the way she was swinging it, she seemed capable of using it.

Munch nodded to them. "Stay with me. The rest of you, help those nearest to you if they seem to be struggling. The Primrose is out there, buying us time. We need to make the most of it."

Something almost like a cheer, yet vented at a murmur, rippled through the crowd and into the passageways out of his sight. These people were frightened, but just the name Primrose and the little flowers that had been passed from hand to hand so often that the petals were falling and the stems drooping had given them enough hope that they were turning the paralyzing fear into hardened determination.

Munch drew the iron rod from the back of his belt. The

blood binding might not have considered it a weapon, but he would make good use of it now.

He tiptoed up the stairs with his four companions at his heels.

At the top of the stairs, he halted in the open doorway and peered into the room.

Two fae guards crouched next to the table in the room, picking up the spilled pieces of what looked like some kind of board game. The board sat on the table while the guards dumped handfuls of pieces on top.

"...really the Primrose?" one guard was saying.

"Don't know. I always thought the Primrose was a man. And fae." The other guard shook his head as he bent to dig a piece out from a crack between the stones of the floor.

Between their search and their conversation, the fae guards were far too distracted to even glance in Munch's direction. All, it seemed, thanks to Brigid.

He suppressed a grin and stalked forward, raising his iron rod. He kept his footsteps soft, light, the tread of an outlaw practiced in sneaking up on those guarding the tax shipments.

He came within a few feet of the fae, and only his shadow falling across them gave away his presence behind them.

One of the fae started to turn, his hand dropping to the sword at his side.

Munch swung his iron rod and clubbed the fae on the side of the head.

The fae sprawled on the floor, but he shook his head, just stunned.

So Munch clubbed him again, and this time the fae stayed down.

The other fae guard sprang to his feet, but Munch's companions rushed him. The young woman swung her wooden club while the young men punched the fae. The guard went down beneath their combined efforts, stunned but not unconscious—or possibly dead—like the fae Munch had taken on.

Munch divested the fae he'd knocked down of his weapons, then checked the fae's pulse. It was there, though the fae had a nasty bump rising on his head.

Munch glanced up and found the stairwell crowded with faces. He hauled the fae from the floor and passed him to the people mobbing the stairs. "Pass him along and lock him in the nearest cell. We don't want him to alert the other guards when he wakes up."

If he woke up. An iron rod to the head wasn't healthy.

The others hauled the second fae to his feet and passed him to the crowd as well. The two fae were quickly hustled out of sight, passed from person to person down the stairs.

Munch buckled on the fae's sword, and one of the young men did the same with the other sword. They handed out the daggers they'd taken so that a few more of the people were armed.

A few weapons racks lined the walls of the tower room, and Munch snatched up a bow and a quiver of arrows, testing the draw weight. He'd be much better able to defend these people armed as he was now with bow and sword.

He glanced over his shoulder at the others. "Pass the word along that those who can fight are to grab a weapon as they go through."

Those closest to him nodded, then leaned back to murmur the instructions to those behind them. He had a feeling that the most argumentative of the men would be the first to push their way to the weapons.

Munch crept to the door and cracked it open, peering around the courtyard.

This tower wasn't far from the castle gate, though the gates were now shut and the drawbridge raised.

That complicated things. He'd have to take the tower and lower the drawbridge before they could escape.

He turned and faced the people again. The tower was even more crowded as more and more of the former captives poured into the room from the stairs.

Munch gestured to his four companions. "Come with me. We have to take the tower and lower the drawbridge."

The young woman grinned and hefted her club again. She had a dagger stuffed into her sash as well. The three young men nodded, their jaws tight.

Munch faced several of the other able-bodied men and women, who had also claimed weapons. He especially focused on the men who had argued earlier. If he made them feel like they had a crucial role, they would see that it was done instead of fight against his orders. "Keep the rest of the people here until the drawbridge starts to lower. We'll just give our escape away if a whole bunch of people start milling around the court-yard without a way to escape."

The others nodded, then took up positions near the door.

Munch cracked the door open wider, then slipped outside. His four volunteers followed him, and thankfully they took the hint and copied his movements, sticking to the shadows along-side the walls.

Only a few fae patrolled the wall, though their gazes remained fixed on the sky and the outside of the castle, not on the courtyard.

That was sensible. This was the Realm of Monsters, after all. Even these monstrous fae had reason to fear the monsters contained in this realm. Nor would they have any reason to think that their prisoners were in the process of escaping.

Munch crept along the wall until he reached the base of one

of the two towers that braced either side of the gate. Based on the chains from the drawbridge, this one held the crank that would raise and lower the bridge.

The door was shut, though when he tested the latch, it moved easily. It made sense that the guards wouldn't lock the tower as it was more important for them to move about freely in case of a monster attack.

Holding his breath, he lifted the latch and eased the door open only a crack. The hinges squeaked, but they didn't groan or creak.

Releasing a long breath, Munch peeked inside. The room at the base of the tower remained empty.

He opened the door wider, then slipped through, the others following close behind. Once inside, he drew an arrow from the quiver and nocked it to the bowstring, though he didn't draw it just yet.

A glance at his companions assured him that they, too, had their weapons ready. Unlike the guards in the dungeon tower, these were unlikely to be distracted. Munch would have to hit them hard and fast to take the tower before anyone else realized what was going on.

Munch started up the stairs with careful footsteps on the stone. The others behind him weren't as quiet, but the scuffing was faint enough that hopefully they could still surprise the fae guards.

The stairs curved, winding upward in a way that would put Munch and his companions at a disadvantage if the fae noticed they were here.

But the stairs above remained empty, and after a few heartbeats, the opening of the doorway above came into sight.

Munch shook his head, suppressing a grin. These fae really should take a few security tips from Guy. There should be a door in every opening, no matter how much of a hassle it was to keep opening and closing doors, since that made it much harder for outlaws to sneak around.

Pressing his back to the inner wall, Munch eased upward until he could see inside the room.

Four fae guards were inside. Two of them peered from the arrow slits into the dead, nighttime forest while one lounged near the crank for the drawbridge chain. A fourth was sprawled on a cot, seemingly asleep.

Across the way, a door led onto the parapet over the gates, connecting to the other tower. There were likely two to four fae in that tower too, and they would likely respond once they realized there was trouble here.

With a deep breath, Munch lunged into the room, stepping to the side to make room for his companions and keep his back to the wall. He drew his arrow, pointing it at one of the guards near the windows. "Surrender and keep your hands away from your weapons."

The fae guards whirled and reached for their weapons.

Well, he'd given them a chance to surrender. Munch shot the first fae guard in the neck above the line of his chain mail tunic.

Even as the fae fell, Munch had another arrow on the string. This fae tried to dodge, but Munch still downed him.

The other two fae guards were on their feet, swords drawn as they raced toward Munch and his four companions. He didn't have time to get off another shot.

Instead, he dropped the bow, drew his sword, and stepped forward to meet the fae. He blocked the fae's strike, the blow jolting all the way up his arm.

These fae were strong. Far stronger than any human guard he'd ever fought as an outlaw.

Munch gritted his teeth and dodged another swing, even as

one of his companions gave a cry of pain. Munch couldn't look away to see which one.

He had to end this quickly. If he was having this much trouble, they would be struggling. They were simply villagers and farmers. Strong, yes, but untrained in weapons the way he was.

Munch ducked, then stabbed forward in a move he'd practiced with Robin many times. It caught the fae off-guard, and his sword jabbed into the fae's stomach. The fae's chain mail stopped the blow from piercing, but the thrust was hard enough to double him over. Before he could recover, Munch brought his sword up and sliced the fae's neck.

Munch whirled and joined his two companions who were still standing. One of the young men lay on the ground, curled around his stomach and blood pooling around him. The young woman knelt next to him, blood pouring down her arm.

Munch's attack took the fae by surprise, and Munch stabbed him under the arm, driving his sword into the fae's chest.

As the fae fell, Munch turned to his two standing companions. They were gaping at him, their eyes round.

This was likely their first fight, besides whatever resistance their village had managed when the fae attacked. Their first time feeling the danger, seeing the blood and gore, dealing out death.

But he couldn't give them time to come to terms with it.

He wiped his sword off on a dead fae's tunic, then sheathed the weapon. As he raced across the room to grab his bow, he pointed at the crank. "Lower the drawbridge."

The two young men nodded and ran to the crank. It took them a moment of fiddling before they figured out they had to over crank it a moment to release the pressure on the wooden chock holding the gears in place, before they could start cranking the drawbridge down.

Munch drew an arrow and positioned himself where he would have a clear shot of the door to the other tower. He spared a quick glance to the wounded man and the young woman helping him. "Keep pressure on that wound. Bind it up if you can."

That injury didn't look good. The young man would need a physician. Even then, he might not survive.

The door burst open, and two fae raced inside, brandishing their swords.

Munch shot both of them, one after the other, dropping them in the doorway.

The two young men at the drawbridge crank halted, gaping at him again. One of them raised a hand, gesturing weakly. "You just…"

"Did what I had to do. Keep cranking." Munch nocked another arrow to the bowstring. No, he didn't like the blood or the killing. But he'd spent years as an outlaw, then more years as a forester, fighting fae monsters. He could handle this, and he'd do what he had to do to protect these innocent people from the fate that awaited them if he didn't take action.

Right now, these young men were looking at him how people usually looked at Robin. Or Will. Or even Guy. In all his time comparing himself to his siblings, Munch had never paused to realize just how competent he'd become.

The young men shook themselves and kept cranking. Foot by foot, groaning as it went, the drawbridge lowered.

When no more fae came from the second tower, Munch moved across the room and peeked out the window into the courtyard.

A crowd of humans poured from the dungeon tower, racing to the gate. Those with weapons formed a line on either side, hurrying the people along and protecting them in case of attack.

Four of the men reached the gates and lifted the bar holding the gates shut.

The drawbridge thunked to the ground on the far side. No sooner had it touched earth than the captives raced across it.

"Let's get out of here." Munch hooked his bow over his shoulder, then waved to the two healthy young men. "Help him up."

The two young men supported the wounded man between them and headed for the stairs. The young woman glanced back, then hurried after them.

Munch claimed a sword and dagger from one of the fallen fae. He stabbed the sword through the gap in the gears, making sure the sword bit deep into wood so that it was wedged tight. He stabbed the dagger through the links of the chain and into the wooden gear.

That should delay any fae trying to raise the drawbridge.

Munch hurried down the stairs, catching up with the others at the bottom. Together, the five of them rejoined the escaping humans.

Others stepped forward to aid the wounded man, who drooped pale and limp.

Munch glanced at him, but there was nothing he could do. He was no trained physician, and the others were already binding the wound and staunching the bleeding.

Except for the wounded man, this escape was going well. Perhaps he might even pull this off.

He glanced toward the lit window in the keep. Was Brigid up there? How was her distraction going? She had a plan to get herself out of there, didn't she?

He should—

Screams pierced the night. Shrill and rising, coming from the people who had already crossed the drawbridge and were nearly to the dead forest.

Three harpies, barely visible as dark shapes against the midnight-blue night sky, swooped down from the sky, grotesque grins on their human-like faces as they dove downward, passing out of Munch's view. But the utter terror in the people's screams told him enough of what was happening.

Munch cursed under his breath. Perhaps he should have stayed in the tower where the height would give him a better shot at the empty plain between the castle and the dead forest.

With Brigid off distracting Lord Chauvlyn, he was the closest thing these people had to a leader. They needed to see him and hear him give orders. He couldn't just stand up in the tower and shoot arrows, staying in the background as he'd always done.

Harpy screeches and human screams filled the air, ringing throughout the nighttime castle.

If the fae weren't already alerted that something was wrong, they soon would be.

Munch would have to do something, but how far would the blood binding allow him to go? He could still feel its clutches around his heart. Brigid hadn't managed to break it yet.

Gripping his iron rod in the last three fingers of his right hand, he raced onto the drawbridge, shouldering aside a few of the people as gently as he could. Once they saw who he was, they made room for him.

Pain lanced up his legs as soon as he stepped out of the shadow of the passage beneath the walls. Gritting his teeth, he gripped the iron rod tighter and forced himself forward until he could step off the drawbridge. He stepped to one side so that he wouldn't block the flow of people exiting the castle. A few steps backwards placed his back to the castle wall, relieving some of the pain.

He wasn't trying to escape with the others. He just needed to see what was happening to protect them.

Fumbling to both clutch the iron rod and draw an arrow from his quiver with his right hand, Munch nocked an arrow to the bow he'd taken, then released. The arrow took a harpy in the wing, and it shrieked as it flapped higher into the sky.

If only he had his iron-tipped human arrows. These fae arrows didn't kill the monsters as quickly, nor was the bow as familiar as his own.

The former captives still poured from the dungeon, raced across the courtyard, and onto the drawbridge. But those on the drawbridge were trying to halt, turn, and run back into the castle. Several people fell while others were pushed into the sludgy, green moat.

"Stay calm! Stick together and head for the rift!" Munch shouted, but no one seemed to hear him over the screams and the shrieking harpies.

Whatever calm determination the people had gotten from the stories of the Primrose had fled in the face of danger. The entire crowd teetered on the edge of utter panic, and there was nothing Munch could do about it but shoot another harpy and shout encouragement to those nearest him.

A growl came from the forest, then a pack of lean, black wolves, their mouths dripping with foam, raced from the forest.

Blast and bother. He was one forester. He couldn't protect everyone. He couldn't even run out to face those wolves head-on.

The people who had been halfway to the forest turned and ran, screaming, for the castle, colliding with those still pouring from inside.

The few villagers with weapons valiantly took up positions as a rear guard. But their fae-made daggers would be no match for the wolves bearing down on them.

The resonant clang of a bell tolled from somewhere in the keep behind them.

In a blink, fae appeared on the castle's parapets, bows aimed over the heads of the villagers to rain arrows down on the wolves. Hoofbeats thundered, and a dozen fae riders on the frenzied, feral horses raced into view from the other side of the castle, cutting between Munch and the far-off rift that would take them home.

Munch nocked an arrow to his bowstring, but he didn't draw it as he placed his back to the castle wall.

This had been a trap. Lord Chauvlyn had been prepared for an escape attempt, and now Munch and the others were surrounded.

Munch had failed. Again.

Lord Chauvlyn turned away from the window, a slow smirk spreading across his face as he stalked toward Brigid. "All your prattle was just the distraction, wasn't it? That's your plan."

He said it with the satisfaction of someone who had suspected as much all along.

So this was the game. While she had been attempting to distract him, he had been stringing her along, toying with her like a basilisk with its prey, before he unleashed a trap of his own.

Blood magic was fueled by blood, yes. But terror made it more potent. Being captured once was frightening enough for the imprisoned humans. But to have escape snatched from them for a terrifying second time? That would feed the fear, the despair, so that when the blood rites took place, the magic unleashed would be dreadful in its power.

Lord Chauvlyn might have the satisfaction of trapping her, but she wouldn't let him see how it had rattled her.

"Perhaps. It was a good attempt. Sink me, but you were rather distracted for a while, there." Brigid lifted her foot and inspected it before she rubbed her boots together to dislodge a few more clumps of dried muck from the leather. Dirt showered onto the floor in a light patter.

From where she sat on the desk, she couldn't see out the window. How far had the captives gotten? They could become hostages or get caught in the middle of battle if things went wrong. Well, more wrong.

Lord Chauvlyn grabbed her upper arm and hauled her to her feet. "Clever. But not clever enough, Primrose." He dragged her across the room and shoved her to face the window, pinning her between the window and his body. He drew a dagger and pressed its cold, sharp edge against her neck. "Look at what you have wrought, Primrose. Take in your failure."

Through the wavy glass and her own reflection, she could see the dark shapes of people moving about the courtyard.

Screams rang through the glass while people were piling back into the castle as fast as they had been hurrying to leave. Harpies swooped through the sky, and wolves slunk from the edge of the forest.

She'd promised these people escape, and instead she'd led them into even worse danger. She'd failed them, and now they'd die, either at the claws of the monsters or hands of the fae.

"It seems the dangers of the Realm of Monsters are too much for your little escape." Lord Chauvlyn's hot breath hissed against her ear.

Brigid's heart pounded in her throat as she fisted her hands in her skirts. There were far too many wolves and harpies for Munch to fight off by himself. She couldn't see him from here, though she assumed the arrow that flew upward and shot a harpy had to be his. He was fighting the losing battle that she, in her hubris, had led them all into.

Someone pounded on the door behind them. "Lord Chauvlyn! The prisoners are escaping!"

Brigid craned her neck to peer over her shoulder just in time to catch the satisfied smirk twisting Lord Chauvlyn's features. The knife scraped against her skin but didn't draw blood.

He met her gaze, then called to the guard, "Give the signal."

"Very good, my lord." Bootsteps hurried away.

Seconds later, the toll of a bell reverberated through the stones of the tower.

Fae popped into view along the walls, their bows drawn. A squad of guards on the meat-eating horses galloped around the castle, cutting the escaping humans off.

"Did you really think I didn't plan for one of your so-called epic escapes, Primrose?" Lord Chauvlyn spun her to face him, still gripping her upper arm with one hand while he pressed that knife to her neck with the other.

"I suppose this one didn't turn out to be quite so epic." Brigid swallowed back the roughness in her throat, glancing back at the frightened people freezing in place in the courtyard.

They had been recaptured. Even as some of the fae drove off the wolves and shot the harpies, the rest surrounded the people. Somewhere down there, Munch would be forced to surrender.

Munch. He'd feel like a failure all over again. He wouldn't see how heroic he'd been, defending these people and attempting this escape against such impossible odds. This defeat wasn't Munch's fault.

It was hers.

Lord Chauvlyn pressed the knife even harder against her neck. A line of pain sliced against her skin as hot blood trickled down her throat. The fae lord's dark eyes burned into her as he leaned close enough that their foreheads nearly touched. "Don't you understand, Primrose? I have you. I have outmaneuvered you at every turn. There is nothing you can do to save yourself or those pathetic humans. You are mine."

Chapter Twenty-One

Finally. The words Brigid had been waiting for. It had taken long enough. She was starting to get worried that she'd lost her touch.

She met Lord Chauvlyn's gaze…and grinned. Lifting her arm, she wrapped her hand over his on his knife's hilt. As soon as their fingers touched, a glow surrounded their hands. The manifestation of the beginning of a binding.

Lord Chauvlyn's eyes widened, his mouth falling open in a dawning realization.

Before he could pull away, she tightened her grip, still grinning. "Thank you, Lord Chauvlyn. I accept your claim to join your Court."

The glow surrounding their hands winked out as a deep pressure of magic bore down on them for a heartbeat before the binding clicked into place and the feeling vanished.

Lord Chauvlyn stumbled back from her, ripping his hand out of her grip. "What? No. No, you couldn't possibly…how?"

"Easy. Your guards didn't capture me entering the dungeon. They caught me leaving it." Brigid tugged on her sleeve, straightening the rumpled fabric. "I joined the humans at the circle in the Tanglewood. While I am a human, I'm officially a part of the Court of Knowledge. The laws of bindings and snatchings apply to me as they would to any court-bound fae. Therefore, you snatched me—a willing participant—from my court into yours, forming the beginning of a binding."

That had been the tricky thing to arrange. She'd needed him to snatch her for just this reason. But she couldn't let him know that he'd snatched her, or he would have done what was necessary to make sure to form the captive binding instead of leaving it open, waiting to be completed with a variety of bindings.

Lord Chauvlyn remained frozen where he was, knife dangling in limp fingers, as if he was too deep in the grips of gaping horror to so much as move, much less process what he was hearing.

"I wasn't sure if it would work for a bit there. I was growing worried I'd have to marry you." Brigid leaned against the windowsill behind her.

"Marry me." Lord Chauvlyn's deadpan astonishment came out as a statement, even if his wide eyes held a question.

"Well, yes. Snatching a willing person from another court is a common way to start the marriage binding." Brigid gave a languid shrug, using the movement to hide that she was digging in her magic pocket. "And you are the storybook version of a handsome, dark, brooding fae. But I find your personality and morals rather lacking. Not to mention that my heart is claimed by another. So I was rather relieved when you mentioned that your master had put you in charge until he returned. That meant you have the authority to claim me as part of your court."

Lord Chauvlyn made a strangled noise in the back of his throat.

"Now that I'm a part of your court, you can't hurt me. Oh, sink me." She reached up and touched the trickle of blood from the cut on her neck. "It seems you already have. Such bad timing."

It was a bit of a gray area, since he had technically hurt her before the binding was complete. But fae bindings loved the wiggle room in grays areas. She was still bleeding, still injured, and he had been the one to do it to her. That should be enough.

His eyes widened, and he raced to join her again at the window. This time, he flung the window open so that their view of the courtyard, castle walls, and the desiccated plain beyond was unhindered by their reflections in the glass.

Even as they watched, a black, twisting rift opened between the humans and the fae riders, a rift that had formed because Lord Chauvlyn had drawn the blood of a member of his court, something that went against the Laws of Bindings.

"This really couldn't get worse for you, unless you broke other bindings lately. Have you, Lord Chaupinton?" Brigid tilted her head, as if considering. "Such as the laws of hospitality, perhaps?"

Lord Chauvlyn's face whitened still further. Because, of course, he had broken the laws of hospitality. Twice, in fact, just that night. He'd been a guest of the Court of Knowledge. Yet he had stolen Munch from his hostess. Then he'd stolen Brigid from the court itself.

"Oh, dear, you have, haven't you? Sink me, but I believe that rift will probably lead right to the court you offended so they can exact their payment for your violation." Brigid gestured at the window and the rift beyond.

From the rift poured Munch's siblings, including Robin and Guy with arrows already nocked to the strings of their bows. Squads of swordmaidens raced from the newly formed rift, led by Queen Hippolyta, followed by Meg, Basil, and a few of the other librarians with King Theseus at their head.

The army that poured from the rift quickly spread out and surrounded the humans, standing between them and the fae riders near the forest. Munch's siblings faced the castle, their arrows not yet drawn but still providing a warning to the fae archers on the wall tops.

But it was a stalemate. A bloodbath would result the moment the first person lifted their sword or released the first arrow.

"But...this is impossible." Lord Chauvlyn gaped first at the rift, then at Brigid, as he stumbled back from the window. "We're in the Realm of Monsters. The Laws of Bindings don't apply here."

"That isn't exactly true." Brigid rolled her shoulders in another shrug, hiding her hands behind her back as she dug into her pocket. "The Realm of Monsters is still bound to the Fae Realm even as it is bound to be separate from it. The moment you grounded that rift in the Court of Revels, creating a permanent circle between the two realms, the laws of the Fae Realm began to filter in here even as some of the chaos of here seeped into there. You've begun, in essence, to form your own court here in this castle, even as you still kept a foot in the Court of Revels. Thus, a few of the Laws of Binding have begun to work here as well."

"No." Lord Chauvlyn gaped at her for a long moment before his face twisted, hardening into taut lines. "No!"

He lunged for her, stabbing with the knife. But now that she was protected as a member of his court, the knife went astray before it ever reached her. Instead, he stumbled past her, and his knife slammed into the wall hard enough to send it flying from his hand.

He would still be able to use trickery on her, and he could

still hurt her if he did it by "accident." There were still plenty of things he could do to her.

"Tut, tut, Lord Chautterton, such temper. I believe I already recommended calming teas as a way to soothe such wild passions?" Brigid forced herself to remain nonchalantly leaning against the wall with her back to the window, as if utterly unconcerned with his attempt on her life.

Behind her back, she gripped the rope and grappling hook that she'd been slowly pulling from her magical pocket for the past few minutes, hooked the grapple on the windowsill, and dropped the rope over the outer wall of the castle keep so that it dangled into the courtyard far below.

He whirled on her, clenching and unclenching his fists. "I might not be able to hurt you, but you won't escape me. Nor will those pathetic humans you love so much. If I give the word, a battle will break out. People will die. Is that what you want, Primrose?"

"No, it isn't. Believe it or not, I'd prefer there to be no bloodshed this day. Not even yours." Brigid gave another shrug and pushed away from the window. "I have no intention of escaping. When I walk out of here, it will be with your blessing."

Lord Chauvlyn snorted and crossed his arms. "I will never give such a blessing."

"Perhaps you won't give it, but I believe you will bargain for it." Brigid reached into her pocket, and this time she drew out a slim, basket hilt rapier. Such a slim weapon didn't deal out the damage of the larger swords and weapons still favored by many of the fae—such weapons were more effective against monsters, after all—but she preferred the lightness and quickness of this type of blade.

She held out the rapier to Lord Chauvlyn, hilt first. "Bargain with me, Lord Chauvlyn."

He took the rapier, wrapping his hand around the hilt and inspecting the weapon with a glint in his eyes. It was well made; the Court of Swordmaidens tolerated nothing less. "It is to be a duel, then?"

"The duel will end when one of us disarms the other." Brigid drew her own rapier from her pocket. The leather wrap of its hilt fit against her palm, familiar from her many practices with the swordmaidens.

Not that she was *that* good. She wasn't incompetent, exactly. Hippolyta would never let her carry the weapon if she was dismal at it. But she was still far better at evading rather than actually fighting.

But evading was exactly what she intended to do now. She just had to hold off Lord Chauvlyn long enough for Munch to arrive.

Munch would arrive. She hadn't told him the plan—she couldn't be sure how this part would play out until she got up here—but she knew him. He would come for her. All she had to do was stall long enough.

Lord Chauvlyn's mouth curled into a slow smirk. "That doesn't forbid bloodshed, Primrose. I can disarm you once you are dead."

"I suppose that's true. But as I said, I have no wish for bloodshed this day. Not even yours." She kept her tone light, even as she resisted the urge to swallow. "But you forget. You cannot harm me. I am a member of your court, as you are of mine."

"Then I suppose your blood is safe this day." Lord Chauvlyn ran his thumb lightly along the edge of the blade, but something in his expression remained dark and calculating. "What shall the terms of our bargain be?"

"If I win, I and all those I claim as mine will walk free from this place to return from whence we came." Brigid resisted the urge to glance over her shoulder. Based on the lack of sound from outside the window, the stalemate remained in place as each side waited for a signal to attack.

"And if I win?" Lord Chauvlyn lowered his sword to peer at her over it.

"Then I will surrender myself to you to bind as you see fit." It was so terribly hard to keep her easy smile in place as she pledged those words, knowing what they'd mean if she lost.

But she was prepared to go through with it, if it came down to it. From the moment she became the Primrose, she knew her life might be the sacrifice she'd have to make. She was at peace with that, if this was the price she'd have to pay.

"It is a bargain." Lord Chauvlyn stated, holding her gaze as he said those words.

As the magic built between them, she slid into a fighting stance, her left leg pointed forward, her right leg anchoring her. "It is a bargain."

With those words, the bargain binding settled on them, more unbreakable than the walls of the castle around them.

MUNCH GAPED, leaning against the firm stones of the castle wall behind him, as Robin and Guy shot the remaining harpies, dropping them from the sky. The rest of Munch's brothers shot the wolves, downing almost all of them before the rest fled, yipping and howling, into the dead forest.

The swordmaidens sprang forward, swords and spears warning off the fae riders while the librarians took charge of the frightened people, calming them down and organizing them into a huddled mass, protected by the swordmaidens.

Humans remained in the courtyard and on the drawbridge,

frozen where they stood, glancing from their rescuers outside to their captors on the walls.

Queen Hippolyta faced the fae lined up on the wall tops. "Lower your weapons."

One of the fae in the center of the wall shifted. He eased back on his drawn arrow, but he didn't take the arrow from the string. "No. We await orders from our lord Chauvlyn."

"I suppose we are at an impasse, since we await orders from the Primrose." Queen Hippolyta rested her hands on her hips as King Theseus joined her, staring down the fae on the walls.

Robin strolled around the edge of the crowd until she reached Munch's side, a smirk on her face. "We heard you'd gotten yourself into a spot of trouble."

"You came." Munch swung his gaze from Robin to his brothers lurking just behind her. Each of them wore a little red flower pinned to the front of their shirt. Now that Munch was looking, he could see that everyone, from the librarians to the swordmaidens to even the king and queen, had wild fae primroses pinned to their clothes.

"Of course we came." Will pushed forward to slap Munch on the back. "You know Robin has wanted to take a gander at the Fae Realm and the Realm of Monsters for years. She leapt at the excuse."

Robin tossed back her head and barked a laugh. "Right you are. And what fun it has proven to be!"

"Fun." Will shook his head. "If you can call waiting around the Fae Realm for a rift to open, then leaping through without even knowing what was on the other side *fun*."

How had Brigid managed to arrange all of this in those short few hours between leaving the Library and joining the captured humans at the circle? How had she even known that a rift would form?

It was all too much to comprehend, and his mind was still

stuck on the sight of his family, so impossibly standing here in the Realm of Monsters.

"You came." Munch couldn't help but repeat the words. Yes, Robin had wanted to come to the Fae Realm for years. But her love for her children and her people had always held her back. "You left your children behind."

What if they were stuck here for years? Would those children grow up without parents?

Will shook his head and pointed back the way they'd come, where the new rift still twisted black against the rotting forest. "The children and our wives are back in the Fae Realm at the House. We've been assured that time moves the same between the Fae Realm and the Realm of Monsters. So even if we miss years in the Human Realm, at least we will all be together."

"They will likely have a few stories of their own to tell." Alan grinned, his fingers flexing on his bow as if he really wanted one of his instruments in his hand. "The House, that talking pony Buddy, and Brigid's siblings seemed a bit harried when we left."

"I would've loved to stay and try out more of that food." Tuck sighed and dropped a hand to his ladle, where it was hooked in his belt.

Munch whooshed out a breath of relief at that. At least they hadn't risked their children growing up without parents.

But that would have taken a great deal of effort, hustling all the children through the circle into the Fae Realm on short notice.

"You did all that. For me. But I'm just..." He trailed off, not sure if he dared say the rest out loud. He was just Munch, the youngest and least competent sibling. He'd understand them going to such great lengths for Robin or Will. After all, they'd done just that when Robin had married Guy and they thought her in danger.

But Robin was the oldest, the only sister, and their leader. She was special. Will was the second-in-command. He, too, was special. In fact, all of them were far more special than Munch.

"You're just what?" John crossed his arms and eyed Munch, frowning.

"He means he's just the little brother." Marion rolled his eyes and slugged Munch's shoulder. "Get over it. I have. So you're one of the little brothers that Robin bosses around relentlessly. So am I. Big deal."

"What Marion means is that you're our brother. Doesn't matter if you're the oldest or the youngest. We look after each other." Will gestured around their circle, all seven of them facing each other. "We always have and always will."

Munch sagged against the wall behind him. He'd always known his siblings cared for him, but he'd never realized how *important* he was to them. Just as important as any of the rest of them in their family.

They had come. For him. He mattered to his family. He didn't have to prove himself or earn his way into their love through dashing deeds. He already had it.

Munch cleared his throat, glancing between each of them. "Thanks."

With a slight rumble and a zapping sound, the rift behind them snapped closed, vanishing as if it had never torn between the realms.

Will frowned, deep furrows etching into his forehead.

Robin barked another laugh. "Basil and Meg explained that rifts were torn by evil deeds. I suppose the love of siblings is enough to repair one."

"That's all well and good, but how are we going to get back?" Marion jabbed a thumb at where the rift had been, then shot a glare at Munch as if he blamed him for the rift's disappearance.

"There's another rift, deeper into that dead forest." Munch pointed in that direction. "It's anchored with stones like a faerie circle and connects to another anchored rift in the part of the Tanglewood that belongs to the Court of Revels."

"And here I was hoping we'd have a grand time of it fighting monsters on our way out of this place." Robin heaved a sigh.

"You still might." Munch pushed away from the wall, and pain shot down his back into his legs. Right. He was still blood bound to Lord Chauvlyn.

What did it mean that Brigid hadn't managed to break the blood binding yet? Was she still distracting Lord Chauvlyn? Or had she been captured? Hurt? Killed?

Munch couldn't leave, and not just because of the blood binding. He couldn't leave Brigid behind.

He pushed another step away from the wall. "Keep the people safe. I need to go back for Brigid."

Robin nodded, then tossed back her cloak, revealing a second quiver clipped to her belt.

His quiver. The one Lord Chauvlyn had forced him to leave behind in the Tanglewood.

Robin unclipped it and held it out to him. "Then you'll need this."

The fae-made bow and arrows he'd taken in the dungeon were a poor replacement for his own weapons. He tossed them aside, then reached for his quiver, his heart beating harder. Would the blood binding let him take up his weapons again after it had forced him to cast them aside?

He braced himself as his fingers closed around the quiver. But nothing happened. No agony shot through him. No numbness to his fingers.

He'd been ordered to take off his weapons, but he'd never been forbidden from putting them on again.

Grinning, he shoved the iron rod into the quiver and buckled the belt around his waist. Will passed him his sword, Alan a handful of his daggers, and John strung Munch's bow before handing it over.

Munch ran his fingers over his bow, feeling every polished groove and straining curve of the familiar weapon. With this bow in his hand, he was whole again.

Robin gestured toward the castle gate. "We can handle things out here. Go get your lady love."

"She's not—" Munch started to say automatically, but he cut off the words. He wasn't sure what Brigid was to him anymore. But the way she'd looked at him in the dungeon as she'd claimed him had done something to his heart, and not just because of the spark of a magical binding. The binding went far deeper than that.

"Sure, she's not." Robin smirked, but her gaze flicked away from him a moment before the shadow of wings swooped over them, accompanied by a piercing shriek. Robin laughed, nocked an arrow, and spun on her heel as she drew the arrow back. "Wonderful! Another flock of harpies!"

Leaving his siblings to take out the harpies and any other monsters who might descend on them during this stalemate, Munch leapt for the drawbridge, using the chain to swing himself firmly onto the wood.

As his feet touched down, he shoved between the people, still huddled where they stood, unsure of what to do now.

He raced around them, hopping over some of those who had decided to sit down while they waited to either be rescued or recaptured.

As he reached the courtyard, he drew the iron rod from his quiver once again. He was still blood bound, and he'd need all the help he could get if he was to resist and get Brigid out of there with the rest of them.

No one tried to stop him as he sprinted across the courtyard, not even Lord Chauvlyn's fae minions. They seemed as frozen with indecision as the humans.

As Munch reached the keep, he discovered a rope dangled from one of the upper windows as if waiting for him.

It could be another one of Lord Chauvlyn's traps. But something deep inside of Munch's chest told him that Brigid had put this rope here. For him.

This time, he was doing exactly what she wanted him to. She wanted him to come to rescue her. He wasn't going to mess up her plans or betray her if he climbed this rope.

Clamping the iron rod between his teeth and securing his bow on his back, he gripped the rope in both hands and began to climb.

The sisal of the rope bit against his palms while his muscles strained with the effort of climbing the rope. But he pushed himself to climb faster, his muscles honed with long years of climbing ropes, trees, and castle walls as an outlaw and forester.

As he neared the window above, the clash of weapons rang from the room inside, followed by Lord Chauvlyn's growl and Brigid's light chuckle.

Only a few more feet. Munch gritted his teeth around the iron rod in his mouth and pushed himself upward.

At the top, he peeked over the windowsill.

Lord Chauvlyn lunged, a rapier in his hand, as he stabbed with perfect form at Brigid.

She danced backwards as if unconcerned, flicking Lord Chauvlyn's rapier to the side with her own rapier. "Good show, Lord Chaubertin. Perhaps you should become a fencing instructor if being an evil minion doesn't pan out."

The fae lord huffed another snarl. His gaze swung past Brigid to land on Munch where he peeked into the room. In a moment, Lord Chauvlyn's face smoothed into his thin smirk. "I would not be too confident if I were you, Primrose. I might not be able to harm you, but there is someone who can."

Lord Chauvlyn gave a flick of his wrist.

Chapter Twenty-Two

A power seized Munch, and he found himself all but dragged over the windowsill into the room as if by puppet strings. He stumbled to his feet, staggering a few steps under the weight of the power gripping him.

No. He refused to be just a puppet in this fae lord's hands. He bit down on the iron rod until his teeth ached and his mouth filled with a metallic taste.

He fumbled for the straps holding his bow to his back, then drew an arrow from his quiver. He nocked an arrow to his bowstring.

Yet, as he drew it back, he couldn't aim it at Lord Chauvlyn. Despite his best efforts, he found himself swiveling, the broadhead pointing at Brigid's chest instead.

Her gaze focused on him, sad rather than frightened. "I see, Lord Chaullin. Your blood bound is under your power but not of your court. You can't harm me, but you can order him to do the deed."

"Precisely." Lord Chauvlyn's dark, flat tone held far too much satisfaction. "I could have him kill you here and now. Or, perhaps, I'll have him shoot you in the arm."

Munch found his aim switching to point at Brigid's upper arm.

"Or the leg. Somewhere non-fatal."

Munch's aim dropped to point at her calf. It was better than at her chest, but his heart still pounded so loudly in his ears that he could barely hear Lord Chauvlyn's smug voice.

"I rather like the thought of you surrendering yourself to me." Lord Chauvlyn stalked another step closer, his rapier still in his hand. "I will enjoy binding you to me, Primrose, and making you pay for every humiliation you've dealt me."

Munch ground his teeth on the iron bar, but he couldn't make his fingers do more than tremble as they gripped his bow and the drawn arrow.

The iron bar wasn't enough to fight the binding in his blood.

But he couldn't let Lord Chauvlyn use him as a weapon to harm Brigid. He wasn't sure what Lord Chauvlyn meant by her surrendering and being bound, but whatever it was, Munch couldn't let it happen. He knew far too well how terrible such a binding was.

How could he fight it? All it would take was a twitch of Lord Chauvlyn's fingers, and Munch would release this arrow at Brigid.

No.

He bit down harder on the iron rod.

No.

He inched his aim downward inch by painful inch.

No.

He couldn't shoot Lord Chauvlyn. Nor could he allow himself to shoot Brigid. That left only one option. Hopefully it would work.

With numb fingers and pain bursting in his head, he forced his arms the rest of the way down. And released.

With the awkward angle, he hadn't been able to hold the arrow at full draw. Still, it had plenty of power as it shot across the short space and slammed into his own foot, piercing the leather, his foot, and into the wooden floor beneath.

He screamed around the iron rod in his mouth as pain lanced through him.

As his bow slid from numb fingers, he dropped to one knee, his foot still pinned to the floor. He took the iron rod from his mouth, gripping it in one hand, and pressed his other hand to his wounded foot.

But he gathered his strength and glared at Lord Chauvlyn. "No, I will not harm her. You might have claimed my blood, but she has claimed my heart from the very first time I met her."

With something like a snap inside his head, the crushing weight of the blood binding fell away from his heart.

He sagged over his injured foot, dragging in gasping breaths.

He was free.

BRIGID RELEASED A LONG BREATH. Wonderful, heroic Munch. Shooting himself in the foot had been a step more drastic than what she'd hoped would be necessary to free him, but effective, in the end. With his brother-in-law's experience with fae, he would have known that putting iron in contact with his blood would have been the most effective way to disrupt the blood binding long enough for it to be broken.

In this case, it had been broken by the far stronger binding now singing between them.

That was something she'd have to deal with after they got out of here.

Across from her, Lord Chauvlyn's face darkened, and something almost like a snarl built in his throat before he lunged at her, his rapier stabbing wildly.

Brigid dodged, keeping her rapier raised defensively between her and the enraged fae lord. In this state, he might just be able to hurt her unintentionally, thus getting around the court binding.

When he lunged again, she danced back a few more steps until her back hit the wall. She was cornered, trapped against the wall with no more space to evade.

Lord Chauvlyn's snarl twisted into a smirk as he stepped in close, pressing his rapier against her neck and pinning her hand with her rapier against the wall.

She stilled, not fighting his grip. There was no way she could overpower him to get free. Besides, pinned to the wall would work. She needed him to get close.

Lord Chauvlyn's hot breath wafted over her face as he leaned close, panting. "I have you now, Primrose. You can't escape."

"Unhand her." From behind Lord Chauvlyn, Munch's voice rang hard and strong.

When Brigid peeked past Lord Chauvlyn's arm, Munch was standing again, bow in his hand, arrow drawn. His foot was still pinned to the floor, bleeding, but he stood straight and tall, a deadly blaze filling his eyes.

Her heart beat harder, her knees getting a little wobbly at seeing Munch—her Munch—in full protective anger on her behalf.

Lord Chauvlyn's back and features stiffened. As if he'd forgotten that, while Munch was injured, he was far from incapacitated. He swung his gaze to Brigid. "So this is how it ends. He is not bound to do me no harm as you are. All you have to do is ask him to shoot me, and you will win."

She forced a light laugh, keeping her muscles relaxed in Lord Chauvlyn's grip. "Sink me, but you have a worse memory than I have. I told you, Lord Chaubertin, that I have no wish to shed your blood today."

"Then we are at a stalemate." Lord Chauvlyn held her gaze, studying her as if looking for a hint of what she had planned. "You can't overpower me to take my sword, but I can't move to take yours without your young man killing me."

"It would seem so. But your problem, Lord Chauvlyn, is that you couldn't help but underestimate me." She spoke softly into the space between them, their faces only inches apart. "You see a pretty slip of a human girl, and you can't help but assume I'm just as frilly and silly on the inside as I appear on the outside. As if frills and pretty things are somehow worth less—and are by their nature more foolish—than the sensible and practical and plain."

His dark gaze locked with hers, his grip still tight on her wrist.

Behind him, Munch didn't move, waiting on Brigid's signal.

She leaned in even closer, her voice dropping to a whisper. "Even when you knew better—when you *knew* I was the Primrose—you couldn't help but dismiss me. But don't you know, Lord Chauvlyn, that it's the foolish things like love and mercy and hope that will conquer the world?"

With that, she leaned in, ignoring the rapier blade pressing against her throat, and pecked a light kiss on his cheek.

He froze, his breath catching. Utterly distracted from the way she wrapped the fingers of her free hand in the basket hilt of his rapier.

For just a moment, she caught a glimpse of a different face beneath the one she always saw. Instead of the handsome features of a fae, the Lord Chauvlyn she saw now had weary lines etched into skin that was not quite perfectly smooth, a hairline that was receding at the temples, and a nose that had a bump in the center.

Then Lord Chauvlyn's eyes widened, and the glamour slammed into place once again.

Even as he all but threw himself backwards, she used his own momentum to pluck his sword free of his nerveless fingers.

As he stumbled a few more feet away from her, still gaping, she swept into a curtsy as best she could with a rapier in each hand. "Thank you, Lord Chaullertin, for such stimulating conversation this evening and for this entertaining rapier practice. But I must take my leave. I fear my young man is bleeding onto your rug, and you wouldn't want the blood to set. As per our bargain, I will take him—and all I have claimed—and leave."

Munch stood tall and strong, the tip of his arrow still aimed at Lord Chauvlyn.

Lord Chauvlyn touched his cheek, then let his hand slowly drop to his side as he sagged against the wall behind him. "Just give the order. Let him kill me. You've won."

And this was exactly why she wouldn't kill him, despite what he'd done. Right now, she held far too much pity for him. It was foolish, perhaps, to leave an enemy alive to strike another day. Especially one who knew her secrets.

But hers had always been a mission of mercy, not of justice. Justice would have to come from someone else.

Brigid slid first one rapier, then the other into her magical pocket before she faced the fae lord, holding his gaze so that he'd see her heart in her eyes. "Take the mercy, Lord Chauvlyn, and enjoy a taste of the things you named foolish."

Lord Chauvlyn gusted out a breath, staring at her for a long moment before he shook his head. "You claimed all the humans in my dungeons, didn't you?"

"Every single one." Brigid strode to Munch's side, then rested a hand on his arm, letting him know that it was all right to lower his bow now. "And all those who stepped through the rift are mine as well. You won't be able to see it from here, but they wear my sign."

At least, they did, if Brigid's instructions had been followed to the letter.

Munch shot her a glance, then his stance relaxed. He lowered the bow, easing the tension on the arrow, though he didn't put it back in his quiver.

Lord Chauvlyn shook his head again, as if even now he couldn't quite believe that a young, human girl had been able to manipulate the Laws of Bindings so completely in her favor. "Of course you did and of course they are." He heaved a breath. "A bargain is a bargain."

Striding to the door, Lord Chauvlyn flung it open. As the guards standing there turned to him, he barked, "The Primrose and the humans are free to leave. Do not detain them."

Before the guards even had a chance to acknowledge his order, Lord Chauvlyn slammed the door in their faces and stalked across the room to the window. He gave the rope and grappling hook a scowl before he leaned out the window, shouting orders to the men assembled on the wall tops.

Finally, Brigid turned to Munch. As much as she wanted to yell at him for shooting himself, she couldn't when it had been the bravest—and probably the smartest—thing he could have done in that moment. "Thank you for coming back for me."

"I didn't do a whole lot. Again." Munch spoke between gritted teeth. After another glance at Lord Chauvlyn's back, he slid his arrow back into his quiver, hooked his bow over his shoulder, and knelt, his expression twisting as the movement tugged on his pinned foot.

Brigid knelt and dug into her pocket. That medical kit had

to be in there somewhere, underneath the rapiers, her disguise, various other random items, and the stacks of papers she'd shoved in there during her discussion with Lord Chauvlyn. "You broke the blood binding, and you provided the means I needed to win that duel and my bargain. That was more than enough."

"How good are you with a rapier?" Munch gripped the shaft of the arrow in both hands, drew in a deep breath, and snapped the shaft.

"Not very. I mean, it's my best weapon. I'm competent. Mostly." Her fingers closed over the medical kit, and she drew it out of the pocket. "Lord Chauvlyn is far better than I am. He would have won, if it had been a straight duel. But I was counting on you interrupting and making sure that it didn't stay a simple duel."

Munch shook his head, then groaned as he lifted his foot up and off the arrow shaft. The bloody shaft and arrow head still remained buried in the floor in the middle of a puddle of blood.

How she hated the sight of blood. The thick, globby feel and the metallic, musty stench. Her stomach lurched, and she looked away so that she could fumble with the medical supply. "We should take the time to tend to that. Can you get your boot off? I'm sure there's something in here we can bind it with."

Munch's hands stilled her fingers on the kit. A glow surrounded their hands when they touched, and Munch's mouth quirked with a lopsided smile at the sight before he lifted his gaze to meet hers. "I'll be fine until we get back to the Fae Realm. I don't want to waste time here."

"We can take the time. Lord Chauvlyn and his men won't stop us." Brigid blinked, hating that a tear trickled down her cheek. She'd even known that it might take shedding Munch's blood to break his binding, but she'd hoped against hope that she could wiggle him out of it without that part somehow.

Munch glanced at the fae lord, still yelling his orders out the window, then lowered his voice. "Your bargain is with him, not his master. If his master arrives, then all of this is off. Besides, those people below are still in danger from the monsters, and some are already more injured than I am. They need a physician or whatever you have in the Fae Realm."

He was right, of course. His injuries—and the injuries of the others—would be better treated once they reached the healers in the Fae Realm.

She blinked back the last of her tears, drew in a shaky breath, then nodded. "All right."

Munch dug out several wads of bandages from the kit, then stuffed them into the holes in the top and bottom of his boot, as if unbothered by all the blood and pain he was likely in. Once he had staunched the bleeding as much as he could without taking off his boot, he swiped his bloody fingers on his trouser leg, then held out a hand to her. "Let's get out of here."

She stood, then took his hand and pulled him to his feet.

When she started for the door, he shook his head and hopped toward the window. "The rope will be quicker. And easier. I don't relish hopping down all those stairs, and it's my foot that's injured, not my hands. If you can lower yourself down?"

Brigid nodded. She'd manage. Forcing a smile onto her face, she strolled up to Lord Chauvlyn. "Please move aside, Lord Chaubloon. We require the use of this window."

The fae lord sighed, then complied. He crossed his arms and leaned against the wall next to the window.

Brigid gestured to the rope. "You first, Munch."

He opened his mouth, like he wanted to argue, before he snapped it shut and hopped to the window.

Smart man. She would have countered his argument if he had tried, but this was much faster. While she appreciated that he likely wanted to be all chivalrous and let her, as the lady, go first, she didn't want to leave him up here alone with Lord Chauvlyn. The fae lord might be bound by his bargain to let them leave, but she wouldn't put it past him to try to get around the bargain somehow.

Munch grunted and grimaced as he maneuvered his injured foot out of the window before he dropped outside, gripping the rope. He quickly began lowering himself down with awkward hops, bracing himself with his good leg against the castle wall.

When he was most of the way down, Brigid turned to Lord Chauvlyn and gave him one last cheeky grin. "We'll meet again, Lord Chauvlyn. Next time, I hope it's under less dire circumstances. Perhaps over a nice, calming cup of tea?"

"Just leave, Primrose. Gloating doesn't become you." Lord Chauvlyn waved a hand to the window without ever shifting his arms from their position crossed over his chest.

"Believe it or not, I'm not gloating. I'm genuine in my offer, if you should find yourself so inclined to give up your current pursuits." She perched on the windowsill, then swiveled to dangle her legs outside. Chomping chimeras, but it was a long way down. Best not to look.

Instead, she glanced over her shoulder at Lord Chauvlyn one last time. "I figured it out, you know. Why you always wear black. It's a protest, of sorts, against the vain frivolity of the Court of Revels. Your court has forgotten that revelry doesn't have to be empty, meaninglessly drowning sorrow in parties and pretending that tragedies don't exist. But you, I fear, have forgotten that life isn't all death and sorrow. There's true joy. There's still hope. Life isn't all black."

She hoped today would give him something to think about.

Perhaps he'd reconsider his loyalty to that master of his. Maybe he'd cease stealing humans and attempting blood rites.

"Just...go," Lord Chauvlyn growled, his stare dropping to the floor rather than focused on her. His jaw worked, even as he hugged his crossed arms as a barrier over his chest.

Or maybe not. That was up to him and the hardness of his heart. She had done what she could and shown him an example of love and mercy. That was all she could do.

She grabbed the rope and dropped over the edge. The sisal bit into her soft hands, but she gritted her teeth and began lowering herself down. At least with her leggings, she didn't have to worry about wardrobe mishaps due to her knee-length skirts and those looking up toward her from the courtyard below.

Her arms began to burn only a few yards down, but she forced herself to keep going. Queen Hippolyta would ship her off to the Court of Swordmaidens and put her through another rigorous training session if she knew how much Brigid was struggling with this.

She kept going, little by little. Her fingers were growing numb, her palms burning from rubbing against the rough rope.

Her fingers slipped, and she half-slid, half-fell, her feet losing their purchase on the rope.

Strong arms wrapped around her, steadying her before she could drop more than a few inches. "I've got you."

She froze, still gripping the rope, before she looked up into Munch's rich, brown eyes. He was braced against the keep's wall, balanced on one foot, as he held her tight.

Right. She was only a few feet from the ground. Peeling her fingers from the rope, she rested her fingers against his shirt instead. "Thank you. Again."

He grinned, his grip tightening as if he didn't want to put her down. But then he glanced around them, sighed, and set her gently on her feet. "Lead the way, Primrose. You have hundreds of people to finish saving."

She turned, pulling one of his arms over her shoulders as she did, and faced the courtyard.

The fae on the battlements had lowered their weapons, staring from her to where Lord Chauvlyn now once again stood at the window.

The humans in the courtyard had clustered in the center, huddled together like sheep fearful of the surrounding wolves. They blinked at her with trusting eyes, waiting for her word.

If they were the sheep, then she was the sheepdog who'd just rendered the wolves fangless.

She flashed a grin and gestured toward the castle gates. "Please exit in an orderly fashion. It's time to go home."

Chapter Twenty-Three

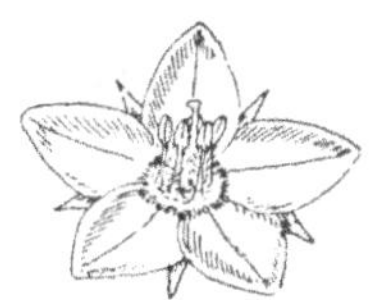

Munch hopped through the dead forest, the rotting moss squelching under the boot of his good foot with every awkward jump. He leaned on his brother-in-law Guy, not daring to set down his injured foot and risk getting any of that stinking sludge covering the forest floor into his wound. Who knew what kind of infection he'd get then?

As much as Munch would've liked to be at Brigid's side in her moment of triumph, he would only hinder her right now. Not to mention that he was far too heavy for her to bear his weight for the entire walk.

Instead, he limped at the rear with his family. Robin and his brothers had taken up the rear guard while Queen Hippolyta's swordmaidens guarded each side of the clustered group of humans. King Theseus's librarians walked among the humans, helping the young, injured, and old. A reminder that not all the fae were cruel and bloody like Lord Chauvlyn, his master, and his minions. There were fae like King Theseus, Queen Hippolyta, and all of those in Brigid's league who had stepped forward to protect the helpless and weak.

"Hydra!" Alan shouted from their right, and Robin and Will raced off in that direction, bows in hand and already reaching for arrows.

"Sorry you're stuck with me." Munch winced as his good foot came down hard on an exposed root and nearly twisted beneath him. Only Guy's steadying grip kept him from face-planting into the muck. "You can pass me off to someone else. Or give me a walking stick."

Standing half a head taller than Munch, Guy didn't even stumble under Munch's weight. Framed by his small, close-cropped beard, Guy's smile pressed thin but real. "You're wounded. The monsters will flock to the scent of blood, and you need someone with you who can defend you." Guy's gaze focused past Munch, then he swerved to place Munch next to a tree. "Speaking of that, stay here a moment."

Divesting himself of Munch's arm, Guy had his bow out in a blink and nocked an arrow.

Munch steadied himself against the tree, fumbling for his own bow as Guy drew the arrow, sighted for half a breath, and released, taking down the wolf that had been stalking through the undergrowth toward them.

Nocking his own arrow, Munch leaned his left shoulder against the tree as he drew and released. His arrow flew through the dead forest before taking another wolf through the eye.

Guy glanced at him, tipping his head in a nod, before a shriek from the sky drew his attention. In one swift motion, Guy drew another arrow, raised his aim, and released.

The large bat creature squawked, folded up its wings, and plummeted to the ground.

"I returned just in time." Robin sauntered out of the dead forest to join Guy, walking her fingers up his chest before flicking his cheek lightly. "I always appreciate a man who looks good with a bow in hand."

Guy's smile widened and warmed as he wrapped an arm around Robin's waist.

Munch sighed and leaned his head back against the tree behind him to stare up at the sky. If only Munch weren't wounded. Then maybe he'd be with Brigid and she'd start looking at him the way Robin had been looking at Guy. And maybe they'd figure out if their second attempt at a kiss would go better than their first. If Brigid would be all right with that.

Would she? Munch had seen the glow surrounding their hands. He had a hunch what it meant, but he wasn't sure where she would want to go from here. They'd danced around their attraction for years, never stepping over the lines they'd drawn between them after that one, brief kiss when they'd been eighteen.

But that had been when he hadn't known her secret. Would things be different now?

"Come on. Let's keep moving."

Guy's voice next to him startled Munch enough that he jumped, though he covered the movement by jerkily shoving his bow into place on his back. "Yes, of course."

Guy raised an eyebrow as he pulled Munch's arm over his shoulder once again. "It isn't wise to be inattentive here in the Realm of Monsters."

No, it wasn't. Munch shook his head as his sister and brothers raced off again, chasing off a chimera this time. Time to change the topic. "I know this is the Realm of Monsters, but does it seem like there are more monsters the closer we get to the rift?"

Guy's gaze swept over the dead forest. Ahead and to their right, a group of swordmaidens fought off a charging bull monster that plowed through trees as if they were kindling.

The bull swung its sharp, arched horns, but the swordmaidens nimbly dodged, using their spears to stab at it from a distance.

Some of the humans screamed, but the librarians kept them moving forward, still protected by the rest of the swordmaidens and Munch's siblings.

"Fae monsters must be attracted to rifts. It would explain why so many pour through whenever one opens up." Guy's mouth pressed tight, a darker look descending across his eyes. "With this rift anchored as you described, that would explain why we have all experienced trouble with so many monsters lately."

"I'm surprised there hasn't been more of a problem." Munch grimaced, both at the dead forest around them and the pain throbbing in his injured foot.

"The fae here likely have been keeping some of the monsters at bay so that they could travel freely through the rift themselves." Guy reached for his sword as an unusually large rat creature skittered at them out of the undergrowth.

Guy swung his sword, catching the rat in the shoulder. It tumbled a few feet away, hissing and snarling. But before it could charge again, Alan's arrow zipped from the forest and took it through the heart.

"That would explain it." Munch hopped a few more steps, breathing a sigh of relief as the black standing stones of the rift came into view between the trees.

Brigid must have already gone through with the first group of humans. Each fae librarian or swordmaiden stepped into the rift accompanied by five or six humans, all of them holding hands so that they wouldn't get separated during the crossing. Stumbling through into the Realm of Monsters was one thing, but getting back in one piece was something else entirely. It was a good thing they had so many fae on hand to help escort these humans through.

To the side, Robin, Will, and John stood back-to-back as they kept a pack of wolves at a distance. To the other side, Alan, Tuck, and Marion drove off a scuttling mass of those rodent creatures.

Munch eyed the rift, his stomach sinking even as two more groups of fae and humans leapt inside.

They couldn't leave the rift like this, anchored and ready for the banished fae from this realm to stroll into the Fae Realm whenever they pleased. Just unmooring it from the other side wouldn't be enough to fully close it. Someone would have to stay behind on this side to close it.

And, once again, he knew exactly who it had to be. There was no one else who could.

He hadn't even told Brigid a proper goodbye. There hadn't been time in the chaos of hustling the humans out of the castle and through the dead forest.

So much for all his daydreams.

At least for now. Munch drew himself straighter as he took in the rift, the standing stones, the dead forest. He was a forester. If he got stuck here, then he'd just have to find a way out again. Perhaps he could follow the monsters to wherever the next rift opened up. He'd find his way back eventually.

Or Brigid would come and find him. She was the Primrose, after all. If anyone could bend the rules of the realms, it would be her.

"Guy." Munch swallowed at the way his voice had gone tight. He wanted to tell his family goodbye, just in case. But he didn't dare say too much, in case Guy tried to stop him. "Tell her it was my choice."

Guy's gaze swung from the attacking monsters to focus on Munch. "Pardon? What is your choice?"

Munch gave a shake of his head, as if there wasn't time to explain now, keeping his gaze fixed on the rift. If he met Guy's gaze, his brother-in-law would likely figure out what Munch was planning.

The last of the humans and fae stepped into the void, leaving only Munch, his siblings, and Guy on this side of the rift.

Munch dropped a hand to his quiver. A few more minutes, and then he'd have to watch his family leave without him. And he couldn't even tell them goodbye.

He'd be on his own, trying to close a rift and fight off monsters at the same time. All while injured.

But it had to be done. Whoever Lord Chauvlyn's master was, he needed to be denied this easy access to the Fae Realm. For the sake of both humans and fae.

Guy opened his mouth, as if to press Munch for an answer, but Robin raced toward them, halting next to Guy. Thoroughly distracting Guy from whatever he had been about to say.

Grinning recklessly, Robin nocked an arrow and shot another wolf with barely a glance in its direction. "This has been fun, but I suppose it's time we call a retreat."

Guy reached out and snagged Robin's hand, pulling her close. Will gripped Robin's other sleeve, and the rest of them took hold of each other.

But as they tensed, poised before the void of the rift, preparing to leap, Munch loosened his grip on Guy as subtly as he could.

As everyone else stepped forward, Munch hopped backward, sliding out of Guy's grip. Guy's eyes widened, and he half-turned back toward Munch, reaching to grab him.

But Munch evaded Guy's grasp, his fingers merely grazing Munch's sleeve before the rift snatched him away. In a heartbeat, Munch's family disappeared.

Leaving Munch alone in the rotting forest with packs of monsters closing in from every side.

Wolves growled from his right. Rodents skittered and gnashed their large front teeth to his left.

There was no time to panic or stand there frozen with indecision.

Munch dove for the nearest obsidian standing stone, placing his back to it a wolf leapt at him. He nocked an arrow, drew, and released. The wolf yelped, falling back with the arrow lodged in its chest just a little off from where Munch had been aiming. Not a great shot, but it bought him time.

The standing stones were too large for him to move by himself so he wouldn't be able to destroy this circle as much as he would've liked. But hopefully he could make it nigh impossible for any fae to anchor a rift to it ever again.

Taking another arrow from his quiver, he jammed it into ground at the very base of the standing stone. Then following that tug of instinct, he touched his hand to the blood spilling from his boot, then smeared his blood on the standing stone.

One down. Five more stones to go.

A rodent scurried in this time, and Munch shot it. At this range, the arrow went all the way through the creature, pinning it to the ground as it died.

At least he had plenty of arrows. He'd come into the Fae Realm with twenty-four arrows in his quiver, and up until the last few minutes in this dead forest, he'd reclaimed all the arrows he'd shot.

Though he wouldn't want to be wasteful with his shots. If he did get stuck here, then every iron-tipped arrow in his quiver would mean the difference between life and death for him.

He hop-lunged to the next standing stone, falling against it, before twisting to bring up his bow and shoot another wolf before it could get too close. Jamming another iron-tipped arrow at the base of the stone, he swiped his blood across it before he had to nock an arrow and shoot yet another wolf charging toward him.

This was taking too long. Forget trying to hop and spare his wound. If he didn't move faster, the monsters would get him long before an infection would.

He gritted his teeth and raced for the next stone. Pain tore through his foot with each step. If he cried out, at least there was no one to hear him except for the monstrous creatures, which closed in as if the renewed scent of his blood and his sounds of pain drove them to a frenzy.

Placing his back to the stone, he had to shoot three rodents and stab a wolf with his sword before he had the space to take an arrow from his quiver and repeat the process of stabbing it into the earth and smearing the stone with blood.

Three stones down. Three more to go. Halfway there.

Taking up his sword again, he faced the pack of rodents that skittered between him and the next stone. There was no help for it.

With a yell, Munch charged and stabbed a rodent. Another rodent scrambled at his leg—his wounded leg, of course—then bit his calf. Not wishing to use his bow as a club and risk damaging it, Munch had to twist to bring the hilt of his sword down on the rodent's head, clubbing it several times before it released his leg.

Sweeping his sword in front of him, Munch raced forward, gaining the relative safety of the standing stone. Stabbing his sword into the ground at his side, he nocked, drew, and released three arrows in rapid succession, downing three more rodents.

With all the blood in the air, the remaining wolves were howling and snarling as they savaged the dead bodies of the rodents. At least that kept them distracted as Munch jabbed an arrow into the earth next to this standing stone. The wound in his foot must have reopened with all this movement, and blood gushed from the holes in his boot and from the bite in his leg, making it all that much easier to swipe blood across the stone.

The wolves and rodents hardly seemed to notice him as he lunged for the fifth stone. Two harpies screeched and swooped down on the carcasses, screaming at the wolves as if about to start a fight of their own.

It would be all the better for Munch if they did. If they were too busy killing each other, they wouldn't pay him any mind.

He repeated the process with the fifth stone and sprinted for the sixth, his blood staining his footprints in the muck while blood ran down his leg from the rodent bite.

After jamming an arrow at the base of the last standing stone and smearing the stone with blood, Munch leaned against it, catching his breath for just a moment.

The rift remained, still dark and swirling in the center of the circle of stones.

Now for the tricky part. If this worked as he hoped, then he'd close the rift. He might even get a split second to save himself before the rift closed.

If this didn't work as hoped, he might just unleash more power than he had reckoned with. Blood had power. It was why blood rites and bindings were forbidden—and so sought after by those seeking power.

But this blood was freely given. Both in the tower when he'd chosen to shoot himself rather than risk Brigid and now when he'd smeared it on the stones. More than that, he hadn't shed his own blood seeking power for himself but out of love for those he was trying to protect.

If anything could not only unmoor this rift but also close it, then surely blood given freely and self-sacrificially could.

With a final glance at the monsters, Munch slid his bow onto his back, gripped his sword in his right hand, and drew out his iron rod, clutching it tightly. With a deep breath, he raced forward until he was very nearly at the rift.

He stabbed the iron rod into the mucky ground hard enough that it sank through the layers of rotting vegetation into something hard and solid beneath, sticking fast. "By my blood freely given, I break this circle and unbind this rift."

A rumble tore from the rift, then quaked through the ground beneath his feet. With a deafening crack, each of the stones split apart, tearing through the center of his smeared blood down to the arrows lodged at their bases. In front of him, the rift quivered, making that same sound the rift by the castle had made a heartbeat before it had closed.

Without taking even a second to draw a deep breath, Munch threw himself into the rift.

Chapter Twenty-Four

Brigid stood at the edge of the anchored rift in the Fae Realm, keeping her smile plastered in place as she welcomed the humans into the realm and assured them that it was safe to go with Queen Hippolyta's sword-maidens and King Theseus's librarians to the castle, where they could rest and have their injuries tended until it was time to depart for the Human Realm.

Somewhere in the Realm of Monsters, Munch was taking up the rearguard with his family. He was injured, but surely he would be all right. His family wouldn't let anything happen to him.

But Brigid wouldn't be able to relax until everyone was free of the Realm of Monsters. Especially Munch.

Finally, Minnie stepped from the black tear in the fabric of the realms with six shivering and crying humans in tow. The swordmaiden saluted Queen Hippolyta. "These are the last of the humans. Well, the captive humans. The human foresters are behind us yet."

"Very good. Please remain here, Minnie. Rosaline will

escort these humans to the castle." Queen Hippolyta gestured to Rosaline, who was leaning against a tree still gathering her breath after running through the Tanglewood on her return trip from the castle. This would be her second trip, and that was after a night that had already been an eventful one for her.

Brigid hadn't had time to explain anything to anyone before leaving. So it had been Rosaline who had reported to Queen Hippolyta, explained the need to wear wild fae primroses, and helped organize everything once Basil and Buddy had fetched Munch's siblings from the Human Realm.

Brigid didn't have time to give Rosaline more than a nod in thanks for all she'd done before Robin of the Greenwood stepped through with her husband Guy and her brothers in tow.

But not all her brothers. Munch was missing.

Heart pounding in her throat, Brigid stumbled forward. "Where's Munch?"

Guy was staring back the way they'd come, his fingers outstretched as if grasping for something. He slowly turned to Robin, his hand dropping, his face twisting with something almost like pain. "He said to tell you that it was his choice. I didn't understand what he meant, but then we were leaving and he just let go. I tried…"

Munch's brother Will spun on his heel, as if ready to throw himself back into the rift. "We need to go back for him."

"No." A hard, deadly look tightened Robin's features as she dropped her hand to the hilt of her sword. "Munch knew what he was doing. He stayed behind to close the rift. He's doing his duty as a forester and protecting the realms—especially the Human Realm—from monsters. We need to let him complete this mission on his own."

Will's jaw worked for a moment, then he nodded. A few of

Munch's other brothers swung their fists, as if angry in their pain and fear. But none of them argued against Robin's verdict.

No. Brigid lunged forward. No, they couldn't just leave Munch in there. He was wounded. If Robin wasn't going to go back through the rift to get Munch, then Brigid would. She might not have Robin's skills with weapons, but she was the Primrose. She could navigate the borders between the realms as few people—fae or human—could.

Hands snagged her, then tugged her back before she had a chance to touch so much as a pinky to the rift. When Brigid turned, prepared to fight whoever was holding her, she found herself facing Queen Hippolyta.

The fae queen shook her head, her grip on Brigid tight enough to prevent any thoughts of tearing free. "You can't go back for him. You'd risk getting stuck between the realms if he closes the rift while you're inside."

"But he's still in there! He could get stuck, and he can't navigate the realms like I can!" Brigid clenched her fists, everything in her wishing she had the strength to wrench free of Queen Hippolyta's grasp.

"He's a forester." Robin moved to join them, her hand still on her sword, her gaze focused on the rift before them. "He's not ignorant when it comes to walking the realms."

Brigid forced herself to nod, but she fixed her gaze on the rift. Any moment now, Munch would come striding through. Or hopping, given the state of his injured foot.

Breathless seconds, then minutes stretched by. The rift remained, swirling dark and empty before them.

Queen Hippolyta eased some of her hold on Brigid and signaled to the swordmaidens who remained on guard around them. "Toss those ropes over the stones. Prepare to pull them down."

"Wait!" Brigid nearly managed to wrench her arm free this time, twisting to face Queen Hippolyta, though her gaze was too blurred with tears and panic to focus on the queen's gaze. "Please. Give him a few more minutes. He will get through."

She had to believe that.

Queen Hippolyta nodded, a strangely soft look in her eyes. "I will. I merely wish to be ready to pull down the circle the moment he is safely through."

Right. Of course. They wouldn't know what might follow him through. Nor would they wish to leave this circle standing a moment longer than necessary, especially if the rift was unmoored in the Realm of Monsters.

The swordmaidens threw loops of rope over the tops of the standing stones, threaded the ropes through pulleys rigged on nearby trees, and gripped the ropes in readiness to pull the moment their queen gave the order.

Munch's siblings waited, staring at the rift with their hands on their weapons as if they willed their brother to stroll through that rift.

Brigid gripped Queen Hippolyta's arm as if the fae queen was the only steady thing in that forest. Any moment now. Surely Munch would come through any second now. If there was any strength in their hearts, any truth to the binding that had started between them, then surely he'd find his way back to her.

A figure tumbled through the rift, then rolled on the moss of the Tanglewood, stopping in an ungainly heap of limbs and weapons.

For a moment, no one moved, staring at the figure lying on the moss. Then Munch raised his head, swept a glance over all of them, then let his head flop back to the ground with a groan that sounded more like one of embarrassment than of pain.

"Munch!" Brigid darted forward, released from Queen Hippolyta's grasp.

"Pull down the circle!" Queen Hippolyta barked the order, then raced to the nearest rope and took a hold, pulling along with her swordmaidens. At one of the other ropes, Minnie strained, looking able to pull down one of the stones all by herself.

Brigid knelt next to Munch and reached for his hand. "Are you all right? Are you hurt? Uh, more hurt?"

"A rodent tried to take a piece of my leg, but that's it." Munch pushed onto his elbows, then gestured at his family. "Well, stop gawking and help them. I'm fine."

"You heard him. We can't let them have all the fun." Robin dropped her hand from her sword, grinned, and sprinted for a rope. "Come on, John! Let's show them what you got!"

With growing grins, his brothers and Guy joined the swordmaidens at the ropes. John, the tallest and brawniest of his brothers, seemed to be competing with Minnie to see who could pull the most weight.

Brigid probably should've joined them, but she wasn't going to be as much help as the swordmaidens or Munch's family. Instead, she stayed by Munch, working to wrap a scrap of cloth around his bleeding leg.

With a grinding groan, the first standing stone toppled, followed by another. They landed with whumps on the layers of moss and loam. As soon as each fell, the swordmaidens on those ropes dropped them and raced to join the others still straining to topple their stones.

As the last one teetered, Munch gestured to a spot just shy of the inky blackness of the rift. "Robin! Your iron rod. I jabbed mine in the ground on the other side."

"Ah, yes. That should keep the fae from forming a circle here again." Robin drew her iron rod from her quiver, bounded past the fallen stones, and stabbed the iron rod into the ground, putting her back and shoulder muscles into the swing. The iron rod sank into the ground nearly up to where she grasped it, settling just as the final stone thudded to the ground, sending a vibration through the moss and into Brigid's toes.

The rift constricted, twisting in on itself with a faint rumble, before it winked out, vanishing as if it had never been.

Brigid released a long breath, the tension of the night draining from her. From the moment Lord Chauvlyn had strolled into the reading nook, she'd been wound tight, lost in her plots and plans and disguises.

For this moment, she could simply be herself. Not the Primrose, the humans' hero, the manipulator of bindings, the plotter to out-think all plots.

But Brigid. The girl who enjoyed pretty dresses, daydreamed about a handsome young forester, and thought that, maybe, if things turned out right this night, she might even get her second kiss.

Munch pushed himself all the way upright, brushing at his clothes. His efforts just smeared his shirt with more muck from the Realm of Monsters and flakes of dried blood from the layers that seemed to coat his hands.

"Are you truly all right? We were getting worried for a few minutes there that you wouldn't make it through." Brigid reached for him but hesitated, not quite sure where to put her hands.

In this moment, she felt how few her twenty-one years truly were. Sure, she could outwit fae far older, but that was a familiar script compared to the entirely new one she found herself reading when it came to Munch.

Munch stopped brushing at his clothes, lifted his gaze to hers, and held out his hand. "I was worried there for a minute too. But then I realized I had this in my pocket, and I found my way back home."

On his palm rested a rather wilted and worse-for-the-wear red flower.

"Where did you get this?" She touched it but didn't take it from his palm.

His fingers closed over hers, his grip warm and gentle despite the flakes of blood and coating of dirt. "From your tower. I went there after I tried to warn you about Lord Chauvlyn. That's how I finally figured out you were the Primrose, though I should have put it together far sooner." He gave her hand a squeeze, still holding her gaze. "I'm sorry I always assumed otherwise."

"And I'm sorry I never told you." Brigid blinked, dropping her gaze down to their hands, which glowed in the darkness of the night. "Every time I saw you, I wished I could confess the truth. But I just…didn't dare."

"You were right not to. I was an unbound human. I was a danger to you if I were caught. Just look at what happened tonight."

He was being far too understanding. Brigid swallowed, still unable to look at him. "It isn't like I haven't trusted unbound humans before. Your sister has known the truth for years. She trained me in walking the faerie paths, after all. If I'd told you the truth, you might have made different decisions tonight. If I'd trusted you fully before tonight, I might have done things differently."

But she hadn't dared show that deepest part of herself to Munch, knowing that he had far more power to hurt her than anyone else. She had been content to continue dancing around their attraction, unwilling to cross that line, because if she did and he rejected her, it would hurt far more than anything that Lord Chauvlyn and all his ilk could do to her.

"Perhaps, but we'll never know. And that's all right. I have no intention of dwelling on what-ifs when everything turned out just fine in the end." Munch's hand reached for her, but he stopped short of touching her cheek, curling his fingers as if he'd remembered how dirty and bloody they were at the moment. "Brigid. Look at me."

She finally gathered enough courage to raise her head and meet his gaze. All she found there was a deeper love than anything she'd seen in the years they'd known each other.

Munch leaned slightly closer, their hands still clasped between them. "I think—"

Whatever he had been about to say was cut off by Robin's boisterous laugh as she dropped down next to Munch. "Just look at that leg. We need to get you patched up before it gets so infected even the fae can't save that foot."

Right. There would be time for romance later. Hopefully. Maybe. The rest of Brigid's night was going to be busy, taken up with escorting the humans the rest of the way on their journey home to the Human Realm.

But Robin was right. Munch's foot was coated in grime and blood. It needed to be tended sooner rather than later.

Brigid stood, brushing at her skirt, as Robin and Guy pulled Munch upright, each of them taking one of his arms over their shoulders.

Together, they set off through the Tanglewood toward King Theseus's castle.

As they hiked, Brigid drew in a deep breath of the sweetly floral, magic-heavy air of the Tanglewood, free of the rotting stench of that dead forest in the Realm of Monsters.

Home. As it had been from the night Basil and Meg had stolen her family away from the Human Realm, it now was hers again after those moments in the Realm of Monsters.

As handy as it had been that Lord Chauvlyn couldn't harm

her, staying a part of his court had risks, especially the risks that came with being bound to that court's king. Brigid wouldn't be free to continue as the Primrose under any fae ruler except King Theseus or Queen Hippolyta.

For that reason, she'd asked King Theseus to officially claim her as part of his court once again as soon as they'd stepped through the rift back into the Fae Realm. Since she'd gone back through the rift alongside Basil and Meg, that had counted as Basil "snatching" her from her previous court, much as he'd snatched her and her siblings from the Human Realm five years ago. It had been enough to start the binding that King Theseus had completed.

Home. For five years, she'd been snatching humans back from their captivity in the Fae Realm to return them to their homes in the Human Realm.

Yet for her, there was no going back there. Slowly but surely, this place had claimed her heart. This was home, for all its wildness and dangers. She loved it with every fiber of her being.

The Tanglewood seemed to be in an accommodating mood that night, for it deposited them on the main road to the castle after only a few minutes of hiking. Shortly, they were ushered inside, and Munch was helped to one of the cots the fae healers had set up in the palace's great hall.

Healers already bustled between the injured humans, doling out healing potions made from the magical plants of the Fae Realm, cleaning wounds, plastering poultices of more magical herbs, and wrapping bandages.

Brigid found herself shoved to the background as the fae healers surrounded Munch, cutting off his boot, then his shirt when they realized he had bites on his arm and back from the vicious meat-eating horses.

As the healers worked, Munch eyed his siblings with that

stubborn set to his jaw that Brigid was beginning to recognize. "You all should go. I'll be fine here, and Brigid can take me to the Human Realm in the morning. There's no reason that you have to stay."

"I can stay. The rest of you go." Will crossed his arms and glanced at the others. "Robin, you and Guy have to return as soon as possible. You're the duke and duchess. Not only do you have a dukedom to rule, but you also have to be there to welcome back all these villagers and see to it that they return to their homes safely."

"No, I'll stay." Alan shook his head and waved to Will. "You're the head of the foresters. You can't be gone from the Human Realm for too long either, especially if there's trouble after tonight. I don't imagine those fae are going to be all too happy that we foiled their plans."

"No, I will stay." Tuck gestured to Alan. "The king commissioned you to sing at his daughter's birthday in a few months. You can't risk angering him by missing it, if you haven't missed it already by staying here as long as you have."

"You can't stay, Tuck. There's no telling how the castle is faring without its head cook." John grasped his tall quarterstaff, opening his mouth as if to make the same offer as the others.

"Don't even say it." Marion rolled his eyes and grimaced. "Look. I'll stay. The village can get along without a tailor for a few months."

Brigid hung back, not wishing to leave Munch but also unwilling to join in this family discussion. She really ought to be over there with Queen Hippolyta, organizing the first group of humans to return to the Human Realm.

But she couldn't bring herself to leave Munch's side just yet. Couldn't she be selfish for just a few more minutes before she returned to her role as the Primrose?

"None of you are going to stay." Munch's voice rang more

unyielding than she'd ever heard from him. Even the healers paused under the force of his commanding tone. "I might be your little brother, but I'm not helpless and I don't need you all looking after me. I'll be perfectly fine here."

Robin glanced from Munch to Brigid, then back to Munch. As she did, something in her eyes and posture shifted, as if she'd come to some understanding. She shared a look with Guy.

Guy's expression, too, changed, and he nodded. He faced the others. "Munch is right. We should leave. The danger is over. We need to return to our realm before too much more time passes."

There was some grumbling, but soon all of them clasped Munch's shoulder, murmured farewells, and shuffled off.

Robin grinned at Brigid. "We'll gather everyone left at the House, then we can take the first batch of people through the faerie circle. I might not get us as close to the time we left as you would, but I'm a fair hand at navigating the circles, if I do say so myself."

Brigid nodded, grinning back. Robin was more than a fair hand at it. If there was anyone who could walk the faerie paths as well as Brigid could, it was Robin. "All right. I won't be far behind you with the next bunch."

As the others moved off, Brigid hesitated at Munch's side. This felt like a moment to say something to him. But what should she say? There wasn't time for the discussions about bindings, secrets, and revelations that they needed to have.

Munch waved to the crowds of people, already being organized into groups by Queen Hippolyta and King Theseus. "Go, Primrose. You have a rescue to finish. I'm not going anywhere." He pointed down at his foot. "Or if I do, I won't be hobbling far."

He was right. The Primrose still had a duty to complete this night. These people had been snatched from their homes, held captive, and been frightened for far too long. It was time to restore them to their homes before they lost too much more time in their own realm.

When Brigid turned and faced the crowd, it was with an easy smile and a light laugh.

Chapter Twenty-Five

Brigid stepped through the faerie circle back into the Fae Realm, her bones aching from the long night and the four trips back and forth she'd already done.

Dawn was breaking through the trees of the Tanglewood, touching tender beams to the carpet of tiny red flowers growing at her feet. Perhaps it was her imagination, but more wild fae primrose than normal flourished around the faerie circle this night.

In the Human Realm, Guy, Robin, and Munch's siblings had returned a mere two weeks after they had left. Quite the feat of realm walking, especially with a group of returning villagers in tow.

Brigid had been only a few days after them with the second group, only losing a week in total by the time she brought the last group through.

She took a moment to lean against a tree and close her eyes. If only she could collapse into her nice, soft moss bed in the House and sleep for a week.

But she had one more trip through the realms to make that night—well, morning now. She still had to return the wounded villagers and their immediate families who'd stayed with them to the Human Realm.

Including Munch.

A deeper ache stabbed her heart at having to say goodbye to him. Yes, she'd see him again, but they'd go back to the same meet-every-few-weeks-or-months thing that they'd been doing for years.

It wouldn't be the same. Not after they'd had these last few days in the Fae Realm and all the moments they'd shared.

Not to mention there was that pesky matter of the half-finished binding between them. It had been necessary to create it to break the blood binding to Lord Chauvlyn. But this binding, too, would need to be broken for him to return to the Human Realm. It could be done, but such breakings always left scars. Things between them would never be the same again.

She pressed her fingers against the rough bark of the tree, trying to force her weary legs forward once again. No sense in just standing there stewing about what would come. She would do what had to be done, then she'd cry into Buddy's mane, lean into her family's warmth, and survive the aftermath.

But her legs didn't seem to want to listen to her. Almost without realizing it, she let her eyelids close as she leaned her head against the tree. She'd rest here for just a moment. Just a single moment.

Hoofbeats thumped on the moss, and Brigid forced herself to look up. There, as if her thoughts had conjured them, were Buddy, Meg, and Basil walking toward her, weaving between the trees at the edge of the Tanglewood.

She used the tree to prop herself more upright. "What are you doing here?"

Basil gestured back toward the quaint little fae village. "We thought we'd help with the last trip through the circle. You'll need the extra hands with the wounded."

A lump formed in Brigid's throat. Silly exhaustion. She didn't want to burst into tears at something as simple as an offer of help, but there she was, blinking back tears and swallowing hard. "Thank you for coming. Not just now, but back in the Realm of Monsters."

Even with all her planning, she hadn't expected that. She'd asked for Queen Hippolyta and her swordmaidens, but King Theseus and his librarians had been a surprise to even her. Basil and Meg's presence even more so. They'd risked their lives for her.

She pushed away from the tree, tottering a few steps.

Meg rushed forward and reached out, steadying her. "Capering carp, you're dead on your feet. You should get some sleep before you attempt another trip between the realms. It wouldn't hurt to let the wounded rest a few more hours."

"The longer they stay here, the more time they'll lose in their own realm." Brigid shook off Meg's hand and strode forward a bit more steadily. Once every single human was safely home, then she could collapse.

His brown coat shining in the morning sunlight, Buddy clopped alongside her, his fuzzy body radiating warmth and that comforting horse smell. "Bother and nonsense. They'll lose more time if you get lost on the faerie paths."

"I never get lost. I have the primroses to guide me." Brigid draped an arm over Buddy's back, hoping the others wouldn't notice how much she was using his solid warmth to steady herself and gather strength. There was just something soothing about the talking pony companion.

"Buddy and I can take them through the circle, if you're that worried about it." Basil gave a small shrug, momentarily wrinkling the shoulders of his librarian coat before it smoothed out again. "We'll lose more time in the Human Realm than you would, but it won't be much more. Not if I have Buddy with me."

Brigid dug her fingers into Buddy's mane, so very tempted to let her brother-in-law take on this burden for her.

While fae or humans just stumbling through a circle would be at the mercy of the magic to spit them out in whatever time or place the magic between the realms saw fit, a realm walker like her could navigate the faerie paths and come close to erasing the time difference between the realms. Talking animal companions, like Buddy, could navigate the faerie circles in nearly the same way, making travel through the faerie circles easier and safer than they would be otherwise.

"I'll be fine, but thank you." Brigid already felt better, soaking in Buddy's warmth and strength next to her.

Meg glanced at her, then shared a look with Basil.

Brigid suppressed a sigh. The two of them were more determined than ever to help her on this last trip through the circles.

Oh, well. She was thankful. They were right. She was dead on her feet, and the wounded would need help, even after several hours of rest and healing.

Perhaps it would be better, saying farewell to Munch when they weren't alone.

Buddy nipped at the muddy hem of her red, embroidered skirt. "Never do that to me again."

"Do what? Go off into the Realm of Monsters and walk into a trap with just my wits to get me out of it?" Brigid patted the talking pony's back as they tramped through the last few ferns at the edge of the Tanglewood and stepped onto the path that led through the village and back to the castle. Having been traveled by so many humans in the past few hours, the moss was more trampled and travel-worn than usual.

"No. Leave me with a horde of hooligan children for hours."

Buddy snorted and shook his head. "I've never given so many rides in a row in my life. Who do they think I am, a witless, non-talking pony at a carnival show? You'd think they'd never seen a pony before."

"They'd certainly never seen a *talking* pony before." Brigid drew in another deep breath of Buddy's musky, horse scent. Now that she was looking closer, she could see the remnants of braids and a few bows still stuck haphazardly in his thick mane and tail.

Meg laughed and leaned over to pat Buddy's neck. "Most children four years old and younger are hooligans."

"Addy and Morgan aren't." Buddy stated this with the utter certainty of an uncle speaking about his two favorite nieces in the whole wide world. In his eyes, they could do no wrong.

"That's because they inherited Basil's goodhearted nature." Meg grinned and reached for Basil's hand.

Basil clasped her fingers, his neck going a bit flushed as if he was embarrassed. "They could have gotten their sweet temperaments from you."

Buddy gave an even louder, horse snort through his large nostrils. "No, if they are sweet and mild-mannered, then they definitely got that from you, Basil. If it were up to Meg, they'd be the hooliganest hooligans of the lot."

Brigid hadn't thought she had the energy for laughter after that long, wearying night. But here she was, half-draped across a pony's back, stumbling her way through the early morning and laughing into his mane. "Hooliganest isn't a word."

"Shush. I said it, so thus it's a word." Buddy twisted his head around to nip at her skirt again, giving it a firm tug with his large, blunt teeth before he let go. "Besides, it isn't really the children's ages I had a problem with. It was the *number* of them."

Brigid opened her mouth, but she paused. She didn't really

have a comeback for that one. All of Munch's six older siblings had gotten married in the past five years, and most of them had one or two children at this point, depending on the length of time they'd been married. Except for Marion, who didn't have any children yet since he'd only been married for a few months, and Alan, whose wife was expecting their first.

Add in Addy and Morgan, a late-night awakening, a trek through the realms, and the impossibility of sleeping in a strange place, and that would result in a large pack of cranky, hyper children four years old and under.

Maybe Buddy had a good reason to grumble. Brigid would take her night facing the Realm of Monsters over the night he'd had.

By this time, they were nearing the causeway that would lead them to the castle and Library, set on the hill overlooking the village.

"Oh, I have something for you, Basil." Brigid reached into her magical pocket and pulled out the wad of papers she'd taken from Lord Chauvlyn's desk in the Realm of Monsters. "I hope there's something helpful in this. I didn't get a chance to look at it while I was surreptitiously stealing it."

Basil took the papers from her, his forehead furrowing. As he paged through them, his brows lowered, then rose. "Do you know what this is?"

"If my guess is correct, they give the identity of Lord Chauvlyn's master, who is one of the two fae you've been looking for." Brigid sagged a bit more heavily against Buddy.

That much hadn't been hard to deduce. The three fae had been kicked out of the Fae Realm for performing forbidden blood rites. Not to mention that they originally had come from the Court of Revels.

Now there was a mysterious master gathering humans to

perform a blood rite, using a rift anchored in the Court of Revels to do it.

It didn't take someone with even half of Brigid's intelligence to put that one together.

Basil nodded, then slid the papers into a pocket of his librarian coat. "It's Claudius. At least we now know he's still in the Realm of Monsters, where he's supposed to be after his banishment."

"True, but that clearly hasn't stopped him from scheming. The last few days have shown that he can cause a whole heap of trouble even while he's in the Realm of Monsters." Meg's mouth pinched as she reached for Basil's hand, clasping his fingers in a way that made Brigid ache all the more for a hand of her own to hold.

Not just any hand, but one with fingers callused from a bowstring and strong from years of wielding a sword.

Basil nodded and patted his pocket. "I'll let King Theseus and Queen Hippolyta know. At least we know who we're dealing with now."

Yes, that was something. And Brigid wouldn't be facing him all on her own. She would continue to rescue captured humans, but that was only a portion of this fight. King Theseus and Queen Hippolyta would take it from here when it came to actively countering Claudius's next move, whenever it came.

They reached the causeway to the castle, and Brigid fell silent, not wishing to give away that she was breathing hard as she leaned against Buddy. Her calves burned from just this slight uphill as she felt every mile she'd walked that night.

Buddy's hooves clopped on the marble floors as they stepped inside, heading for the double doors to the castle's great hall. While still guarded by swordmaidens, the doors stood open, showing the remaining bustle inside.

Six pallets lined up against one wall for the people, including Munch, who had been most grievously injured during the escape. Only one, the man who had been stabbed during the fight to lower the drawbridge, had been touch and go through the night, but before Brigid had left with the last group of humans, the fae healers had told her that they expected he would pull through.

The immediate families of those who had been wounded had remained behind, unwilling to be separated from their loved ones.

King Theseus and Queen Hippolyta stood just inside the great hall, talking to Head Librarian Marco, the head healer, and several of the squad leaders among the swordmaidens.

With a glance toward Brigid, Basil turned in that direction, inserting himself in the circle and rocking back and forth on his heels as he waited for a moment to interrupt.

Brigid dug her fingers into Buddy's mane. "Let's—"

A door slammed against a wall from somewhere in the Hall of Anywhere Doors.

Brigid jumped and leaned even more heavily against Buddy as she peered past him in that direction.

Next to Basil, both King Theseus and Queen Hippolyta reached for their swords, but they didn't draw them. All the swordmaidens in the vicinity dropped into fighting stances, weapons in hand.

King Oberon of the Court of Revels stormed from the Hall of Anywhere Doors into the entry hall of the castle. His dark brown curls didn't so much as twitch from their coif despite his furious pace while his scowl barely moved his cheeks and upper lip from their tight, too smooth perfection, as if someone had attempted to sculpt the perfect face with magic and succeeded a little too well.

Today, he wore a white ruff around his neck that poofed out so far that he likely couldn't see much but straight ahead of him. The fluttering layers of silk that draped over him—they were too sparse and draping to be called a shirt—were dyed a mix of greens and blues that shimmered like dragonfly wings as he moved. The effect gave a great view of his almost too well-defined pectoral muscles that clashed with his jiggling paunch.

Around his middle he wore a very tight, very short pair of pants that left his legs entirely exposed from his flabby thighs all the way to his thick calves. His feet had been slipped into sandals that seemed to be made of grass with teeny-tiny straps only over his toes so that the grass sole slapped the marble floor with every step.

At his heels trotted the three-foot-tall, green-skinned sprite Puck. The sprite wore clothing that was identical to his sovereign's, except that his were entirely in green from a light green ruff to emerald shorts that were barely darker than his skin, making it almost look like he wasn't wearing anything at all.

"Walloping wildcats, what does *he* want?" Meg crossed her arms and glared, a grimace of distaste curling her mouth.

"Nothing good, I'm sure." Buddy snorted, his upper lip curling as if he'd gotten a whiff of rotten hay in his food trough. "The Deplorable Duo are always up to some mischief." He used his mocking nickname for King Oberon and Queen Titania.

Brigid let a grin brighten her face. With the fae king present, she needed to wear her mask. "I know I've complained about Lord Chauvlyn's basic black, but, horrific hydras, I don't really blame him for choosing black when *that's* his other option. I'll have to tell him that the next time I see him."

Meg shot her a look. "I hope that won't be anytime soon. Especially now that we know Claudius is his master. I'm not sure Lord Chauvlyn can even count King Oberon as his king anymore, now that he's given his loyalty to his new court in the Realm of Monsters."

Come to think of it, that meant that Claudius had probably counted as Brigid's king for a few minutes there.

Brigid suppressed a shudder. Good thing King Theseus had snatched her back into the Court of Knowledge as soon as possible. Who knew what terrors a king like Claudius would have unleashed on her once he discovered a human was a member of his court? He might not have been able to outright kill her, but there was a lot he could do besides kill her, especially given the power a monarch held over the members of a court.

King Oberon stomped across the marble hall—his sandals flip-flopping ridiculously loudly with every step.

Puck bounded ahead, skidding to a brief halt in front of King Theseus and Queen Hippolyta. "My good King Oberon wishes to speak with you."

"I can see that." King Theseus's dry tone contrasted with Puck's overly exuberant declaration.

The flapping of King Oberon's shoes ceased as he halted inches from King Theseus. "What is the meaning of this, Theseus? What is this I hear that you let your wife tear down a circle on *my* court's side of the Tanglewood? You know the laws. You are not to meddle with my court or anything inside my borders. To do so means war."

"War and weeping. Weeping and war," Puck echoed, taking up a station just behind King Oberon and a little to his left.

King Theseus crossed his arms, unflinching under his fellow monarch's ire. Granted, King Oberon was hardly an intimidating figure even when angry. But that didn't mean he wasn't dangerous. With his sprites, he could wreak havoc quite effectively across the courts if he wished.

Still, King Theseus's hard eyes never wavered as he met

King Oberon's gaze. "For one, I don't *let* my wife do anything. She makes her own decisions, and I have full confidence in them. If she pulled down a circle, then it was the right thing to do. Two, do you really wish to threaten me with war, Oberon?"

Theseus gestured from Queen Hippolyta, dressed in chain mail and bristling with weapons and fury, to the swordmaidens and librarians who were closing around them. Even the librarians had their clubs and staffs out now, including Basil.

When Brigid glanced to Meg, her sister gripped her shepherd's staff in her hand, looking far too eager to brain Oberon a good one if King Theseus gave the word.

A smile seemed ready to break onto King Theseus's face before he stuffed it down, turning back to King Oberon. "Just because we are a court of peaceful librarians doesn't mean that we are helpless any longer. We have training and powerful allies. If it came down to it, there are others among the courts who would stand with the Court of Knowledge in a war with the Court of Revels."

King Oberon's perfectly square jaw worked, the cleft in his chin deepening with his scowl. "I have powerful allies as well, Theseus, and they will crush your little band of bumbling librarians and women waving swords pretending to be warriors."

Queen Hippolyta made a noise like a snarl in the back of her throat. She stepped forward, starting to draw her sword.

King Theseus didn't try to restrain her or stop her. He merely held out a hand to her, not touching her as he met her gaze. Giving her the choice to either continue forward and attack King Oberon or listen to King Theseus's silent counsel offered in that one, gentle gesture.

Hippolyta's mouth pressed into a tight line, but she shoved her sword back into its sheath with a sharp snap.

King Oberon smirked at that. As if it confirmed all his

preconceived notions of King Theseus's "control" over Queen Hippolyta. Behind him, Puck grinned, showing off his rows upon rows of fang-like teeth.

King Theseus shook his head, then nonchalantly waved. "You mean your allies in the Realm of Monsters? The ones that the Primrose just single-handedly defeated to rescue hundreds of people from their clutches? Those allies? Forgive me if I'm not intimidated."

Brigid couldn't help but lightly chuckle to herself. King Theseus might not be as visibly angry as Queen Hippolyta, but his sarcasm gave him away. He was *furious*.

King Oberon's clenching fists joined his working jaw. "Just a minor setback. Mark my words, the Primrose will be caught. You can't harbor him forever."

Brigid nearly startled at King Oberon's use of *him* to refer to the Primrose. Of course. If she hadn't been so tired, she would've realized it sooner. King Oberon didn't yet know she was the Primrose. Word would spread soon enough. Lord Chauvlyn would wiggle back into the Fae Realm eventually. Or one of the librarians would let something slip to a library patron. Too many people had seen her tonight. Her anonymity was gone.

That didn't mean she'd have to stop being the Primrose. She'd just have to get sneakier about it.

Some things would be easier. King Theseus and Queen Hippolyta had openly backed her by going into the Realm of Monsters to rescue those humans. They couldn't go back to their appearance of deniability.

There was no point in hiding anymore. They'd tried to appear neutral to avoid war with the other courts. But right now, war—at least with the Court of Revels—might be inevitable.

Brigid had known she could be dragging her court into war

the moment she'd asked Queen Hippolyta for reinforcements to enter the Realm of Monsters. With blood rites involved, she'd deemed the risk necessary, and Queen Hippolyta had agreed.

King Theseus must have also agreed because he didn't waver under King Oberon's accusation. "He won't be caught. But if he is, ten more will rise in his place. Not everyone in the Fae Realm celebrates cruelty the way you do."

"Mischief and mayhem. Mayhem and mischief," Puck recited, humming to himself as he rocked back and forth on his heels behind his king.

A weight settled onto Brigid's shoulders that she wasn't sure she'd be able to shake, especially if this did indeed turn into a war. She'd become the Primrose to save lives, not cause a war. Instead, had she traded human lives for the lives of the fae who would be killed in this war, should it come?

She clenched her fingers in the reassuring warmth of Buddy's mane.

He swung his head around and nudged her with his nose. "This isn't your fault. With Claudius involved, this war was coming whether you did anything or not."

She released a long breath. Buddy was correct. If she had done nothing, then Claudius would have been free to gather humans and conduct the forbidden rites. Even if he hadn't succeeded in abolishing the Laws of Bindings, such rites would have torn a rift the likes of which the realms had never seen. The death and destruction would have been incalculable. Standing on the edge of the Tanglewood as it was, the Court of Knowledge would have been the first court to fall. The Great Library, all the precious, stored knowledge of the realms, and all the librarians who worked here would have been wiped from the Fae Realm.

This war wasn't on her, if there was a war. It wasn't on King Theseus or Queen Hippolyta either.

The fault lay with Claudius, Lord Chauvlyn, King Oberon, and fae like them who reveled in the cruelty they dispensed on both humans and fae alike.

King Theseus stared King Oberon down, his eyes as hard as Queen Hippolyta's sword. "You came in here to complain about me breaking laws, but what about your lawbreaking? You anchored a rift in your court, opening the way for monsters to spill unhindered into our realm. You gave leave for a band of rogue fae to use your court as a waypoint."

King Oberon puffed up like a chimera with its lion fur rubbed the wrong way, sputtering. "Well, I never—"

King Theseus stepped forward, not giving King Oberon a chance to gather himself. "Your emissary broke the laws of hospitality and stole from my queen and from my court. If anything, our actions tonight in destroying the circle were our due justice for the wrongs done us."

"Now, I don't—"

King Theseus crowded King Oberon's space, as if the two kings were about to come to blows. "And what's this I hear about you associating with Claudius? Whom, I might add, you banished years ago after he tried to take your crown and court. Why would you willingly ally yourself with him? What did he offer you that would be worth the risk?"

"As if you don't know." King Oberon jabbed a finger into King Theseus's chest. "It's the same reason you've allied your-self with the Court of Swordmaidens."

"The safety of my people?" King Theseus didn't back down under King Oberon's poking finger.

"Power." King Oberon stated it as if it should have been beyond obvious. "Now that you have it, thanks to bagging yourself a warrior wife, I've seen the way you've been eyeing my court. For the past five years, you've been digging your claws into my business more and more. I had to defend myself somehow before *you* steal my crown."

"We share the Tanglewood between our courts. We're both Summer Courts. Of course our business is tangled together." For the first time, King Theseus's voice rose in pitch. "I have no designs on your crown. I'm a fellow monarch. I *can't* steal your throne any more than you can steal mine. Frankly, I'd love to ignore you and your miserable excuse for a court. But you have a way of making your business my business. The chaos of your court inevitably spills into mine and, unlike you, I actually care about my people."

This time, it was Queen Hippolyta's turn to reach out a hand. Though Brigid wasn't sure if it was a restraining gesture or an offer to take King Oberon out if King Theseus gave the word. Knowing the fae queen, it was probably the latter.

King Oberon's face mottled red as he seemed to swell in his rage.

Puck stepped forward, his tiny green fists clenched at his sides. "Just give me the word, my great King Oberon! I'll unleash torment and terrors. Terrors and torment."

For the first time, Head Librarian Marco stepped forward into the conversation, giving a little cough and smoothing his long white beard. "There will be no need for that, now. There's been no harm done this night."

"She *broke* a circle in *my* court." King Oberon pointed at Queen Hippolyta with all the flourish of a petulant child complaining about a broken toy.

"And saved both the courts from the continuing flood of monsters." Head Librarian Marco sniffed and looked down his long, slightly crooked nose at King Oberon. "Do you really want to start something as messy as a war? Wars have a terrible habit of getting in the way of parties and revelries. Now, if your sprite will come with me, we have a nice new play that was just written by the Right Honorable Acting Troupe here in the Court of Knowledge. If you take it back now, a troupe in your court would have enough time to practice to put on a show this evening."

Brigid leaned away from Buddy to whisper to Meg. "Nick Bottom wrote a play?"

That was the bad part of being gone from the Court of Knowledge so often. Sometimes she missed the mundane parts of life in a court.

"Yes. Unfortunately." Meg's mouth wavered between a grin and a grimace. "Let's just say the only one day of practice Oberon's people are going to get won't make the play any worse."

Nick Bottom was a goblin who, along with several of his friends, had moved from the Court of Goblins to the Court of Knowledge to pursue a career in the arts. But just because they wanted to be actors didn't mean they were any good at it.

And if their writing skills were as bad as their acting...Brigid almost felt sorry for the poor residents of the Court of Revels who would be forced into that production.

"What? I thought Nick Bottom's play that we watched years ago was hilarious." Brigid kept her voice light, her expression too innocently open.

"The play was a tragedy."

"Oh, yes, it was." Brigid couldn't help it if her grin widened. "There were plenty of tears."

"Because we laughed until we cried. At the death scenes, I might add." Meg shook her head, though she, too, was grinning.

King Oberon's huffy anger vanished in a blink, though his face was so unnaturally smooth from so many magical alterations that only the raising of his brows and the gleam in his eyes gave away the change from anger to intrigue. "A new play, you say?"

"Never performed before. Not even in the Court of Knowledge." Head Librarian Marco leaned a bit closer, lowering his voice as if to impart a great secret. "I've been told by those who have witnessed the Right Honorable Acting Troupe practicing it that it is a spectacle to behold."

Meg snorted. "Nick roped Basil into watching a preview. It's a spectacle, all right. Spectacularly bad."

"Remind me to be gone on their opening night here in the Court of Knowledge."

"Oh no you don't. If I have to sit through it, then you do too." Meg gave Brigid a stern look.

"Librarian Basil!" Puck bounded past Head Librarian Marco and King Oberon to where Basil had been standing, trying to hide in the background from the moment King Oberon had stormed into the entry hall. Puck tugged on the hem of Basil's black coat. "You can take me to find this new play!"

Meg sighed, then started in that direction, though her voice held a note of something that was almost like fondness. "I'd better go help them. It's going to take two of us to keep Puck from tossing books off the shelves or otherwise causing chaos and angering the Library."

Brigid understood. Puck was a disaster wrapped up in a pint-sized package, not to mention a touch evil if turned loose. But it was hard not to be a bit fond of the sprite. He did every-thing with such a cheerful exuberance. Granted, he demon-strated the same cheerful exuberance when tormenting someone to insanity as he did when fetching a book from the Library. So, not a great role model for children. But something about him just made a person smile. Most of the time.

Within a few more minutes, Head Librarian Marco had King Oberon laughing as he escorted him back toward the Hall of Anywhere Doors to return to the Court of Revels while Puck fetched the play.

"And that's how wars are averted." Brigid released a breath and leaned more heavily against Buddy.

"By treating King Oberon like the spoiled child that he is?" Buddy snorted, then bared his teeth briefly at King Oberon's back before the king and head librarian disappeared into the Hall of Anywhere Doors.

"No. Well, yes. I was going to say by bribing him with the things he loves: parties and revelries."

"Perhaps King Theseus should send over a case of the finest faerie fruit wine. That's what he loves the most." Buddy flicked one of his ears in the direction of the Hall of Anywhere Doors.

"Not Queen Titania?" Brigid tried to hide her grin. She didn't think she succeeded.

"Perish the thought. No. He definitely loves wine far more than Queen Titania." Buddy snorted, shaking his mane. "There are a great many things King Oberon loves more than Queen Titania. Himself, for one. Then again, there's a great many things that Queen Titania loves more than Oberon. That's why they are the Deplorable Duo."

"Right as always, Buddy." Brigid pushed off him, though she gave his broad, muscled neck a scratch. "Still, sending a case of wine wouldn't hurt. Hopefully King Oberon and his court will get too drunk to notice how bad the play is."

Not that she really trusted King Oberon's taste in the acting arts, considering his taste in fashion. He might think Nick Bottom's play was the best piece of literature ever written.

To each their own. Art was subjective like that.

Buddy shook his mane again, then cocked his head to indicate where King Theseus and Queen Hippolyta had turned away, talking in low voices. "Not sure the two of them are in any mood to send over so much as a case of wine in what could be construed as an apology."

No, they weren't. Even now, Queen Hippolyta's hand remained clenched on her sword's hilt, her eyes flashing, while the muscles at the corner of King Theseus's jaw were knotted.

And perhaps Brigid had misspoken earlier. That war had been averted…but only for now. King Oberon was too volatile to be appeased by plays and parties for long. Eventually, he'd erupt again.

Truthfully, this had been building for years. Even before the disastrous Midsummer Night five years ago when Brigid and her family had arrived in the Fae Realm. The incidents between the courts just kept piling up, and it would have to come to a head eventually.

Regardless of what happened with the Court of Revels, they were at war with Claudius and his cronies. They'd dealt him a blow, but he would try again. He was getting bolder, to even attempt something like this. If anything, this defeat would just make a fae like him more determined than before.

Brigid pushed away from Buddy's warmth. "In that case, I'd better get moving. I'd like to get all these humans out of here as soon as possible."

Chapter Twenty-Six

Munch sat on his pallet, leaning against the wall and munching on a bowl of fruit one of the fae healers had scrounged for him. Next to the bowl, he had a tray with the fae version of scones, sweets, and other treats, and he was slowly working his way through sampling them all.

As he plucked another slice of a turquoise citrus-like fruit and stuffed it into his mouth, Brigid flitted into the great hall in the wake of that argument between fae kings that had nearly escalated to a war.

That argument just helped solidify what Munch had already been turning over in his mind. He just needed to talk over a few things with Brigid.

Brigid halted for a moment to speak with the head fae healer before she nodded and headed straight for Munch, that customary wide but empty smile on her face.

She wore the same knee-length red dress embroidered with flowers with the pink leggings beneath. But her boots were grubby with streaks of mud all the way up to her knees. Beneath that empty smile, her eyes were smudged with dark circles, and a weariness lingered in the lines of her face.

The only reason he didn't look just as bad was that one of the fae potions he'd been given had sent him right off to sleep for hours. While the stuff had looked like a disgusting, milky sludge, it had tasted sweet—almost too sweet.

"You look beat. You should rest a while." Munch gestured to the pile of blankets next to him. The fae healers had prepared a little too well for the injured and hadn't needed nearly as many pallets or blankets as they'd feared.

"Walking the realms always takes it out of me." Brigid sank onto the blankets and leaned her back against the wall behind her. "But never fret, I have one more trip to the Human Realm in me yet. I'll get you back to your family before too many more weeks pass over there."

"I'm not worried about that." Munch wanted to reach for her, but he didn't want to start that whole glowing hands thing again. He had other things he wanted to discuss before they got up to *that*. "I mean, yes, I want to see my family again. But they'll be fine if I take a few more days to do it."

"Probably, but their families won't be." Brigid gestured to the rest of the line of pallets. The healers were going down the line, distributing last doses of healing potions, checking wounds, and getting the injured ready to travel. "The healers say we'll be able to leave soon. How's your foot?"

"Nearly healed." Munch lifted his bandaged foot and swiveled it around. The movement pulled a little tight, but it didn't hurt. He'd probably be able to walk on it when they left, even though he might limp. The bites on his arm, back, and leg were entirely healed, just a bit pink and tender.

Fae healing potions were amazing stuff. A mere few hours later, and his wounds were nearly healed. Sure, the potions didn't work quite as well on him as they would have a fae. If he'd been a fae, he likely would have been completely healed by now.

Still—he glanced down the line of injured on the pallets—it seemed like he had healed faster than the others. Did it have something to do with that glowing hand thing between him and Brigid?

Now wasn't the time to ask.

"Good. I'd hate for you to go lame because you shot yourself in the foot." Brigid's smile flashed back onto her face, though it wasn't as bright as it usually was, as if she was too weary to fully fake the mask.

"Wouldn't be the first time, though it's usually more metaphorical than literal." Munch shrugged, glancing over the sweets on the tray. Which one should he try next? "And if I'm not shooting myself in the foot, I'm putting my foot in my mouth. Especially when it comes to you."

"Not all the time." Brigid's genuine smile peeked through. "You said some pretty nice things earlier tonight." Both the masking grin and genuine smile faded. "Did you mean them?"

Like when he'd said she had claimed his heart long ago? Yes, he'd meant that. He just wasn't sure if he could gather the courage to say it again.

"Of course I did." Munch couldn't bring himself to look at her, and he instead picked a frosted square sweet of some kind off the tray.

He and Brigid lapsed into silence, and he let the moment linger as he gathered his thoughts and stuffed the treat in his mouth. Surprisingly bitter, and he chewed and swallowed quickly.

There was so much they needed to talk about, and he wasn't sure where to start. After all the progress they'd made, he didn't want to go bumbling into this.

He drew in a breath and glanced at Brigid. "Why did you

give Lord Chauvlyn mercy last night? You could have handled it differently. You had Queen Hippolyta and her swordmaidens on hand. Or you could have asked me. Even if you didn't want to kill him, we could have taken him captive. So why did you let him go?"

Brigid rested her head against the wall behind her, staring unseeingly into the great hall. "When my sister Meg was snatched, we spent eight months wondering what had happened to her. Sure, it all turned out all right, but I couldn't shake the burning fury and fear and helplessness of those months."

It didn't seem like an answer to his question, but he didn't interrupt.

"I let those emotions fuel me when I became the Primrose." Brigid sighed and shook her head. "But I quickly figured out that anger is a rather bad motivation, and Queen Hippolyta made sure to train the anger out of me. It turns out that whacking a pole with a sword until my arms burned and my blisters seeped is very therapeutic."

Munch was never going to complain about Robin's early morning archery or sword practices ever again. "And that's when you made love your motivation?"

"It started out as love for the people I was helping." Brigid drew her knees up, hugging them. "I ache for their sorrow at being separated from their families. I hurt for the cruel way they are treated in this realm. And I want to soothe their tears after the torments they've suffered here."

Of course she did. Munch had gotten a taste of what humans suffered in the Fae Realm. And he hadn't been captured that long.

Brigid rolled her shoulders in a shrug and waved at the others in the room. "But it has become so much more than that. Now, I do this not just because I love my own people but because I love the Fae Realm and its people. This place is my home, and it's filled with many fae who aren't cruel. Like Basil or King Theseus or Queen Hippolyta or many of the librarians. The many decent and honorable fae shouldn't have to bear the collective guilt of those who aren't."

"So you do this out of love for them." Munch curled and uncurled his fingers, wishing he dared reach for Brigid's hand.

"Yes." Brigid rocked back and forth slightly as she hugged her knees. "Tonight, I realized that I do it out of love for the cruel fae like King Oberon and Lord Chauvlyn as well. Maybe not love, exactly, but I pity them, and perhaps I want to try to save them from themselves. What kind of presumptuous person does that make me?"

"It doesn't make you presumptuous. It makes you a hero." Munch gave in and rested a hand on her arm. When she shot a glance at him, he gave a slight shrug. "Sure, you might have a bit of a complex. Robin had one too, for a while there, thinking she had to save everyone and that no one else but her could do it. But that doesn't mean you aren't a hero. There's nothing wrong with pitying your enemy and extending him mercy. Just as long as you are prepared to give justice when the time comes."

"I think that's where King Theseus and Queen Hippolyta come in." Brigid gave another one of those tiny wiggles of her shoulders, as if she didn't have the energy to put into a full shrug. "Lord Chauvlyn said something to me last night. He claimed that it wasn't possible to love without selfishness. Even the most noble of people love for what they can get out of it."

"What did you tell him?" Munch wasn't sure he wanted to examine that thought too closely. It rang far too close to his own realization about his drive to be a hero.

"That maybe it's hard to love without selfishness, but I still have to believe it's possible. Even if I know I don't love as unselfishly as I should, I'm still going to strive to be better." Brigid sighed and rested her chin on her knees. "But it was rather disheartening to be called out by Lord Chauvlyn, of all people. Worse, he was right. I'm not the gloriously unselfish hero I'm made out to be. There's a part of me that's doing this because I love the satisfaction I get out of it rather than because I'm unselfishly, self-sacrificially loving the ones I'm helping."

Her words were so raw that, for a moment, Munch wasn't sure how to answer.

For years, he'd lifted her up on a pedestal, loving her from afar as if she was some kind of unattainable paragon.

But that had never been love. Not really. He'd been in love with an idea of her, an idea that turned out to be utterly false. Worse, he'd built that idea of her so solidly in his mind that it had blinded him to the truth of her. He hadn't been able to guess that she had the ruthless cunning to be the Primrose until the truth had been smacking him in the face.

But now, he saw her. Her goodness. Her heroics. Her flaws. Her mistakes.

This time, he reached out and clasped her hand. That golden glow surrounded their fingers again, but he wasn't going to flinch away. When Brigid tilted her head to look at him without lifting her chin from her knees, he squeezed her fingers. "Perhaps none of us love as we ought. Tonight, I realized that I only wanted to be a hero for the acclaim I would get out of it, not for any truly heroic reason. But if we realize our faults, if we've been given a heart that knows better than to wallow in the selfishness and hardness that is so often the default, then we can strive to do better. Maybe we won't do it perfectly, but it's a beginning."

Brigid heaved a sigh that gusted over their clasped hands. "Thanks, Munch. You can be rather wise when you want to be." She paused, her eyes widening as if she realized how that might sound. "Not that you aren't wise. Or that you're unintelligent most of the time. Or...ugh. Now I'm the one with my foot in my mouth. I can banter with Lord Chauvlyn just fine, but when it comes to you, I'm just...argh."

She dropped her forehead onto her knees, though she didn't tug her hand free of his.

He laughed and gave her fingers another squeeze, wishing they were at a point where he could draw her into his arms and hold her. "It's rather nice to see the shoe on the other foot for a change."

"Ha, ha." She tipped her head to peek at him again. "Do you think we can dispense with the foot comments?"

"Now that I no longer have one foot in the grave, I think so."

She sat up straighter so that she could give him a scathing glance. "You were never dying. It was just a little arrow to your foot."

"It was a very large arrow, thank you very much. Smart man that I was, I grabbed an arrow with a whacking great broadhead rather than one of my practice arrows with their tiny, non-barbed heads. If not for the fantastical fae healing potions you have here, I probably would have gotten gangrene and lost the foot if I'd been in the Human Realm." Munch tried to hold on to a woebegone expression as he held up the bowl of fruit. "But at least I've been showered with all the culinary delicacies the Fae Realm has to offer while I recover from my grievous injury."

"So I see." Brigid leaned forward a bit to peer around him. "You wouldn't mind sharing, would you?"

Right. She probably hadn't had anything since before they'd been brought to the Realm of Monsters.

Munch set the bowl between them, then picked up the tray

and set that in front of her as well. "Help yourself. Even I won't be able to polish off all of this by myself."

To make sure she wouldn't feel uncomfortable stuffing her face in front of him, he selected a dessert that appeared to be made of some kind of crumbling, pink pastry base with an orange-colored whipped topping that he hadn't tried yet. When he popped it in his mouth, it had an unexpectedly mild, vanilla-y taste, given the brightness of the colors. Hmm. Not his favorite. He still preferred the purple-pink pastries filled with some kind of dark purple jelly.

Brigid took one of the scone-like items and took a bite, leaning back against the wall again and shifting so that she sat with one leg folded, the other stretched out next to the tray of food.

They ate in silence for a few minutes, watching the bustle in the rest of the great hall. The other wounded humans seemed to be in no hurry to get moving. They'd have a few more minutes to talk before it was time to leave for the Human Realm.

And that meant they had one more thing they had to address before they went anywhere.

Munch swallowed his last bite, wiped his fingers on his trousers—it wasn't like a few crumbs and stickiness was going to hurt them at this point—and lifted his and Brigid's clasped hands, which still glowed. "Does this mean what I think it does?"

Brigid swallowed, her gaze swinging away from him. "Don't worry, it's just the beginning of a binding. We can break it so that you can return to the Human Realm without a problem."

"What if I don't want to break it?" Munch kept his focus on her, wanting to catch every flicker of her reaction.

Brigid stilled, her posture going careful and controlled, as she faced him. "But you love your family. This binding would mean you'd live in the Fae Realm."

"I know. And I do love my family. But it's time I forged my own life, and I think that life is here. With you." Munch rubbed his thumb over her knuckles, and for a moment, the glow around their fingers brightened. "And it isn't like I will never see them again. I know you. You're still going to be the Primrose. We'll be back in the Human Realm often, returning rescued humans to their home."

Five years ago, he'd been too young to make this decision. He'd needed a few more years of growing and maturing.

But now he was ready. Sure, it wasn't an easy decision. There would be times when he'd get homesick for his family and the Greenwood. This change wouldn't be without cost or pain.

Brigid was worth it. Their future would be worth it.

"You'll miss so much. Even with my best efforts moving between the realms, time still moves faster there. You'll miss seeing so much of your siblings' lives and the lives of your nieces and nephews." Brigid's eyes were wide, her posture poised as if she was ready to tug her hand free of his and bolt. "I can't ask that of you."

"You're not asking. This is my choice." Munch held her gaze as he shifted to grasp both of her hands in his. "I can't go back to only seeing you for a handful of hours every few weeks or months. These past few days have made me realize that my place is here in the Fae Realm. With you."

She gaped at him, seemingly lost for words. Perhaps her exhaustion was catching up with her. Or maybe she was just trying to figure out a way to turn him down gently because she didn't feel the same way he did.

He rubbed his thumb over her knuckles. Her hands were so small and soft in his. "After tonight, your secret is out. Your missions are going to be even more dangerous. I'm asking to be the person at your back, ready to step in to fight if things go sideways. If that's what you want."

She blinked rapidly, her amber brown eyes filling with an emotion he couldn't read. "No, no. I mean, yes. You're the man I've wanted at my side for so long. It's just…" She trailed off, shook her head as if she was trying to knock the words loose, then glanced at him. "I never thought this would actually happen between us. I always had my secrets, and I never thought you'd give up your family for me."

"Well, it looks like it is happening. If you want it to." Munch held up their clasped and glowing hands. "This proves it."

Brigid laughed—her real laugh, not the tinny one she used as the Primrose. "You do realize what this binding is, right? It's a marriage binding. And while we might be on our way there, we aren't quite there just yet. We could leave the binding unfinished for a while, but it's dangerous to leave a binding half-done, and you're going to need the protections of a full marriage binding if you're going to live here."

Munch shrugged and squeezed her fingers. "I'm all right with courting and taking things slow after we're married, if you're good with that. It worked out for my sister and brother-in-law."

"For my sister and brother-in-law as well."

"See, it's practically a family tradition." Munch grinned and gestured at the fae bustling around the room. "What could be more fae-like than doing things backwards and finish falling in love after getting married? We're way ahead of where either of our sisters and brothers-in-law were when they got married. We're not strangers, we're not trying to kill each other, and we've been wanting to fall in love for years. We just haven't had the opportunity to do it yet."

"Well, when you put it that way, how could I possibly say

no?" Brigid shifted against the wall so she sat a little closer to him, their shoulders just brushing. "And this is the Fae Realm. No one is going to blink an eye at us getting married after only being truly together for a few days. The fae do it all the time. This realm has a way of speeding up such things."

"That it does." Munch held up their clasped hands again. "So…how does this work? I'm assuming we should finish this binding sooner rather than later?"

"We…could do it right now." Brigid peeked at him, then her gaze dropped to their clasped hands. "I'm not sure what stepping into the Human Realm might do to the unfinished binding. It might start fraying it. It should reforge when I snatch you back into the Fae Realm, but…"

"Right now is fine by me." Was this how Robin always felt right before she did something particularly reckless? Because right now, Munch was so filled with a restless energy that he would jump off a cliff if Brigid asked him to.

"You do realize it will be Midsummer Night a few nights from now, right? With all these shenanigans that Lord Chauvlyn, Claudius, and King Oberon have been pulling, it's bound to be a bad one." Brigid winced and gave a little shudder.

"Bring it on." Munch patted his quiver, grinning. A little monster attack was nothing he couldn't handle. "All the more reason you need a forester at your side."

She met his gaze, a warm, trusting smile on her lips and beaming in her eyes. When she spoke, her tone held a note of utter sincerity. "My hero."

In that moment, he could have taken on the entire Realm of Monsters just to make sure she kept looking at him like that. As if he were dashing and heroic.

He glanced down at himself. He wore only one boot. His trouser leg was cut away, as were parts of his shirt. His clothes in general were muck-smeared, monster-blood-spattered, and torn. He probably didn't look or smell all that great after his ordeal being captured and thrown in the dungeon. And he was sitting on a pallet in a hall with both fae and humans bustling about. Hardly the look of someone who was dashing and heroic.

He couldn't do anything about his appearance or his clothes. But he could do something about the setting.

He clambered to his feet, wincing only slightly when he tested out his bad foot. Walking would be doable, though he'd be going nowhere fast. "Come on. Let's find a more romantic corner of this Library of yours."

He'd been dreaming of this moment for years. As had she, it turned out. It might be a little rushed, but he was going to do it right.

When she glided to her feet, still holding his hand, she met his gaze with sparkling eyes and a grin that set his heart pounding.

Yep, now that he had her—the real her—he had no intention of ever letting her go. And, by the way she gripped his hand and all but dragged him toward the doors that led to the Library, she felt the same way.

Chapter Twenty-Seven

Brigid tugged Munch through the Great Library, curbing her hurry due to his limp. He didn't wince or complain at the pace.

A few librarians glanced at them before turning away with stifled grins and knowing gleams in their eyes. At this rate, Meg and Basil would probably hear the news from a gossiping librarian before Brigid had a chance to tell them in person.

A few bookwyrms slithered from the shelves, chirruping and chattering as if the Library itself was celebrating with them. Brigid stopped to pet a few of them, but she didn't take the time for all of them. Not yet.

She led Munch through the winding shelves until they reached the far dark corner where the waterfall reading nook tucked into its cozy little spot.

Munch glanced at her, his eyes widening with question. "Here?"

It probably seemed a strange spot to pick. This reading nook was where Lord Chauvlyn had figured out her secret and she had figured out that Munch had unwillingly betrayed her.

But this nook was far more than that. It was secluded, private, and still one of her favorite places in the entire Library.

"I still love it." Brigid shrugged as they ducked around the waterfall and stepped into the space.

As she had hoped, the inside was empty at this time of morning, filled instead with the steady background roar of the waterfall, the chorus of frogs, and the buzzing of the flitting dragonflies.

She faced Munch, still holding his hand, her heart beating harder in her chest.

What were they thinking? Sure, they'd known each other for years. But this was a big step. A permanent one. Not a choice to be made on a whim. Even if the Fae Realm was the place for whims and leaping without looking.

She swallowed and fumbled for her pocket with her free hand. "Um, well, I guess we'll need some string."

"Brigid…" Munch reached out and held both of her hands in his once again. His grip remained strong, sure, even as his eyes searched her face. "We don't have to leap into this quite this quickly. We can return the others to the Human Realm first, then see what happens after we return."

"I know." Her mouth still felt far too dry, her head a little light.

But as she turned that option over, something in her rejected the idea before she could even give it much thought.

No, she was sure about this. She and Munch had been falling in love one brief visit at a time for years. The only way for them to be together and get to know each other more deeply was for him to make the choice he was making now and stay in the Fae Realm. And the only way for him to safely stay in the Fae Realm was for him to either be bound to a Court or marry into a Court. With the binding already started between them, the second one made the most sense.

She met his gaze, her words coming out in a whisper that she wasn't sure he'd hear over the waterfall and frogs. "I don't want to let you go. Not this time."

The corner of his mouth quirked with that slightly lopsided smile of his. "Me either. I've waited five years for you to look at me like you are now."

She'd put on a lot of masks, disguises, and façades over the years. But right now, she couldn't hide the way his words tugged at her heart.

"But Brigid—" He squeezed her fingers, his smile dropping. "Before we do this, I need you to promise that you won't use me like a pawn again. I know why you didn't tell me the truth earlier and why you kept me in the dark for most of tonight about your plans. And I understand that there may be times when you won't be able to tell me everything. But if I'm to be your partner in this mission of yours, then I can't be—I won't be—just the dupe you move about on your whims."

She dropped her gaze down to their joined hands, unable to meet his eyes when he was searching her soul like that.

He had a valid point. She read people, and that made it easy to manipulate them to get her way. She'd done it tonight with Lord Chauvlyn. And, yes, even with Munch a few times there.

It was one thing to out-think her enemies and bend them to her plans. But it was unhealthy if she did that to her family and to the man she married. She tried to be careful with Basil, Meg, and the rest of her siblings. She'd have to be just as careful with Munch.

What would it be like to have Munch at her side, a true partner in this? She'd never had someone she could fully confide in when it came to her work as the Primrose. Even with the support of her League, her family, and her king and queen, she had still been alone when it came to carrying the burden of her mission.

But with Munch, she would finally have someone with whom to discuss her plans, her fears, her hopes in a way she never had with anyone before.

And she could be that person for him in return. She could encourage him in a way even his family—as much as they loved him—had never been able to. If given the chance to step out of their shadow, he'd find a new confidence and thrive in a way he never had before.

She met his gaze once again, stepping a little closer with their hands still clasped between them. "I promise."

And there was that lopsided grin again, the one that made her want to lean into him and forget all about her responsibilities, if just for a few more minutes.

She released his hands and dug into her pocket, pulling out a red hair ribbon. That would work. "Ready?"

"Ready." Munch grinned right back at her.

They tucked the red ribbon between their palms as they clasped their right hands.

Brigid wound her half of the ribbon around their clasped hands and her wrist. "With this binding, I pledge myself to you."

His grin falling into that serious look that drew his brows together over his deep brown eyes, Munch wound his half of the ribbon around their hands and his wrist. "With this binding, I pledge myself to you."

The glow surrounding their hands brightened, and a tingle spread from Brigid's fingers and up her arm.

She and Munch fumbled to tie the two ends of the ribbon together with their free hands. They hadn't left much in extra length, and it kept slipping from their fingers.

"Who knew tying the knot would be the hardest part of getting married?" Brigid tried to loop her end of the ribbon through his. But their hands bumped, sending the ribbon slipping from both of their grasps once again.

Munch shook his head, then chuckled. "We're terrible at this."

Perhaps it was the lack of sleep. Or the absurdity of standing there in the reading nook, struggling to tie a simple knot.

But a giggle burst out of her before she could stop it. And once she started, the giggles just kept coming harder and faster until she was doubled over, crying with the force of her giggling and gasping out breaths between her laughter.

Munch braced his free hand on his knee as he chuckled right alongside her. "If we're this bad at just tying the knot, do you think our kissing has improved?"

Brigid wrestled her giggles somewhat under control to partially straighten. "I hope so! That first kiss was disgusting."

"And awkward." Munch grimaced.

"And too much spit." Brigid only somewhat exaggerated her shudder. Their first kiss when they'd both been eighteen had been a truly awful first kiss. Or, well, as awful as any first kiss usually was without some fae, Midsummer magic to help it along.

Munch's chuckles died away, and he straightened, rubbing at the back of his neck. "I haven't kissed anyone except you."

"Me neither." Brigid swiped at the wetness of the giggle tears on her face. Without practice, neither of them had likely improved any at kissing over the years. They'd find out once they finished tying this knot. She picked up her end of the ribbon. "Let's forget about kissing until we get this bothersome knot tied."

This time, they finally managed to tie a knot without dropping the ribbon.

"Yes!" Munch pumped his fist as soon as the ribbon slid into place. "Got it!"

The growing magic coalesced around their hands, then sank into their skin. With a glinting flash that sent sparks dancing in front of Brigid's eyes, the ribbon parted and disappeared, sinking into matching red-gold lines around both of their wrists.

And just like that, after three years of falling for him—well, five years on his side of things—they were married. Perhaps they still had some courting and relationship building to do, but they would get there. It would be a lot easier, now that he could safely stay in the Fae Realm with her. They had the luxury to take their time to build this into something as solid and lasting as the magical binding now linking them together.

Munch lightly rested his hands on her waist and tugged her closer. "I guess this is the moment when we find out if our second kiss is better than our first."

Brigid wasn't quite sure what to do with her hands as she leaned in closer, standing on her tiptoes just as he was leaning down. Their noses bumped for a moment, and then there was the awkward shuffle as they tried to figure out who was going to tilt their head which way. And then the kiss...

They both pulled back at the same time and just blinked at each other. Brigid pressed a hand over her mouth.

"That was...better." Munch drew out the last word, as if it was the most tactful thing he could think to say.

"Yes." Though that wasn't saying much. "Still too much spit."

Munch nodded, then eyed her as if torn between hope and apprehension. "Maybe we should try again? For more practice?"

She was game to try. She liked Munch. A lot. Surely that would translate to a good kiss eventually, right?

This attempt involved a lot less nose-bumping and

awkward fumbling, and she found herself tilting her head just a bit more.

There. Almost. It wasn't a spark, exactly, but it at least felt like there should be a spark that hovered just out of reach. A spark that would be attainable, eventually.

She drew back. "That was better." It wasn't even a stretch this time.

"Yes." He grinned at her, a hint of the outlaw in his eyes. "Again?"

She was up for that, so she wrapped her arms around his neck and kissed him again.

When they finished kissing that time, it was Brigid's turn to grin. "Again. I think I'm getting the hang of it."

After that, they kissed until Brigid was breathless, light-headed, and giggling so hard she couldn't kiss anymore. Not that it mattered since Munch, too, was laughing. The kisses were still mildly bad, but she didn't care. This was Munch. She'd take a bad kiss with him over an amazing kiss with anyone else any day.

She rested her forehead against his shoulder, trying to catch her breath and get her giggles under control.

He wrapped his arms around her, holding her. "I guess practice does make perfect. Just think, by our fiftieth kiss, we might actually get the hang of this."

"Fiftieth?" She lightly smacked his arm as she pulled away. "Way to be optimistic."

"Just being realistic. It took us five years just to get to our second kiss." His chuckle was as warm as the look in his eyes.

"It was only three years for me."

"My point still stands." Munch took her hand in his again, holding them up so the golden lines around their wrists caught the light. "We'll do things in our own time, even if it takes years to get where we need to be."

"Let's hope it's not years this time." Brigid wrapped her arms around his waist and leaned against him. At least this part didn't feel nearly as awkward and unpracticed as kissing did. "I've waited for you long enough as it is."

"I waited longer." He wrapped his arms around her, his chuckle light and teasing.

"True." Brigid grinned up at him. "I guess one more important question remains."

"What's that?" Munch's grin faded as his eyes studied her face.

"What do you want me to call you? I know the nickname Munch isn't your favorite."

He grimaced and shrugged. "I don't have any better ideas. There aren't a whole lot of good nicknames for Mungoe, and I really don't want to be called Mung, Munnie, or Mun."

"True. There aren't a lot of options." She tightened her hug around his waist. "Maybe something like Mungus?"

His grimace deepened, as if he'd tasted something foul. "Definitely not. Makes me sound like some kind of fungus."

She winced. Yes, it did. "Just let me know. This is your chance to reinvent yourself. You can take on any name you want here in the Fae Realm."

This time, his chuckle held a wry note. "Good point, but I'm afraid I'll probably stick with Munch. For old times' sake." His laughter faded as the soft brush of his sigh stirred her hair. "My mother loved the name Mungoe. It's one piece of her I always carry with me. And my family might tease, but Munch is the name they gave me. It might be an annoying nickname, but it's *my* annoying nickname."

"In that case, I'll happily call you *my* Munch." She rested her head against his shoulder and released a long breath. "I have every confidence that here in the Fae Realm, you're going to live adventures that will put the stories of that other Mungoe to shame."

"I doubt that, but it would be nice to feel worthy of the name." Munch lightly rested his chin on her head, holding her tucked close.

Something in her relaxed for the first time in years. Probably for the first time since she had taken on the guise of the Primrose.

Safety. That was what this feeling was. Basil and Meg supported her as best they could, but they couldn't offer the shelter that Munch could. He would charge into battle with her and for her. Mostly for her. She would much rather let him take on all the weapon wielding from now on.

She soaked in the moment for another few heartbeats before she heaved a sigh. "I suppose we'd better get back to the others. We've already lingered for far too long as it is."

A nagging prickle itched at her. Should they have taken this much time, knowing that there were people depending on her to get them back home? It was fine to take up her own time, but what about theirs?

Munch nodded, and he held her hand as they strolled back through the Library, through the Hall of Anywhere Doors, and into the entry hall of the castle.

There, they found the remaining humans gathered around Basil and Meg. A young woman perched on Buddy's back, bandages wrapped around her leg, while several people were on stretchers, carried by their family members.

"I'm sorry for the delay." Brigid hurried toward them, Munch at her side.

"We just located another stretcher and gathered the last one here, and Basil just finished sending Puck on his way. So we haven't been waiting long." Meg shrugged, her gaze dropping down to Brigid's and Munch's clasped hands.

Brigid smiled and held up their hands, showing the red-gold rings around their wrists. "I took Munch to my favorite nook, and we tied the knot."

Meg gave a small squeal and leapt forward into a hug. From over Meg's shoulder, Basil gave Munch that *I approve but I'm still keeping an eye on you* big brother look.

Brigid hugged her sister back as best she could without letting go of Munch's hand. Hopefully Munch's family would take the news well, especially considering that Munch would be leaving them for the Fae Realm.

"At least you had the decency to do it somewhere romantic." Buddy nudged Basil with his nose as Meg let go of Brigid.

Basil shifted and gave a small cough. "Meg said she was fine with it."

"I am." Meg rejoined Basil, grinning up at him. "A moonlit pony ride was plenty romantic."

With one last glance at Munch, Brigid straightened and faced the people, plastering on her Primrose smile. "All right. Who's ready to go home?"

MUNCH SHIFTED from foot to foot as Robin and Guy finished greeting the rescued humans, organizing them into groups, who would be escorted back to their home villages.

He'd thought Robin had guessed what was going on between him and Brigid before she'd left. But that didn't stop his stomach from churning at telling his family about his decision to stay in the Fae Realm.

Ever since their parents had been killed when he had been only eight years old, his family had been close. His older siblings had essentially raised him.

How was he going to say goodbye? Even if it wasn't going to be for forever?

But he was twenty-three years old. Nearly twenty-four. It was time to set out on his own.

Finally, Guy shook the last man's hand, and the various groups of guards and rescued people departed from the hall.

Next to him, Brigid also fidgeted. Their palms were getting uncomfortably hot and sweaty, but he didn't want to let her go. She was the only one left at his side, since Meg and Basil had stayed behind at the faerie circle with Buddy.

Marion wandered over to them, then lightly punched his arm. "Finally. You've been mooning over her for ages."

"Welcome to the family." Will halted next to Brigid and nodded to her. "Glad to see Munch finally got his head on straight."

Alan joined them and held up his lute. "So, tell me. What is your tale of epic love so I can write it into my next ballad?"

John and Tuck drifted closer, both of them giving him gruff nods and slaps on the back.

"I, um…" Munch glanced around at all of them. They'd all picked up on the fact that he and Brigid were together now. That much was obvious by the way he was holding her hand.

But the rest of it? He wasn't sure how to tell them.

"Your stuff is already packed for you to take back to the Fae Realm with you." Robin sauntered over, her hand lightly clasped in Guy's.

Munch sighed. "You knew." He'd thought she had, but he hadn't been sure.

"It was as plain as heads on a hydra that you wouldn't be coming back to stay." Robin's face and tone remained uncharacteristically serious, despite the lightness to her words. "I'm jealous, you know. Just think of all the adventures you'll have in the Fae Realm."

"What she means is that we'll miss you." Guy tilted his head in a serious nod, made more somber by the way his black beard framed the deep grooves around his mouth.

Munch couldn't help but smile. Who would have guessed, with his overabundance of big brothers as it was, that Guy would turn out to be the additional big brother he needed.

He had gained yet another big brother in Basil when he'd married Brigid. Now that was a strange thought. Mild-mannered fae librarian that he was, Basil was the exact opposite of any of Munch's other big brothers.

"Yes." Robin held his gaze, only a hint of her customary smirk lingering on her face. "We're glad you've finally found the place where you can live your life to its fullest adventure."

Munch cleared his throat, not wanting to admit just how tight and choked his voice had gone. "I'll miss all of you, but I'll be back."

"We'll visit often." Brigid glanced around at his family, speaking quickly as if worried that they would be angry at her for taking him away. "I'll make sure that we don't lose too much time when crossing the realms."

"And we can pass messages through the faerie circle." Munch swallowed and glanced at Will. "I'll miss working as a forester. I'm sorry I'll be leaving you short-handed."

"We'll be fine. Besides, you're still going to be a forester." Will reached into his quiver and pulled out an iron rod. It was too shiny and rust-free to be the one Will had carried for years. Instead, this one gleamed in the light beaming down from the high windows of the Great Hall, highlighting the bow and arrow symbol stamped into the iron. "As the head of the foresters, I'm appointing you as the first forester stationed in the Fae Realm."

"And as the duke of Gysborn, I approve of this appointment," Guy added, a hint of a smile softening his stern features.

Munch let go of Brigid's hand so that he could take the iron rod from Will with both hands. Its heft mirrored the weight of the appointment he was being given. "Truly?"

"Of course. As foresters, we can only do so much on this side of the faerie circle to protect humans from fae and fae monsters." Will waved to the iron rod, still holding Munch's gaze. "Just think of how much more effective we can be with you working on that side of the circles. Especially when you're teamed up with the Primrose."

When he'd made the decision to stay at Brigid's side in the Fae Realm, he'd thought he'd have to give up his family, his work as a forester, everything.

But that wasn't the case. He would still have his family, even if they would have to keep touch from afar more often than not. And he would still be a forester, working to protect the Human Realm from incursions by the fae.

This. This was what he'd been searching for all those times when he'd felt such a restless drive welling up inside him.

Robin was right. With Brigid beside him and their shared mission to pursue in their own unique ways, he would find the adventure of a lifetime in the Fae Realm, the place he was always meant to be.

Epilogue

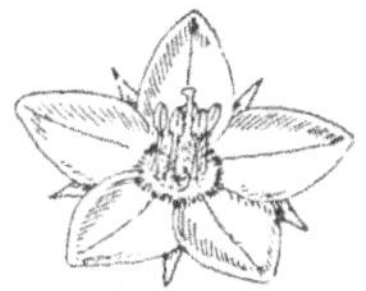

ONE YEAR LATER

A cloaked figure darted along the upper balcony of the glittering ballroom in the Court of Ice. The entire palace had been formed of ice, from the gleaming, deep blue of the ballroom floor to the delicate icicle railings of the balcony above.

The figure paused in a shaft of light, his face still hidden both by his red mask and the black of his cloak's hood. His cloak was pulled so tightly around him that nothing of his clothing underneath could be seen.

"The Primrose! There! Get him!" The king's guards pointed, then raced as fast as they could for the nearest set of stairs. The ice cleats attached to their boots gave them purchase on the slick surfaces of the palace.

Smiling as the guards raced past her, Brigid minced her way across the ballroom. With the hair of a white wig piled on her head and a white mask on her face that paired with the light blue of her gown and the white fur that trimmed her cloak, she appeared to be someone from the Court of Ice attending their monarch's Midwinter Masquerade.

Little did anyone know that two human children hid beneath the ginormous hoop of her skirt, shuffling along in time with her. Seriously, one could hide just about anything under a hoop skirt. It made such a convenient fashion choice at times.

As she reached the court's Anywhere Door, the guards standing there gave her only a cursory look over before they waved her onward. After all, they knew exactly where the Primrose was. Their fellow guards were chasing him even now.

A black-clad fae lord stood next to the Anywhere Door, his hands clasped behind his back. His gaze remained elsewhere, as if he was searching for any attempt of the cloaked figure to reach the Door.

As expected, Lord Chauvlyn had returned from the Realm of Monsters several months ago, thinner and more dour than he had been before. Less expected had been that he had kept the identity of the Primrose to himself. Everyone still seemed to be looking for a fae man, and neither her fellow librarians nor Lord Chauvlyn seemed in a hurry to correct them.

She suspected Lord Chauvlyn kept her identity to himself because her capture had become so personal to him that he wanted to capture her himself, even if that meant sabotaging everyone else's chances.

Or, maybe, he'd taken some of her words to heart. Perhaps he had a small niggling squeak of a conscience that returned her mercy with one of his own. Doubtful, but she could hope.

Whatever his reasons, Brigid would use his silence to her full advantage.

She rested her hand on the latch of the Anywhere Door, thought of the Hall of Anywhere Doors, then pulled it open. Just before she stepped inside, she glanced over her shoulder.

"Fancy meeting you here, Lord Chauvertin. Sink me, but I must be going. I would dearly love to catch up sometime."

The fae lord straightened as if he'd had an icicle dropped down the back of his pressed, black shirt. He whirled, gesturing wildly for the nearby guards. "The Primrose! Guards!"

She laughed, then stepped through the Anywhere Door before any of them could move, closing it firmly behind her.

Lord Chauvlyn would be livid. He wouldn't be able to chase after her. Thanks to the tense, near-war between the Court of Knowledge and Court of Revels, all the members of the Court of Revels had been barred from using the Anywhere Doors.

Even if Lord Chauvlyn tried, the magic wouldn't let him enter. She'd heard he'd tried to get himself adopted into another court, but the other courts were trying too hard to be neutral to take in a member of the Court of Revels right now. They didn't want to risk angering the Court of Knowledge and have their own Anywhere Door access taken away.

As soon as Brigid and her charges stepped into the Hall of Anywhere Doors, she turned and set her hand on the latch, thinking of the House she shared with Munch. Their House was next to Meg and Basil's in the village, though Brigid was thankful that her House seemed to be less grumpy than Meg's House. Still, Brigid's House still had its quirks.

Even as Brigid stepped through, she faintly heard the sounds of an Anywhere Door opening farther down the Hall and guards from the Court of Ice shouting as they poured through.

She laughed to herself, finished stepping into the cozy safety of her snug little House, and closed the Door behind her.

Around her, her House gave a warm little shudder, like a mother hen fluffing up her feathers before taking her chicks under her wings.

"All right, children. It's safe to come out now." Brigid

bundled her skirts into her arms and lifted the hoop high enough that the two children, a brother and a sister, could crawl out from their hiding place underneath.

As the children blinked first at her, then wide-eyed at the House around them, a branch extended from the ceiling and brushed first at the girl's hair, then at a smudge on the boy's sleeve. Both children jumped, then pressed against Brigid.

She smoothed one hand over the girl's hair and rested the other on the boy's shoulder. "Don't be alarmed by the House. It can be overly affectionate, but it means well."

In the kitchen, a cupboard door flew open, and a branch reached inside, pulling out a tray piled high with food that would be safe for the children to eat. The branch reached into the cupboard again and again and again, disgorging such a bounty of food that the children would never be able to eat it all.

"Really, House. What have I told you about pulling in more food than we'll need?" Brigid placed her hands on her hips, staring down the cupboard.

The House gave a small, chastised tremble before the branch started grabbing trays of food and stuffing them back into the cupboard until only two trays remained. Still more food than they'd need, but close enough.

Brigid steered the two children into seats and coaxed them into picking out food. They hesitated at first, likely remembering all the times they'd been forced to eat faerie fruit or other food that would cause them pain or terrors. But once they nibbled on the first few bites, they both seemed to realize this food was safe to eat. They dug in as if they hadn't had a decent meal in days.

They likely hadn't.

The Anywhere Door opened again, and this time Munch swept inside, shutting the door quickly behind him. His white cloak swirled around him for a moment, settling around the guard uniform of the Court of Ice that he wore.

Both children froze, wide-eyed.

"It's all right. This is my husband." Brigid crossed the room and laughed when Munch pulled her into his arms. "Did you have any trouble?"

"None at all. Just like you knew he would, Lord Chauvlyn drew all the guards off the chase for me to chase after you." Munch rested his hands on her waist, his grin matching hers. "I flipped my cloak to the white side, switched my mask to a white one, and joined their ranks. They were too busy to even notice an extra guard among them, and I slipped away as soon as we reached the Hall of Anywhere Doors. Last I saw, King Theseus, Queen Hippolyta, and Head Librarian Marco had the situation well in hand."

"Good. We'll wait a few hours for the furor to die down, then we'll get these little ones back to the Human Realm. If we time it right, we might even be able to join your family for supper." Brigid leaned into him.

"I'd like that." Munch's hold on her tightened for just a moment. The only sign he gave of how much he still missed his family, even a year later. But even when he was homesick and missing his family, he still chose her each and every day.

She sneaked a peek over her shoulder. Both children had gone back to eating, and the House had several branches hovering about, holding out napkins or shifting plates closer when the children struggled to reach.

When she turned back to Munch, he pulled her closer still. "Another brilliant plan, Primrose."

"Another daring escapade, Forester." Brigid tilted her head toward him.

He glanced past her, then seemed to decide that the children were distracted enough. He leaned down and kissed her.

Perhaps it was their fiftieth kiss. Or a hundredth. She'd stopped counting long ago. It no longer mattered how many kisses they'd shared. Munch had been right. They had, indeed, gotten the hang of kissing. In fact, they were quite good at it, if she did say so herself.

Free Book!

Thanks so much for reading *Forest of Scarlet*! I hope Munch and Brigid made you laugh and even surprised you a time or two! If you loved the book, please consider leaving a review on Amazon or Goodreads. Reviews help your fellow readers find books that they will love.

If you ever find typos in any of my books, feel free to email me at taragrayce(at)taragrayce(dot)com.

If you sign up for my newsletter, you'll also receive the free novella *Steal a Swordmaiden's Heart.*

This novella tells the story of how King Theseus of the Court of Knowledge won the hand of Hippolyta, Queen of the Swordmaidens.

If you don't wish to sign up for my newsletter, Steal a Swordmaiden's Heart is available on Amazon, though it isn't in KU like the rest of the series.

Sign up for my newsletter now

NIGHT OF SECRETS

Love is a distraction when the Library is on the line.

Despite being humans living in the Fae Realm, Viola, along with her brother Sebastian, have achieved their dream to become librarians and establish their own outpost library in the Court of Islands. When an attack on their way to the outpost separates them, Viola arrives alone, not knowing if Sebastian is alive or dead.

To preserve their dream and investigate what went wrong, Viola uses a fae glamour to be both herself and her brother. She didn't count on falling for the island's handsome fae ruler, Lord Orsino. But he's in love with Olivia—the same fae lady who Sebastian had been courting. Too bad everything only gets more complicated from there.

Can Viola navigate this tangled web of love to save the outpost library and find her brother? Or will an old enemy threaten not just Viola and the outpost but also the Great Library itself?

Inspired by Shakespeare's *Twelfth Night*, this standalone fae fantasy romance features fae rom-com hilarity, a girl in disguise, and a magical fae library, perfect for fans of K.M. Shea, Sylvia Mercedes, and Sarah K.L. Wilson.

Preorder on Kindle Today!

If you missed the previous adventures and would like to read more about Basil & Meg, Guy & Robin, or read about Brigid and Munch's meet cute, pick up *Stolen Midsummer Bride, Bluebeard and the Outlaw,* and *Wild Fae Primrose* today!

Stolen Midsummer Bride

Steal a bride. Save the library. Try not to die.

Basil, a rather scholarly fae, works as an assistant librarian at the Great Library of the Court of Knowledge. Lonely and unwilling to join the yearly Midsummer Revel to find a mate, Basil takes the advice of his talking horse companion and decides to steal a human bride instead.

Bluebeard and the Outlaw

Marriage: the ultimate heist.

Robin of the Greenwood spends her days robbing from the rich to feed the poor. When Robin discovers the Duke Guy "Bluebeard" plans to marry again, she conceives a plan for a final, big score. The lord is notorious for killing his

wives, but Robin has no plans to be dead wife number four.

Wild Fae Primrose

A stolen bride's sister. Robin Hood's little brother. A mission to fight the fae.

If you would like to see Brigid's and Munch's meet cute and their first awkward kiss, check out the companion novella, *Wild Fae Primrose*, now available on Amazon!

Enjoy this collection of stories that bridges the time gaps between *Stolen Midsummer Bride* and *Bluebeard and the Outlaw*, providing backstory for *Forest of Scarlet*!

Acknowledgments

Thanks so much once again for picking up one of my books! Your support is the reason I can keep writing and publishing, and each sale and review means so much!

As always, special thanks to everyone who made this book possible.

My family: my dad, my mom, my brothers, and my sisters-in-law. A special thank you to Meghan for a certain quote. You know the one. ;)

My friends: Bri, Paula, Jill. Thank you for celebrating every writing and publishing milestone with me.

My writing friends: Molly, Morgan, Addy, Savannah, Sierra, and many others. This book wouldn't be what it is without your help brainstorming and chatting and cheering me on.

My proofreaders: Tom, Mindy, and Deborah. Thank you for carving time out of your busy lives to polish up my books so I don't completely embarrass myself (any mistakes that make it past you are totally my fault).

All of you guys are the best team an author could ask for!

Also by Tara Grayce

COURT OF MIDSUMMER MAYHEM

Stolen Midsummer Bride
Steal a Swordmaiden's Heart
Forest of Scarlet
Wild Fae Primrose
Night of Secrets

A VILLAIN'S EVER AFTER

Bluebeard and the Outlaw

SACRIFICED HEARTS

Mountain of Dragons and Sacrifice
Of Dragons and Stone

TETHERED HEARTS

Ties of Bargains

Middle Grade

PRINCESS BY NIGHT

Lost in Averell